ENDORSEMENTS

"*Resistance* is the best Fantasy book I have read. It is full of colorful, but realistic characters, villains who will do anything to get their way, and a conflicted half-breed who finds what he never knew he needed. I highly recommend this book for Fantasy lovers, and even for those who do not usually read Fantasy."
—FAITH BLUM, AUTHOR OF *A MIGHTY FORTRESS*

"A thoroughly engrossing story with amazing worldbuilding and a theme usually left to historical or science fiction. Good work, Jaye. You've made at least one fan very happy!"
—KENDRA E. ARDNEK, AUTHOR OF *THE ANKULEN*

"*Resistance* is one of the best fantasies I've ever read. Not only does it hold a meaningful message, it is filled with inspiring characters who will take readers on an adventure they will never forget."
—JACK LEWIS BAILLOT, AUTHOR OF HAPHAZARDLY IMPLAUSIBLE

"The minute I picked up this book, I couldn't put it back down! *Resistance* quickly became one of my favorite books!"
—MERCY, MERCYRAY.BLOGSPOT.COM

"After loving the author's previous series, *Makilien*, I was wondering how *Resistance* could top it. I was not disappointed. The story pulls you in from the first word to the last, and shows how God is ultimately the one we should put our trust in. Jaye held me captivated until the very end; I couldn't get enough of this book!"
—KATIE E.

"This is such an incredible book! I couldn't put it down any more than I can fly; definitely ranks as one of my favorites. Highly recommended for readers of all ages!"
—YSA R.

"A stunning story…even after the last page, the impact remains. With fantasy concepts, Christian allegories, Ancient Rome-like times, and a futuristic touch all rolled into one, *Resistance* tells a powerful story of young men and women staying faithful to their God, despite the evil raging against them, and Him. I am captivated, and long to read more!"

—SHANTELLE H.

RESISTANCE

RESISTANCE

ILYON CHRONICLES – BOOK ONE

JAYE L. KNIGHT

Living Sword Publishing
www.livingswordpublishing.com

Resistance
Ilyon Chronicles – Book 1
Copyright © 2014 by Jaye L. Knight
www.ilyonchronicles.com

Published by Living Sword Publishing

Proofread by Amber Stokes
www.editingthroughtheseasons.com

Ilyon Map © 2014 by Jaye L. Knight

Cover Images
© Kjolak - Dreamstime.com
© AMCphotos - Dreamstime.com
© kjpargeter - Depositphotos.com
© smaglov - Depositphotos.com

All Scriptures are taken from the New American Standard Bible, Copyright © 1960, 1962, 1963, 1968, 1971, 1972, 1973, 1975, 1977, 1995 by The Lockman Foundation. Used by permission. www.Lockman.org

ISBN 13: 978-0-9837740-4-4
ISBN 10: 0983774048

To my one and only King.

And to my brothers, Jacob and Sam, for the little bits of
inspiration you provided (unknowingly) for Kaden and Liam.

PRINCIPAL CAST

Aertus (AYR - tuhs)—Arcacia's male moon god.

Aldor (AL - dohr)—Kalli's husband. An old friend of Rayad.

Altair (AL - tayr)—Kyrin's family name.

Anne—The daughter of Sir John Wyland.

Aric (AHR - ick)—Emperor Daican's head of security.

Aros (AHR - rohs)—Rayad's white horse.

Collin—A young man from Tarvin Hall with an interest in Kyrin.

Daican (DYE - can)—The emperor of Arcacia.

Dagren (DAY - gren)—An Arcacian army captain bent on capturing Rayad and Warin.

Daniel—Daican's son, the prince of Arcacia.

Davira (Duh - VEER - uh)—Daican's daughter, the princess of Arcacia.

Elôm (EE - lohm)—The one true God of Ilyon.

Goler—An Arcacian army captain and bitter rival of Trask.

Grey (GRAY)—The baron of Landale.

Henry Foss—Daican's secretary.

Holden (HOHL - den)—A former informant for Daican with an intense hatred for ryriks.

Holly—A maid at Auréa Palace.

Jace—A half-ryrik former slave and gladiator.

Jasper—A gladiator owner and former master of Jace.

John Wyland—A retired knight.

Kaden (KAY - den)—Kyrin's twin brother.

Kalli (KA - lee)—Aldor's wife. An old friend of Rayad.

Kyrin (KYE - rin)—A young Arcacian woman with the ability to remember everything.

Laytan—The owner of the mercantile in Kinnim. Father of Rebekah.

Lenae (LEH - nay)—A widowed Landale woman.

Liam—Kyrin's older brother and an Arcacian soldier.

Maera (MAYR - uh)—Kyrin's dappled buckskin horse.

Marcus Altair—Kyrin's eldest brother and an Arcacian army captain.

Marcus Veshiron (Veh - SHEER - on)—Kyrin's grandfather and an Arcacian general.

Meredith—A young girl from Tarvin Hall. Like a little sister to Kyrin.

Mick—A resistance member from a wealthy mining family.

Morden—A young man in Kinnim whose father is mayor.

Morris—Baron Grey's secretary.

Niton (NYE - ton)—Jace's black horse.

Peete (PEET)—Kinnim's sheriff.

Rayad (RAY - ad)—An Arcacian man wanted by the emperor for being a rebel.

Rebekah—A kind young woman in Kinnim.

Richard Blaine—A knight and old family friend of Daican.

Sam "Endathlorsam"—A talcrin man and Tarvin Hall's wisest scholar.

Solora (Soh - LOHR - uh)—Daican's wife, the queen of Arcacia.

Tane "Imhonriltane"—Sam's nephew.

Trask—Resistance leader and son of Baron Grey.

Trev—A member of Daican's security force.

Tyra—Jace's black wolf.

Videlle (VI - dell)—The head mistress of Auréa Palace.

Vilai (VI - lye)—Arcacia's female moon god.

Warin (WOHR - in)—An Arcacian man active in the resistance against the emperor. Lifelong friend of Rayad.

William—Kyrin's father and an Arcacian army captain.

Zocar (ZOH - cahr)—The head master of Tarvin Hall.

LOCATIONS

Arcacia (Ahr - CAY - shee - uh)—The largest country of the Ilyon mainland.

Arda—An island country off the coast of Arcacia. Inhabited by talcrins.

Ardaluin Bay (Ahr - DUH - luin)—The large bay off of Arcacia's western shore.

Auréa (Awr - RAY - uh)—Daican's palace in Valcré.

Dorland—Ilyon's easternmost country. Inhabited by cretes and giants.

Falspar—Troas's neighboring city. Rayad's birthplace.

Fort Rivor (RYE - vohr)—Arcacia's largest military fort located southeast of Valcré.

Ilyon (IL - yahn)—The known world.

Kinnim—A small forest town in central Arcacia.

Landale—A prosperous province in Arcacia ruled over by Baron Grey.

Marlton Hall—Home of Sir John Wyland.

Samara (Sa - MAHR - uh)—A small country north of Arcacia.

Sidian Ocean (SI - dee - an)—The body of water surrounding Ilyon.

Tarvin Hall—An academy set up to train children for the emperor's service.

Trayse River (TRACE)—The river separating Arcacia from Dorland.

Troas (TROH - as)—One of the largest cities in southern Arcacia.

Valcré (VAL - cray)—Arcacia's capital city.

Wildmor—An untamed country of vast forest. Inhabited by ryriks.

RACES

Cretes—A short tree-dwelling race with long dark hair, brown skin, and large, colorful eyes. Known for their aloofness and ability to train dragons.

Giants "Dorlanders"—A very large race that stands between seven to nine feet tall. Known for their quiet nature and aversion to conflict.

Humans—The primary inhabitants of Arcacia and Samara.

Ryriks (RYE - ricks)—A fierce and savage race with black hair and almost luminescent blue eyes. Known for their quick rage and violence against other races.

Talcrins—A tall race with dark skin and metallic looking eyes. Known for their love of knowledge.

Further information found in the Race Profiles
at the back of the book.

ILYON

N
W   E
S

SAMARA

AMBERIN
STONEHELM

SINNAI MTS.

SIDIAN
OCEAN

ARCACIA

GRAYLIN VALLEY

DUNLOW

KINNIM

VALCRE

LANDALE

ARDALUIN BAY

MERNIN
FORT RIVOR

KEATON

FALSPAR
TROAS

ARDA

For the LORD is a great God
And a great King above all gods.
- Ps. 95:3

For the LORD will judge His people
And will have compassion on His servants.
The idols of the nations are but silver and gold,
The work of man's hands.
They have mouths, but they do not speak;
They have eyes, but they do not see;
They have ears, but they do not hear,
Nor is there any breath at all in their mouths.
Those who make them will be like them,
Yes, everyone who trusts in them.
- Ps. 135:14-18

FLEEING. RAYAD CRUNCHED his brows down. At this age, he should have been retired and living comfortably, but no. He was a wanted man.

His gaze darted from one person to another in the milling crowd while his heart knocked his ribs in a strong, elevated rhythm that hadn't slowed in more than a day. What he wouldn't give to be sitting in the cool shade of his front porch right now, admiring the farmland he had worked for so many years. But it was all gone now, along with that familiar life.

He skirted the outer edge of Troas's arena and kept to the shadows of the stone and weathered wood walls, which were in sore need of repair. It would be just his luck to have them collapse on him. Faded red banners fluttered overhead, far too festive even in their tattered state. No one should celebrate what took place here, but the roaring cheers inside disagreed with him.

A glimpse of gold fabric sent a kick to his innards. His hand jumped to his sword hilt, but the blade remained sheathed. He wouldn't use it unless he had no choice. Once in twenty-four hours was enough. He still hadn't found time to scrub all the dried blood from around his fingernails yet.

He spun around in search of a different route and grimaced at the only alternative. The arena. He ducked behind a group of wealthy merchants and joined the flow of spectators who would cover his retreat to the other side. Shadows engulfed him, and he blinked as his eyes adjusted. If the walls were going to topple, now would be a very bad time. Hot, humid air descended and burned his nostrils with the musty odor of hundreds of bodies crammed into the enclosed space. He wrinkled his nose and tried not to breathe too deeply. The roar of the crowd deafened him and added to the unpleasantness. Masses of screaming people packed the stands above him. Their thumping feet rained dust down into his eyes. He hated to imagine what caused such a commotion. Time to find the nearest exit.

He set out on a determined course, but people congested the path. They pushed and shoved with little show of courtesy. Rayad bit back a grumble when they forced him to stop and wait for the way to clear. He peered through the crowd for any sign of the distinctive gold and black uniforms of the emperor's soldiers, but everyone blended together in this mass—grimy peasants and silk-clad nobles alike. Though it worked in his favor, it didn't help his mood. After a sleepless night on the road, he wanted to finish here and be on his way to safer country.

He balled his fists. If these people had no concern for civility, then fine. He shoved through them, squeezing past the horde of sweat-dampened bodies until he hit a group of bulky men who refused to budge—blacksmiths and woodsmen, by the look of their worn leather jerkins and rough linen shirts. He scowled and glanced through a small open window to his left, down into the arena some ten feet below. Though he had no desire to witness the grisly sport, his eyes stuck there.

Two sparsely armored men circled each other and passed close to his vantage point. One, a tall blond brute he wouldn't have relished messing with, carried a short sword and a large, round shield riddled with dents and notches. The other had his broad back to Rayad with a long sword outstretched in front of him. Spots of crimson stained the men's clothing. Their gusty breaths reached Rayad even up here—proof they'd been fighting for a while.

In a blink, they crashed together and drew an uproar of cheers from the crowd. The screech of metal set Rayad's teeth on edge, and his fingers tingled as if the swords rested in his hands. He set his eyes on the man with the long sword. His mouth dropped open. The fighter was just a boy—no more than sixteen or seventeen years of age! Still, he was tall—at least as tall as Rayad, if not taller. Fierce determination and concentration drew his face taut. Though a path had opened for Rayad to move on, a strange investment in the outcome of this fight willed him to stay.

The two fighters clashed again. Rayad followed every move the young man made. Such skill in spite of his youth; such explosiveness and strength behind his attacks. He'd be more than a match for most men. Each move appeared as natural as breathing, his blade placement precise and murderously quick. Impressive. This boy was no brawling fighter, which was so common in the arenas.

Back and forth, blows landed with the shriek and clang of metal. Rayad leaned over the edge of the window, careful not to trust it with his full weight. His eyes remained fixed on the young fighter. While he couldn't, in good conscience, wish for the other man to die, he found himself pulling for a victory for the younger man. The gladiator's bare arms and shoulders bulged with thick muscle and glistened with sweat as he swung his sword blade in a blurred arc. Beads of moisture dripped from his chin and the ragged ends of his black hair. Exhaustion dogged both men, weighing on their movements and slowing their pace. The excitement in the stands heightened with anticipation for the imminent conclusion. Rayad's breath grew shallow.

From somewhere, the young man summoned a hidden reserve of energy. Sword raised, he drove into his opponent. The blond fighter staggered and struggled for an advantage against the ear-ringing downstrokes of his rival's blade. The rain of blows continued in its ferocity until he lost his balance and crashed to the ground. A thundering of cheers erupted when the young man positioned himself over his fallen foe, poised to deliver the killing blow.

The young man's eyes turned to the stands. His chest heaved. One by one, the people jabbed their thumbs toward their throats and chanted in unison for the fallen man's death. The rhythmic outcry pounded into Rayad's ears. Of course they wouldn't call for mercy. A crowd this invested would want bloodshed. Rayad shook his head. He shouldn't watch this, but something held him there—some pull to see the fight to the end—though he would probably regret it later.

The young gladiator's gaze shifted to the officiator of the games. The overweight lord slid from his seat and shambled to the edge of his viewing box where he held out his fist. With increased vigor, the crowd called for death, all eyes on the lord's outstretched thumb. In an almost contemptuous motion, he jerked it toward his throat. The crowd broke into cheers.

Rayad let go a long sigh, a dull ache in his chest. No one, especially someone so young, should be forced into murder. But what did he expect? The world seemed to thrive on this sort of cruelty.

At first, the young man did nothing. His sword point still hovered over his kneeling opponent's chest. Rayad's own heartbeat slowed as the young man's eyes dropped from the stands. He raised his sword higher. The crowd, now hushed, leaned forward.

In a blur of motion, the young man spun his sword around and smashed the hilt into his opponent's head. A solid blow, but not a lethal one. The man went limp and fell senseless to the dirt. Rayad's lungs released their held breath. All fell silent for a moment, but then boos and jeers poured from the spectators. Turning in a slow circle, the young man glared at them. With a flick of his wrist, he tossed his sword aside and marched toward one of the gates. Half-eaten food and garbage pelted him along the way, and the angry, hate-filled shouts continued well after he was out of sight. Rayad glanced once at the officiator. A scowl put deep lines in the man's pudgy forehead. He ought to be down in that arena fighting for his life. Maybe then he wouldn't be so quick to condemn a man to death.

Rayad tore himself from the opening and shook the images away as he emerged outside the arena on the far side. A den of madness and evil. That's what his father had always said about the games. And he'd known it firsthand as a slave and caretaker of the horses often used in gladiatorial fights. Though he'd earned his freedom and turned that knowledge of horses into a lucrative business of breeding and training the animals, he was a rarity. Most enslaved men involved in the games never escaped the bloodshed of the arenas.

Rayad thanked his Creator he never had to have a part in it. Men were not supposed to kill each other for sport. It wasn't the way of Elôm. But the knowledge of Elôm had died to mere myths in the minds of many in Ilyon these days, with Arcacia leading the way. If that weren't true, he wouldn't be in this mess.

Setting his mind again on what he must do, he came upon the local market. Stalls and carts lined each side of a narrow street between the rough stone buildings and clogged traffic nearly as much as in the arena. He grumbled under his breath, good and tired of so many people. He couldn't reach the forest again fast enough. Red and gold overhangs shadowed the path from the sinking sun, but it also trapped the hot, stifling air beneath. Not even an overburdened spice cart could cut the stench of sweat. How he hated cramped and dirty markets—and he'd seen enough of them in his days of trading and selling horses. Yet, once again, the unpleasant crowd provided necessary cover.

Near one stall at the end of the lane, his eyes caught on a shadowed figure, and he murmured a silent prayer of thanks. He slipped through the remaining people, sidestepping a pair of grubby children who raced by, and joined the other man in the shadows.

"Ah, Warin, you're here." Rayad clasped the man's thick,

bracer-protected forearm. Splitting up to disguise their trail had been wise after all. At least they both still drew breath.

"Thank the King you made it." Warin kept his deep voice low. "I was beginning to worry."

"I took it slow and made sure to cover my trail. The emperor's men are everywhere." Rayad glanced around. No sign of gold and black uniforms here . . . yet. "We're probably ahead of any messengers from Falspar, but we can't be too careful."

Warin agreed.

Rayad returned his eyes to his friend as his heart sank. Would they really part here for the last time? This grimy, undesirable place in the middle of nowhere? They were like brothers—they'd grown up together, worked together. He'd never expected their lifelong friendship to end like this.

"Have you made up your mind on where you'll go?"

"I figure I'll head west." Warin inclined his head in the direction the sun would soon set. "If there are others like us, I'll find them." He paused, and his eyes turned hopeful. "You still plan to head north?"

Rayad hated to disappoint him, but gave a firm nod. "It's been too long since I've seen Kalli and Aldor."

A smile hinted through Warin's beard. "You're sure you don't want to join me?"

Tempting, he had to admit, but Rayad shook his head. "I think it's time for a little peace. I'm getting too old for this."

Warin chuckled. "You know I don't believe that. You only have a few years on me, after all . . . but I don't blame you. You ought to have some peace by now."

The two of them clasped arms again.

"Take care," Rayad said, squeezing his forearm. "Maybe I'll get bored and come find you one day. May the King protect you."

"You too. I'll keep a lookout."

They traded their final goodbyes and parted. Making his best attempt at optimism, Rayad used the opportunity of the market to purchase the last of his provisions and returned to the stable where he'd left his horses. He stowed his supplies and paid the stable boy before leading the animals outside. His eyes made a quick sweep for soldiers before he turned to mount his reliable white gelding.

"Time to get out of here, Aros."

Once he was in the saddle, the horse promptly obeyed his every command. The one beside him, however, balked at first. Rayad tugged the lead rope and grumbled. "We're not doing this now."

The young ebony-coated stallion followed, though the subtle arch of its neck still spoke of stubbornness. *Ornery creature.* Was the beast even worth the trouble? He was getting too old for a good number of things, including dealing with fiery young horses. But the stallion was all that remained of the proud bloodline his father had started so long ago . . . the only one not stolen from him.

Forcing aside his nerves, Rayad maintained a casual pace toward the northern outskirts of Troas, one of the largest cities this far south. It lay just north enough to avoid nighttime attacks by the monstrous cave drakes inhabiting the Krell Mountains on Arcacia's southern shores.

Beyond the outer buildings, he spotted the forest, but first he had to pass through the open meadow scattered with tents and wagons. Heavy, barred wagons mostly—gladiator wagons—all gathered for the games. Many stood empty, but a few contained men with faces and eyes either void or glaring their cold hatred. Rayad diverted his gaze and focused on the road, but he ground his teeth. What was happening to this world? Oh, for the days long past when the inhabitants of Ilyon had served and worshipped their true Lord—millenniums ago, before the ryriks had led the revolt against their Creator and changed how everything was created to be.

The road meandered its way toward the trees, urging Rayad to ride faster. He glanced over his shoulder, just to be sure no one followed, and tried to shrug off the clinging claws of paranoia. A raised voice drifted through the air, and he whipped his head around.

"*. . . worthless creature . . . teach you to defy me . . . do as you're told . . .*"

Rayad snorted and shot a glance at the stallion beside him. Probably another troublesome beast of burden. He rode past a tent and found the source of the shouting—a stout man dressed in flamboyant red linen and an ill-fitting leather doublet. The man raised a horsewhip, spitting out a string of curses, and brought it hissing down—not upon some hapless animal, but on another man kneeling in front of him with one arm chained to a stake. Rayad's gut wrenched. It was the same young gladiator he'd seen in the arena. He pulled Aros to a halt.

The man beat the gladiator without mercy. Rayad cringed at every stinging impact, but the young man made no sound and barely flinched. Infuriated, the man with the whip took him by the hair and yanked his head up. Blood dripped from the gladiator's chin.

"How many times do I have to tell you? You could be a sensation. You please the crowd, do you understand?"

To punctuate these words, he backhanded the gladiator across the chin. In a defiant move, the young man tried to rise, but he received a solid fist to the ribs and sank back to his knees, where the man with the whip proceeded to beat him again.

Rayad squeezed Aros's reins, and the leather dug into his palm. Common sense told him to move on, that he could do nothing, yet every bone in his body willed him to act.

"Excuse me," he called out before the man could strike again.

The man with the whip spun around, his face flushed nearly purple. Rayad slid off his horse and marched up to him. Another massive hulk of a man stood nearby next to a wagon with the faded and peeling red words *Jasper's Gladiators* painted along the side.

"What's the meaning of this?" Rayad demanded of the man with the whip.

His flaccid face knotted in an ugly scowl. "None of your business. He's my slave."

Rayad planted his fists on his hips and glared down at the man who stood a few inches shorter. "Slave or not, no man should be treated in such a manner."

Jasper let out a cruel bark of laughter. "He's no man."

He reached for the gladiator's hair again and yanked it up on the side. Rayad's breath snagged halfway up his throat. The young slave's ear came to a noticeable point.

Sneering, Jasper shoved the gladiator's head away as if he were the most disgusting thing in Ilyon. "He's half ryrik."

The mixed blood slave looked up, and his sea-blue eyes almost glowed behind the strands of hair that fell in his face. His gaze locked with Rayad's. Defiance and danger flashed in the cold, diamond-hard light, but deeper writhed the shadows of a tortured soul.

"He gets just what he deserves; now go about your own business."

The coarse voice snapped Rayad to attention. He broke eye contact with the gladiator as Jasper raised the whip again. Before it found its target, Rayad grabbed it.

"Enough!"

Scowl lines sinking deeper, Jasper tugged on the whip, but Rayad held fast. The man balled his fist and took a swing at his chin. Rayad caught him by the wrist and, in one fluid motion, landed him on his back. The man at the wagon pulled out his sword and stepped forward, but Rayad was quicker. In an instant, his own sword flashed out of the scabbard and rested at Jasper's throat. The other man paused.

"This is between me and him." Rayad's tone and glare left

no room for argument. The man remained where he stood, but watched closely, sword ready.

Rayad stepped away from Jasper. The smaller man scrambled to his feet, his red face bunched like a child ready to throw a fit. He reached for his sword, untrained fingers fumbling, but froze at Rayad's next words.

"How much do you want for him?"

Jasper's expression morphed from rage to confusion. "What?"

"How much do you want for the boy?"

Jasper eyed his slave, and the gladiator peered at the two of them, his bruised and bleeding face a cold mask, void of emotion.

With a harsh laugh, Jasper turned back to Rayad. "You'd pay for such an animal?"

Rayad narrowed his eyes and battled the impulse to go ahead and let the man try to fight him. Let him see how it felt to be on the receiving end of someone who held all the power.

"He may be half ryrik, but he's also half human." Thinking better of letting this turn violent, he slid his sword back into the scabbard and turned to his horses to dig in his saddlebags for his money pouch. He weighed the small leather bag in his hand. Not much to show for a lifetime of hard work. He faced Jasper again. "I'll give you two-fifty for him."

Jasper's mud-colored eyes squinted greedily. "How about three hundred?"

"I only have two-hundred fifty."

Jasper darted a glance behind Rayad. "Throw in the black horse and you can have him."

"The horse is not for sale."

"Then there's no deal."

Rayad's fingers itched to reach for his sword again. Instead, he turned to his saddlebags once more. This time he pulled out a dagger of the finest craftsmanship. He hesitated, hating to part with it, but in the end, he'd rather keep the horse.

"I'll give you this and the money."

At the sight of the weapon, Jasper nearly drooled. "All right, it's a deal." He sneered at the slave. "He won't amount to anything anyway."

Jasper snatched up the dagger and the money pouch with a wicked grin begging to be wiped away with a fist. He reached into his pocket and tossed a key into the dirt at Rayad's feet.

"I wouldn't set him loose if I were you. He's likely to run off, or even more likely, slit your throat and ride off with your goods."

With these parting words, Jasper and his bodyguard strode away toward the city. Rayad faced the young gladiator whose piercing eyes trained on him like some wounded, mistrustful animal. He took a step closer, and the slave rose to his feet, confirming his impressive height. His hair, as black as one of the crows that scavenged nearby, framed his face in straight, uneven layers ending at his strong jaw. A hint of stubble traced his bloodstained chin. Though almost hidden behind a hard mask, his youthfulness peeked through, just as Rayad had seen in the arena.

The young man eyed him up and down, clearly taking in his strengths . . . and weaknesses.

Elôm, what have I gotten myself into this time?

Keeping his voice calm and non-threatening, Rayad asked, "What is your name?"

The young man didn't even blink at the question. A long silence stretched between them. With a sigh, Rayad gave up and bent down for the key.

"Jace." Though hinting at youth, his voice was deep and powerful.

Rayad straightened.

"My name is Jace." The young man's eyes glinted and measured his every reaction.

"I'm Rayad."

He gave Jace a look-over. Though missing his armor now,

11

blood stained Jace's sleeveless tunic from his right shoulder down his side and oozed along his left arm. Rayad glanced at the key in his hand and back to Jace as he weighed his options. Best to start right out with the truth.

"I have no notion of whether or not I can trust you. But I do want to help you and see your wounds are properly tended. I'll leave you chained until then, but when I'm done, I'll release you. After that, it's your choice. You can run or come with me. You're no longer a slave."

Jace's hardened expression barely changed, but his eyes flickered with the many thoughts racing through his mind. If only Rayad could know what those were.

He turned and unbuckled his sword belt to hang it over Aros's saddle. This destroyed his plans for a quick getaway, but what choice did he have? He couldn't just let the boy run off, wounded and unprepared. It would defeat the purpose of freeing him. He glanced at the key again and tucked it away in his saddlebags. At least this way Jace wouldn't try to kill him until after he'd dressed his wounds. He gathered up his medical supplies and waterskin and turned back to Jace.

"Why don't you kneel down so I can take a look at your back and other wounds?"

Jace's eyes flashed to Rayad's face, pained in their intensity and distrust. No doubt this young man had known a lifetime, short as it might be, of hateful mistreatment. Rayad softened his normally rough tone. If he were going to help him, he would have to break through the first layer of his defensive wall at least.

"I have no intention of harming you." He gave a dry chuckle. "Actually, I have no doubt you could outmatch me if you wanted."

Jace's tense face relaxed a little. He cast a wary glance around the camp and dropped first to one knee and then the other. Rayad knelt beside him and lifted the back of his threadbare tunic. He ground his teeth together. Angry, red welts covered Jace's back. Numerous other scars left from old wounds added to the stomach-turning sight. Rayad drew in a deep breath and checked the wound on Jace's shoulder. Despite the amount of blood, the long cut was superficial.

"I think this would be easier if you took your tunic off," he said quietly.

Jace reached up with his free arm to pull his tunic over his head and let it hang on the chain. A grimace crossed his face—the first show of any pain. Their eyes caught, and a burst of anger flared in Jace's, erasing the embarrassment. Rayad gave him a sympathetic look. "Feeling pain isn't a weakness."

Jace looked away, clenching and unclenching his jaw.

Neither spoke as Rayad carefully cleaned and bandaged the wounds. Though Jace tried to hide all hint of pain, his breathing became labored. When he finished, Rayad rose, and Jace slipped on his tunic as he pushed to his feet. Rayad returned the supplies to his saddlebags where he pulled out the key. He turned it in his fingers and glanced skyward. *Give me wisdom to handle this.* It could cost him his life. But wasn't a whole garrison of soldiers bent on taking it anyway? If he had to go one way or the other, this would probably be quicker than anything they planned. He turned to Jace, and the young man lifted his wrist. With silent prayers still running through his mind, Rayad unlocked the chain. It fell to the ground with a clatter, and he tossed the key away.

"You're free."

Jace's eyes darted around the area—first to the trees, then to the horses, and finally back to his rescuer for a moment. Rayad sensed the energy building inside him. Energy no doubt fueled by volatile ryrik blood. Any moment he could bolt . . . or attack. There'd be no stopping him either way. Rayad masked his apprehension with a conversational tone.

"Listen, you can go if you wish, but people would probably suspect you're a runaway, and you could be enslaved again. If you come with me, I can offer you a good, warm meal and better prepare you to go on your way."

Jace's restless gaze fixed on him, but offered no answer. Rayad grabbed the horses' leads and looked off toward the city. The sun had sunk behind it now. He wouldn't get much farther today.

"Why don't we head into the forest and find somewhere out of the way to set up camp for the night?"

He headed for the trees. After a few yards, he glanced back to find Jace following. Perhaps he did have a chance at helping this young man.

A good distance in, Rayad veered off the road and found a suitable clearing a couple of hundred yards into the forest. Any snooping soldiers wouldn't bother to look here. But it also left him at Jace's mercy. The young man appeared only too aware of this fact.

"We'll camp here," Rayad murmured, and forced himself to turn to the horses, half-expecting to find himself strangled from behind. Tension squeezed his muscles, and an uncomfortable sensation of pressure built around his throat. A minute or two passed, and he relaxed. He looked over his shoulder. Jace just stood and stared at him as if seeing some foreign life form.

Rayad pulled the saddle from Aros's back. "I won't force you to do anything, but if you feel up to it, you can gather some firewood while I tend the horses. Don't strain yourself—just enough to get the fire going. Then I'll start supper."

He went on with his work. A moment later, Jace walked off. Soon, Rayad had the horses hobbled and grazing, and he cleared a place for the fire. He rested back on his heels and peered into the quiet shadows of the forest. Not a sign of Jace. Maybe he was gone for good, or just waiting in the forest until night fell. And why not? It would be easy to steal the horses and get away in the dark. *This is in Your hands, Lord, whatever happens.* Still, he'd just as soon not have to walk all the way north and find a way to survive without supplies or money.

His stomach grumbled in response to such thoughts, and he reached for his pack to dig out his food supplies. When he looked up again, Jace walked just outside the camp. His muscular arms encircled a bundle of wood, and he approached with impressively quiet steps.

Rayad let a small smile grow and rose to his feet. "Thank you."

Jace blinked. He'd probably never heard that before.

"Just set it down, and I'll start a fire."

Jace did so and stood back, watching. Murmuring to himself, Rayad put together a meal of rice, beans, and meat—not a feast by any stretch of the imagination, but filling. He dished a generous portion into a bowl and offered it to Jace. The young man took it and sat opposite him across the fire. After the first ravenous bite, all else seemed forgotten for the moment.

Less intent on his meal, Rayad studied his interesting new companion. First glance would lead most to see Jace as fully human, but for someone familiar with ryriks, the similarities went beyond his pointed ears. Coal-black hair, intense blue eyes, and strong build—clear signs of his ryrik blood—not to mention the flashes of anger characteristic of a ryrik. But how many other traits and tendencies did the young man share? The bloodlust? The deep hatred for other races? The fits of rage that could be sparked by anything?

Rayad shook his head. Only Elôm knew what other traits Jace might possess or how prominent they might be. Rayad would have to discover that for himself. He'd never before heard of anyone with mixed ryrik blood. Women never lived to tell of ryrik attacks, yet here Jace sat.

Jace downed the contents of his bowl and set it aside. His eyes snagged on the sheathed sword propped up next to Rayad. Their gazes met. Rayad tried to gauge what lay behind the iron-like shell that portrayed such hardness, yet hid such pain. Murderous intentions? Maybe, but Rayad had seen that in men before and found none of it in this young man.

Well, he'd know the answer soon enough. He reached for his sword. Jace's whole body tensed, ready to spring, and light flared in his eyes. Rayad laid the sword on the ground between them, the hilt just a foot away from Jace's hand. He had only to grab it. Considering the swiftness Rayad had witnessed in the arena, the young man could have the deed over and done with in a moment.

"If you intend to kill me, get it over with. I won't be able to stop you, and I won't sit up all night watching you." He had too far to travel to play guard night after night. He needed alertness and rest should other foes discover his trail.

Jace's dark brows dipped low over his eyes. "You're not afraid?"

"Of dying? Not really." Rayad settled against his saddle, resting in the complete truth of his words. He didn't particularly care to die now, but he didn't fear it. "I've lived a full life, and I'm a firm believer in King Elôm."

Jace stared at him for a long, drawn-out moment. The fire crackled fitfully between them.

"Why?" the question came at last.

"Why what?" Rayad asked.

"Why are you doing this for me—a half ryrik?" Jace grimaced, and the mask slipped to reveal the true agony that lived inside him. He nearly choked on the words. "An animal. All hate me."

He hardened again, but that look left a dull ache in Rayad's heart as if bruised. "I'm not so sure of that," he said softly. He cleared his throat. "As for your question, I don't hold with cruelty or injustice. And you may not understand, but I feel compelled to help you." How could he not when his father had lived a similar sort of life? He would do the same if he were here. He'd been a rare type of man—always going out of his way to help those less fortunate. "It's up to you whether or not you accept my help."

Firelight danced in his gem-like eyes as Jace considered Rayad's words. His gaze fell on the sword, and he gripped the hilt, lifting it up. Rayad only watched him. Jace stared at the weapon before deftly tossing the hilt in the air and catching the sword around the scabbard. Eyes back on Rayad, he offered the hilt.

"I won't kill you."

Rayad took his sword and smiled faintly.

A ROBIN WARBLED in the branches overhead. Rayad shifted under his wool blanket as sleep wore off. His eyes popped open. Well, he was alive. Now, would Jace and the horses still be there? He propped himself up on his elbow. The two horses stood beneath the trees where he'd tied them. The stallion nipped at Aros who snorted and stomped his hoof in warning. Rayad gave his own little snort and rolled over to peer through the thin tendrils of smoke rising from the fire's embers. Jace lay on the other side, wrapped in an extra blanket.

Rayad sat up. The young man did not stir. In his sleep, Jace's face had relaxed entirely and revealed an almost heartbreaking look of innocence. Sympathy rose inside Rayad. With no children of his own, something took hold of him he'd never experienced before—a desire to show this young man a true home and life away from cruelty—to show him something other than hatred.

But a frown tugged at his brows. What did he have to offer? He had no family, no home, no money, and absolutely no experience with this sort of thing. After a long moment of contemplation, the answer came clear as the sky overhead. He knew Elôm. What could be greater than that knowledge? He rose to his feet, ran a hand through his short hair, and rolled up his bedroll. He may turn out to be horrible at this parenting thing, but he could give it a try . . . if Jace would let him.

He chuckled softly to himself at the humor in it. One moment he was running for his life, and the next he was taking in a troubled young man, and a half ryrik one at that. *I'm sure You set that all up*, he easily conversed with his King and Creator. *I just haven't the faintest idea why yet.*

Though Rayad worked quietly to pack his supplies, Jace jerked upright. He stared around the clearing, his eyes confused at first, but then his gaze landed on Rayad. He breathed out a long breath. The tension returned to his face.

"Sleep well?" Rayad asked.

Jace just stared at him, as usual.

"Yes," he murmured at last.

"Good. When we've eaten, we can be on our way." Rayad paused. "That is, if you'd like to join me."

"Where are you going?"

Rayad almost smiled at the lack of suspicion in his eyes. "I have some old friends who live a few days north of here near Kinnim. I hope to stay with them for a time until other arrangements can be made."

"You have no home?"

Unwanted memories stirred Rayad's mind, still too fresh to leave behind. "No, not anymore . . . I'm on the run."

Surprise perked Jace's expression.

"I'm wanted by the emperor's men," Rayad explained. If Jace joined him, he had to know the truth since it could endanger him as well. And if Jace decided to turn him in, well, he was willing to risk it. He'd already placed himself at Jace's mercy. "They want me for speaking out against his desire to force Arcacia to worship his false gods. They consider me a rebel . . . among other things. What about you? Is there someplace you'd rather go?"

Jace looked away, hiding his face, and shook his head.

Rayad let him have a moment. He pulled a good bit of jerky and hardtack from his pack and offered it to him. The young man took it without a word, but Rayad picked up the smallest spark of gratitude.

"My friends," he went on, "they're an older couple." Jace glanced at him, and Rayad smirked. "Yes, older than me, and very kind. They live on a small farm about ten miles from the nearest village, so there won't be many people, and no one to come looking for us. So, would you like to join me?"

Jace swallowed and raised his yearning, yet hesitant eyes. "I don't think your friends would have me." His voice dropped lower. "I'm a killer."

Considering what he'd seen of Jace in the arena and during supper last night, Rayad felt confident enough to say, "I don't believe that."

Doubt lingered in Jace's expression, and Rayad assured him, "I know Kalli and Aldor will welcome you. Trust me, you'll never meet kinder or gentler souls."

Rayad smiled in memory of how the two, as a young couple, had shown up at his parents' home during a raging storm with hardly more than the clothes on their backs and about to deliver their first child. They'd worked on the farm long enough to get back on their feet before setting out to establish their own place and had kept in touch over the years. It would be real good to see them again.

With a slow nod, Jace accepted his words.

Following their brief breakfast, Rayad retrieved Aros to saddle him. Then he went for the stallion. The moment he loosed the rope from the tree, the horse pranced around and yanked against the lead.

"Oh, don't you start with me." Rayad scowled. Didn't he have enough to contend with without always having to fight the cantankerous beast? And his sire had been so well behaved. He would gladly have traded the two, yet the stallion's wild nature was to thank for preventing the animal from being stolen. That was his only consolation in this—the thought of how much trouble the emperor's soldiers must have faced before giving up on the horse. Hopefully he'd sent them back to the barracks with a few bruises.

"Come on," he commanded and tugged the lead toward Aros.

But the stallion planted his feet and would not budge.

"Well, if you aren't the most stubborn, ornery . . ."

He flicked the end of the rope at the horse's hindquarters. The big, black animal jumped sideways, but still refused to move. Rayad's hackles rose. After all the many years he'd spent training horses with his father and on his own, he'd developed great patience and knowledge where the animals were concerned, but this one tried it like no other. He glared at the beast, convinced it stood there mocking him.

"Can I try?"

Jace's sudden appearance startled him. Surely he couldn't be serious, but the young man stared intently at the belligerent horse. Rayad shook his head in reluctance and handed over the lead. What did he have to lose?

"Just don't let him go or it'll take us all morning to catch him," he warned. "And beware. He's never liked strangers."

Rayad stepped back to watch, skeptical, but interested. He just hoped the horse wouldn't take a bite out of Jace. The ill-tempered thing had tried that on occasion with Warin. The stallion eyed Jace and laid his ears back. He gave his head an angry toss and snorted. This didn't look good.

"What's his name?" Jace asked.

"Niton."

"Niton," Jace repeated, his deep voice making the name sound especially rich and noble.

Not that the animal deserved it. Something like Beast would have been more appropriate had Rayad known what the horse would grow into. And he probably would've sold him just as soon as he was weaned.

At his name, Niton's ears rose and pricked forward. He blew out loudly a couple of times before his breathing quieted. Jace remained still until the stallion calmed. He then approached slowly and spoke in a soothing tone that contrasted starkly with his usual cold and sullen manner. Coming up next to the horse, he laid his hand on the stallion's neck. Niton didn't even flinch. Rayad's mouth dropped open. Jace stroked Niton's neck and shoulder and, with the slightest prompting, led him straight to Rayad, who gawked at them.

"How did you do that?"

Jace shrugged with no hint of beguilement or trickery. "I've worked with horses before. I like them." His voice dropped lower as he ran his hand down Niton's face and looked into one of his dark eyes. "They don't know what I am."

Rayad stared at the two of them. In all his long years, he'd never come across such a surprising mystery as Jace. Still taking it in, he turned for his other horse.

"We best get moving. Aros can bear both of us."

"Can I ride Niton?"

Rayad stopped and turned again. Voice flat, he said, "Niton's never had a man on his back, and the way things are going, I doubt he ever will."

One of Jace's brows rose in a black arch, and Rayad wished to take back his words. He'd just given the young man a challenge. He blew out a sigh at Jace's unwavering look. "All right, it's your body," he conceded, his own bones aching. "But like I said, don't let him go . . . if you can help it."

Jace's expression transformed into a small but determined smile. He tossed the end of the lead over Niton's neck and tied it to the halter. At the stallion's side, he took the rope reins and a handful of Niton's thick mane in one hand. Rayad stepped forward to offer to help him up, but Jace sprang from the ground and swung himself onto Niton's back despite the horse's significant size. Agility—another ryrik characteristic.

At the sudden, unfamiliar weight, Niton pranced in place. Jace sat with all the confidence of an experienced horseman as the stallion took a few skittish steps backward and reared. He laid the reins across Niton's neck and made him turn to the right. After circling a few times, Jace brought him to halt. Now Niton stood as calm as Rayad had ever seen him.

Mouth open again, Rayad looked from the horse to Jace whose eyes held a bit of smugness. He shook his head. "You have quite a talent, Jace."

He reached for Aros. After mounting, he nudged the gelding, and they started for the road. Jace moved Niton up beside them, and Rayad glanced at them again. This was sure to be an interesting adventure.

JACE DREW IN a deep breath and let it out slow, focusing his senses. He pressed his back against the rough trunk of a swamp maple. A grunt rumbled from behind the tree as something large rooted in the brush. Each beat of Jace's heart thumped stronger than normal. The beast was close. He flexed his fingers around his bow and quieted his thoughts. Success would only come with precision. In one smooth motion, he swung around the tree and drew back the bowstring.

A massive pickerin boar stood a mere thirty feet away. Its coarse black hair came to a stiff ridge down the center of its back, which reached up past Jace's waist. A breeze carried its soured stench to Jace's nostrils, and he took a glance at the animal's wrinkled head. At the end of its long snout, four eight-inch tusks protruded with razor sharp tips. He'd never come across one this size before. It would be a fine prize if he brought it down, though most hunters would never have taken on such a beast alone. But he wasn't most hunters, and he wasn't out here for sport.

He peered down the arrow shaft and aimed for the pickerin's shoulder. A heart shot was the only way to bring it down quickly and safely. He took another silent breath to steady himself. Though the animal angled away from him, its head shot up in alarm. It sniffed the air with a loud snort. A cold shiver raised the hair along Jace's arms, and his heart punched his ribs in warning. The pickerin spun around the very moment he released his arrow. With a *thunk* the shaft penetrated, but too far to the right, near the boar's neck. Jace scowled. Squealing more in rage than pain, the pickerin charged him.

He groaned and dashed deeper into the trees. Though quick as a deer in the forest, he couldn't lose the enraged boar as it crashed through the brush right behind him. He scanned the terrain ahead and scrambled for a plan that wouldn't get him gored to death. Maybe, if Rayad was nearby . . .

Launching over a tangle of roots, he came down on a thick bed of dead leaves. Dampened from a recent rain, they slipped across a slick rock. He hit the forest floor hard. Hooves pounded behind him, and he rolled to his back. Hot blood pumped all through his body as the animal bore down on him. When it drew close, he kicked it under the chin. The pickerin took a step away, shaking its snout.

He clambered to his feet and yanked out his hunting knife. This time he did not turn and run. He faced the pickerin and stared the animal down. The boar stomped its hooves, snorted, and charged again. Jace tightened his grip on the knife and waited for barely a moment before sidestepping. The pickerin raced past him. Pain sliced across his left knee, and he sucked in his breath, but his aim was perfect. The long blade of the hunting knife pierced the pickerin's tough hide and sunk deep into its flesh just behind the shoulder.

He yanked it out again and spun around to watch the animal. One of them was going down in this clearing. The boar skidded to a halt and scrambled for footing as it came at him again. But this time it only made it a couple of feet before collapsing and lying still. Jace stood poised for another attack. When a full few seconds passed in silence, he let out a sigh and relaxed. Still cautious, he approached the downed pickerin. Convinced it was dead, he wiped his knife in the grass and returned it to the sheath in his boot. Now Aldor wouldn't lose any more of his sprouting crops—crops they would need come winter.

Jace cast his gaze about for his bow. When he found it in the leaves, he brushed away the mud and fastened it back to his quiver. Footsteps approached from a distance, and he straightened. Rayad appeared and made his way through the thick trees.

"You found him," he said as he came to stand next to Jace and eyed his muddied clothing. "Did he give you much trouble?"

"Some. I tried for a clean shot, but he moved as soon as I fired." He shook his head. He'd even had the wind to his advantage. Most game didn't prove to be such a challenge.

Rayad's gaze dropped to the blood staining the edges of the tear in Jace's pants. "Your leg."

"Just a scratch."

The older man's graying brows drew together and put worry lines in his forehead. "Just make sure you have Kalli take a look at it. You don't want it getting infected."

Jace responded to his serious tone with a half smile, and Rayad's frown deepened. "Now don't you give me any of that talk about becoming overly protective and fussy in my old age. I have every right to show a little concern now and then."

Jace let a full smile develop and chuckled, drawing a smile from Rayad as well. Yes, after three years, the man did have that right considering the trials Jace knew he'd put him through. It had taken him a long time to adjust to life beyond slavery and respond to care and concern instead of hatred. The memories of his former life still clung to him more strongly than he wished, but in the midst of the hard times, he'd come to know a peace altogether foreign to him. Though not always constant, at times such as this, he was content.

A far-off look occupied Rayad's face. Apparently, Jace was not the only one letting his mind wander. He eyed him in amusement. Rayad blinked, and his frown resurfaced when he realized he had been caught reminiscing, which did no favors for his argument about getting old.

"Come on," he said with a growl that drew another chuckle from Jace. "Let's get this animal gutted and back to the farm. Kalli will be pleased. I bet she'll make pickerin stew tomorrow night."

Jace's stomach growled, prompting him forward.

With the hefty pickerin boar hanging from a long branch between them, Jace and Rayad emerged from the forest into a small, cleared valley of lush farmland. Fields of rich, dark soil blanketed with the bright green of new crops stretched out before them. Even after three years, the sight hadn't dulled for Jace. It was the first place he'd ever learned the definition of home—the one place in all the world he felt free and happy.

When they neared the barn ahead, Aldor came from the garden. He grinned, his white teeth matching his snowy beard. "You found him. Excellent! I was getting worried we'd lose our spring crop."

"You shouldn't have to worry now," Rayad replied, "unless there's another one in the area. But with this big guy around, I doubt it."

"He's a big one all right. Haven't seen one this size in years. We'll be eating good this summer. I'll get the smokehouse fired up first thing." He eyed the animal's wounds. "Two shots to bring him down, huh? Not bad, considering his size."

Jace shook his head and shifted the pole on his shoulder, hating to admit, "My first shot missed. I had to take him down with my knife."

Aldor glanced toward Rayad. "Can't say I've seen that done before."

"He didn't leave me much choice," Jace responded. He'd only done what he needed to stay alive and kill the boar.

They carried the pickerin into the barn and laid it down. A loud bark echoed from behind them. Jace turned as a black wolf bounded into the barn. She stopped at the pickerin and sniffed before emitting a deep growl. Jace knelt beside her and ruffled the thick fur around her neck.

"Easy, Tyra. You don't have to chase him out of the fields anymore."

The wolf nuzzled his face and wagged her tail.

"Let's see your leg." Jace took her foreleg in his hand. The linen bandage remained in place, and only a little blood had seeped through from the tusk wound she'd acquired in her last confrontation with the pickerin.

It took all three of the men to hoist the boar up from one of the rafters to butcher. Tying off the rope, Jace caught movement out of the corner of his eye and looked to the door as Kalli entered the barn. While her husband was tall and fit, and surprisingly strong for his advance age, the matronly old woman was shorter and rounded. Laugh lines creased the corners of her eyes and around her mouth. Her very presence warmed the barn and filled Jace with peace.

"My, what a fine catch!" she exclaimed. "Thank the King for giving us two fine hunters to bring back such a prize."

"Indeed," Aldor agreed with his wife.

"It was all Jace," Rayad said, nodding. "I only showed up after the fact."

Kalli beamed at Jace, and heat rose into his face at the praise. "And for that, I shall make your favorite—pickerin stew."

He grinned, though he hadn't done anything spectacular. Actually, he'd done a poor job of it by not taking the pickerin down with his first shot.

Kalli's demeanor changed to one of concern, and she clucked, "Jace, you're bleeding."

He glanced at his leg. The bloodstain was barely the size of his hand. "I'm fine."

She placed her hands on her ample hips. "You'd say that on your deathbed. Now, come to the cabin and we'll have a look at it."

If anyone was overly protective and fussy, it was Kalli. Jace gave her a winning smile—one she couldn't refuse. "I'm sure it'll be fine until we're done."

Kalli's eyes narrowed, though Jace didn't think she was capable of truly being cross with him. "Well, all right, but you just make sure you let me tend to it when you come in. Pickerin wounds are a nasty business."

"I will," Jace promised, rubbing Tyra's head. Looked like they would both get medical attention tonight.

He glanced at Rayad. The older man gave him an *I told you* look. Jace rolled his eyes, and this time Rayad chuckled.

KYRIN ALTAIR'S PULSE betrayed her, drumming in her ears and causing that too familiar ache to throb at the base of her skull. The buzz of a hundred different conversations droned around her and joined with the pounding of blood in her head. She gritted her teeth. She should have known this would happen. Why had they ever come near here, especially now?

The sweeping central square in the heart of Arcacia's capital city of Valcré always teemed with people, as colorful merchant stalls and carts offered a vast variety of exotic and unique wares, but today, the crowd size had more than doubled. Nearly half the city had gathered to witness the spectacle. People pressed in close and jostled each other for a good view.

With quiet pleas of "excuse me," Kyrin squeezed her way through the crowd, searching. Most people ignored her, almost suffocating her with their nearness, but a few moved aside when they noticed her gold and black government-issued uniform. The constant tug of small hands holding tightly to the back of her long jerkin assured her that Meredith hadn't fallen behind. She shuddered to think how difficult it would be to find a little girl in this mass.

Confronted with a solid wall of male backs, Kyrin stopped. The closeness of the people trapped the breath in her lungs, and her vision mottled. She pressed her palms to her eyes and focused

31

on breathing. She wouldn't lose it now. Sweat beaded on her body and plastered her hair and clothing to her skin. *Just breathe.* She fought to tune out the crowd for even a brief respite, but the pounding headache made it impossible to focus.

"Do you see her?" the small voice came from behind.

Kyrin's head snapped up, and she outwardly composed herself. She looked over her shoulder at the petite little blue-eyed girl and forced a smile. "No, not yet."

She had to keep moving, keep searching. They stepped around the men and drew ever closer to the raised wooden platform that commanded everyone's attention. Kyrin adamantly ignored it. She rose up on her toes to gain a better view through the crowd, and a flash of gold caught her eye.

"Kaden!"

Please, let him hear me. She called again through the bodies in front of her and released a loud breath when the dark-haired young man turned in her direction. Taller than many of the men around him, he spotted them and pushed his way through to meet her and Meredith. Just having him near soothed her quaking insides.

"Did you find her?" he asked.

Kyrin shook her head. Kaden's dusty blue eyes, identical to her own, turned to ice, and his jaw muscles bunched.

"I swear, when we—"

"No, you don't," Kyrin cut in, giving him a warning look, though threats of her own flitted through her mind. She grimaced and pressed her fingers to her throbbing temples. Why couldn't she be normal? "Let's just find her and get back."

Her brother's eyes narrowed. "You all right?"

"I will be when we get out of this crowd."

Kaden huffed and scanned the area again. At last, he announced, "There she is."

He moved to the left and pushed his way through far less politely than Kyrin had. She and Meredith stayed on his heels and kept to the cleared path he made, which quickly closed up behind them with grumbling onlookers. When they broke out of the sea of bodies next to another young woman in government uniform, Kyrin cut around in front of Kaden just before he could go off on the girl.

She put her hands on her hips. "Elise. Where have you been? We're going to be late."

The blonde girl spared the three of them little more than a glance and said pertly, "We have time."

So much for respecting the fact both Kyrin and Kaden had two more years on her fifteen.

Meredith tugged the girl's arm, her voice mournful. "Come on, Elise. I don't wanna miss lunch. I'm hungry."

Elise shushed her before catching Kyrin's hard look.

"What? Don't you want to see?"

Kyrin's gaze shifted to the platform. A wood block, about knee-high, sat in the center, though she averted her eyes from the dark stains bleeding down the front. Her focus rested on the huge man who towered beside it, but a leather mask hid his face. He gripped a massive broadsword, its sharp point resting on the platform as he waited.

Kyrin swallowed the lump in her throat and looked away. "No."

"Oh, come on. It's—"

A murmur swept through the crowd and pulled Kyrin's attention back to the platform where five men climbed the stairs. Her stomach tightened. Four of the men bore the uniforms of Arcacian military—black and gold, just like her and her companions. The man between them, however, wore a pair of stained linen pants and only a leather jerkin—the exact opposite of their clean, professional appearance. But his fearsome features commanded all the attention. He stood a good five inches taller than any of the guards who held the heavy chains attached to his shackles. Taller even than Kaden. Long, greasy strands of thick black hair fell around his hard face, which bore the bruises of recent beatings, and an unusual amount of black hair covered his muscular arms.

Kyrin swallowed the thumping of her heart in her throat as the man peered at the crowd. His eyes unnerved her. They flashed a startling, almost luminescent blue as if an icy light glowed behind them. She could have found them beautiful if not for the man's hideous sneer.

Meredith shrank against her, and Kyrin put her hands on the girl's shoulders.

"Come on, let's go," she urged Elise, and Kaden added firmly, "Now."

They'd seen enough ryrik executions, and this was no sight for Meredith. It would give her nightmares for sure. She didn't need one more thing to frighten her.

But a wave of jeers and hisses from the crowd drowned them out.

"Murderer!" a man shouted.

From nearby, a woman cried, "Soulless monster!"

The shouts rose up with growing intensity and loathing. Even Elise joined in. Kyrin shifted as a chill raised goose bumps under her sleeves. While she carried no sympathy for the ryriks considering how many people, particularly women and children, they brutally murdered, the crowd's hostile reaction unsettled her. People shouldn't be so eager to witness death. Perhaps they would not be if the details forever implanted themselves in their minds whether they wanted them or not—the way they did for her.

The guards shoved the ryrik man forward and forced him to his knees with a sound kick to the back of the leg. Though the ryrik showed no reaction in his expression, Kyrin caught the subtle twitch of a muscle in his jaw. His gaze swept the thousands of faces gathered to watch his demise. An intense fire burned in his eyes. He wanted to kill every single one of them, and given half a chance, he would. Thank goodness for the chains and guards.

The executioner stepped forward and lifted his sword into the air. The ryrik swallowed, and sweat glistened on his forehead. Kyrin's eyes trailed one bead of moisture that rolled down the side of his face and seeped into his beard. The guards forced the ryrik's neck down on the block. Kyrin bent down toward Meredith. She took care to keep her voice calm.

"Just face me."

The child buried her head against Kyrin's stomach. She covered the little girl's ears and turned her own eyes away. She wouldn't let such sights add themselves to the ever-growing collection of memories that would never leave her, ever. Yet, the scowling, jeering faces of the crowd were little improvement. Not much different from the ryrik, really. If only she could forget such unpleasant experiences, but they stuck as permanently as the ones she wished to keep. She caught Kaden's stormy eyes, and held them.

It all concluded in a disturbingly swift moment—a life brought to an end. The crowd erupted in whoops and cheers. Enough was enough. Kyrin snatched Elise's arm.

"It's time to go." She turned to Kaden. "Lead the way."

She took Meredith's hand and held her close to shield her from the gruesome view of the platform as they worked their way through the people again. The crowd bumped and pushed them as most people turned to leave. Even with Kaden in the lead, they made slow progress. Kyrin once more found herself battling to breathe normally. With her free hand, she grabbed Kaden's jerkin to make sure the crowd didn't separate them.

When they broke out into a less cramped intersection, Kyrin released a long breath, letting the tension drain. She let go of Kaden and brushed away the damp wisps of hair clinging to her face. From here, they had a perfect view of Auréa Palace. Settled on a hill overlooking all of Valcré and the Ardaluin Bay, it stood tall and majestic with its support columns and magnificent towers rising toward the sky, the golden-hued stones soaking in the sun. But such a familiar, everyday sight lost much of its majesty.

However, the edge of a skeletal-like structure farther to the right did give Kyrin pause. The Draicon Arena. Under construction by Emperor Daican's masons for over three years now, the monument to his father would dwarf most other structures in the city once it was completed—all for the purpose of gladiatorial games. Kyrin grimaced. She didn't want to think any more about death today.

Meredith squeezed her hand, and Kyrin shifted her focus to another large complex a little nearer. She cast a glance at the sun and winced. As the oldest of the group, she took responsibility for them and would no doubt have to explain things to Master Zocar if they arrived late. How did she always get stuck looking after Elise?

"We have to hurry."

She looked down at Meredith. Her short legs would never be quick enough. Kaden followed the same line of thought, as usual. He scooped Meredith up, and the little girl wrapped her arms around his neck.

"Let's go," he said.

Kyrin took the lead and hurried up the street between the multiple-story shops and merchants' homes that populated this area of the city. Elise jogged to catch up, bouncing her perfect, golden blonde ringlets—the very opposite of Kyrin's straight and plaited dull brown locks. Not that she was jealous.

"Relax," Elise said. "We have plenty of time."

Kyrin huffed. "You always say that."

Despite Elise's protests, Kyrin maintained their fast pace. They would not be late if she could help it. By the time they reached their destination, Elise panted behind them, not sharing Kyrin and Kaden's athleticism. Kyrin rushed them toward the large, arched gateway that passed through a twenty-foot wall. Huge black and gold banners hung on either side. One depicted a brawny, stern-faced man wielding a broadsword, and the other a shapely woman with attire far too revealing, in Kyrin's opinion, and hair flowing down to her feet—Arcacia's two moon gods, Aertus and Vilai. She glanced at Kaden, but he was certainly more concerned about missing his lunch.

Beyond the wall lay the complex Kyrin had seen from the intersection. Tarvin Hall. Between the main building, outbuildings, and training fields, it occupied many acres and sat right in the palace's shadow. This was home—at least the home Kyrin and Kaden had known since the age of seven, along with any other child deemed remarkable or particularly privileged.

They jogged through the gate to find the front courtyard empty and ran up the wide stone steps to the front door of the main building—a massive, three-story structure. Inside, the silent, empty halls echoed their hasty entrance. Kaden set Meredith down, and they strode through the corridors, the little girl running to keep up.

At the dining hall, they came to an abrupt halt, and Kyrin grimaced. *Great*. The tall doors stood shut, and a murmur of voices filtered through them. Lunch had started.

Her eyes shifted from the closed doors to a lone figure beside them. Master Zocar stood tall and proud like one of the grim-faced statues in the courtyard, and just as commanding. Though thin, almost spindly even, Kyrin didn't doubt his strength. She'd seen him sparring on the training fields. A retired general, he'd headed this program for all the years she had attended, and demanded utmost respect. The younger children were convinced one glance from his smoldering, dark eyes could shrivel them on the spot. He moved toward them now with slow, precise steps.

"Uh-oh." Meredith pressed up against Kyrin and grabbed her jerkin. Kyrin patted her shoulder.

Master Zocar's gaze landed first on the little girl and then pinned Kyrin. She suppressed a grimace. While she no longer feared the man, not a single person at Tarvin Hall liked to face him when in the wrong, and she and Kaden found themselves in that position more than most.

37

"Late for noon meal, are we?" His voice filtered out, low and even, not giving away any emotion.

Zocar stood firm on order and discipline and ran Tarvin Hall much like the military he'd once commanded. After all, wasn't that what they all were? The emperor's own personal army, groomed from early childhood to do his bidding? Of course, this was considered a high honor, and Master Zocar held them all to a standard of perfection. His own appearance attested to that— always impeccably dressed and groomed—his uniform pressed, and his shoulder-length silver hair neatly framing his face. He would look better with it cut short, but now was not the time for such thoughts.

The silence lengthened, and Kyrin shifted.

Master Zocar's thin brows rose. "Well, what do you have to say for yourselves?"

Kyrin bit the inside of her lip. She glanced at Kaden and willed him not to say anything. He returned her look with his own warning message in his eyes, but Kyrin chose to ignore it.

She faced Master Zocar again and straightened. "It's my fault. I should've made sure we were back sooner."

Kaden let out an audible sigh. Kyrin could almost feel him frowning at her.

"Is that so?"

Now Meredith drew breath and opened her mouth to speak, but Kyrin nudged her. Dear Meredith, always ready to come to her defense. But if Kyrin understood anything here at Tarvin Hall, it was that tattling made enemies, and she wouldn't let the girl come under fire for her. She already made a prime target for the other young students.

"Yes, sir," Kyrin answered with a reinforcing nod. "I'm the oldest and was responsible."

Master Zocar peered at her as if trying to draw out the truth. "Well then, you four know the consequences. No lunch, and an assigned chore to occupy your afternoon."

"Sir?"

"Yes, Kyrin?"

"Let them have their lunch. I'll take the punishment, and do multiple chores if I have to."

Another long silence followed, and Kyrin watched his eyes. The man was a master at thinking things over without the slightest hint of his thoughts showing in his expression. Even she had difficulty reading him at times, but had no doubt of his answer.

Eyes fixed on Kyrin, he said, "Meredith, Elise, Kaden, go find your seats."

He turned to open the door of the dining hall. Meredith's face drooped as she looked up, but Kyrin gave her a quick smile and coaxed her forward.

"Go on. I know you're hungry."

"What about you?"

Kyrin shrugged. "Not really." After this morning, the knots still hadn't released from her stomach.

Meredith bowed her head and shuffled away. Elise passed by next. They traded glances, and Elise's chin tipped up. Kyrin met it with a cold stare. No doubt Elise would have found a way out of this punishment anyway, the ungrateful manipulator. Heat prickled up inside Kyrin, but she refused to let it take hold. After all, she had done this for Meredith and Kaden and contented herself with that. The two girls entered the dining hall. Kaden, however, didn't budge.

"Kaden, if you please." Master Zocar motioned to the door.

Kyrin stared expectantly at her brother, but he refused to look at her. *Stubborn.*

"Sir, I'll do the chores. Kyrin can eat."

Kyrin shook her head. "I'm the oldest."

"By three and a half minutes."

Kyrin narrowed her eyes. Why did he always have to insist? But she supposed if they weren't both stubborn, Tarvin Hall's instructors would have separated them growing up. According to their authorities, family connections and interaction distracted them from their studies and duty to the emperor. However, regardless of any rules or consequences, they stuck together. Always had, always would.

"Very well," Zocar decided, "you'll both do the chores."

Kaden flashed a triumphant smile, and Kyrin rolled her eyes. He just couldn't leave well enough alone. She returned her gaze to Master Zocar and caught the tiniest hint of amusement twinkling in his eyes. After all, how many times had they gone through this?

She sighed. Time to get it over with. "The courtyard?"

Master Zocar gave a brief nod. "Then I would like to speak to you . . ." he paused and specified, "*just you*, in my office."

"Yes, sir."

She turned and walked back down the corridor the way they had come. Kaden's footsteps echoed beside her. Outside, she stopped at the top of the steps and stuck her hands on her hips. Kaden should have let her take responsibility for this. She refused to look at him and frowned down into the courtyard. In the center, a circular area of etched stone about fifteen feet in diameter portrayed another depiction of Aertus and Vilai. As a high traffic area, it required cleaning every few days.

She descended the steps, and Kaden followed her across the courtyard to the maintenance shed. They each filled a bucket from the well and grabbed a hard-bristled brush. On hands and knees, they scrubbed the stones, working the bristles into the grooves. Such tedious, tiring, and sometimes painful work. Kyrin still bore bruises on her knees and scabs on her knuckles from last time. And experience had taught her it would take them over an hour to clean it to Master Zocar's satisfaction. Students learned at a young age that shortcuts only made more work. Better to overdo than fail Zocar's expectations.

In some ways, Kyrin didn't mind the work. It offered them a time of quiet away from all the activity of living at the bustling Tarvin Hall, but sometimes it left too much time for thought. Thoughts that often drifted toward home—their true home they'd left ten years ago. They could be there now, if only they'd been born normal. How could they help it if they'd learned to read as well as their eldest brother by the time they were four? And Kyrin certainly hadn't chosen to be so aware of small details or able to remember everything that ever entered her head. Still, when they turned seven, the emperor's men brought them here to spend their childhood developing their dedication and service. Forget their home, parents, and other brothers or the cherished days of unconcerned play. Only normal children experienced such things.

"So . . ."

Kaden's voice snapped her attention back to their work. She looked over at him. He had a contrite little smile on his face. Apparently, her wandering thoughts had caused her to ignore him for longer than she'd intended. "You're impossible."

"So are you."

A smile pulled at Kyrin's lips. She fought it for only a moment before it won, but she attempted to force it away. "You just keep your eyes on your work."

They'd agreed a long time ago that Kaden would focus on Aertus's side of the etching while Kyrin took care of the indecent Vilai.

Kaden snorted. "It's not like it isn't right in front of me every day." He shook his head. "It's stupid anyway."

Kyrin peeked around to make sure no one had overheard him disrespect the goddess. "You know, you could've just let me do this myself. You must be starved by now."

He shrugged, though she'd never known him not to be hungry. "You could've just let me tell Master Zocar it was Elise's fault we were late."

Kyrin dunked her brush in her bucket and let her shoulders sag. "And make more enemies?"

"At least the right person would've been blamed instead of you . . . again."

Another little smile tugged Kyrin's cheeks. He might be impossible at times, but without him, she wouldn't have survived the last ten years. "Let them all blame me. It's not like I can sink any lower in their estimation between being an Altair and branded for life as the ultimate snitch."

Kaden's expression darkened, a sharp ring to his voice. "Grandfather was the traitor. I don't see why we all have to live with his shame. And it's not your fault Master Zocar and the other instructors use you all the time."

"I know," Kyrin sighed. Every time they brought her into their offices to ask about the other students' behavior or to tell her to keep an eye on someone, she hated it. "But why fuel the fire?"

Kaden made a face and went back to scrubbing. They could complain all they wanted, but when had that ever changed their circumstances?

AT THE END of the half-hour lunch period, the doors of Tarvin Hall opened, and students poured into the courtyard on their way to various activities. With them came the inevitable sneers and snickering directed at anyone under punishment, though they were especially harsh toward Kyrin and Kaden. It always bothered Kaden the most. They managed to ignore it for a while, but when someone stopped near Kyrin, she tensed.

"So the snitch got caught breaking the rules again?" The male voice dripped with contempt. "I thought the snitch was too good to break rules."

Kyrin clamped her jaw shut and looked toward Kaden. His expression tightened, his fingers fisting around his brush. She gave him a shake of her head and pled with her eyes.

A foot knocked against Kyrin's bucket and tipped it over. Dirty water splashed everywhere. She jerked back, but not fast enough to prevent it from soaking into her pants and the long ends of her jerkin. Kaden threw down his brush and jumped up. Kyrin scrambled to her feet. The two young men stood chest to chest. Kaden's taller stature contrasted highly with the other young man, but his opponent didn't back off.

"Do you have a problem?" Kaden demanded, his voice taut.

"It was an accident," the other replied too innocently.

Kaden scoffed. "Sure."

"You going to do something about it?"

Kyrin's eyes slid to the group forming off to her right, ready to back the young man up. Kaden could take any one of them, but not all at once. If things escalated, she would have to watch him get beat up and then further punished for fighting, again. All for her sake. Before it could spiral out of control, she took her brother by the arm. The iron-hard muscles in his fore-arm tensed under her fingers.

"Kaden," she said gently, but with a tone of warning. "It's fine. Just leave it alone."

Neither young man moved, their gazes still warring against each other. Finally, smirking, the other young man ambled off. Kaden's muscles bunched harder, and Kyrin tightened her grip. She said his name again, urging him to listen, and his gaze dropped to her. "It's not worth it."

Kaden huffed. "I'm tired of how they all treat you. We're not children anymore."

Kyrin gave him a grateful look and shrugged to release the tension. "As long as I've got you, I'm fine. Now, let's finish up."

With a final glare toward the bullies, Kaden turned back to work with Kyrin, who breathed out a sigh. How many similar situations had ended with Kaden in the infirmary nursing painful cuts and bruises? More than she could count on both hands twice, and each one she could recall in vivid detail.

Some time later, they rose, stretching their sore knees, and returned the buckets and brushes to the shed. Once inside the Hall, Kyrin went straight to Master Zocar's office. She smoothed her still wet jerkin and knocked lightly on the huge mahogany door. At his permission to enter, she slipped inside and let the door close with an echoing click. It took a moment for her eyes to adjust to the dim interior, made more so by the dark wood furnishings and drapery. It gave the space a feeling of gloom that a child would find menacing. Intentional, no doubt. It had certainly terrified her at first. But she smiled now at such memories because

Kaden had always been right there with her, holding her hand and making her feel protected. Now, however, she could handle Master Zocar on her own.

"Please, sit," he told her.

Kyrin took a seat in the hardback chair in front of his wide desk. At one time, she and Kaden had both fit sitting side by side in this chair. It still left her feeling small.

Elbows on the desktop, Master Zocar steepled his fingers and peered at her through half-closed eyelids. It was an old habit of his used to intimidate, but the effect was lost on Kyrin. Realizing this, he moved his hands to the arms of his chair and said, "This is already the second time this month you've taken the blame for someone else."

Kyrin said nothing. Of course, he would know exactly what she had done earlier. Little escaped him after all this time.

"Why would you do that?" he asked when she did not speak.

"I just wanted to make sure Meredith and Kaden got their lunch."

One corner of Zocar's mouth rose a fraction as if in triumph. "And not Elise?"

Kyrin shrugged.

"You know, anyone else would've been happy to blame her for being late."

She considered her conversation with Kaden. No one else had their reputation—one exacerbated by almost everything they did. "It seemed like the best way to handle it."

Master Zocar narrowed his eyes and tapped his fingers as if trying to find an answer to an impossible question. He never had understood her or her brother. While everyone else competed for their own interests and achievements, she and Kaden fought for each other and the weaker children at Tarvin Hall. It did nothing to help them reach their full potential, as Master Zocar continually pointed out, but she didn't expect anyone to understand their reasons.

Finally, he gave up his scrutiny. "All right, you may go."

"You don't have any extra chores for me?"

"No. Now, go down to the kitchen and get something to hold you until supper. I won't bother giving Kaden permission since I know he'll end up down there anyway."

Kyrin's expression fell, her conscience bruised. "We don't mean to undermine your authority, Master Zocar," she said softly. At least, she didn't. Kaden had far less respect for the authority at Tarvin Hall, though, on rare occasions, he did confess his contrition over this.

Zocar just waved off her apology. Though dictated by discipline, Kyrin had long suspected he had something of a soft spot for the two of them. Not that he'd ever admit such a thing.

"Go on now."

Kyrin rose and stepped to the door. Hand on the cold, ornate knob, she glanced back. "Thank you."

Zocar nodded, and Kyrin let herself out. In the hall, she pulled the door closed and turned to face Kaden, who stood against the wall waiting for her. A look of defiance already lurked in his eyes.

"So what are we doing next?"

"What if the chores are only for me?"

"I'm still helping."

She shook her head and moved past her brother. "You have to stop doing that."

"What?"

"Defying Master Zocar." She looked over her shoulder and caught that familiar look of stubbornness, but deep down he surely agreed with her. Before he could attempt any weak argument, she said, "Come on, he told me we could get something to eat."

Kaden's expression brightened. It always did at the mention of food.

The kitchen staff showed little reaction to their entrance. Kyrin found Kaden here nearly every day, despite the rules against it. No one ever mentioned it though. The motherly head cook loved to feed him due to his appreciation for her cooking and his ready compliments.

After a quick snack, which for Kaden turned into a full meal, they wandered back upstairs with a couple of hours yet before supper.

"I think I'll head out to the training field," Kyrin said.

Kaden grinned at her. "Feel like beating something up?"

She laughed. They might be twins, but she wasn't that much like her brother. "No, I just enjoy practicing."

"Yeah, I suppose I'll head out there too. Last time Kurt and I sparred, he said I needed to practice more. Apparently, I was sloppy."

Kyrin glanced sidelong at him. He didn't lack practice. That much she knew. A skilled swordsman for his age, he just didn't apply himself most of the time.

They parted and turned toward the opposite ends of Tarvin Hall. Along the way, Kyrin passed several other students ranging in age from six to twenty years old. All wore identical uniforms—black pants, gold shirts, and black jerkins, though the boys' jerkins ended at the waist while the girls' fell longer, coming to a point at their knees.

The east wing of the Hall held the girls' dormitory. At the one door leading into it, a hefty woman stood guard, tall and rigid. She barely took notice of Kyrin, but kept a watchful eye, ready to chase off any boy who might try to sneak past.

Down an incredibly long, polished wood hall, Kyrin climbed a staircase, and then another to the third floor. In the middle of this hall, she opened the door to her room. Two rows of three bunks rose one after another up the wall on the right. To the left stood a large wardrobe and a long table. A girl with flaming red hair that nearly reached her knees, the envy of the whole floor, sat on one of the bunks while a second pretty, blonde-haired girl stood at the window—Yara and Milly, two of Kyrin's room-mates. Their conversation ceased as she stepped inside.

"What happened?" Milly asked. "Where were you during lunch?"

Both girls appeared genuine. These two usually treated her civilly, at least to her face, though they tended to be a bit flighty and spoke of little besides their latest crushes or gossip. It always miffed them when Kyrin didn't join in.

"Kaden and I were out with Elise and Meredith. Elise got distracted by an execution in the square."

Yara wrinkled her nose. "And she got out of trouble again?"

Kyrin didn't answer. Like Master Zocar, they would never understand. She walked to the wardrobe and pulled open the doors. Each girl had a shelf of neatly stacked clothing. Kyrin took great care to make sure the stack stayed straight and folded when she pulled out her training uniform. The girls' head mistress would have a fit if one of her daily inspections turned up something out of place.

While she changed into the new uniform, which was similar but sturdier than the usual one to withstand the rigors of training, Yara and Milly resumed their conversation. Surprisingly, it didn't center around boys, but rather the big evaluation and ceremony three days from now.

"I wonder how many will be chosen?" Milly said. "Surely more than last year. Do you think so, Kyrin?"

"I'm sure. Master Zocar hasn't been especially hard on everyone for nothing."

Yara agreed, and she and Milly speculated on who would be chosen. Kyrin had her own guesses, but she did not share them. Talk of the promotion ceremony made her queasy. All through the year, reports went to the emperor's men on the students' progress. From the nineteen- and twenty-year-olds who completed their training, those with the most skill or talent received a promotion to specific positions within Arcacia's most prominent cities. Anyone left over filled smaller government roles.

Only a couple of years remained until Kyrin's promotion. How she wished to slow down the time. Not only would it mean separation from Kaden, but also a new, unfamiliar life. Though it might be everyone's highest goal to achieve promotion, Kyrin wouldn't mind if the officials overlooked her when the time came. What could she offer anyway? Acute observation skills and a perfect memory didn't seem particularly useful. If only they'd think her useless and send her home . . . with her troublemaker brother, of course.

She stuffed her damp clothes in the hamper and left Yara and Milly to their speculations. Outside, behind the Hall, the steps led down into a sweeping area with five separate training fields. Most existed for the young men and their weapons training. The riding arena took up the most space. At the creation of Tarvin Hall, they'd used it to train the students in dragon riding, not just horses. But the mysterious cretes, the only race with the skills to train dragons, had stopped dealing with Arcacia years ago. Only the very wealthy owned dragons these days, and those dwindled.

She caught another glimpse of the Draicon Arena out past the wall, a better view than on the streets, but she locked her focus on the building settled at the edge of the smallest training field. Inside the sunlit interior, the air glittered with dust particles and tickled her nose with a mixed scent of dusty wood and oiled leather. Large tables and shelves sat along the walls, but it did not contain as much equipment as the other buildings. The young women had no training in swordplay or the use of such weapons, with the exception of archery and self-defense using a quarterstaff.

At a tall wooden box, Kyrin inspected a collection of smooth oak staves. She pulled one out to weigh in her hand. Satisfied, she walked out to the training yard. A few of the older girls and trainers practiced nearby. They glanced her way, but then ignored her.

In one corner by herself, Kyrin took the staff in both hands and moved through the different stances she'd learned over the years, paying careful attention to her posture and fluidity. She came out to practice so often, her hands and feet moved almost without thought. She enjoyed this exercise. It was almost like dancing, but more precise, and helped calm her mind.

Caught up in the movement, the refreshing air of the outdoors, and the warmth of the sunshine, it startled her to turn and find another person standing a few feet away. The sandy-haired young man responded to her surprise with a broad, flashing grin.

"You look excellent," he praised. "One of the best I've seen."

"Thank you, Collin." She let the end of her staff rest on the ground.

Of everyone at Tarvin Hall, he would surely be the number one choice for promotion at the ceremony. At nineteen, he excelled in his training and showed extraordinary leadership and teaching skills. He'd trained the young men and women for years already. No doubt his promotion would place him as a lieutenant in Emperor Daican's army where he would work his way to captain in record time, and, eventually, general.

Kyrin's eyes shifted to the staff in Collin's hand. He was equipped to spar and had another set of sparring armor tucked in his other arm. He followed her gaze, and his grin widened.

"Thought you'd like someone to practice with."

Kyrin bit back a sigh. She enjoyed her solitude, but Collin would insist if she tried to decline. He was persistent that way, and far too confident in the effect of his persuasive grin. Yet, he had a way of being endearing despite his over-inflated ego and propensity for flattery.

"Sure," Kyrin responded, but when she glanced over at the other girls, she caught their envious and disapproving frowns. Collin was the catch of Tarvin Hall, and he soaked up every bit of the attention.

Rolling her eyes, she took the sparring equipment from him. Thick leather bracers protected her forearms, gloves protected her knuckles, and greaves covered her shins. A leather breastplate protected her ribs. While none of it would be effective in a real fight, it did help deflect an accidental blow.

Lifting her staff from the ground, she faced Collin. He took a step back. With another wide grin, he bowed gracefully at the waist. Oh, the resentment Kyrin sensed drifting her way, but she didn't spare the other girls a glance. Instead, she held her staff in her favored defense position.

"After you, my lady," Collin said. His voice always held a distinct tone of mirth.

Kyrin reacted with a swift and powerful downward attack. The shattering crack of the two staves echoed across the field. After the successful block, Collin countered with his own swift attack. But Kyrin responded almost before he completed his move. After so many sparring sessions with him, he'd become easy to read with every one of his moves cataloged in her brain.

Back and forth, they traded blows. At first, it was hard to look on Collin as an opponent with the grin still attached to his lips and his eyes twinkling. He enjoyed this far too much, but as the match wore on, his expression grew more focused, and Kyrin pushed every advantage she had. Soon, they both panted with exertion. Kyrin's forearms and shoulder muscles burned, but she never let up on her attack.

A good several minutes later, their staves came together in an unspoken draw.

"Very well done," Collin told her, his grin resurfacing. "You've become a master since our first lessons."

Kyrin couldn't keep from matching his grin. "Thank you. You taught me well, but you could've had me during the match."

"Could I have?" Mischief sparked in his eyes at his feigned ignorance.

"I lost my balance, and you hesitated."

Collin leaned on his staff. "What can I say? I'm a gentleman."

Kyrin chuckled lightly. Ridiculous charmer. "Thank you, sir, for an excellent workout."

"Any time."

Kyrin tucked her staff under her arm and reached to loosen the laces of her bracers on her way toward the supply building. She didn't dare check the faces of the other girls. When she did look up, Kaden waited at the edge of the field. Moisture glistened on his forehead and darkened his shirt. His expression bordered on a scowl as he stared past her. She glanced over her shoulder. Collin now mingled with the other girls, to their near-swooning delight.

When Kyrin moved past, Kaden followed.

"He likes you, you know."

"Collin?" She shook her head in dismissal. "He likes most girls over sixteen at Tarvin Hall." Half the reason Kaden couldn't stand him.

"Do you like him?"

Kyrin gave a short laugh. "Kaden, really, you know me better than that."

He cast one more suspicious glance back at Collin.

"And anyway, what would you do if I said yes? Threaten him?"

Kaden's mouth opened, but Kyrin held up her hand. "Never mind, don't answer that." It would probably be more than a threat considering Collin's cockiness.

After depositing the equipment in the supply building, Kyrin and Kaden walked back to the Hall. When they entered, they met Master Zocar.

"It's about time for afternoon worship," he announced. He eyed their sweaty, rumpled uniforms. "After you've changed, join us."

Kyrin stiffened.

When neither replied, his eyes narrowed a bit. "It's been at least a year since I've seen you two at the temple."

Kyrin's heart beat much harder than she wanted it to. Why did her mind have to go so blank? Before she could formulate a reply, Kaden spoke up in a calm and casual manner.

"We can pray and worship much better when we're alone and it's quiet. It's distracting with so many people. We notice too much around us. Especially Kyrin."

Master Zocar's eyes slid between them, and he didn't speak for a long moment. Kyrin held his gaze steadily whenever it turned to her and resisted the intense urge to swallow.

At last, he nodded. "All right, but I expect you to spend the next hour in prayer and reflection."

"Yes, sir," Kaden responded, almost too dutifully.

Master Zocar gave them one final semi-stern look and strode away.

Once he was far down the hall, Kyrin blew out a sigh, glad Kaden had taken over.

"So how much longer do you think we can hide the fact we're followers of King Elôm?" he murmured.

Kyrin shook her head and her shoulders drooped. "I think the bigger question is what will happen when we're found out?"

NIGHT HAD FALLEN by the time the men finished with the pickerin. Rayad helped Aldor close up the barn, and all three of them stopped at the well on their way to the cabin. Tyra followed, licking her lips contentedly while her sides bulged with pickerin meat. Once cleaned of blood and hair, the men went inside. The savory smell of beef soup and fresh bread greeted them, and they found Kalli bent over at the hearth. She hummed a happy tune as she stirred the contents of the steaming cast-iron pot hanging over the flames of the large fireplace.

She straightened. "I bet you men are hungry. Sit down, all of you."

"Smells delicious," Aldor told his wife as he and the others took their seats around the hardwood table.

"It sure does," Rayad agreed. Far better than anything he used to make living on his own. He hadn't eaten so well since his mother passed decades ago. In fact, it was his mother who had helped Kalli hone her cooking skills.

Kalli smiled in appreciation and turned once more to the hearth. She stirred the soup again and reached for the handle, but Jace pushed back his chair to stop her. "Let me help you."

He took the heavy pot for her and set it on the table.

The old woman gave his arm a gentle squeeze. "Thank you, dear."

A smile rested on Rayad's lips. What a kind soul Jace turned out to be, especially when it came to Kalli. The two of them adored each other. Considering how despicably ryriks treated women, Rayad thanked Elôm every day for this. After all, he'd been the one to bring Jace into their home, but Jace would far sooner harm himself than the old couple. Any fears Rayad had in the beginning, Jace had laid to rest a long time ago.

Kalli took her seat, and Aldor led them in a short but sincere prayer to their Creator and Provider. When he finished, they eagerly passed the food around. All the work springtime brought made them hungry. While they ate the hearty meal, Rayad said, "I think I'll ride into Kinnim tomorrow. Aros has a shoe loose, and it's been a while since I've heard the latest news."

He never liked to be kept in the dark too long about Arcacia's current affairs. He didn't trust the emperor to keep things peaceful.

"Good," Aldor replied. "I could use a few things."

Rayad looked across the table at Jace, who appeared too busy with the meal to heed the conversation. "Do you want to join me, Jace?"

His blue eyes rose briefly, but an answer was slow in coming. He went to great lengths to avoid towns and other people. It had taken Rayad a full year and a half to convince him to come along the first time. He tried to coax him out of his comfort zone when he could and help him develop more trust toward people, but seventeen years of being treated like an animal wouldn't erase easily.

When Jace did speak, it was almost too quiet to hear. "Sure."

Rayad gave him a smile, thanking Elôm for the progress they had made. It may look small to an outsider, but for them, they'd climbed mountains, one painful step at a time, with many dark valleys in between.

Jace took another wet bowl from Kalli and wiped it dry with the dishtowel. Behind him, Rayad and Aldor discussed what supplies they needed from town. He grimaced, his stomach already winding up in a knot. He should never have agreed to go along. No visit had ever been comfortable despite Rayad's encouragement. He simply had no place in the general public—but he wouldn't back out now.

"What's the matter, dear?"

Jace looked down into Kalli's plump, motherly expression. "Nothing." He gave her a weak smile. "I'm fine."

She tipped her head with a look of gentle scolding. "Now don't be fretting about those people in town. They're fools if they judge you before they know you. It's their loss, not yours."

Jace's smile strengthened. No other person in the world possessed the ability to cheer him up like Kalli. She had a way of making everything seem all right no matter what the circumstances.

Once the two of them finished with the dishes, Kalli instructed him to sit down again so she could tend his wound and fussed over how long they'd waited. By her estimation, it was only moments away from festering and causing his death.

Jace bit back the urge to grin and rolled up his pant leg. "See, only a scratch." He hoped no laughter came through in his voice.

Kalli shook her finger at him. "Even a scratch can become infected. Those pickerins aren't clean animals."

Jace didn't argue, allowing her to dote on him. After all, without a mother growing up, he could use every ounce of Kalli's love. Tyra sat at his side and rested her head in his lap until it came time for her turn.

"Well, I've got an early start tomorrow," Aldor said as the evening grew late. He pushed back from the table. "Best get to bed."

"I'll just be a few minutes," Kalli told him.

He rose, as did Rayad.

"I think I'll turn in as well." He looked at Jace. "What about you?"

"After I take Tyra out."

Jace left the table and stepped out onto the wide front porch. Tyra followed. The nighttime chill in the breeze sent a shiver across his skin, and Jace drew a deep breath of the fresh air. He liked the quiet and stillness of the night. While Tyra tended to her business, Jace glanced over the farm. Though well past dark, to his eyes everything appeared as more of a twilight. He looked up at the two large moons overhead, their silver and bluish light competing with the stars. Far off in the trees, a wolf howled. His gaze fell on Tyra, but she walked toward him, uncaring of the life she could have in the wild.

"Ready to go in?"

She glanced up, crystal blue eyes glowing, and he turned back to the door. Yet, when he gripped the knob, a cold sensation prickled the hair at the back of his neck. Behind him, Tyra growled. He looked over his shoulder. The wolf stared off at the woods across the clearing. Another menacing growl rumbled from her throat, and Jace peered into the shadowed trees. An unexplainable churning took hold of his gut, but nothing appeared out of place.

For a while, the two of them just stood watching and listening. Eventually, Tyra joined him at the door. Jace released a pent-up breath, and his stomach settled a little. Probably just another wolf or a bear, but for most of his life he'd had to watch his back, never trusting anyone. Even now, it was difficult to live without such suspicion. With one last sweep of the farm, he followed Tyra into the cabin and bolted the door securely.

Kalli had gone to bed, but left a candle burning on the table. Jace's smile crept out. Even after three years, she still forgot he didn't need light to see in the dark, but he appreciated her thoughtfulness. He blew out the flame and climbed the stairs to his room. Tyra trailed behind.

His small bedroom held little more than his bed and a dresser, yet it was the first private room he'd ever had. The first private sanctuary he could call his own. Tyra found her place on the old rug at the foot of his bed and, after turning a few times, nestled in for the night. Before preparing for sleep, Jace walked to the window and opened it wide so either he or Tyra would be able to detect anyone or anything prowling around the cabin. Braced against the sill, he peered out at the forest. Another chill tickled his arms, but he tried to convince himself it was only the breeze.

With quiet strictly enforced after dark, Kyrin treaded the halls with care. Light still peeked under many of the doors along with whispered voices. She left the girls' dormitory behind and slipped outside, relishing the coolness of the night. Sleep eluded her, and another headache threatened to take hold. Ever since the confrontation with Master Zocar about their worship practices, she felt jumpy. Kaden seemed unconcerned, but then he always would in order to comfort her, even if he worried privately.

She glanced at the gate, which stood closed this time of night, and crossed the courtyard. To the right of the Hall rose another impressive circular building with many windows. Warm, glowing light from dozens of candles streamed through the glass.

At the entrance, Kyrin pushed open one of the double doors. The old hinges creaked, and the musty but pleasant scent of books and scrolls wrapped around her as she walked inside. She stepped out from under the ornate archway that supported a huge balcony overhead and shadowed her small form. In the center of the building, towering shelves filled to bursting with books surrounded her. How long must it have taken to write and collect them all? Tables and chairs for studying claimed most of the open spaces. Kyrin never grew tired of the sight. Tarvin

Hall had one of the most magnificent libraries in Arcacia, and how she loved it. It was the one and only good thing about living here.

"Ah, my young pupil returns."

The deep, rumbling voice filled the space. Kyrin turned. Just emerging from under another archway was a man of impressive stature, his skin dark and rich like freshly tilled soil. Kyrin had to tip her head back to look into his bright eyes, which gleamed the color of the emperor's finest gold, flecked with copper. He had the build and bearing of a formidable warrior, yet, as a talcrin, he was much more a scholar than a fighter and held the position of Tarvin Hall's wisest instructor. Kyrin never could guess his true age. Mid-forties, perhaps, but whenever she asked him, his response was always a smiled, "Old enough." A good foot or more taller than her, his presence intimidated many, but for Kyrin, it brought calm, and she smiled.

"Good evening, Endathlorsam." Most Arcacians would never bother to remember the talcrins' lengthy traditional names, but Kyrin liked to use his on occasion as a sign of respect toward him and his people's culture. After all, there weren't many talcrins around since most lived on their secluded island country of Arda.

He grinned with straight, sparkling white teeth. "You're the only person here to ever use my true name."

"I like it," Kyrin said with a shrug, "but I do like Sam too."

He chuckled, and his metallic eyes shone with fondness. "Have you come for another night of reading and study?"

Kyrin did not answer immediately, and Sam gave her a knowing look. "Or, perhaps, for discussion?"

She nodded, and Sam guided her to a grouping of couches and chairs. Kyrin sank down onto the couch and its familiar comfort while Sam occupied the stuffed chair across from her.

"What's on your mind?" the talcrin asked gently.

Though Sam would have warned her had there been others present, her eyes swept the room before settling on his face.

"Master Zocar has noticed Kaden and I don't visit the temple anymore."

Concern flickered in his eyes, though his expression remained unchanged. Sam was the only other person in Valcré whom Kyrin knew to be a believer in Elôm. If it weren't for him, she and Kaden would never have learned of Elôm in the first place.

"He asked us to join them this afternoon," she went on. This was one time she did fear Master Zocar.

"What did you say?"

"Kaden told him it's easier to pray and worship when we're alone." She frowned. "While that's always been true, I feel like it's becoming more of a lie since it isn't the real reason we've quit, and I don't know what we'll do if he starts pressing us."

A slight frown creased Sam's forehead. "Has he made any more comments recently?"

"No."

Sam tapped his fingers against his leg in silent contemplation, and Kyrin waited. The situation didn't present as much difficulty or danger for him. As one of the instructors, no one monitored his temple attendance like the students. One of the primary goals of Tarvin Hall was to see its pupils firmly devoted to not only the emperor, but the gods as well.

"I can't give you the perfect answer or solution," Sam said at last, and Kyrin gave a short nod. The beliefs they'd chosen presented growing danger, and they knew this from the beginning. "The best thing is to pray. You can be sure Elôm won't abandon you in this. Ask for His wisdom. It may be that Master Zocar won't approach you again, but if he does, I'm sure Elôm will direct you if you seek His guidance."

"I'll do that. I just wish I had stronger faith." She prayed as often as she could, but still found herself so uncertain most of the time. Unlike her mentor, who displayed only strength and trust.

The talcrin gave her a gentle smile. "You will. Keep following the King and it will grow." He held her gaze, his eyes searching her own. "Now, what else is bothering you?"

Kyrin lifted her brows. "I hope I'm not that apparent to everyone else."

Sam's smile widened. "I just know that look in your eyes."

"It's all this talk about the promotion ceremony . . ." She cringed before admitting, "I'm scared, Sam. Kaden and I could be promoted in only two years. I don't want him taken away from me too. He's the only family I've had all this time."

"I know it's a difficult thing to consider, but remember, you don't know what will happen tomorrow, let alone two years from now. Elôm is always at work. You don't know His plans for you."

Kyrin ducked her head sheepishly. Even now, she struggled to let her faith work. "You're right. It's just been on my mind more than usual with the ceremony so close. I—"

The squeak of hinges cut her off. She and Sam looked toward the entrance. A moment later, Kaden came walking out from under the archway. He gave Kyrin a half smile.

"I had a feeling you were here."

He walked up to the couch, and Kyrin scooted over to give him room as he dropped down beside her.

After nodding at Sam, he asked, "What're you two talking about?"

"I told him about Master Zocar, and we were just talking about the ceremony," Kyrin answered.

The deep frown that crossed her brother's face matched her feelings on the topic. "I'll be glad when it's all over for another year."

Kyrin agreed and picked at one of the seams on her jerkin. "I just wish we were born to a normal, poor family with no reputation and no special talents. Then we wouldn't be here."

Sam's voice drew her eyes up. "Don't forget, Kyrin, or you, Kaden, that King Elôm created you two exactly the way you are.

Every detail about you, He designed. He gave you your talents for a reason. It may take you a lifetime to discover why, but there is a purpose."

Right there, Kyrin prayed for Elôm to show her that purpose. "I know. But it's hard sometimes. I feel so useless here. I want to serve Him, but how can we when we have to hide our faith?"

"By doing exactly what you know He desires of you. You may have to hide what you believe, but you can still serve Him, even here, with the way you respond to your situations and live your everyday lives. It may not seem important to you, but it is to Elôm. In all you do, even attending to your studies and doing your chores, you're to do it for Him. That service is pleasing to Him. You may not like it, but unless they lead you to do something you know is wrong, He even desires for you to serve and follow the authority of the instructors here at Tarvin Hall as well as the emperor."

Kyrin side-glanced at Kaden. He stared at his lap, but she still caught the guilty expression. He would not speak, but Kyrin nodded at Sam.

"Again, you're right. Thank you. It might not be exactly what we wanted to hear, but it's what we needed to hear."

Sam's smile returned. "Take heart, Kyrin. Your faith has already grown since you first believed."

Comforted, Kyrin smiled too.

"Now," Sam said, his voice rising a little, "it seems you two could use some good news."

Kaden's head snapped up.

Breaking into a wide grin, Sam told them, "I received word today that your father is in the city."

Kyrin sat up straighter. "He is?" Her heart fluttered, and her thoughts raced ahead. This opportunity wouldn't slip past them.

"He arrived this morning."

"How long will he be here?" Kaden asked.

"For a few days. He's staying up at the fort and meeting with some of the other captains."

Kyrin's pulse now pounded a fast rhythm. "Do you think we can see him?"

"I'll see what I can do," Sam promised.

Kyrin grinned at her brother, who smiled back. The memory of their father's face erased all the worries she carried. At the moment, nothing was greater than the possibility of seeing him. Her gaze jumped back to Sam. "He doesn't know Kaden and I believe yet, does he?"

Sam shook his head. "I haven't had a chance to tell him."

"Just think how excited he'll be," Kyrin said. She almost shivered with the anticipation. According to Sam, their father had been a secret believer in Elôm for several years. How wonderful to share the same faith.

For another half an hour, she and Kaden sat with Sam, talking of their father and how they might arrange a meeting. So few of the children at Tarvin Hall ever saw their families during their stay.

Before it grew too late, she and Kaden bid Sam goodnight and left the library. Outside, under the light of Aertus and Vilai, they slowly crossed the courtyard. Kaden breathed out a heavy sigh as they neared the Hall. Kyrin looked up at him. She did not expect his frown after the news about their father.

"What's wrong?"

Kaden stopped and stuffed his hands in his pockets as he stared down at the stone underfoot. He gave a halfhearted shrug and spoke in a low whisper. "I know I shouldn't be so defiant. It's just . . . I hate what they're doing here, you know? Taking young, innocent children away from their parents to brainwash into the emperor's service."

Kyrin couldn't help the small smile that lifted the corners of her lips. It was never easy for her brother to admit his faults.

"I know it's hard to respect Master Zocar and obey the authority here, but I think doing it as a service to Elôm will make it easier. We just have to remember it."

Kaden nodded, and she squeezed his arm, giving him a wider smile.

"SOMETHING BOTHERING YOU?"

Jace pulled his eyes from the forest alongside the road and shook his head. "No."

He didn't mention the incident the night before, but it still lurked in his thoughts. What had caused him and Tyra to feel such unrest? He hadn't felt that way on the farm before. He glanced down at the wolf trotting beside Niton. The two of them had walked the farm before leaving this morning, but hadn't picked up anything out of the ordinary, so he tried to put it out of his mind.

"I know you hate going into town," Rayad said as he looked over at him, "but it's good to keep up with the happenings in Arcacia. We don't want to be completely oblivious to what's going on around us."

Jace remained silent, perfectly content to ignore the world and its people as long as they did the same. To stay at the farm in seclusion for the rest of his life suited him just fine. He'd seen enough of the world to last him a lifetime.

Midday, he and Rayad emerged from the forest. Just ahead lay a sprawling village of quaint, mostly single- or two-story buildings constructed of gray weathered wood. A couple of farms and planted fields spread out to the right, but forest trees rimmed the open area. Nothing like Arcacia's largest cities; otherwise Jace would have refused to come altogether. At least the forest stood nearby. It offered him a sense of security and shelter—an escape should he need to seek it.

He halted Niton at the forest's edge and looked down. "Stay, Tyra."

The wolf cocked her head and then sat down.

"Good girl."

He hated to leave her, but most people held the belief that black wolves were evil—much the same as they felt about him. He scowled. They didn't know evil like he did.

He nudged Niton forward again and followed Rayad into Kinnim. They passed the first humble dwellings and shops to find the dirt streets deserted, but commotion drifted from the center of town.

Rayad slowed to let Jace come alongside him. "I bet there's a market today. We'll head to Laytan's first since it's on the way and see if he has everything on Aldor's list."

They followed the dusty and rutted main street to the mercantile, one of the largest businesses in Kinnim. Jace glanced up at the sign over the front overhang. Someone had freshly painted it with crisp white and red letters since his last visit. At the hitching post out front, they tied the horses and stepped up onto the boardwalk. Through the already open door, a mixed aroma of spices, leather, and other dry goods greeted them. A stout man with dark hair and a thick beard emerged from the back storeroom as they stepped farther inside. He wiped his large hands on his canvas work apron and eyed his customers.

"Rayad." His gruff voice carried a tone of surprise, and his eyes landed briefly on Jace with a guarded expression. "Can I help you?"

"Just need to find a few things for Kalli and Aldor," Rayad told him.

He turned to browse the shelves, and Jace steeled himself to approach the counter. Laytan watched him as one might follow the movements of a rabid dog. Jace reconsidered for a moment, but wouldn't give in to the intimidation. He had as much right to be here and do business as anyone. Reaching into the leather pouch on his belt, he withdrew the pickerin tusks and laid them on the counter.

"I want to sell these."

The other man glanced down, though not enough to inspect the tusks fully. Hard expression never changing, he mumbled, "I'll give you ten for them."

Jace shifted his jaw and spoke coolly. "That's what you gave me last time. These are bigger and worth more."

The shopkeeper grumbled. Jace wouldn't put it past him to refuse, but he finally said, "I'll give you twenty."

Jace accepted with a nod, ready to take the money and leave. Better to wait for Rayad with the horses than stand around here with Laytan glowering at him as if he should be locked up somewhere. The man fished the money from his cash box and dropped the coins into Jace's hand. As he deposited them into his pouch, a second person entered from the storeroom.

"Jace!" a musically feminine voice exclaimed.

Both he and Laytan looked up as the shopkeeper's daughter, Rebekah, joined them at the counter. She smiled brightly at Jace, her honey-blonde hair braided away from her face. Her vivid blue eyes caught on the tusks and widened.

"Oh my. When did you get those?"

Jace shifted his weight from one foot to the other. His throat suddenly lacked moisture. "Yesterday."

As comforting as he found Kalli's presence, younger women made him uneasy. Especially Rebekah. She possessed all the best and kindest qualities in Kinnim. Her presence always turned his thoughts to a near useless jumble, and he hated the loss of composure.

Eyes still wide and gazing up at him, she said, "He must have been huge."

Jace shrugged and stared down at the tusks instead of her face. "He was good-sized."

He glanced up, and Rebekah's eyes twinkled with a grin. A moment of silence hung between them.

Laytan cleared his throat and practically growled, "Rebekah, have you finished the inventory?"

"Yes, Father," she answered with a smile still tingeing her voice.

"Well, why don't you check the new stock?"

"Then may I go to the market?"

Laytan hesitated. "Fine."

Rebekah's grin blossomed again, and she kissed her father on the cheek. Just before turning to leave, she smiled once more at Jace. "Maybe I'll see you there."

She disappeared into the back and left a death-knell silence behind. Jace cast a reluctant glance at Laytan. The man's eyes narrowed to a thin warning line, and Jace didn't doubt the threat behind them. Luckily, Rayad chose that moment to approach the counter with an armful of supplies, breaking the tension. Laytan gave Jace one more razor glare before turning to his business. As much as the desire to leave pulled at him, Jace stood his ground.

When they finished the transaction, Rayad bid Laytan a good day, and Jace followed him outside. Laytan's scowl burned into his back on the way out the door. This was exactly why he always stayed at the farm. No matter what Rayad told him, getting out never did any good for anyone, least of all him.

While Rayad stuffed the supplies into his saddlebags, Jace ran his hand down Niton's neck, soothed by the motion. The horse turned his head, no longer the ill-tempered beast Jace had first met, and breathed into his shoulder.

"Don't take it personally," Rayad said, drawing Jace's attention. "You know how protective he is of Rebekah and leery of anything even remotely out of the ordinary."

Out of the ordinary. That summed Jace up perfectly. He

supposed he would be leery too in Laytan's position—just a normal man with purely human blood and a pretty daughter.

"I'll take Aros and Niton to the blacksmith," Rayad went on. "Do you want to meet me at the market?"

Jace shrugged. "I can." The forest beckoned with its promise of seclusion and peace, but maybe he could find a small gift to bring home to Kalli. She rarely came into town. He handed Niton's reins over to Rayad.

"Keep your ears open for any pertinent news," Rayad instructed him.

Jace nodded. If he could do anything, it was listen and observe, and people always had plenty to say. Those aware of his mixed blood seemed to think he wouldn't understand their whispers, or didn't realize he could hear better than full-blood humans.

They parted ways, and Jace followed the main street to the center of Kinnim. In the large, open square, dozens of carts and stalls displayed a variety of wares. Their colorful banners and awnings fluttered in the breeze, which carried the familiar scent of linen and fruit as well as less recognizable foods and spices. Most of the townspeople gathered here to browse or visit with friends. Laughter carried from all corners of the square, but Jace's unease remained. Laughter didn't necessarily mean kind people.

At the edge, he stopped to watch for several minutes and contemplated whether or not it was even worth it. His lungs had trouble expanding all the way. Though this market paled in comparison to some he'd witnessed, the sights and sounds served up many unpleasant memories. Such social gatherings had always boded ill for him.

He shuddered, mouth dry again, as the recollections of those days flooded his mind. Before turning him into a gladiator, Jasper had taken great pleasure in chaining him up and charging people to take a swing at him. *The only time you'll ever have a fair chance at taking on a ryrik,* he would say. No one cared that

Jace was only half ryrik and barely more than a boy. They'd paid well.

Jace curled his fists and shook away the painful memories and Jasper's haunting sneer. He could only hope the man had gone out of business. He never had been wise with his money, risking large amounts on certain gladiators he thought could win him a fortune, like Jace.

With a deep breath, he pushed himself to join the crowd. He made his way to each stall and ignored the obnoxious vendors bent on hawking their wares to anyone they could. Most fell silent once they noticed something odd about him. He might have appeared human, but he hadn't met anyone yet who didn't grow suspicious when they took a closer look. Usually, it took little more than a glimpse of his eyes.

A half an hour after he arrived, light footsteps approached. He ignored them, expecting another shopper to bypass him, but a voice startled him.

"Finding anything?"

He spun around to meet Rebekah's smiling face. His heart gave a nervous thud.

"No. Not really." His gaze swept the area for anyone else who may have joined her, like her father, but the market appeared clear of danger. For now. "I thought you were busy at the shop."

Rebekah chuckled lightly. Besides Kalli, Jace had never met someone so cheerful all the time.

"There wasn't much more to do." She inclined her head. "Come on."

She walked off to the next stall filled with painted and glazed pottery. He followed hesitantly, his eyes darting around the square again. A couple of people had stopped to stare at them. He turned his face away from their scrutiny, but couldn't shake the feel of it wrapping around him.

When he caught up to Rebekah, he lowered his voice. "I don't think your father would approve." Or anyone in this town.

Rebekah shrugged and smiled up at him. "He still likes to believe I'm just a little girl. But he does trust my judgment, and I know I'm safe."

Jace stared at her. How did she know that? Foolish considering she knew nothing about his past.

She too took notice of the onlookers peering at them, but boldly turned back to him as if they were the only two present. He had to admire her confidence and disregard for their disapproval.

"Are you looking for anything in particular?" she asked.

Jace cleared his throat, debating. He really should leave. The last thing he wanted was to muddy her reputation, and if word got back to Laytan, things could get ugly. Someone could be on their way to the mercantile right now, but how did he walk away without being rude?

"I thought I'd look for something for Kalli."

"How are Kalli and Aldor? They always seem like such a sweet couple."

Jace hesitated. How could she be so calm? Every sense warned him to watch his back. "Yes, they are . . . and they're doing well."

They came to a cart spread out with all manner of beaded jewelry.

"What does Kalli like?"

Jace shrugged as he watched her pick up a necklace to admire. "She and Aldor live simply, but I thought I'd surprise her with something out of the ordinary."

Rebekah gave another joyful and musical chuckle, which was surprisingly soothing to his nerves. "Well, the market is the perfect place to find such things."

For the next few minutes, he followed her from stall to stall. It was incredible how she so easily conversed with everyone— even with the more insistent merchants. She always spoke kindly and with a smile, but deftly avoided being sweet-talked into any purchases. It revealed an inner strength and cleverness amidst the sweet innocence. Though his gut still threatened to tie itself in knots, Jace found that she *almost* made this market experience enjoyable. Her abundant joy was contagious, and she managed to pull more than one smile from his set expression—quite a feat for anyone besides Kalli.

Just when he lowered his guard enough to relax, a grating voice sent tension knotting across his shoulders.

"Look what the excitement dragged into town."

Jace ground his teeth together and turned. He should never have stopped watching his back. Wrong move on his part.

Flanked by two of his smug-faced friends, a red-haired young man smirked at him, his eyes harboring all sorts of ill will. Jace barely bit back a sharp retort, but the other man's smirk only grew at his silence. He peered around Jace.

"Rebekah, what are you doing with this . . ." He glanced back to Jace and turned up his wide nose. ". . . half-blood?"

Jace balled his fists. Warmth seeped down his arms and into his muscles, pulsing with the preparation for a fight, but he struggled to still it.

Rebekah came to his side, her face set in a frown that looked entirely out of place. "Stop it, Morden."

He gave her a condescending little grin. "Why don't you run along? We've got business here." The grin stretched wider. "I'll gladly come find you later."

Rebekah put her hands on her hips, glaring at him. She opened her mouth to speak, but Jace beat her to it.

"A gentleman would treat a lady with more consideration."

Morden snorted. "And what would you know about that?"

A blaze erupted inside that Jace struggled to contain. He breathed in hard, cursing the impulses he had to battle so often. He couldn't let it take control of him. Not again.

"Come on, Jace, we still have to find something for Kalli." Rebekah's soft voice quieted his growing agitation, and she tugged lightly on his stiff arm.

His blood still burned hot in his veins, calling him to action, and was almost too strong to resist. He thought of Rayad, who told him time and again to go to Elôm when he struggled like this. He forced himself to turn away from Morden and whispered silently, "Elôm, I need help."

But Morden, who must have caught the movement of his lips just before he turned completely, let out an incredulous laugh. "Are you praying?"

Jace froze. His heart thundered.

"Who could you be praying to? Don't you know? Animals like you have no soul."

An evil pang of doubt knifed through Jace's heart, colder and more painful than the steel of any dagger, robbing the breath from his lungs. His eyes settled on Rebekah's face, but it was her pitying expression that caused the weak grip on his emotions to fail. Heat flared in his muscles. He spun around and smashed his fist into the side of Morden's jaw, sending the man reeling. Regret followed, but it was too late. Morden's friends caught him by the arms and steadied him as he shook his head to clear his vision.

Jace dragged deep breaths into his tightened lungs and waited for Morden's next move. *Just walk away.* The silent plea went out in desperation. If only it would just end here. But satisfaction lit Morden's eyes, and his lip curled in a malicious sneer. He'd been trying to goad Jace into a fight since Jace's first visit to town. Despite Rebekah's protests, Morden shoved away from his friends and flung himself forward. Jace wrapped his arms around the man's torso as Morden's head rammed into his chest and bruised his ribs. He stumbled backward and crashed into a nearby cart.

"Hey!" the merchant shouted as several items toppled over.

But Jace paid him no heed. He twisted his body and threw Morden to the side. When the man recovered his balance, he faced Jace, fists ready. Waves of heat pulsed through every vein and nerve in Jace's body and focused all his senses on his opponent.

They came together again, trading blows and trying to wrestle each other to the ground. Jace gave far better than he received. Morden had nothing on his training, experience, and raging ryrik blood.

Despite his size, Jace moved with speed and agility and avoided most of Morden's blows. The fight ranged over a large portion of the square. Women gasped and scurried away from them, men whooped and hollered, and the merchants scowled while trying to prevent them from coming near their goods. Jace barely noticed any of them. Both he and Morden panted by the time someone shoved between them and an agitated, high-pitched voice ordered them to stop. Neither one intended to give up, but a hard shove to Jace's chest forced him back a step.

His mind still in fight mode, he glared down at the wiry old man standing between them who didn't appear at all intimidated by either man. Peete, Kinnim's sheriff, scowled at Jace first and then Morden.

"What's the meaning of this? Disturbing the peace on market day? Which of you started the fight?"

Morden's finger pointed in Jace's face, and Jace had a good mind to break it. "He did."

Peete pinned fiery eyes on Jace, his bushy, gray eyebrows crunched low. "Is that how it is?"

Jace shook as he worked to halt the flow of hot blood rushing through his limbs. "I hit him first, but I was just minding my own business before he showed up."

"All right, come along with me," Peete ordered.

Jace blew out an angry breath. He only just stopped himself from laying into Morden again when he caught the young man's triumphant grin. It did give him an ounce of satisfaction that Morden would wake up in the morning with a severely blackened eye and swollen jaw. He should have given him worse—he was more than capable—but something had held him back from doing serious harm. He supposed he should be thankful.

Peete prodded Jace to move. "Let's go."

"Sheriff, the fight wasn't Jace's fault," Rebekah hurried to his defense.

Morden scowled at her.

Peete, however, shook his head. "This ain't none of your concern, Rebekah. Why don't you go home?"

Rebekah's face fell as the sheriff led Jace away from the square. He glanced back and caught the word "sorry" on her lips. He gave a quick nod and kept walking, focused on quelling the fire inside him. His gaze shifted around the village as his instincts fought his better judgment. He could easily overpower Peete and escape, but Rayad would disapprove of such action.

When they stepped inside the old, weatherworn jailhouse, Peete gestured across the room. "Put your weapons on the desk."

Jace gritted his teeth and loosened his sword belt. He laid it and his hunting knife on the desk as he watched Peete out of the corner of his eye. The old man was hard to figure. If he considered Jace a threat, he would have taken the weapons earlier. Was he brave, foolish, or just cantankerous enough to think he could take on anyone?

Peete jerked his thumb toward the door at the back of the office. "Now come on back with me."

Down a short hall, he pulled open a cell door.

Here, the flames resurfaced. Jace wasn't a criminal. He set his jaw and ground out, "I may have thrown the first punch, but I didn't start that fight."

"Maybe, but market day's important to the village and I gotta do what I can to keep people from disturbing the peace."

"You could start by arresting Morden."

"Well now, considering his daddy's mayor, I think that would create a disturbance to the peace."

Jace scowled and resisted the urge to hit something or some-one. "So just because his father runs the town, I take the fall even if he's the guilty one?"

"Look, sonny, I'm just doing what's best. Now, you just sit right down and relax and cool your head a bit. I'll go and find Rayad to come fetch you. After that, I suggest you stay out of Kinnim and away from Morden for a while."

Jace snorted. He didn't plan to visit Kinnim again anytime soon, if ever. With a grumble, he entered the cell. Peete locked the door, and Jace sank down onto the rickety cot. It creaked under his weight and threatened to give way. When Peete's footsteps had left the jail, Jace leaned back against the wall and released a great sigh. He reached up and brushed his sleeve across his face to wipe away the blood dripping from his nose. A lucky swing by Morden. He shut his eyes in an attempt to close off his mind to what had taken place, but Morden's words wriggled through his defenses to torment him.

The last of his anger cooled, but a deep, gnawing ache replaced it. Was it true he had no soul? Most people didn't believe he could—not when ryrik blood beat through his heart. And there was no denying his blood. It was the heat that drove him every time anger kindled the fire. Hard as he tried, he rarely succeeded in stopping it. His throat constricted, and a heavy, familiar burden pressed down on him.

"Elôm," he whispered, but stopped in the dead silence.

Were his prayers even heard?

He shook his head and tried to dispel such thoughts. Rayad would call them all vicious enemy lies. If only he could trust that. But ever at the back of his mind remained the possibility he could be wrong. Condemnation at again giving in to his anger joined the struggle and made for a long wait in the cramped cell. He hated being closed in—trapped with his fears and unable to escape.

The growing dark cloud in his mind lifted a little when the jail door opened. Voices poured in, Rayad's gravelly with irritation.

"Where is he?"

"This way," Peete mumbled, sounding a bit cowed. He might have been more than happy to throw his weight around with Jace, but Rayad was a different matter.

The two men came into the hall, and Jace rose from the cot. Rayad reached the cell first. His tone evened as he examined Jace through the bars. "Are you all right?"

Jace glowered at Peete, but nodded. The sheriff unlocked the door, and he stepped out of the cell. Rayad touched him reassuringly on the shoulder, and they followed Peete to the front office. There, Rayad's voice sharpened again.

"Next time, Peete, bring him to me. Don't just lock him up like some criminal."

"Just doing my job."

Rayad scowled at him and walked to the desk to collect Jace's weapons. "Maybe if you put as much effort into punishing the right people, things like this wouldn't happen in the first place."

Peete sat down and leaned back in his chair with a sour expression. "How're you so all-fire sure he ain't responsible for that fight?"

Jace glared, and Rayad gave the sheriff a cold, level gaze. "I know Jace, and I know Morden." He handed Jace his weapons and motioned toward the door, his voice laced with contempt. "Let's go. I've had enough of this town."

Jace couldn't agree more. He hated towns, and he hated people. As far as he was concerned, he was done with them for good.

Outside, the two of them mounted, and Rayad asked, "You're sure you're all right?"

"I'm fine," Jace responded, but did not look him in the eyes. It wasn't the fight that had done any damage. He'd suffered far worse in the past.

They rode in silence. On the outskirts of town, Jace glanced over at Rayad. The older man said nothing about the fight and didn't appear upset, but the guilt inside Jace was unrelenting.

"I know I shouldn't have hit him . . . it just happened before I could stop myself." He swallowed. He'd even prayed right before he did it, but it hadn't helped at all. Was the prayer even heard? Did it prove what he feared? Cold, the very opposite of the heat from earlier, washed through him.

Rayad's voice pulled him back from these damaging thoughts.

"Imagining what he said, I would've hit him too." Jace stared at him, and Rayad amended, "Now, it wouldn't have been right, but I think my irritation would've won out."

But Jace could find no comfort in that. Irritation wasn't the driving force behind his actions. It was rage. The deep burn of it still lingered in his chest like a monster waiting to be roused. A monster he could never defeat.

At the edge of the forest, Tyra waited for them under the shade of an evergreen. When they reached her, she trotted out and took her place beside Niton. Jace looked down at her and smiled a little, some of his anxiety alleviated, but not all. Too many questions assaulted him to find peace—questions that sometimes lay dormant, but never truly left him.

A mile into the forest, he opened up again. "Why aren't my prayers answered?"

Rayad's forehead creased. "What do you mean?"

"I didn't want to fight. I didn't want to give in to anger again. I prayed to Elôm for help." Jace hung his head. "A moment later, I hit Morden."

"Unfortunately, just because we pray not to do something doesn't mean we always won't. We're imperfect and always needing to grow. You've believed in King Elôm for little more than a year now. Give yourself time. He's working in you, and eventually, looking back, you'll be able to see it. And remember, our growth is never complete here. Look at me—I trusted in Elôm when I was a boy, but I'm not even close to all I'd like to be. You know me. I can be impatient, stubborn, ill-tempered, but I know Elôm is still working in those areas."

Despite these words, Jace bit back an outcry of frustrated desperation. They didn't relieve the churning in his mind or offer a definitive answer to his questions.

"What is it, Jace?"

He swallowed, his throat squeezing around his words. Was he even ready for the answers? "What if my prayers aren't heard?"

"King Elôm hears all the prayers of His children. He hears yours."

"But . . . what if I'm not one of His children . . . what if I have no soul?"

Rayad pulled Aros to a halt. Niton stopped beside him. Jace gripped his reins and waited almost fearfully for Rayad's response.

Voice calm, yet strained, Rayad asked, "Is that what Morden said to you?"

Jace stared down at Tyra, who looked up at him, so calm and patient.

"Jace." Rayad's voice was deathly serious now. Jace lifted his eyes. "It's not true."

Jace matched his tone as he looked him in the eyes. His ribs throbbed where his heart hammered into them. "How do you know? You've always told me that, but how do you truly know? Everyone believes ryriks are soulless."

"Because I don't believe Elôm created an intelligent race of people without souls. And even if He did, you're not a ryrik. You're only half, and I fully believe the human part of you has a soul."

Jace looked away, teeth locking together painfully. No matter how many times Rayad reassured him, the truth remained that no one could ever give him a conclusive answer.

"You're forgetting that even if you can't see it, *I* can see how Elôm is working in you," Rayad told him. "You're not the same young man I rescued or even the man you were a year ago. Your heart was hard when we first met, but Elôm softened it, and you came to trust Him. Since then, I've seen how He's helping you grow. That wouldn't be the case if you had no soul."

Jace stared ahead, trying to see what Rayad did, but all that filled his mind were haunting images of the past and the way the anger still had such control over his life. Any bright spots escaped him. Too weary now to argue, he only nodded, and they moved on again. For the rest of the eight miles, they rode in silence.

When they reached the rise where the forest opened up to the farm, Tyra emitted a deep growl and snarled. The horses halted, snorting and tossing their heads. Ice-cold gripped Jace and viciously twisted his insides. The strong scent of smoke drifted toward them.

"Something's wrong," he gasped.

Tyra took off toward the farm, and Jace and Rayad urged the horses after her.

SMOKE BILLOWED FROM the cabin and settled in a thick gray cloud over the valley. Jace's ribs pressed around his lungs as images of what he might find streaked through his mind. A flood of prayers joined them. Kalli and Aldor had to be all right. But nearing the cabin, his heart stumbled and struggled to beat on. Two figures lay on the ground in the yard.

"No!"

He jumped off Niton's back before the stallion could even slide to a halt and raced toward the nearest figure, where he dropped to his knees.

"Kalli," he choked.

She gave no response, her eyes closed and her face ghostly pale in contrast to the scarlet blood spilled across the front of her dress. Jace darted a glance at Aldor. He lay a couple of feet away with his arm reached out toward his wife. Jace brushed his fingers over Kalli's face. The warmth of life was gone. A chilling blanket wrapped around Jace and smothered him. No, they couldn't be gone. Not now. Not like this. He couldn't lose two of the only people who had ever been family. He needed them. Shaking, he gripped Kalli's arms and willed her to open her eyes.

"Please," he gasped.

His very life seemed sucked away with that one word. Rayad's echoed shout barely registered. Jace's wide eyes jerked up. A man dressed in gold and black loomed above him in the smoky haze. Pale light glinted on an upraised sword. Jace broke from shock and fell back as the sword descended. He tensed, but Tyra jumped between them just before the blade reached him, and her jaws clamped down on the man's arm. He shrieked out a curse and used his free hand to swing his sword. The wolf yelped and fell at his feet.

"Tyra!" Jace's voice broke free.

He jumped up and yanked out his sword. His blade whirred through the air, and the soldier faced him just in time. Emotion exploded hot inside Jace. It surged through his muscles and took over the fighting reflexes ingrained in his body. The man didn't stand a chance. In moments, he fell beneath Jace's sword. Metal clanged from behind. Before Jace could look back, another soldier appeared in the smoke and engaged him in battle.

With Kalli and Aldor's still forms seared into his consciousness, he didn't think, he only fought. He took down two more opponents, and his eyes landed on a third. This man was young—his own age or younger. The soldier took one look at him and dropped his sword in surrender. He retreated, but Jace came after him. He grabbed the young man by the front of his uniform and put his sword to his throat. The young man cowered.

"Please don't kill me! Have mercy!"

Jace's hand shook with the intense struggle to stay his blade. Had these men shown Kalli and Aldor mercy? A helpless, elderly couple, yet they lay slain in their own front yard. His sword pressed down harder, and the soldier sucked in his breath.

"Don't kill him, Jace."

At Rayad's voice, Jace let his sword fall away from the soldier's neck, but he tightened his hold on the uniform and glared down at the young man. His pain-racked voice came out raw and strangled. "You murdered them."

The man shook his head fiercely. "No! I didn't! I swear, I didn't want to kill them. I was only here as an extra man."

Rayad came to Jace's side and set cold eyes on the soldier. "What was your business here?"

The young man swallowed, and his gaze switched nervously between his captors. When his eyes remained on the older man, he asked, "Are you Rayad?"

"Yes, but what business is that of yours?"

The young soldier shuddered at the icy tone. "Our captain . . . he sent us out to find you."

"Your captain," Rayad repeated. "What's his name?"

"Dagren."

Jace had never heard the name before, but Rayad's eyes slid closed in a grimace. When they opened, they trained on the soldier once more.

"Were you sent to kill or capture me?"

"Either," the soldier answered with a wobbly voice.

"And were you ordered to kill anyone with me?"

"Y-yes, but I didn't hold with that."

Rayad's eyes narrowed. "How did you know I was here?"

The soldier hesitated, but Jace gave him a jerk. He would find out who all was responsible for this, and they would answer for it. "Tell us."

"One of the men in Kinnim tipped us off."

Jace's heart gave a sickening stutter, and he pulled the soldier closer. "Which man?"

"His name was Morden."

Jace's eyes went wide. *No!* His pulse spiked. He'd faced him just a couple of hours ago—faced him and let him walk away with not more than a few bruises while here Kalli and Aldor lay dead. A fresh wave of searing heat burst through his chest. Throwing the soldier to the ground, he stormed toward Niton and sheathed his sword along the way. Morden would pay for this.

"Jace!"

But he didn't really hear Rayad. The heat raged through his insides, engulfing everything, including his reason. Rayad ran after

85

him and grabbed his arm just as he reached Niton. Jace ripped out of his grasp. He would not be stopped. Morden needed to answer for this. Kalli and Aldor had to be avenged. But a whisper of warning made it through the roaring haze in his head. He stood paralyzed, caught between a need for revenge and making the right choice.

"Jace," Rayad spoke urgently, "don't do this. You'll be tortured with regret if you do."

Jace panted, his clenched fists shaking. He didn't know if he could stop himself. It was too hard, too painful. *Elôm!* A deep groan of agony clawed up his throat as the full weight of loss crushed him. He slumped over and put his hands to his head.

"They're gone," he ground out. "Kalli and Aldor are gone."

Rayad rested his hands on Jace's shoulders. "I know."

Jace locked eyes with him, desperate for understanding, for relief, for *anything*. "We have to do something."

Rayad's throat worked, and his voice was hoarse. "I know how you feel, Jace, but there's nothing we can do. We can't take this into our own hands. You know as well as I do it would be wrong."

Jace shuddered with every breath, still fighting within himself. The heat started to dissolve, but it left him with pain that was even harder to bear. Everything that had become familiar and good about his life crumbled away beneath him and left him staggering. Rayad squeezed his shoulders, but even his eyes revealed a struggle for understanding.

They turned back to where they'd left the soldier, but he had already run and disappeared in the smoke. Jace's instincts rebelled over just letting him get away. The man had done nothing to save Kalli and Aldor, and to Jace, that made him just as guilty as the actual murderers.

But the young soldier vanished from his mind when his eyes fell on Tyra. He rushed to her side as his heart almost failed to beat. Not her too. His throat closed up. He couldn't bear it. He lifted her head in his hands, and she let out a low whine. She was still alive, but blood soaked the fur around her chest.

"Rayad," he called. His voice scratched with smoke inhalation, and he suppressed the urge to cough.

Rayad hurried to his side and took a quick look at the wolf. "Let's get both of you out of this smoke."

Jace gathered Tyra into his arms, her warm blood soaking into his sleeve, and they retreated from the smoky yard. Behind the cabin, the breeze kept the area clear. Their horses and those of the fallen soldiers had found refuge here. Jace lay Tyra down on the ground while Rayad went to Aros. From his saddle, he brought his medical kit and waterskin.

"Hold her," he instructed. "I'll see what I can do."

Jace held Tyra securely with her head nestled in his lap. Rayad pressed cloths to her chest until the bleeding slowed and he could examine the wound.

"I'll have to stitch it."

"Will she be all right?"

Rayad looked up to meet his eyes. Jace searched them for the truth. "I hope so. I think, if we're careful to tend the wound, she'll recover."

Jace was afraid to let himself feel any relief. If he lost her too . . . He struggled to breathe again. Tyra whined, and he held her still while Rayad worked. When they had bandages wrapped around her chest, they let her rest in the cool grass. Jace rubbed the top of her head between her ears, coughing a few times at the hot needles stabbing into his windpipe.

Rayad rose and looked off toward the cabin. He opened his mouth, but the words were slow to come. "I'll go . . . get Kalli and Aldor."

Jace pushed to his feet to follow, but Rayad put a firm hand to his shoulder. "You should stay out of the smoke."

Jace held his eyes and spoke in a controlled tone. "I need to help."

Rayad set his lips in a grim line. They walked back toward the cabin, which still blazed but was close to collapsing. Thick haze surrounded them. The afternoon sun and roaring flames turned it a dusty orange, and the air shimmered with heat. They came to Aldor, and Jace couldn't move at first. He had seen more dead than anyone his age should have, but it didn't dull the horror of seeing a loved one so still and lifeless. Breathing in, the thick air seared his lungs like poisoned gas.

He gritted his teeth and bent down to help Rayad lift Aldor up. They placed him under a large sugar maple several yards from the cabin. This was one of their favorite places to take a rest while working during the hot summer days. Kalli always brought their lunch out to them. Jace struggled to swallow as they went back for her. He reached her first and gathered her up with great tenderness and care. His eyes rested on her face. He'd give up the whole rest of his life just to see her smile once more. She was the only mother figure he had ever known. From the moment he'd first stepped into her cabin, she'd treated him as family, as her own child.

A crushing force coiled around Jace's chest and cut off his air. His blood heated, but without something to expend it on, it consumed him inside. Pressure rose to his throat and eyes, and they burned with smoke exposure and unshed tears. He'd spent most of his childhood and young adult years learning to suppress all emotion, and now no tears would come.

Rayad's hand rested on his shoulder, and Jace blinked hard. Walking out of the smoke, he laid Kalli gently next to Aldor and stood in silence for a long moment. Just hours ago he'd laughed with her at the table and helped Aldor in the barn, teasing the man over how he talked to their milk cows. He couldn't imagine ever laughing again after this. That part of his life died with them.

"I'll get shovels from the barn," Rayad murmured, his voice far away.

He left Jace in a daze. Even staring right at them, he didn't know how to accept that Kalli and Aldor were gone. They'd welcomed him into their home, their lives, and their hearts. He thought he'd escaped death and the rampant cruelty of the world, but it had shown up here too, right in the only place he'd ever found refuge.

When Rayad returned, Jace took a shovel from him with numb fingers and drove it into the ground. They did not speak. Flames roared and logs crackled at their backs as their shovels bit into the dirt, punctuated by Jace's increasing coughs. They worked for some time until he couldn't take in enough air without a coughing fit snatching it away again.

"Jace."

He didn't acknowledge Rayad and kept digging. He would finish this. Kalli and Aldor had given him everything. The least he could do was help with their burial. Rayad reached out and stopped his shovel. Jace gripped the handle hard.

"Go sit down. I'll finish."

Jace resisted at first, but a fresh coughing fit ripped through his chest like sharp claws and left him too weak. He dropped his shovel and stepped away. His legs buckled when he reached the base of the maple. He leaned back and fought for air, dizzied from lack of oxygen. His lungs burned and seemed to shrink to a size too small for the air he needed. He pulled in a breath, but deep, hacking coughs gripped him again and flayed his throat. He wrapped his arms around his chest and grimaced.

Rayad stuck his shovel in the ground and brought him a waterskin. Jace gripped it with shaking fingers and raised it to his lips. He choked on the first couple of sips, but the water soothed his dry throat. It allowed him a few short moments to fill his lungs with fresh air. But relief was temporary. This time the coughing coated his mouth and spattered his lips with the salty warmth of blood. He wiped it away and caught a glimpse of Rayad's strained look.

Biting down, he fought to control the urge to cough. After a few minutes, it subsided enough for him to get a good breath between each bout, and Rayad returned to digging. Tyra, despite her wound, limped to Jace's side to offer him comfort.

When the two graves were finished, Rayad laid the shovel aside. Jace moved to rise, and Rayad offered him a hand to pull him to his feet. They stood beside Kalli and Aldor. With most of their possessions burned up in the cabin, they had nothing with which to better prepare the bodies for burial. They could only lay them gently in the graves as they were, but they deserved better. Deserved to live out their days in peace and die of natural causes. Not of murder.

Jace gripped his shovel again and worked beside Rayad to fill the graves. The more they covered Kalli and Aldor, the heavier the weight of pain and loss pressed down on him, as if he were the one in the grave being buried. Part of him was. He looked at their faces once more, and when they disappeared, he struggled to hold the shovel.

They stood at the graves for a long while in silence to consider their time with the older couple. Jace had never known peace even existed before coming here. He thought he'd die believing the whole world to be a place of darkness and cruelty. But he'd been safe with Kalli and Aldor—loved, accepted. He sank to his knees as the loss overwhelmed him.

"They're with King Elôm now," Rayad said, his voice breaking. "Any burdens or pains forgotten. And we must not completely despair. We'll see them again one day."

Guilt tore at Jace. "It's my fault."

Rayad turned to him.

"Last night, Tyra and I both sensed danger, but I didn't investigate it." His hands fisted and his nails dug into his palms. Why hadn't he searched out the source? Why hadn't he trusted his instincts?

"You have no fault in this. None. It could've been anything last night." Rayad drew in a halting breath. "If anyone's to blame for this, it should be me. I knew Dagren might still search for me, and yet I stayed here." He shook his head as if pushing away his own guilt. "Listen, Jace, blaming ourselves won't help or undo anything. We can't change the past, though we often wish we could."

THE SUN ROSE clear and brilliant above the forest, but Rayad had never seen such a dreary sunrise. He shifted against his saddle propped up behind him and winced at the stiffness in his joints and muscles. His eyes fell on Jace, and he prayed in earnest that he, at least, could sleep. The coughing fits had afflicted him throughout the night and had not subsided until a little more than an hour ago. Of all things Jace had inherited from his ryrik blood, Rayad couldn't help asking Elôm why this was one of them—this painful reaction to air pollution that was said to be the ryrik's curse for being the first to follow the path of evil.

He rubbed his hands over his face, and his tired eyes traveled across the quiet farm. The cabin that once held so many memories now lay as no more than a smoking, black heap of charred wood and ash. Then his eyes came to the fresh graves and misted. He blinked and swallowed down the knot in his throat. He'd experienced a lot of hardship, but nothing as difficult to under-stand as this. Kalli and Aldor were so innocent—so undeserving of such an end. And Jace. He grimaced. After what he'd suffered, all Rayad wanted for him was peace. Where would they find that now?

Rayad prayed for him with all the words he could find until Jace's sudden hacking cough interrupted him. Jace groaned before waking fully. Moving slowly, he pushed himself up and glanced at Rayad with feverishly glazed eyes. His drawn and pale face concerned Rayad. He'd never been exposed to so much smoke before, though he was no longer coughing up as much blood. At least not enough to worry that his lungs would fill to the point of suffocation, as was the danger with prolonged exposure.

Rising to his feet, Rayad stretched his aching joints. "You just rest. I'll see what I can do about breakfast."

Jace didn't seem to hear him. He focused on Tyra, who lay beside him. Praise Elôm she still lived. To lose Tyra on top of it all would destroy Jace. That wolf was about as dear to him as any person, and a far better friend than most.

From the soldiers' saddlebags, Rayad put together a simple breakfast. He handed a plate to Jace and sat down with a quiet groan. For a long moment, they both just stared at their food. Nothing appeared appetizing this morning. Rayad gathered his thoughts and closed his eyes.

"King Elôm, You know our hearts, that we're grieving. Help our focus to be on You, and strengthen us to endure this. Thank You that we're able to come to You in times of need, and thank You for providing a life after this one, and the comfort of that."

He had to clear his throat before taking a bite of his breakfast. It settled tastelessly in his mouth, and he swallowed it down hard. He forced another bite and looked at Jace. The young man wasn't much interested in food either, but Rayad didn't have the heart to try to get him to eat. Most of it went to Tyra.

Once the plates lay empty, Jace stared at Rayad. Any spark of hope was hidden by a thick curtain of sadness and fatigue.

"Now what?"

Rayad rubbed his forehead, unsure of what future lay ahead after this. He could only focus on the moment. "We'll gather rocks for the graves so no animals get into them. We can bury the soldiers at the edge of the forest." Beyond that, he didn't know. Now that the emperor's men had located him, he and Jace couldn't stay to work the farm. They would have to move on, but where would they go? Wherever they had to. But first things first.

"I'll go hitch the wagon."

Rayad started to rise, but Jace stopped him.

"Who's Dagren?" He peered at Rayad with a need for answers—a reason for the death of innocent lives. "Why is he so determined to find you?"

Rayad settled into place with a heavy sigh, and his mind journeyed back to where this had all begun. "Captain Dagren commands a barracks north of Falspar, where I'm from. For years, Emperor Daican has hinted at his desire to enforce the worship of Aertus and Vilai. My friend Warin and I were quite outspoken in our opposition to it. After a while, his men grew tired of us and targeted me as the instigator. Once they stole my livestock and destroyed most of my farm as warning, I knew they would come for me next, either to kill me or take me to be killed. Call it foolish stubbornness, but I wasn't just going to stand by and give up everything left in my possession, including my life."

He paused to relive the memories. Had he made the right choice? How would things be different now if he'd backed down or chosen to flee sooner? Only Elôm knew. "Warin joined me and we stood our ground. There was a fight. Men were killed . . . including Dagren's son. Of course, Dagren would stop at nothing after that to have our heads, so it was either flee or face the whole garrison. Warin went off west somewhere, and I came out here."

He shook his head. He should have known it wouldn't end there. "Obviously, Dagren has not given up on his hunt for revenge. And once he hears of this failure, it'll just motivate him to try harder."

His gaze rested on Jace, who looked so lost. "I'm sorry. I know this is the only home you've ever known, but we can't stay here."

Jace's expression hardened. "Why? Why can't we stay?"

"More men will come."

A flame jumped into Jace's eyes and was the only bit of light Rayad had seen all morning. "Then we'll stand and fight them like we did now."

"Jace." Rayad's voice extended sympathy and understanding. Of course Jace would want to fight for this place, same as he had fought for his own home. "We can't face them all. Eventually, they'd overwhelm us, and it would only result in many dead. There's a time to stand and fight, but it isn't now."

The fire drained from Jace's eyes, and his shoulders slumped.

Rayad rose again to head to the barn, which was the only thing left standing of the life they'd both come to love. He looked back down at Jace, his words rough. "We'll get through this."

When Rayad returned with the wagon, Jace climbed up beside him, his muscles aching as if he'd been pummeled, and they drove off to the rock piles around the fields. It took them most of the morning to collect enough stones for the graves. Jace worked without speaking until sweat rolled down his face and back. Nauseating waves of heat followed by icy chills alternated through his body. At times, faintness almost sent him to his knees, and the coughing spells persisted in their frequency. By the time they finished and sat in the back of the wagon to rest, he verged on collapsing.

"We'll see what supplies we can put together," Rayad said as he leaned against the side of the wagon. "We'll take the extra horses to Kinnim and sell them to the blacksmith. Then we can buy whatever supplies we lack from Laytan."

Jace's eyes darted to him. "We're going to Kinnim?" What if they ran into Morden? An inkling of the rage from yesterday coursed through his blood.

Rayad gave a slow nod. "We need the money." He paused. "You don't have to go into town."

But Jace hung his head. Any bit of heat died, requiring too much energy to sustain it. He wouldn't have the strength to face Morden even if he wanted to. "I'll be fine."

Rayad slid off the wagon. "We should get moving. We don't want to leave a fresh trail for Dagren's men."

"Where will we go?" Jace had seen many places, but how could anywhere come close to this? Another cold shiver passed through him. The world was a dark place outside this valley. Could he face it again? Nausea threatened to turn his stomach inside out.

"I'm not sure. East, maybe. The farther east we go, the farther we'll be from Daican's influence."

He climbed to the wagon seat. Jace remained still, not sure if he could move. Back at the barn, Rayad drove the wagon inside to unhitch. Forcing his limbs to work, Jace slid down, but every movement felt as though he were partially detached from his own body. Right now, he just didn't want to feel *anything*.

"Why don't you gather the horses," Rayad told him. "I'll release the rest of the animals."

His voice stuck in his throat, Jace walked outside. The seven soldiers' horses grazed behind the barn with Aldor's second plow horse. He patted the large, blue-roan workhorse on the side and focused on anything but having to sell the familiar animals. Working numbly, he tied them all together and led the whole string around front.

When he reached the open yard between the barn and the remains of the cabin, he froze. A strange man had just dismounted a tall, roan horse. Jace's senses sharpened in an instant as his mind shot warning signals through his nerves. People didn't drop by for visits way out here, and after what just happened, he wasn't about to trust anyone. Dagren could have sent this man too, even if he didn't wear the black and gold of the soldiers. Jace didn't know him, and that made him an enemy until proven otherwise.

He dropped the horses' rope and moved his hand to the hilt of his sword, his fingers finding their familiar place on the cool leather grip. At the same time, the man turned and spotted him.

"Hello there." His voice was deep and friendly but did nothing to ease Jace's suspicions. A pleasant face could hide all sorts of evil.

The man stood and waited for a reply. He was tall and broad with the stance of a warrior—a formidable opponent if he chose to fight. His short hair and thick beard were dark chestnut, but peppered with gray. The silence lengthened between them, and the man shifted. His gray eyes swept Jace up and down. Definitely a fighter.

"I'm looking for a man named Rayad. Is he around?"

This all but a confirmed Jace's suspicions. Why would any stranger be out here looking for Rayad if not to cause him harm? He narrowed his eyes, tightening his fingers around his sword, and withdrew the blade a couple of inches. If this man wanted Rayad dead, he'd have to kill Jace first. "What do you want with him?"

The hint of a smile the man had maintained faded at the ice in Jace's tone. He straightened and planted his feet, resting a hand on his own long sword as he considered Jace. They stared at each other for a long moment and waited for one or the other to make a move.

"It's all right, Jace." Rayad's voice broke into the stare-down.

Jace swung his eyes around to the barn door. Rayad gave him a nod. "He's a friend."

Jace let his sword slide back into place as Rayad walked toward the stranger.

"Rayad." The man blew out a great sigh and visibly relaxed. "Thank the King you're alive."

He held out a hand, and Rayad clasped his forearm.

"Still breathing, by His grace."

Jace eyed the two of them, not quite free of suspicion. Rayad hadn't had contact with anyone outside the area in three years. Things changed. Even old friends could prove to be enemies.

Rayad turned back to him and motioned him over. "Jace, come meet my friend, Warin."

Recognition of the name prompted Jace forward, but he watched the man's reaction closely. Rayad made introductions, and Warin's gaze lingered for a telling moment. Jace tensed. He had to see it—every hint of his ryrik blood that was impossible to hide.

"What brings you here?" Rayad asked, alleviating the awkwardness of the moment.

Glancing once more at Jace, Warin said, "It's a long story, but after we left Troas, I managed to keep tabs on Dagren. A week ago, I received word he'd found you and was sending out men. I set out right away to warn you, but . . ." he glanced at the smoldering rubble behind him, "it looks like I'm too late."

Rayad winced. "They attacked yesterday morning while Jace and I were in town. They killed Kalli and Aldor."

Jace's heart constricted at the words. He still couldn't reconcile it in his mind.

"I'm sorry I wasn't able to reach you in time. If I'd only known sooner."

"You tried."

Warin's eyes swept the farm and landed on the string of horses. "What do you plan to do now?"

"Leave," Rayad answered simply. "Dagren will surely send more men."

"Where will you go?"

Jace caught a glance from Rayad, and that one look set his gut to writhing. Why did he get the sense things were about to change, but not for the better?

"We haven't decided yet."

"Can't say I'm sorry to hear that, because I was hoping you'd come back with me."

"Where to?"

Warin's voice lowered as if he might be overheard by unfriendly ears. "I'm part of a new group. Resistance to Emperor Daican is growing . . . and there's rumor of war."

Jace flinched at the word *group*. Joining up with a band of resistance leaders was not the future he had in mind. Better to head off into the wilderness far away from people. Only there would he find any hope of peace.

But Rayad's face expressed interest. "War?"

"Unfortunately."

Rayad glanced at Warin's horse. Sweat darkened the animal's coat. "Why don't you take your horse to the water trough, and we can sit down so you can tell me what's going on."

Once Warin's horse had taken a long drink and was grazing nearby, Rayad and Warin settled down on a bench while Jace leaned back against the barn, arms crossed, to listen in. His entire future hinged on this conversation. Even before they began, he mentally urged Rayad to send his friend away so they could get on with rebuilding their shattered life.

"So fill me in," Rayad said.

Warin did not speak immediately. His eyes drifted to Jace again. Jace met the lack of trust with a cold look, but Rayad assured his friend, "You can speak freely."

Satisfied with Rayad's word, Warin began, "Emperor Daican has been biding his time, securing his forces, putting men in place, but now he's ready to start making his moves. We already know he's had people killed for not worshipping his false gods, but it was always done quietly. However . . ." He paused again with the briefest glance at Jace and then around the yard. His voice dropped almost to a whisper. "We have allies inside Daican's palace, and we've received word that the next person caught refusing to worship Aertus and Vilai will be publically executed in Valcré. Daican will declare it a crime to practice any other form of religion. He's just waiting for the right incident."

Rayad scowled. "I knew it would come to this."

"Yes, but there's more," Warin went on. "Daican is working to expand Arcacia's borders. The area of Dorland west of the Trayse River has already fallen under his rule. Who's to say he won't try for the rest of Dorland?"

"The giants and cretes would never stand for it. The giants may not be a fighting people, but they won't just let Daican walk in and take over. Not if the cretes have anything to say about it."

"Yes, but even with a combined force of giants and cretes, it would be hard to outmatch Arcacia's military. More than half of Ilyon is already under Arcacia's rule. The fear now is that Daican's trying to control the entire continent."

Rayad sat back, and his eyes registered understanding. "To turn Arcacia into an empire . . ." He shook his head. "I always suspected he had some grand scheme behind changing the royal title from king to emperor."

Jace clenched his teeth. Daican was ultimately responsible for Kalli and Aldor's murders, and if he sought this kind of power, it was one more reason to take to the wilderness where no one could find them.

"There are no set plans for any invasions," Warin said, "but talk is growing. Our greatest fear is Samara. It's sure to be the first place Daican strikes."

"No one has ever breached Stonehelm, and I've heard their king, though young, is a smart and valiant leader. As small as Samara is, their faith has preserved them. Attacking them would be a bold move, even for Daican."

"It's true King Balen leads them well," Warin acknowledged, "but, unfortunately, Samara's faith has grown weak. And, if Daican releases a concentrated flood of men against them, even the strongest defenses might fall under the sheer weight of numbers. Against the entirety of Arcacia's forces, Samara would be overrun. Even King Balen is concerned."

"How do you know this?"

"We have a couple of Samarans in our group. They've joined our efforts to resist Daican." Warin paused with a hopeful look. "We want you to join us."

Rayad glanced up, and Jace gave his head the slightest shake. *Don't.*

Exhaling, Rayad focused again on Warin. "And what's the purpose of your group?"

"There were three of us hiding out near Keaton—all wanted by the emperor's men. We gathered information, mostly. A few months ago, we headed north to Landale. The baron there is secretly a follower of the King, and it's through him we receive our information. When Daican makes his declaration against the followers of Elôm, there will be many people running for their lives. It's our goal to provide shelter and rescue for those we can. The forest outside of Landale is vast, and the baron's son, Trask, has set up a camp where we can all hide. We also plan to train any who are willing to form a militia of sorts. If war comes to Samara, they'll need all the help they can get."

Rayad responded with silence, and Jace could only hope he'd decline. They'd had enough trouble involving the emperor.

After a moment, Warin urged, "If we don't stand up now to resist this, we may not be able to later."

Rayad gave a slow nod, but said, "I need to discuss it with Jace."

Warin looked at him again, his expression free of any hostility or resentment. "Very well."

He rose and walked away toward his horse to leave Rayad and Jace to speak in private.

"I won't go," Jace said, addressing the unspoken question. He'd go off into the wilderness alone if he had to, but he wouldn't get involved with this.

"Why not?"

"Too many people." He grimaced at the very thought of joining a group larger than the three he'd lived with these years. "They won't trust me. *He* doesn't trust me." He gestured toward Warin. The man might not be hostile, but he was wary. "Everyone sees I'm different, and they don't like it."

"Just give Warin time to get to know you. Time is all most people need. You and I didn't trust each other at first either."

Jace shook his head and looked away, crunching his teeth together. It was rarely that simple. Not in Kinnim, not anywhere. People feared him, and that fear usually led to mistreatment. Rayad, Kalli, and Aldor had been exceptions he couldn't count on finding anywhere else.

"Jace," Rayad said quietly. "We wouldn't be going for ourselves, but to serve others. Ilyon is about to become a very dangerous place for those of us who follow the King. You and I are capable of defending ourselves against the emperor, but most are not. There will be hundreds, if not thousands, of men, women, and children who will be at Daican's mercy. If we leave and hide away somewhere as we planned, we'll be turning our backs to all this when we could offer aid and, perhaps, make a difference."

Jace still wouldn't look at him, his eyes set on the nearby trees that beckoned to him. He had to fight every impulse he had to flee the situation.

Rayad rose to stand facing him and pressed on. "You know what it's like to be powerless, and you saw yesterday what happens to those who can't defend themselves from the emperor."

Jace's chest tightened with pain. Powerlessness. Yes, he understood that. It seemed to have control of his spiraling life right now. Uncertainty of the future battled against everything Rayad said. Breathing raggedly, he met Rayad's eyes. He had no true confidence in his words, but he said, "All right."

His insides revolted over what he'd done, but Rayad's slight smile carried pride over the decision. He put a firm hand on Jace's shoulder. "It might not be the easiest choice, but it's the right one."

Jace gave a helpless nod and tried to convince himself that were true.

JACE LET NITON trail behind Aros while he sank deep inside himself—a dark hideaway of old familiarity. He hadn't allowed himself to think when Rayad sold Aldor's plow horses and all but one of the soldiers' mounts. The one they kept was loaded up with their supplies and plodded along next to him. He gathered just enough energy to glance over at the horse, where Tyra lay nestled between two bundles. Satisfied, he dragged his eyes back to the road ahead.

People crisscrossed the main street of Kinnim as they rode toward the mercantile, but the village was quiet with most of the traveling merchants having already gone. Now that the cabin had burned, the only possessions Jace and Rayad had left were the few items in their saddlebags. They didn't even have a spare change of clothes, and neither had any desire to wear the extra uniforms in the soldiers' bags. But Warin kept them and the weapons, saying they could be useful at camp.

At the shop, Rayad dismounted first. Jace slid down next, but it took effort. His entire body hurt, especially his chest. The coughing fits still plagued him despite the cool, fresh air, and he couldn't hope for relief anytime soon. The last time he'd inhaled too much smoke from the smokehouse, he'd been ill for days.

Laytan stood at the counter and frowned when they entered, no doubt surprised to see them two days in a row. His eyes narrowed at the sight of Jace, then slid suspiciously to Warin. He watched them out of the corner of his eye as they moved farther into the shop, but didn't ask any questions. They gathered their supplies—just the basics they would need for the journey. Arms full, they approached the counter where Rebekah's voice sounded from behind her father.

"Are you going somewhere?" She came up beside Laytan and eyed the supplies before turning her questioning gaze to the men themselves.

"We're leaving," Rayad said.

Rebekah gave a delicate frown. She opened her mouth to question them, but Jace's coughing cut her off. Though he tried to suppress it, his lungs burned too fiercely. Rebekah's eyes fell on him. She gasped at the blood spattering his hand when he pulled it away from his mouth. Ignoring her father's grunt of protest, she rushed around the counter and put a light hand on his arm.

"Jace! What's wrong?"

He shook his head and managed a rough, "I'm fine."

"It's the curse, Rebekah," her father hissed.

She shot him a disapproving frown, but her face softened when her eyes returned to Jace. "What happened?"

Jace glanced at Rayad, and his voice caught in his throat. Could he say it? It hurt so much. "Kalli and Aldor are dead . . . murdered."

Rebekah's hand flew to her mouth. "Oh, Jace, I'm so sorry." She shook her head, tears turning her eyes a watery blue. "Who would do such a thing?"

"Rebekah," Laytan's sharp voice cut in, "I think it's time they left." It was more than a friendly suggestion.

The buildup of emotion in Jace's chest brought on more painful coughing and made him gasp for breath. He hated for Rebekah to see it—or her father, since it would only confirm what he said.

Rayad stepped forward and asked Laytan, "Do you have anything that might help him?"

Laytan shook his head, but Rebekah hurried to a shelf and grabbed a dark bottle.

"This might. My grandmother makes it. It does wonders for a cold. Just rub it on your chest morning and night. I think it's the smell as much as anything that helps." She pulled the stopper and held the bottle up for Jace. He breathed in the scent of the remedy. The strong, herby smell did soothe his lungs. She replaced the stopper and put the bottle in his hand. "No charge."

Her father grumbled her name, but her eyes remained on Jace.

He looked down at her and wondered at her kindness. She was one more rare exception to add to the list. "Thank you."

She gave a wobbly smile. "It's the least I can do."

Jace stared at her for another moment. Would he find such kindness and acceptance where he was going? He probably should have tried to get to know her better when he had the chance.

Pulling his eyes away, he turned and followed Rayad and Warin outside, where they packed up the supplies. He took Niton's reins and gripped the cantle to drag himself up into the saddle, settling in with a wheezing sigh. If only he could lie down instead. He glanced up the street, his eyes catching on a familiar figure. His muscles went taut, and his heart paused. Morden had just stepped out of a nearby building. Their eyes locked. A spark flared to life inside Jace. He squeezed Niton's reins in his fist, but the sheer weight of sorrow and exhaustion tamped down the flame. For the first time, he had no real desire to act.

Morden, however, narrowed his eyes, one rimmed in a dark purple bruise, and stalked down the boardwalk. Despite the thorough beating he'd received the day before, he apparently wanted to try his luck again. But then Rayad stepped into view. His eyes landed on Morden and leveled him with such a menacing glare that the young man actually took a step back. Morden's gaze flicked down, resting on Rayad's hand, which gripped the hilt of his sword. Without a weapon of his own and his friends to back him up, Morden stepped away, slowly at first, before scurrying off.

The sun disappeared behind the thick tangle of trees and cast deep shadows across the road. Warin was prepared to ride another mile or two, but coming upon a small clearing, Rayad reined his horse to a halt. Beside him, Jace hunched over in his saddle.

"We'll camp here tonight," Rayad said.

Warin gave an accepting nod. He had no command over his companions. Rayad held seniority anyway, and Warin was quite content to follow the lead of his old friend. Even after three years, it came naturally.

Rayad slowly lifted himself from the saddle and slid to the ground with a grimace. Jace didn't appear any better off, Warin noted, but they probably weren't as used to long days in the saddle.

The darkness deepened around them as they unsaddled the horses and built a fire to heat their supper. A warm meal in their bellies restored some energy. When he finished, Jace rose and went to brush his horse, which left Warin and Rayad alone at the fire sipping coffee. Tapping his fingers on the rim of his cup, Warin peered at Jace across camp and considered the shopkeeper's comment back in Kinnim. There was a story here to be sure. He turned to his friend and lowered his voice so as not to be overheard.

"He's a ryrik."

Rayad looked up, his eyes refocusing as he came out of deep thought. He glanced at Jace and then faced Warin. "No. He's half ryrik."

Warin's brows shot upward. "Half ryrik?" He stared at Jace again. "I didn't think that happened."

"Neither did I."

"Do you know how?"

Rayad poked at the fire and a shower of sparks rose into the air. "No, and neither does he. He was a slave as far back as he can remember. I found him in Troas, right after I spoke to you. He was a gladiator, or at least that's what his master wanted him to be. I saw him, in the arena. Then, on my way out of the city, I came across his master beating him for not killing his opponent. I paid for his freedom, and he's been with me ever since."

Warin shook his head. Remarkable. "Weren't you afraid he'd kill you? I mean, not to sound harsh, but how did you know he wouldn't behave as a full-blood ryrik?"

"I didn't, but I couldn't just leave him there." He stared at Jace. "He struggles with his ryrik blood. With the energy and the anger it causes. But he's no cold-blooded killer. I don't believe he ever was, and he certainly isn't now. He has faith in the King."

"You believe that?"

Rayad's gaze shot to Warin, and his eyes and expression grew cold. Warin held up his hands passively, quick to explain. "It's not that I doubt you, it's just, you know what people say."

The hardness transferred to Rayad's tone. "I've never cared what *people* say. I know Jace has a soul." Then his voice softened, and he said, "It's convincing him that's difficult."

A moment of silence followed. Rayad drank down the last of his coffee and set the cup aside. "I trust that boy with my life. He may appear hard and cold, but that's his shield against the cruelties of this world. It's not easy to earn his trust, but once you do, it reveals a whole different side to him. Underneath it all, he has a very kind, gentle, and generous heart. You just have to get past the pain and scars he bears."

Warin watched the emotions play across his friend's face. Interesting, the way he defended the young man. He knew Rayad better than just about anyone. Rayad had always been the practical, straightforward one—never the sentimental sort—but Jace brought something out in him that Warin hadn't seen before. He loved that young man like a son.

Jace joined them a short time later. He looked from one man to the other, probably sensing the solemn mood that had fallen between them. Hoping to lighten it, Warin turned to Rayad again and asked, "I have to know. That fine animal can't be Niton, can it?"

"He is indeed," Rayad answered with a nod.

Warin whistled. "He sure has matured into an impressive-looking stallion. I hardly recognized him without his ears laid back and his teeth flashing at me. But how did you ever get a saddle on him? I thought that was next to impossible."

"I didn't." Rayad nodded across the fire to where Jace sat next to his wolf. "He did. Actually, the day after we met, he hopped on Niton and rode him just like that. Didn't even need the saddle."

Jace ducked his head, but Rayad continued the praise. "He's got a gift with animals. You should see. People would think that horse is a dog the way he's got him trained. He even taught him to sit and lie down."

At this, Warin let out a laugh. "Really? That beast trained like a dog? That's impressive. I'll have to see it one of these days." He paused as a thought formed. "You know, people would pay good money for horses with that kind of training, if you ever had a mind to get into that sort of thing."

Jace gave a shrug, staring into the fire, but Warin was serious. It could be a good living if one were to pursue it.

KYRIN SMOOTHED NON-EXISTENT wrinkles in her jerkin yet again before her hands stilled. She shook her head and forced her hands back to her sides. *Ridiculous.* The nervous thrill that raced through Tarvin Hall was getting to her. All around, her roommates chattered as they prepared for the ceremony, fussing over their hair and uniforms. She sighed and prayed for it all to end. Then she could focus on helping Sam arrange a meeting with her father before he left Valcré.

But even such thoughts couldn't distract her from the way the room seemed to shrink and lose oxygen. Her heart bashed her chest as if trying to follow the growing urge to escape the confined space. She scolded herself and the panic, but let out a huge breath when the call came to go downstairs. The cascade of young women and girls joined with the boys in the main hall. Though students crammed the area, Kaden appeared at Kyrin's side as the instructors ushered everyone toward the great auditorium.

"Ready for another one of Master Zocar's droning speeches?" His long-suffering tone drew out Kyrin's smile. "You'll have to tell me if he deviates at all from the speech last year."

Kyrin chuckled, but she caught the head mistress giving them a smoldering look. They both fell silent as they entered the grand auditorium. The room had a way of drawing eyes upward, and with good reason. The massive arched ceiling, painted in exquisite, complex designs, towered high above them, making even the largest man appear tiny, let alone Kyrin. Once she'd taken an awed look, her gaze dropped down to the many rows of long benches facing a raised stage at the far end. Enough seating for all of them, totaling almost four hundred. Her stomach gave another uncomfortable flutter.

Everyone knew the drill, filing into the spaces between the benches, remaining with their age groups. The boys grouped to the right side while the girls had the left. Everyone between nineteen and twenty naturally headed to the front.

"See you after," Kaden murmured.

Kyrin nodded. If only he could stay with her. It would help her nerves. But they parted, and she made her way to her place with her roommates. No one sat yet, however. Once all had found their places, a hush fell over the auditorium as everyone sensed the magnitude of the occasion. For a long moment, quiet reigned until Master Zocar ascended the side stairs to the stage, his sure steps and tall stance befitting a former general. How he could look even more imposing than usual was beyond Kyrin. Behind him came a few of the other instructors of Tarvin Hall, as well as several of the emperor's own officials. They walked to the center of the stage and spread out evenly, with Master Zocar in the middle. His penetrating gaze swept over the attendants.

"Students of Tarvin Hall." Though the room dwarfed everyone, it carried his voice all the way to the farthest row. "Today marks a great milestone in the lives of many of your classmates. Today they have reached the ultimate goal that you all spend years training and preparing for. Today they will be granted the greatest of honors in moving on to begin their service to our emperor."

A chorus of applause sounded, and Master Zocar gave the signal to be seated. In one mass movement, they sat straight-backed and attentive. Kyrin clasped her hands firmly in her lap and focused on keeping her knees from bouncing.

With everyone's attention fixed on him, Master Zocar went

on to give a long, drawn-out speech about the majesty of Emperor Daican and the privilege of serving him. Kyrin mentally compared it to the one last year and cast a discreet glance to her right. By chance, she caught Kaden's eye across the main aisle. At his comically raised eyebrow, she fought against a giggle rising inside her and promptly looked away. *Troublemaker.* She glanced at the other students. Though all sat in rigid rows, eyes wandered or blinked in an attempt to stay alert. The excited buzz from earlier drained during this portion of the ceremony.

Her gaze switched to the people onstage with Master Zocar—the emperor's officials in particular. Most had been present last year, though there were a few she did not recognize. They all stood unmoving, faces set, and took the entire thing far too seriously. Not much to see there. But, when she looked to the instructors of Tarvin Hall, she fought a smile. One man found great interest in the ceiling, while another's face screwed up in a battle not to yawn. The head mistress glared at him.

At long last, Master Zocar brought his speech to a close, unaware of how the instructors perked up behind him. Now for the true purpose of the ceremony. Though she and Kaden were safe, for now, Kyrin's stomach still flip-flopped. Anticipation hovered over the rest of the students who waited to see if their guesses would prove correct. Several fidgeting bodies caught her keen sight. She adjusted her sweat-dampened hands on her lap.

One of the emperor's officials stepped forward and handed Master Zocar a scroll. After all, the emperor's men did the choosing after receiving Zocar's reports throughout the year. Though all was quiet, it became even more so, as if everyone held their breath. In the silence, Master Zocar broke the wax seal and rolled open the scroll. The parchment crinkled audibly.

With a satisfied smile, he announced, "Here now are the names of those who have found favor in the sight of the emperor and shall be assigned to special positions within his service. If you hear your name, please rise and join us to receive your commission."

And so the promoting commenced. Zocar read through the list, and his voice echoed out each name. One by one, the students from the front row rose and made their way onstage, where they received a commission for their new assignments. Faces beamed with pride, and more than one person tipped their chin smugly in the direction of their classmates.

Kyrin nodded her head as Master Zocar called up every one of her predictions, including Collin. Though he made an effort to keep a straight face, that grin of his just begged to break out. He accepted his commission and stepped into line with the other promoted students. No doubt his commission assigned him to some prominent position in Arcacia's military. He'd be perfect for it.

The list dwindled, but far more students received a promotion this year than the previous. No wonder Master Zocar looked so pleased. A year of strict scheduling had done its work. Only a few young men and women remained on the benches up front. At the last name on the list, everyone paid great attention, particularly the few remaining students. They leaned forward, ready to jump up and hurry to the stage. It was their last chance, and only one would be called.

"This last promotion is a special circumstance of incredible honor, for Emperor Daican has requested this young woman to serve him personally. She is not from among our nineteen- and twenty-year-olds . . ." Heads slumped, and Kyrin nearly felt sorry for those remaining students, but what a shock. Had this ever happened before? ". . . making her the youngest to be promoted in the history of Tarvin Hall." Master Zocar let a long, suspenseful moment pass. All eyes were riveted on him. It could be any one of them. With a wide smile, he said, "Kyrin Altair, please come forward."

Kyrin's heart faltered, and she went stiff. Did he mean her? Was there another Kyrin at Tarvin Hall? The heavy *thump,*

thump, thump of her pulse pounded in her ears as it struggled with each beat. This couldn't be.

"Kyrin, please rise and come forward," Master Zocar repeated.

An elbow poked into her ribs and snapped her from the daze. She turned to Yara. Everyone had abandoned formality and turned to gape at her.

"You better get up there," Yara whispered.

As if prodded by a sharp object, Kyrin rose a little faster than she intended to. It was as if someone else had taken control of her body and moved her stiffly toward the center aisle. The only clear thought in her mind was the requirement to obey Master Zocar. He'd called her, so she must go.

When she looked up, her eyes locked with Kaden's. She froze. He stared at her with a tangle of emotions that appeared ready to propel him out of his seat. Kyrin swallowed with difficulty. What if he did something foolish? *Stop him, Elôm.* Afraid her own emotions would provoke his protectiveness and lead him to disastrous action, she hid everything behind a mask of calm and ignored how her insides twisted into a hopeless knot.

She gave him a slight nod, hoping to convey acceptance, and moved off toward the stage. Everything would be all right . . . wouldn't it? Though every muscle in her face fought to remain expressionless, inside, her head whirled. For once, she couldn't make sense of anything. This wasn't supposed to happen! She wasn't supposed to face this for another couple of years. And to be requested personally by the emperor? Dizziness tried to tip her to the floor. What could Daican want from her? If only she had more closely followed Kaden's example. The emperor wouldn't have requested the service of a troublemaker. *Oh, Kaden.* She would have to leave him.

Her stomach pressed up toward her throat. She glanced left and absorbed all the many awestruck faces. One in particular stood out, though awestruck wasn't the word for her expression.

Flabbergasted for sure, and certainly not pleased. She pulled her gaze away from Elise's envious stare.

Like walking in a dream, Kyrin reached the stairs and half-stumbled up to the stage. If only it were a dream. She approached Master Zocar, though she couldn't match his distinctly pleased smile. An official came forward and held out a rolled-up parchment, sealed and tied with a gold ribbon—*her* commission. Gingerly, she took it, forcing her trembling fingers to still, and glanced out over the audience. She found Kaden in the crowd, but looked away. His agitated expression pushed tears to her eyes. Her gaze switched to the door. *Run!* The urge gripped her, and her breaths came in short little gasps.

"Please take your place in line, Kyrin."

She flinched at Zocar's voice and turned toward the line of promoted students. Her eyes landed on Collin. His straight face had vanished, and he grinned openly at her. Little comfort that offered. She wanted no part of this. Fighting to maintain control, she took her place at the end of the line.

None of Master Zocar's closing comments registered. Kyrin stared down at the commission in her hand. Her fingers itched to tear it open. What position could it possibly assign her to? Whatever it might be, it had just ripped away everything she'd come to know. Life had always been a set, familiar routine here at Tarvin Hall. And she had Kaden. The emperor had taken her away from her entire family, except for her twin brother, her closest friend in the world. Now everything had turned upside down, and they would take her away from him too.

She trembled, and her vision clouded around the edges. Wouldn't that be the perfect humiliation in this nightmare, to faint in front of everyone? They'd talk about her for weeks. She cast her eyes about, blinking away the fog, and her tears burned hot. Her gaze caught at the back of the auditorium. Sam. Whether he'd been there all along or had just shown up, she couldn't say, but the sight of him was a lifeline. The familiar face of her long-time friend restored her confidence and reminded her of the one most important thing in all this madness—King Elôm.

"I don't understand. The emperor wants me to *read* people?" Kyrin's eyes shifted between Master Zocar and the government official who stood by as she read her commission. She'd never heard of such a job. "Why?"

Zocar deferred to the official. The stern man's gaze trained on Kyrin. "Emperor Daican has many enemies, and it's often difficult to tell who they are. With your ability to detect lying and such, you can warn His Majesty of any potential threats and persons he should be aware of."

Kyrin glanced down at her commission again as if it could explain how she had landed in this mess. The thought of the emperor alone made her knees wobbly, never mind other threats and political intrigue.

At her hesitation, the official narrowed his eyes. "You are pleased to serve the emperor, are you not?"

Kyrin's gaze snapped back to his. "Of course." Her insides flinched at the lie. "I apologize. This is all very unexpected."

"Of course it is," Master Zocar said in breathy exasperation. "This has never occurred before at Tarvin Hall. It's an incredible honor for you and your family."

Kyrin glued a smile to her lips. If she didn't play this right, who knew what could happen. It certainly wouldn't bode well for her personally, and she could only imagine the disgrace it would bring to her already shamed family.

"Now, do you understand everything?" Master Zocar questioned.

"Yes, sir."

But did she? If not, she'd have to figure it out as she went. She didn't wish to try his or the official's patience.

"Excellent. Now, the celebration feast will begin shortly. Go enjoy yourself. Tomorrow morning, your escort will arrive to take you to the palace."

Cold washed through Kyrin with another urge to flee. She gave a respectful nod to both him and the official and turned to leave.

"And Kyrin," Master Zocar added. "Make sure you're on time for this meal."

Kyrin managed a small smile at the rare jest.

Of all the most anticipated events of the year at Tarvin Hall, the promotion ceremony banquet rose to the top. Expert chefs from all around Valcré gathered, at the emperor's expense, to provide the food. The students took full advantage of this and heaped their plates with the exquisite delicacies.

With mountainous meals set before them, they filled the dining tables, and the large hall rang with their enthusiastic chatter. To her great discomfort, much of it centered on Kyrin. Seated with the other promoted students along a raised table at the head of the room, she couldn't escape notice. She kept her eyes down and took a small bite of creamy herb and butter potatoes. It went down hard, catching in her throat and settling like a rock in her stomach.

"Ah, come on, Kyrin, eat up."

Collin's grin flashed at the corner of her eye. He'd clearly manipulated the situation to sit beside her. Could be worse, she supposed. She glanced at his half-empty plate, and that was already his second helping. The thought of so much food stuffed inside her made her sick, and she willed the potatoes not to come back up. She'd avoided fainting, but retching in front of everyone would be just as bad.

"I'm afraid I don't have much of an appetite. Too much excitement."

Collin gave her a smile one might give to a child. "I guess it's not too much of a shame. We'll be eating pretty well after this—the two of us assigned to the palace of all places."

Kyrin managed a brief smile, though it pained her cheeks. Collin had already gone over every minute detail of his assignment to the emperor's security force, and how they'd still see a lot of each other. He found entirely too much pleasure in it. Now Kyrin believed Kaden's suspicion that Collin had more than a passing interest in her. It made her want to bury her head in her arms and forget his existence for a while. Him and the world around her.

Instead, she looked out past her dining companions and sought her brother's table to find him watching her. He'd barely touched his meal either, the surest indication he was upset. Few things could so distract him from the promotion banquet. Her entire being cried out to seek his protection and comfort, but the whirlwind of the celebration had kept them separate so far.

Beside her, Collin spoke again. Kyrin tried to appear busy with her food as he went on about what it would be like to serve the emperor together, and what an honor they'd received. She only half-listened and nodded every so often. The tight ache at the back of her head slowly consumed her attention. *Please, let this end.*

Not until everyone stuffed themselves to the point of bursting did the feast conclude and the dining room empty. Through the commotion, Kyrin caught sight of Kaden in the crowd. He tipped his head toward the Hall's entrance. She followed, but had to pause several times to accept congratulations, even from some of the students who had been less than kind over the years. She tried to treat everyone nicely, but the now-raging headache left her nearly incapacitated. The moment she broke away, she hurried after her brother.

Her footsteps quickened almost to a run, and she left behind the buzz of conversation and outbursts of laughter. At the entrance to the Hall, she slipped outside. The cool night breeze instantly refreshed her and helped the headache. In the light of Aertus and Vilai rising above the wall, she found Kaden waiting at the side of the stairs. At first, they only looked at each other, but then she stepped into his arms, and he hugged her tightly. Face buried in his shoulder, she struggled not to cry, but the tears leaked out. Kaden's heavy breathing echoed in her ear. She gripped him more tightly and never wanted to let go. He was always so big and strong, jumping in to protect and defend her in a heartbeat, listening, sharing, comforting, and encouraging through all the years of their crazy childhood. But soon, that would be gone.

"Oh, Kaden, what happened?"

"I don't know." He pulled away, but his hands remained on her shoulders. "Come on, let's go see Sam."

She followed him across the courtyard to the library, desperate to find comfort there as she usually did. Inside, Sam met them. His golden eyes were warm with understanding.

"I knew you'd be here tonight."

Kyrin gave him a weak smile, but her lips wobbled in the attempt to hold it. "I guess I'm awfully predictable."

Tears needled her eyes again, and she fought them. She was stronger than this . . . wasn't she? Despite her best defenses, a rebel tear escaped and made way for others.

"Sam," she breathed in barely more than a whimper.

He closed the distance between them in less than a stride and wrapped her in his powerful yet gentle embrace, holding her like a frightened child. And that was just how she felt—just like the scared little girl who had hugged her father once more before leaving home behind. All those emotions stored in her memory returned at the thought of once again having to leave the familiar.

She buried her face in the soft suede of Sam's jerkin, and her shoulders shook with quiet sobs. He allowed her to cry and release the pent-up tension and stress that had built throughout the day. After several minutes, she pulled away and used her sleeves to wipe her face.

"I'm sorry."

"No. Sometimes tears are the best thing." His deep voice soothed her.

"I just don't understand."

The talcrin took her gently by the arm and led her to their usual seating. Kyrin sank into the soft cushions of the couch, resting her throbbing head back. Kaden sat beside her.

"I can't believe this has happened," Kyrin continued as Sam took his seat. "I thought . . . I thought I was safe for another couple of years."

"I know," Sam said. "It came as a shock to me as well."

Kyrin wiped her face again. "I don't like it here at Tarvin Hall, but at least it's familiar and Kaden's here, but now . . ." She gulped, and her heart raced. "I leave for the palace in the morning. I'll be serving the emperor, and not from some faraway city or town, but directly. I don't want to do this."

"We'll get you out of it," Kaden said suddenly.

"But how? What could we do?"

"Leave. Run away from Valcré."

Sam's voice lowered in warning. "You'd be fugitives, hunted by the emperor's men."

"So? They can't search all of Ilyon. We could hide somewhere. We could even go to Dorland, or Samara. We'd find somewhere safe."

"We can't, Kaden," Kyrin said quietly.

Her brother frowned. "Why not?"

"We would *never* be able to see our family again. Never see Father, never see our brothers, never see anyone," Kyrin stressed. "And what would that do to our reputation? We don't care how it affects us, but what about Father and the others? We just can't do that to them."

"But how can we do this?"

"I know this is difficult," Sam said, "and frightening for you, Kyrin, especially in light of how we believe, but there's one thing you're forgetting. What has happened today is no mistake. King Elôm has complete control in this, and I can only believe He has a plan for you. It's certainly no accident. He wants you at the palace. And if He wants you there, you can know He will guide you and take care of you. He doesn't expect you to face this on your own."

Sam was right, of course, but fear still fought to overwhelm her in the face of all the changes she would be required to confront come morning.

KYRIN SHIVERED DESPITE the warmth of the Hall. Her empty stomach gave an agitated gurgle, and she rubbed it. She'd skipped breakfast, not sure she could keep anything down. She never did get to sleep either. While her roommates had slept off their giant meal, she'd stared up at the bottom of the next bunk and prayed for some sort of intervention to keep this time from arriving. But it had come anyway.

She knelt down in front of Meredith. Tears pooled in the little girl's stormy blue eyes, and her voice quivered.

"I wish you didn't have to go."

"So do I."

"Will I ever see you again?"

Kyrin shook her head. "I don't know."

Meredith's face fell. She'd only just arrived at Tarvin Hall, and now she would lose her closest friend and protector. Kyrin squeezed the girl's thin shoulders. "Meredith, whenever anyone says mean things to you, don't listen to them. Just because they say it doesn't mean it's true, all right?"

The girl gave a weak nod, and Kyrin pulled her trembling little body into her arms. Meredith was as close to a sister as she had.

"Goodbye, Meredith. I love you."

"I love you too," Meredith choked out with a muffled sob.

Kyrin held her and rubbed her back before she rose. Her escort waited, and she still had goodbyes to say. She gave Meredith the best smile she could manage and turned away. With a silent plea to Elôm, she faced Kaden. His eyes were tired and bloodshot. He surely hadn't slept either, and he still wore yesterday's wrinkled uniform. Without speaking, they hugged tightly. Kyrin fought to stay strong. If she cried, it would make it that much harder for Kaden. She couldn't do that to him, even though she wanted to stand there and bawl like a child.

"I'm only going to the palace," she said, somehow keeping her voice light. "It's just up the hill. I'm sure we'll be able to see each other."

They parted, and Kaden forced a smile. "We'll make it happen. They can't always keep us apart."

Kyrin wasn't so sure this time, but she had no other hope to hold on to. She couldn't allow herself to contemplate not seeing him for months, maybe years. That would surely send her into a downward spiral that she wouldn't be able to control.

She filled her tightened lungs and gathered her fortitude. "Goodbye, Kaden."

He struggled for a moment to reply, his voice deeper than normal. "Goodbye, Kyrin."

Once more, they hugged, but goodbye felt so wrong. They hadn't spoken such words to each other in over ten years.

Before pulling away, Kyrin said, "Please take care of Meredith for me."

"I will," he promised.

That was all the time they were given.

"Come along now," Master Zocar cut in. "They're waiting for you at the palace."

Drawn by habitual obedience, she followed him toward the entrance, but then looked back. Kaden and Meredith stood side by side, watching her go. Tears seared her eyes and nose. Her limbs almost seized up as her heart tried to drag her back to them. An outcry to run pulsed at her core. Perhaps they should have escaped when Kaden suggested it last night. She and Master Zocar rounded a corner, and her brother disappeared. Kyrin gave a short gasp. *Help me be strong!*

Just outside the Hall, they met Sam—a timely distraction. He smiled at her. Zocar would think it to be in congratulation, but Kyrin saw the deeper sentiments hidden behind it—both his sympathy and his encouragement.

"I came to wish you the best," he said. "You're a very strong and capable young woman. I have no doubt you'll do well."

Though hard to believe that completely, a smile finally tugged at Kyrin's lips, and she stepped forward to hug him. It might have been odd to show such affection for one of the instructors, but she couldn't leave without it, and he didn't hesitate to embrace her in return. So quietly that she could barely hear, he whispered, "You'll be in my prayers."

Her smile resurfaced as they parted, though her vision turned watery. "Thank you."

He coaxed her forward. At the bottom of the stairs, two escorts waited with Collin, who grinned at her. But today she had no desire to return the grin.

Here they stopped again, and Master Zocar turned to her. He too gave her a wide smile.

"You've done your family and Tarvin Hall proud, Kyrin," he said in a kinder voice than usual.

Now that it came down to it, she just might miss him.

"Go on now, and serve the emperor well," he told her.

She managed a brief smile. If Elôm required this of her, she would try her best.

She fell in with Collin behind the escorts. The two of them followed the officials out of Tarvin Hall, no longer students. All their study and training had brought them to this moment. They made the uphill march toward the palace. Kyrin's pulse outpaced her dragging feet. She took no notice of the familiar scenery, her head bent until they passed through the palace gate and entered the expansive courtyard. At the foot of the palace, she looked up and stumbled to a halt. She had seen the palace many times from just outside the gate, but never so close. She craned her head back to take in the magnificent splendor of Auréa—four stories tall and with towers even higher. How could it look so infinitely larger and more intimidating here than from outside the courtyard? A cold sweat prickled her body.

"Come along, please," one of her escorts urged.

Kyrin's joints fused. The immense palace doors loomed before them. To pass would be to enter the unknown. An entirely new way of life she wasn't ready to face.

"Come on, it's not some monster waiting to swallow you up."

Her eyes snapped to Collin and that ridiculous grin of his. *That's what you think.* But his calm managed to break the icy bonds that had laid hold of her, and she let out a strangled laugh. She pulled her shoulders back and took the steps one at a time.

Collin nodded. "I knew you were braver than that."

Kyrin glanced sidelong at him. Brave? She wished. She could do with some courage right now. Her thudding heart seemed likely to fail her.

The palace doors swung inward, and they crossed the threshold. Kyrin's mouth fell open as her eyes traveled up one of the many ornate marble columns to the towering ceiling of the foyer. Dizzied, she dropped her gaze back to the floor. But the high polish of the geometric black and gold tiles reflecting the hundreds of candles glittering from their chandeliers didn't help. She squeezed her eyes closed to let her senses right themselves.

The escorts prompted her forward without allowing her time to grow accustomed to her new residence. She opened her eyes and let her gaze settle on two women who stood at the foot of a wide, scarlet-carpeted staircase. The younger woman, who was not too much older than Kyrin, wore a servant's uniform—a simple gray linen gown and crisp white overdress. Despite a pretty, freckle-sprinkled face and cinnamon-colored hair, she completely faded into the background next to the other, middle-aged woman.

This tall lady stood with a palpable air of authority and dignity. Dressed in a deep gold gown and black bodice, she reminded Kyrin of Master Zocar, but female. Her honey-brown hair was gathered up in an impressive arrangement of curls that Kyrin could never hope to duplicate, and didn't reveal any hint of graying with age. With a close look, she spotted the fine lines in the woman's face, but a thick layer of cosmetics hid most of them.

"This is Lady Videlle, head mistress here at Auréa," the escort introduced. "She will show you to your quarters and prepare you for your meeting with the emperor."

Kyrin glanced briefly at him before her eyes went to Collin. He grinned and winked at her as the escorts led him away down the hall. She almost wished he could stay. At least she knew him. She wasn't used to meeting strangers without Kaden.

With a convulsive swallow, she raised her eyes back to the tall, commanding woman in front of her. Lady Videlle had rigid features, yet not as harsh as the head mistress at Tarvin Hall. One blessing to be thankful for.

"Come with me," she said, her voice crisp, though not unkind.

She swept off and practically glided across the polished floor. How could she be so graceful? The only thing to prove she wasn't floating was the sharp click of her heels on the tile. Kyrin's own steps felt clumsy in comparison. She glanced over her shoulder. The servant girl followed a few yards behind with her eyes down. Kyrin's attention swung back to Lady Videlle at the clear ring of her refined voice.

"As you can see, Auréa Palace is large and can be confusing to navigate, but given your abilities, you should have no difficulty once you've been shown around."

Just how much did these people know about her?

"The stairs to the servants' quarters and the kitchen are down that hall, but you'll have no need to go there." She waved her hand as they passed. "Your quarters are in the advisors' wing, along with mine and the other members of the emperor's cabinet."

Lady Videlle looked back at Kyrin, face pinched. "I am to make it clear to you that, while relationships of any type between the staff here at Auréa are not expressly forbidden, it is not encouraged and must never interfere with your duties. Marriage and children are forbidden without the express approval of His Majesty. Should you, at any time, find yourself with child, you are required to see the palace physician to have it dealt with promptly, and it will be at your own expense."

Kyrin almost tripped over herself, and her mouth dropped open again before she snapped it shut. Everyone knew women often took certain drugs to end their pregnancies, but they never openly discussed it at Tarvin Hall. She swallowed on the repugnance of it.

In a wide corridor, Lady Videlle paused and pushed open one of many doors. "This will be your quarters."

Kyrin followed her into a room twice the size of the one she'd shared at Tarvin Hall, and her eyes rounded. Such finery! A large bed and wardrobe drew immediate attention. No more small, claustrophobic bunk or shared cabinet. A dressing table, writing desk, and several other, smaller furnishings filled the space— luxuries she'd never had before. Gold paper covered the walls, warmer than the stark and plain colors of a Tarvin Hall dorm, and a black and gold circular rug lay in the center of the dark wood floor. For the first time since childhood, she had a room to herself, and an impressive one at that.

"Far different from what you're used to, isn't it?"

Her attention shifted back to Lady Videlle at her first attempt at casual conversation. "Very much so."

"Well, in a few days, it will begin to feel like home."

Home. A twinge passed through Kyrin's stomach, but she hid the discomfort behind a slight smile.

"Now, there is much to see to this morning," Videlle went on. "Tonight you will meet the emperor and dine with him and his family, though typically, you will dine with the rest of us. Before that, however, you have a guest to see this afternoon."

Guest? What guest? How could she have one already on her first day?

Videlle did not pause long enough for her to voice these questions.

"First things first, your appearance." She faced Kyrin again, looking her up and down as an artist might scope out her canvas. Her thin, elegant eyebrows slowly dipped down, and Kyrin fidgeted.

"Well," Videlle said at last. "You're very plain."

Kyrin winced. She'd learned years ago to be content without the flawless ivory skin, full lips, and rich, flowing curls so many girls seemed to have. Nonetheless, Videlle's harsh assessment stung.

"Your hair will need work . . ."

Kyrin glanced at her dark, nut-brown braid resting over her shoulder. It certainly didn't match the luxurious sheen of Videlle's hair.

". . . and you are slender enough, but you're not the shapeliest girl. Perhaps you will fill out, but we shall see if our dressmaker can't do something to enhance you in the meantime."

Kyrin's cheeks warmed. She had no desire to look like many of the women she regularly encountered with their revealing gowns and tightly cinched bodices.

"You do have pretty eyes," Videlle added, almost as an after-thought. "Yes, we will try to draw more attention to them."

No one had complimented Kyrin's eyes before. Compared to Yara's striking green or Meredith's darker indigo hues, she never considered her dusty blue particularly attractive. But they were her father's eyes, and that made them special to her.

Videlle crossed the room to the wardrobe. "I will help you

this morning, but after this, Holly will assist you." She gestured to the servant girl standing ready at the door.

Kyrin glanced at her again, and the young woman curtsied.

"She is familiar with the morning routine and will be your personal maid."

Kyrin had to stop herself from gaping. First this extravagant room and now her own maid. Hadn't she just been on her hands and knees scrubbing Tarvin Hall's courtyard? She needed a moment to process this, but Videlle seemed determined to forge right ahead with her duties. She pushed back the wardrobe doors. Gold and black fabric filled the inside, but a few other splashes of rich color peeked out. She withdrew an article of clothing.

"Put this on first and we shall see to your hair and cosmetics."

She handed the white linen shift to Holly, who helped Kyrin change out of her uniform and into the close-fitting, short-sleeved garment. Once it was laced rather tightly in the back, Lady Videlle indicated a chair at the dressing table. Kyrin took a seat, and Holly loosed her hair to brush out the tangles. Despite being in a braid most of the morning, it hung limp and straight.

Videlle held her elbow in her hand and tapped one finger against her chin. "Doesn't look as though it will hold a curl well, does it?"

"No, ma'am," Holly answered quietly.

"Well, you will just have to do your best with it."

Kyrin almost laughed. The poor girl would have quite a challenge. She watched in the mirror as Holly reached for a tall glass bottle of clear liquid. She sprinkled a little of it into her hands and worked it through Kyrin's hair. Whatever it was transformed the dull strands to a rich, shiny brown. So that's how women did it.

Next came an abundance of hairpins and thin, flexible rollers, with which she arranged the top layer of Kyrin's hair up around her head. She used heated rods on the bottom layer to create the perfect, long curls women so coveted. After all, long, elaborate hairstyles were the height of women's fashion. To have it cut any shorter than waist length was a sign of terrible shame. Though Kyrin always found working with her hair a frustration, Holly turned it into what equated to a work of art.

As fascinating as it was to watch, Kyrin focused on Lady Videlle, who used this time to inform her about her position here at the palace. "You will be allowed to come and go as you please as long as you check with either myself or Holly. We will know the emperor's schedule and whether or not you are required."

Kyrin's heart gave a leap. She would still get to see Kaden. Already she wanted to know when she'd have a bit of free time, but she refrained from interrupting.

"For your service, you will be paid a generous monthly sum based on the performance of your duties."

"What, exactly, are my duties?" Kyrin asked as she looked at her in the mirror.

Lady Videlle frowned. "To read people, of course."

"And how and when will I do this? What type of situations?"

"Well," this seemed to be Videlle's favorite way to begin a statement, "no one has ever held your position until now, but from what I understand you will be present at most of the emperor's meetings and important gatherings. You will watch discreetly from the background and relay any pertinent information to the emperor's assistant, who will then give that information to the emperor. Obviously, your main objective is to recognize any threat to His Majesty."

Kyrin was about to nod, but thought better of it since it could mess up Holly's work.

It took close to an hour before both Videlle and Holly found satisfaction with Kyrin's hairstyle. Would they spend every morning in this manner? What a waste of time. But she didn't dare breathe a word of this, of course.

Now Lady Videlle took over to show Holly what she had in mind for cosmetics. At this point, Kyrin could no longer watch the progress in the mirror as the women fussed over her face. Videlle applied generous amounts of cream and powder to Kyrin's skin, much like an artist now with all her brushes and cosmetic palettes.

After a variety of colors and applications, Videlle stepped back to examine her handiwork. "There, you see that, Holly, how the blue and brown brings out her eyes as well as complements her hair?"

Holly nodded studiously.

"That's what I want you to go for."

"Yes, ma'am."

"Can I see?" Kyrin asked. After all that painting and powdering, how must she look?

"Not just yet. Let's first get you into your dress."

Videlle went to the wardrobe again. This time she withdrew a long, gold linen gown similar to her own. It had an attractive cut, and the neckline was not too low, thankfully. Actually, it was quite plain except for the embroidered black ribbon sewn down the length of each sleeve and around the bottom hem.

Holly helped Kyrin into this dress and laced up the back. She also tightened laces on either side of the dress's bodice so it fit as snugly as the shift. Over the dress went a fitted black, suede vest. Kyrin smoothed her hands down the front. She had only worn dresses on special occasions. This would take some getting used to, but the dress was pretty. Maybe dressing up would have its advantages.

This thought vanished the moment Lady Videlle produced a pair of black shoes. Heels. Her shoulders sagged. Only once had she ever worn heels, and it ended in disaster. Of course, it hadn't been purely out of clumsiness. She had been tripped, deliberately, but still. She grimaced at the memory of the ensuing chaos when Kaden had jumped in to avenge her.

"Do I have to wear heels?"

Lady Videlle looked at her aghast. "Well, of course you must. What is a gown without appropriate footwear? Besides, it will add a couple of inches to your height, and that is always a good thing."

Kyrin winced. Five foot seven was just fine. She didn't need to be five foot ten. Now she understood why Videlle was so tall.

"Well, for pity's sake, at least wear them today and when you're with the emperor. If you wish to go without them on your own time, very well."

Kyrin accepted this agreement and stepped into the shoes Videlle set on the floor. Holly buckled them, and Kyrin took a couple of uncertain steps. The instability made her nervous, but she had no choice.

With a final inspection, Lady Videlle smiled. "Well, considering what I had to work with, the outcome is quite satisfactory." She gestured to the full-length mirror in the corner. "See for yourself."

Kyrin stepped carefully to the mirror. She sucked in her breath at her reflection. No more plain, simple Kyrin. Layers of cream and powder smoothed and lightened her skin tone. The pale color brought out the deep crimson of her lip paint and the dusty blue and brown on her eyelids that did indeed draw attention to her eyes. She was beautiful, at least according to the standards of society. Despite how plain she'd been, Holly and Videlle had transformed her image into one any girl would envy.

And yet, Kyrin's heart sank. This would now be expected of her—this painted girl in the mirror. Suddenly, she desired more than anything to be plain old Kyrin.

"I NEED A bodyguard?" Kyrin didn't like the sound of that.

She struggled to keep up with Lady Videlle on their way to meet with Sir Aric, Emperor Daican's head of security, and not fall flat on her face, or worse, break an ankle. The woman didn't seem to notice.

"Yes, of course. Now as part of Auréa's staff, the emperor's enemies are your enemies. Many believe that to harm one of His Majesty's aides or advisors will harm him."

Kyrin's pulse quickened. She'd never worried about her safety with her brother around.

"Now, don't fear," Lady Videlle said as she slowed just a bit. "Emperor Daican's security force is the finest in Arcacia."

A lot of good those words did, coming from a relative stranger. She'd rather have Kaden to protect her.

The two of them entered the meeting room, and Kyrin's gaze did a quick sweep. Comfortable seating filled the spacious area. Lady Videlle said the palace aides often used it for congregating at the end of the day, but never mind the furnishings. Kyrin's attention focused on two men standing proudly in their palace uniforms. The first man, a bit older than the other, stood tall and dark with a stern jaw set. A distinct air of authority surrounded him. The younger man waited to the side, his much lighter features a contrast to those of his superior.

"Sir Aric," Videlle said as she approached the black-haired man. "Thank you for meeting us here."

"Not a problem." His voice was deep and all business.

Lady Videlle turned to Kyrin. "Here she is, Emperor Daican's new observer, Kyrin Altair."

Aric inclined his head politely. "My lady."

"Sir Aric." She studied his face. Though cool and collected, a spark of warmth in his gray-blue eyes hinted at a softer side.

He motioned to his right, and the younger man stepped forward. "This is Trev. He's been part of the security force here at Auréa for three years now, and I've assigned him as your personal guard. He'll be your escort whenever you have reason to leave the palace grounds."

Kyrin eyed her new bodyguard. He reminded her somewhat of Collin in the way he held himself—confident, sure of his abilities—yet without possessing Collin's arrogance. Just a quiet, reassuring confidence. Maybe he would be able to keep her safe. She managed a smile.

Trev met it with his own. "My lady."

His quiet tone surprised her, but it was genuine and encouraging.

"Trev will be at your disposal whenever you should need him," Lady Videlle told her. "Just send word through Holly."

Kyrin nodded her understanding, but getting to know her bodyguard would have to wait. With barely a word of parting, Lady Videlle whisked her off for what she called a "brief" tour of the palace—through winding, turning halls, numerous sitting rooms, libraries, various ball and meeting rooms, up flights of stairs, and back down again. Even Kyrin's head spun at the sheer size and complexity of Auréa's marble and gilded interior.

By the time they finished inside the palace and toured the grounds, a deep ache throbbed just above Kyrin's eyes. She resisted the urge to rub her forehead since it would smudge her cosmetics.

"Well." Lady Videlle finally paused and sounded a bit winded.

"Now you've seen all you need to of Auréa. I trust you will be able to find your way around."

"Yes, my lady," Kyrin replied, though to try to recall it now only intensified her headache.

"Right, then, this way. Lunch will soon be served. We don't want to keep your guest waiting."

And she was off again with that graceful but deceptively fast walk of hers. Thank Elôm that Kyrin had spent so much time wandering the city and at the training fields to have the stamina to keep up, though her heeled shoes fought her every step. If only Videlle would slow enough to allow her to question the identity of her mystery guest. She had no desire to meet anyone else. Between her headache and the new information spinning around in her head, she'd surely make a dreadful dining companion. In fact, the whole idea made her quite uneasy. Kaden was good with people, not her.

She took a couple of deep breaths to clear her mind of all unnecessary information. Dampness built up on her palms beneath her clenched fingers. How very unladylike. She grimaced and forced her hands open, willing them to dry before meeting her guest.

Lady Videlle stopped at the door to one of the parlors and opened it. Before Kyrin could do anything more to prepare herself, the woman ushered her into the room. Her eyes locked on the man dressed in a captain's uniform who rose from the couch. Strong, dark features, dusty blue eyes—Kyrin took in these details in a heartbeat, and all the tension that had wound her so tightly released. Tears rushed to her eyes and a smile broke across her face.

"Father!"

Without a moment's concern for formality, she ran into his arms and ignored Lady Videlle's disapproving sniff. Nothing at all could steal the joy of this reunion. Lady Videlle, the palace—it all disappeared as Kyrin soaked in the warmth of her father's strong, yet gentle embrace. The tears fell, no doubt smudging her eye shadow and leaving dark streaks down her face, but forget her appearance, forget everything. She had her father. It had been so long.

They parted, and Kyrin stared into his smiling face—so kind and handsome, his eyes sparkling with both tears and happiness.

William Altair wiped his thumbs across her face. "It's so good to see you."

"I can't believe you're here," Kyrin breathed.

Off to the side, Lady Videlle exclaimed, "Goodness, child, no need to carry on so. Look at your face. Oh, this will never do!"

Kyrin wanted to ignore the woman, but she came with a napkin from the table and forced Kyrin back a step. She fussed and dabbed at Kyrin's face like a mother would a young child. Giddiness bubbled up inside Kyrin, and she chuckled as she grinned at her father, further flustering Videlle. The woman shook her head and lamented over her ruined appearance.

"There's no hope for it now. We will just have to redo it before you meet the emperor." She stepped away, still shaking her head in dismay. "I will leave you now and inform the kitchen staff you are ready."

Kyrin's father smiled kindly at her. "Thank you, Lady Videlle."

She gave a terse nod and cast one more exasperated glance at Kyrin on the way out.

Once the door had closed, Kyrin released a full laugh and hugged her father again. "I really can't believe it. I knew you were in Valcré, but I never expected to see you here."

"You can be sure I never would have left the city without making a point to see you and Kaden." William held her at arm's length and shook his head. "Look at you. How your mother would love to see you now."

Kyrin's smile wobbled at the lack of feeling that thoughts of her mother evoked. She should feel something, shouldn't she? But her father's presence cheered her again immediately.

"It's been a long time," she murmured.

"A very long time."

"I'm just glad it's you. I'm not sure how I would have handled someone else."

With a sympathetic look, William asked, "How are you holding up?"

Tears pricked her eyes again. How could she adequately answer that question? But she refused to cry again. She swallowed and spoke through a rough voice, "It's been . . . overwhelming."

"I can only imagine. I was shocked to receive the news."

"You and me both. I never even considered that anything like this could happen."

Her father motioned to the couch behind them, and they both sat. His eyes turned serious now, the way Kaden's often did when they talked.

"How do you feel about this? It's certainly an incredible honor . . ."

His voice trailed away as he studied her face. Kyrin glanced around the room to assure herself that they were the only two people present before her eyes returned to her father.

"Yes, to those who would wish for it, but . . . I have no desire to be here." Her voice dropped lower. "Though I guess this is where King Elôm wants me."

Her father's eyes grew delightfully large, but just as he was about to speak, the door opened. Servants entered bearing trays of food for their lunch. Kyrin and William rose from the couch to take seats at a small table. No one spoke as the servants set out their plates and poured each a glass of red wine from a crystal decanter, but William did give them a kind thank-you as they departed. When the door closed again, Kyrin and her father sat in silence for several seconds after the sound of footsteps died away. Then the conversation resumed in earnest, their meal all but forgotten.

"How long have you known about Elôm?" William asked, his voice lowered, yet animated.

"A little over a year."

"Who told you?"

"Sam did."

"And Kaden? What about him?"

"Him too. We don't disagree on much."

William let go a long sigh. "I can't tell you what good it does me to hear that. I've been wondering what I'd say or how I'd explain things to the two of you in the short time we have. I knew I had to say something since it's so uncertain when we'll see each other. But how did you know I believe?"

"Sam told us that too."

"Good old Sam."

Kyrin nodded vigorously. "He's been such a good friend to Kaden and me, and so helpful when we struggle with things. Without him, we'd still be lost."

"This brings me great comfort. For so long, I've wondered if I alone in our family would know the truth."

"What about Mother and the rest of the boys? Have you spoken to them?"

Her father winced. "Your mother is not yet ready to listen. She's fearful of what it could mean for us, and it upsets her if I say anything around Michael and Ronny."

Kyrin's forehead wrinkled, and a small flame burned in her chest. Her father should be able to talk to her little brothers about something so important. No one should prevent him, and she was tempted to say so, but she held her tongue. Instead, her thoughts turned to her two older brothers. They were adults and could choose to listen on their own. "What about Marcus and Liam?"

"I've used the opportunities I've been given, but it's a very delicate situation. I never know what I should say or what might be too much." William paused, and the fine lines in his face deepened. "The trouble with Marcus is his devotion to his duty as a soldier. To believe in the King, he would have to realize that his loyalty and dedication to the emperor and his gods are for naught. I'm afraid it would take a miracle."

Kyrin considered her eldest brother. During the years of their childhood together, he had always played the soldier. He'd dreamed of becoming a renowned general like their Grandfather Veshiron. And all these years he'd worked toward that goal, not knowing what such dedicated, almost worshipful, service to the emperor cost. Her father was right. Marcus's loyalty and ideals would never sway easily, even if his soul stood at risk.

Kyrin pressed her fingers to the deep ache in her stomach. "Maybe Elôm will give us a miracle."

A small smile lifted the corners of William's mouth. "We will pray so."

And Kyrin did, right there in the quietness of her heart. She and her family had lived such separate lives for the past years. She didn't want the eternity that followed this life to be the same. These days it was her only hope they would ever be together again.

"So what about Liam?"

Her father's face and voice softened. "Liam is different. I can speak my mind more freely with him. He never says much, but always listens. You remember how he is. He gives a lot of thought to things before making up his mind. I think he's open. I just need to find the right way and time in which to explain to him. It won't be easy with his situation. He could never hide such beliefs as well as I can."

Kyrin hung her head. Why couldn't they just serve their God in peace? It didn't harm anyone.

"Don't worry," her father said. "I'll use every opportunity I can to speak to them. All of them."

She looked up. Her heart beat heavily. "Just be careful."

A grimace flashed across her father's expression as if he knew something, something dreadful, but he warded off questions by hiding it behind a smile. "I will. Now, what do you say we eat?"

Kyrin hesitated, still wondering about his reaction, but maybe she didn't want to know. She had more than enough to think about already. She looked down at the cooling food, which a moment ago sat forgotten, and picked up a spoon to try the light-colored soup in the bowl before her. It had a creamy chicken broth with dumplings.

"Mmm, Kaden would die for this."

"Still has a large appetite?"

"Voracious." Kyrin laughed. "And I know why. Wait until you see him. He's definitely inherited Grandfather's height. I'm afraid he's surpassed you now."

William shrugged. "How can I complain about healthy, growing boys?" He took a bite of his soup, and once he swallowed, he said, "Speaking of the General, I have a surprise for you. Your grandfather is coming tomorrow."

Kyrin paused, her spoon hovering over her bowl, and stared at her father. An odd surprise, considering. But her father smiled and his eyes twinkled.

"He's bringing Marcus and Liam with him."

Kyrin's spoon dropped with a splash into the soup, and a huge grin took hold of her face. "Really?"

William nodded in confirmation. "They would've been here today, but the General had a few things to see to."

Just when Kyrin thought she'd exhausted her tears for the day, they blurred her vision, and anticipation swallowed up her appetite. Her voice a little shaky, she said, "I might not be happy with everything that's happened, but at least it's allowing me to see all of you."

For the remainder of the meal and throughout the afternoon, Kyrin sat with her father and caught up on the years they'd been apart, talking of home and her brothers. For those blissful hours, her promotion slipped to the back of her mind. With her father, she felt safe and confident. But, to her dismay, evening fast closed in on them. Long before she was ready, Lady Videlle entered the room.

"Kyrin, it is time for you to prepare for your meeting with the emperor."

Kyrin looked to her father. "Will you be at supper?"

"No," William told her with regret. "This is a private meeting."

They rose from the couch, and Kyrin wanted to latch on to her father and not leave his side. He gave her an understanding look and pulled her into a gentle embrace. Whispering in her ear, he said, "Just be yourself. Be kind, but cautious. You'll do fine. Always remember, you're not alone. You never will be."

They parted, and Kyrin gave him a teary smile. She quickly composed herself and turned to follow Lady Videlle. She glanced back once to catch her father's calming smile, and it instilled in her courage to face what was to come.

BACK IN KYRIN'S room, Holly went to work fixing her cosmetics while Lady Videlle rattled off a mind-numbing list of etiquette and details for Kyrin to remember. Most of them Kyrin knew already, and Videlle's constant talking frayed her already worn nerves. Still, she fought to remain calm. Her father's words replayed in her mind, bringing comfort and reminding her of the higher power in all this. She prayed fervently for strength and wisdom.

After Videlle's drawn-out fussing, she finally declared Kyrin ready to meet the emperor. Kyrin glanced in the mirror. Her face displayed a fresh layer of cosmetics, perhaps even thicker than before, especially on her eyelids, which left them sticky. But she surely couldn't complain about it now.

"Come along then," Videlle said. "We must not keep His Majesty waiting."

Off they went through the palace. Kyrin focused on her heart, keeping it from racing, and tried to stop her palms from sweating again. This was when it really mattered. The Emperor's first impression of her meant everything. He was the most powerful man in Ilyon, and not only her ruler, but now, her employer. She summoned all sorts of comforting images to her mind—her father, Kaden, and Marcus and Liam. She just had to make it through tonight, and tomorrow she would see her older brothers.

This helped right up until she spotted the massive doors ahead. The last several yards dragged at her feet. Her tongue swelled up in her mouth, and she swallowed repeatedly. What if she couldn't speak when she needed to? She could make quite a fool of herself if she bumbled her way through this. They paused as two servants took the ornate door handles and swung the doors open to admit them into a spacious room adorned in rich, burgundy velvet and gold accents. Now Kyrin's heart did pound.

Two men stood at the far end of the room, but one look at their rich clothing made it clear which man was the emperor. Both turned. Kyrin caught only a glimpse of the emperor's face before Lady Videlle stopped and sunk into a low and graceful curtsy. Kyrin promptly moved to imitate her, though she couldn't claim such gracefulness. Her unsteady footwear threatened to topple her.

"Your Majesty," Videlle said, her voice low with reverence.

Slowly, they straightened, and Kyrin let out the breath trapped in her lungs. The emperor had closed the distance between them with the other man a few feet behind. Kyrin's gaze lifted, con-necting with the emperor's, and stopped. Her mouth almost fell open. Warm, amber-brown eyes met hers—not at all cold or steely like she'd anticipated. In fact, nothing about this man matched her expectations. Though she'd seen him on occasion, it had been at a great distance.

He wasn't tall, not like Kaden, but he was fit. This showed even through his royal garments. Dark hair brushed his broad shoulders, and his strong face sported a neatly trimmed beard. Kyrin often heard women, even some of the older girls at Tarvin Hall, speak of the emperor rather breathlessly. She never understood why until now. Emperor Daican was a very hand-some man. Could he really be the man she and Kaden spoke of so often as their enemy? Those golden-brown eyes of his, twinkling in the warm glow of the candles on the wall, could not be less threatening.

Whether anyone else spoke in those brief few moments, Kyrin would never know, but she started at Lady Videlle's introduction.

". . . present to you Kyrin Altair."

"Miss Altair." Daican's smooth but strong voice hung between them. He gave her a perfect, charming smile that for all the world looked genuine.

Kyrin's mind swirled dizzily with the uncertainty of how to feel—relieved or terrified. Where was the cruel-hearted man responsible for stealing her and Kaden away from their family? Nothing coincided with the assumptions she had created, and it nearly choked her ability to think. But somehow, she managed a response.

"I am pleased to meet you, Your Majesty."

She even broke into a smile. How could she not when he smiled so openly back at her?

"And I, you," Daican replied. "You've been of great interest to me for some time."

"Really?" The question slipped from Kyrin's mouth, and she winced. "I apologize, Your Majesty. So many go through Tarvin Hall, I never considered you would personally take interest in them."

The emperor chuckled softly. "I'm afraid I don't have the time to spare to read reports on everyone, but there are a few my advisors bring to my attention, and you happen to be one of those few."

Kyrin still couldn't imagine why her, but she refrained from asking this question. Instead, she spoke with great care. "I am honored. I never considered myself extraordinary at Tarvin Hall."

"Oh, but your talents are quite valuable, particularly at this point in time. People are deceiving and can hide their intentions so easily . . ."

For the briefest moment, Kyrin's insides turned to ice. If this was exactly what the emperor was doing, he did a frighteningly good job of it.

". . . but you know what to look for," Daican continued. "You pick up on things others miss. You can catch the subtle hints to one's intentions."

Kyrin studied the man for just such hints. However, she could find nothing to give him away—no clues that his kind and welcoming manner cloaked dishonesty. She did get a distinct and rather uncomfortable feeling that he was fully aware of her attempt to read him. Deciding any further scrutiny would be folly, she recalled her father's words and recovered her smile. "I hope I prove as valuable as you're expecting."

"I'm sure you will." Daican glanced behind him. "Where are my manners? Miss Altair, this is Sir Richard Blaine, my chief advisor and an old family friend."

The man stepped forward. Grim-faced, he did not offer a smile, and just nodded his head stiffly. Kyrin curtsied, a shiver skittering across her skin. While Daican presented warmth and friendliness, this man embodied everything she had expected of the emperor. He was slightly older than Daican, and a hair taller, with thinner, more severe features. His cold gray eyes left a hollow feeling inside her.

"Ah, my dear."

Kyrin focused again on Emperor Daican, thankful for the distraction. He smiled animatedly with his eyes set across the room. Kyrin turned as a courtly woman approached. Long, dark hair cascaded past her shoulders, held back by a golden circlet, but smoky eye shadow brought all the attention to her jade green eyes. She moved with mesmerizing poise and grace that almost put Lady Videlle to shame. Kyrin would be afraid simply to move in front of her. She bore a stunning resemblance to the more detailed depictions of Vilai, like a painting come to life, though she was a bit more tastefully dressed. Though middle-aged like Daican, her maturity only seemed to give her a more dignified air. Even Kyrin's newly transformed look fell far short of this woman's natural radiance.

Kyrin glanced down and smoothed out the wrinkles in her vest. The gold fabric of her dress seemed to have lost a bit of its vividness. She looked up again, and her eyes settled on a second woman this time. Near Kyrin in age, she too bore rich dark hair and green eyes, possessing all of the older woman's finest features, but her facial structure more closely resembled Daican.

The young woman looked Kyrin's way, and her deep green eyes seemed to bore right into her soul. Kyrin's breath grew shallow as irrational thoughts popped into her head of all her secrets spilling out. Was this what people felt when she studied them? She hoped not. It didn't feel good. She swallowed, trying to moisten her throat, and dropped her eyes again before looking to Daican.

"Miss Altair, this is my wife Solora, Queen of Arcacia." Daican spoke with a tone of true adoration and brushed his finger down the older woman's smooth arm. Pride elevated his voice when he gestured to the younger woman. "And our daughter, Princess Davira."

Kyrin curtsied low again. "Your Majesties."

Neither responded, their mysterious, exotic eyes taking measure of her. Kyrin fought not to fidget. Would they find her as lacking as Lady Videlle had upon first examination? Her hands grew damp, and heat prickled her back. She inwardly thanked Daican for breaking into the awkward silence as he smiled at her once again and put her strangely at ease.

"I do hope you're hungry. I'm sure you'll find the fare of Auréa to your liking."

"Yes, my lord, on both accounts."

"Excellent."

He offered his arm to his wife, and Kyrin followed the royal couple and the princess to the dining room. Along the way, Daican leaned close to his wife to murmur near her ear. Kyrin didn't catch his words and had no desire to overhear, but Queen Solora's answer was more audible.

"He left just after breakfast. Aric said he hasn't returned yet."

A cold shadow passed over Daican's face, and his jaw clenched as he looked away from his wife.

In the grand dining room, servants pulled out chairs for the four of them at an enormously long table overhung with crystal chandeliers. Daican sat at the head, of course, with Solora to his right and Kyrin beside her. Davira had a seat directly across from Kyrin. The space to the emperor's left was set, but remained curiously empty.

The meal commenced with much more pleasantness than Kyrin had anticipated all day. Most of her nerves calmed within the first few minutes. The emperor continued to amaze her with his talkative and even witty personality. Though Solora and Davira seemed to deem her too far beneath them to engage in personal conversation, Daican had no such reservations, and even managed to make her laugh several times. They talked about Tarvin Hall, the palace, and Valcré in general. At one point, he asked, "Were you surprised to see your father?"

Kyrin grinned, quick to relive the moment. "Completely, and I couldn't have been happier."

Daican smiled in turn with a knowing look. "You two are close?"

"Yes, my lord, very close."

"I was close to my father as well," he said with a nod. "He died when I was seventeen. Your age, correct?"

"Yes, my lord." Kyrin sobered with the thought of losing her father so young. "I'm sorry. That must have been difficult."

"Indeed," Daican said quietly. "It is very young to have the rule of a country placed on your shoulders. My father had great vision for Arcacia. His life was cut too short, but I've dedicated my life to establishing the legacy he was working toward. Not just for myself and my children, but for him also. I want my rule to reflect his greatness."

Odd as it seemed, Kyrin felt compelled to say, "I think he would be proud."

Daican's magnetic smile returned. "Thank you." But then his eyes slid to the empty seat beside him and sparked. "If only all children felt the same as you and I."

Kyrin glanced at the chair, and pieces she had not yet considered fell into place. The emperor also had a son, Daniel. Now the queen's answer to her husband's question made more sense.

Daican's annoyance vanished as quickly as it had appeared, and his gaze switched to Davira with another look of pride. "We're close, aren't we?"

Davira smiled lovingly at him, though something about her sent a chill down the center of Kyrin's back. "Yes, Father."

Attention returned to Kyrin then, and Daican asked about her afternoon with her father and discussed the coming visit from her grandfather and brothers.

A short time later, the doors to the dining room burst open. Everyone looked up with a start. A young man in his mid-twenties strode into the room. One look at his dark, short-cropped hair, fit build, and amber eyes left no doubt about his identity, though he stood a bit taller than his father. Prince Daniel garnered most of the whispers and female giggles at Tarvin Hall. Inheriting all of his father's good looks, he had the added benefit of youth that made him irresistible to nearly every young woman within a hundred leagues. And he was decidedly unattached.

Kyrin stared wide-eyed at him, though it had nothing to do with his looks. She was the only woman she knew who wasn't smitten with the prince. No, the man drew her gaping with his behavior. He tromped around the table, pulled out his chair, and sat down hard.

"Sorry I'm late." He barely glanced at his parents as he snapped open his napkin and laid it on his lap. "I had to dispatch a group of bandits on the way back. A dreadful waste of time."

"Daniel," his mother warned sharply.

The prince's brows rose as his eyes settled on her. "What? Don't believe me?"

A devilish smirk broke out on his lips.

"You were to be here on time." Daican spoke with a sharp edge to his voice, and his eyes glinted as he glared at his son.

"Like I said, I was detained by unforeseeable circumstances," Daniel replied without looking at him.

"And your men will confirm that?"

Daniel just shrugged and motioned to the nearby servants. "I'm starving. Never had lunch."

"Have you even washed up?"

Kyrin caught the way the emperor's fist squeezed the life out of his napkin.

Daniel raised his dark eyebrows to his father now. The prince wore a hunting outfit with a couple of small twigs and leaves still clinging to it. His dark hair flipped out at odd angles from riding, and the distinct smell of pine, earth, and horses drifted across the table.

"First you scold me for being late and then get after me for not taking the extra time to wash."

Kyrin couldn't imagine using such a flippant tone with her own father.

Complete silence settled over the table. Daican and his son glared at each other in an intense battle of wills.

At last, the emperor ordered in a low, controlled voice, "Out." He then added more forcefully, "I'll not have you disrupting this meal."

"Suit yourself."

Daniel shoved his chair back, tossed his napkin onto his empty plate, and strode out of the room exactly as he'd entered. Silence fell again. Kyrin didn't dare to move and draw attention to herself. If only she could sink into the cushion of her chair out of sight. To witness a heated argument between the royal family on her first night in Auréa was not an ideal way to begin her service.

She peeked at Daican, who glared at his plate, and then

glanced across at Davira. Fire seethed in the princess's eyes. Beside her, the queen breathed slow, measured breaths. In a moment, Daican composed himself and once more turned a calm expression to Kyrin.

"I sincerely apologize, Miss Altair. My son has an unfortunate habit of forgetting his place."

"I understand, my lord," Kyrin murmured.

From that point on, the meal lost a little of its pleasure, though the emperor did his part to keep things light. When they finished for the evening, Daican bid her goodnight with his hope that she would find her position in Auréa agreeable.

Kyrin left the dining room with a keen desire for rest. As pleasant as the meal turned out to be, the weariness of the day descended and weighed heavily on her shoulders. She couldn't wait to get the shoes off her pinched and aching feet. Holly waited in her room and helped her change and wash up for bed.

A gentle tap came at the door just as they finished, accompanied by her father's voice. Holly opened it to him and bobbed a curtsy. She glanced back at Kyrin.

"Will there be anything else, my lady?"

"No, Holly, thank you."

The young woman left the room, and William closed the door.

Kyrin sank into one of the padded chairs at the end of her bed and rubbed her feet. Her father took the seat across from her.

"Now you look more like the Kyrin I remember."

They shared a smile.

"I'll hate having to wear that stuff every day."

Her father rested back in his chair with curious eyes. "How did it go?"

She stared at him in silence for several seconds. If not for the vivid memories, the last couple of hours would have seemed like a strange dream. "I'm confused. He wasn't at all what I expected. He was so . . . nice. He was kind to me and easy to talk to, and even funny." She hesitated. "It's difficult to see him as an enemy. He is our enemy . . . isn't he?"

William leaned forward to rest his elbows on his knees. "I don't think that's something that can be answered by a simple yes or no, especially not by me. I don't know him well enough for that. Like you, in my personal experiences with him, he's been very kind. But I do know he is opposed to the teaching of Elôm and has done things you and I would never approve of, so that requires caution from us."

The rich food Kyrin had eaten churned in her stomach as her encouraging outlook on supper faded. Her father reached out and took her hand, squeezing it securely, the way he had when leading her around as a child.

"Don't worry. You're a smart girl. You'll figure this out."

THE NEXT MORNING brought much more anticipation than Kyrin had expected for her second day in Auréa. She sought her father the moment Holly finished with her hair and cosmetics, after a mighty battle not to fidget with impatience while the girl worked. She and her father took breakfast together and remained in the privacy of the drawing room to talk while they awaited the rest of Kyrin's guests.

She chuckled at a story he told of her younger brothers, and then tipped her head a little as her eyes caught on a dark leather cord peeking out from around his neck. "You still wear it."

He looked down and reached into his collar to withdraw the cord. A shiny, dark-flecked stone hung from it, matching the blue of their eyes.

"Always."

Kyrin gazed at it. Such a small, insignificant object, yet it represented a much different time of her life.

"It was so long ago, but I still remember asking Carl to help me make it for you, almost like it was yesterday." The old gardener's smiling face played in her mind, and a half smile touched her lips. She didn't think of him as often as her father or brothers, but she did miss him. He'd always been like family. She couldn't have made the parting gift for her father without him.

"It must be a remarkable thing to have all your memories so clear."

Kyrin's smile faded. The quickest and clearest memories to jump to her mind were ones of goodbye, of cruel words, and of nighttime tears. "Not always." Her throat ached, and the sting worked its way up into her nose, then her eyes. "I just wish I had more memories of home."

William put his arm around her shoulders and kissed her hair just above her ear. "So do I."

"If only Kaden and I had realized what was at stake. We could have hid our learning abilities and how we pick up on things."

"Ah, your mother wouldn't have wanted that. She always wanted to see you become something more than you could have back in Mernin."

Kyrin tensed under his arm, and her ribs pressed into her lungs. "Only because that's what Grandfather wanted." Her voice matched her taut muscles.

"Perhaps, but that's only part of it." William pulled away enough to face her. "Really, Kyrin, she's very proud of you and Kaden."

Kyrin let these words rest in her mind and bit back the urge to argue. Maybe he was right.

"Keep in mind," he went on, "had you and Kaden never come to Tarvin Hall, you never would have met Sam, and you might not have followed the King now."

The tension released, and Kyrin drew a full breath. A smile even worked its way to her lips. "True. I hate how things are, but no knowledge of Elôm would be far worse in the end."

He patted her shoulder. "Very much worse."

They grew silent at a knock on the door. A footman stepped into the room. "Excuse me, Miss Altair, your brother has arrived. He's in the parlor across the hall."

Kyrin had just enough restraint to retain some semblance of dignity and not dash from the room to meet him. Who knew when Lady Videlle or a member of the royal family might be nearby to witness her actions. But she did share a huge grin with her father as they left the couch. At the parlor door, she let herself in and closed it just enough to hide her father, for now. Kaden stood in the center of the room with his gaze lifted as he scanned the rich, albeit dark, interior. His eyes dropped to her and rounded.

"Kyrin."

If he intended to say anything else, her enthusiastic embrace cut him off. She squeezed him tightly and relished the sense of security he brought.

"I know I just saw you yesterday morning, but it already feels like such a long time."

She pulled away and took a step back to let her brother look her over. Slowly, his forehead furrowed.

"Wow," he said, but his voice was dull.

"You don't like it."

Their eyes met, and Kaden hesitated. "No." He was quick to say, "Don't get me wrong, you look beautiful, it's just . . . it's not you."

"I know," Kyrin put him at ease. "I don't like it either, but I don't have much choice."

"We never do," Kaden muttered and half-scowled. "So, why was I summoned?"

Giddiness fluttered in Kyrin's chest. "To celebrate my promotion."

Kaden cocked an eyebrow, and Kyrin laughed, enjoying the ability to surprise him. "Don't worry, part of this you will like."

She hurried back to the door, peeking around it to grin at her father, and then pulled it open fully as she turned to watch Kaden's face. At the way his quizzical expression transformed into one of open shock, a pleasant warmth surrounded her heart.

"Father."

They met near the door, where William hauled Kaden into his arms, and they traded a crushing embrace. Tears pushed to

Kyrin's eyes, and she dabbed the corners. She wouldn't ruin Holly's work this time.

William held his son at arm's length, his eyes beaming. "Look at the fine young man you've become." He glanced at Kyrin. "I'll say he's grown."

She chuckled again as she watched them with delight—the two men she held most dear.

Kaden shrugged. "I guess I've put on a couple of inches."

"You've probably caught up with Liam now."

"He's got the Veshiron height too, huh?"

"Yes, you two certainly inherited your grandfather's stature, and it won't surprise me if Michael and Ronny have as well, especially Michael. Already tall and lanky for a twelve-year-old."

Kaden shook his head. "Man, I'd like to see them. Michael probably doesn't even remember us."

"I'm afraid not."

"A bit much to expect, I guess," Kyrin said. "He was only two, and Ronny was just a baby."

She imagined his little body, so soft and cuddly in her arms, and his big brown eyes, like their mother's. If only she could hold him again, but he was no longer a baby. Just what did her brothers look like now, ten years older?

Kaden crossed his arms. "I assume since they haven't shown up at Tarvin Hall, Kyrin and I got all the special talent in the Altair family."

"They're smart and quick learners, but nothing out of the ordinary," their father confirmed.

Kaden glanced toward the closed door and lowered his voice to a sober tone. "Good."

William gave a nod of silent agreement, but smiled to lighten the mood. "Come, let's sit down. We've got a lot to talk about."

Kyrin would cherish the next hour and a half for a long time afterward. She could have spent days with her father and Kaden, reminiscing and talking of home. With them, she was free to be completely herself. Because of this, she experienced a mix of both disappointment and excitement when they received word that the remainder of her guests had arrived. This time, they all met in a larger sitting room.

The moment she passed through the doors, tears burned the back of Kyrin's throat. Her eyes misted at the sight of her older brothers' smiles. Liam stepped forward first, and Kyrin hugged him for all she was worth, for once glad of her shoes to give her a little extra height.

"Oh, Liam, it's so good to see you!"

She let out a quiet laugh at his strong embrace that bordered on painful.

"Sorry," he said a bit bashfully as he let her go.

Kyrin waved off the apology and grinned up at him. The long six years since their last brief visit had transformed her brother from a rather awkward fourteen-year-old to a tall, muscular young man like Kaden. No more awkwardness there. He appeared strong and capable in his soldier's uniform, yet the quality of innocence Kyrin always loved so much about him didn't seem to live in harmony with the image he presented. Something about it caused her heart to ache, and she squeezed his arms with a gentle smile before turning to her eldest brother.

"Marcus."

His embrace was more measured and careful, exactly as she expected of him.

"I'm so glad you're here," she murmured near his ear.

She gave him a wide smile and blinked away the sting in her eyes. Four years had changed him too. Both her older brothers had become men, and Marcus looked very fine in his captain's uniform. It fit him like a second skin, unlike Liam. He had the unmistakable air of someone with authority—calm, collected, and quietly confident, yet possessing a warm smile that could charm anyone. Kyrin loved the way his brown eyes lit up as they did now.

"Kyrin," a deep, powerful voice boomed out.

Her gaze jumped to the tall, massive-bodied man behind her brothers. Though his deeply lined face and white hair gave away his years, his impressive stature still possessed the strength of youth. Marcus Veshiron, or the General as most called him, was impossible to overlook. He dwarfed Kyrin and looked down on most men, except for Liam and Kaden who neared his height, yet were still a bit shy of it.

Kyrin pushed a smile to her lips, though it took effort. "Grandfather."

He stepped forward and took Kyrin into his arms, but the embrace lacked true warmth.

"Congratulations, my dear. What an incredible honor you've brought to your family. You and Marcus both. At last, the Altair line is showing promise."

The smile died on Kyrin's face, and her molars fused together. She glanced at her father, but he shook his head dismissively.

Kyrin worked her jaw loose and forced the smile back to her lips as she turned to Marcus. "Father told me about your promotion to captain. Congratulations. I know how hard you've worked for it."

Marcus gave her a look of appreciation, but their grandfather spoke first, beaming with pride.

"Indeed he has. Proving every day to be a natural leader."

"Natural or not, I am just pleased to be where I am," Marcus said.

"As you should be," the General replied. He nodded at Kyrin. "Both of you."

With another fake smile, Kyrin moved toward a nearby couch. The conversation would surely be long, and her heeled shoes already cramped her feet. If only they weren't buckled on, she could kick them off under her dress where no one would notice. "Why don't we sit?"

She sank down onto the cushions with a prayer for patience.

Her father sat to her left and Liam to the right while the other men found comfortable chairs facing them.

"So, tell me, Kyrin, you've met the emperor?" her grandfather questioned, his eyes alight.

"Yes. I dined with him and his family last night."

"Impressive, isn't he? A brilliant leader."

Kyrin considered the question and measured each word carefully before speaking. "He's certainly different than I was expecting."

"How so?"

"He's much more personable than I imagined. I wasn't expecting one of such high authority to be so kind to me."

Her grandfather chuckled at her—a condescending type of laugh that made her feel like a child. She quietly cleared her throat and brushed her hands across her skirt. Glancing at Kaden, she noticed how intensely he watched her. No doubt, she would have to explain her praise for Emperor Daican.

"A remarkable man." The General's voice hummed with admiration. "There is no greater honor than to serve him. I mean to see each of you reach prominent positions of service."

Kyrin cringed inwardly and sensed Kaden bristling across from her. If this conversation went any further, things were liable to get ugly. She opened her mouth to change the topic, but her grandfather's voice cut her off as he pinned icy gray eyes on her twin.

"Speaking of which, it has been brought to my attention on numerous occasions that your conduct at Tarvin Hall has been less than acceptable."

Kaden's face grew dark, and his eyes sparked. Kyrin closed her own for a moment. Trust everything to fall apart when the Altair men and the General came together. She begged Elôm to put a restraint on her brother's mouth.

"You receive reports on me?" Kaden asked with an edged tone to match their grandfather's.

"Of course," the General replied.

"I thought those reports went to the emperor's aides only."

The General sat up even straighter. "I make it my personal business to know how my grandchildren are progressing. And I'll have you know, I'm far from pleased with your actions."

Kaden barely managed a syllable before the General spoke over him. "All this disobedience, fighting, and disregard for authority is appalling."

"Do you even know why I was fighting?" Kaden demanded.

Kyrin barely held her tongue from jumping to his defense. After all, most fights had come from defending her from cruel tormentors.

"It makes no difference. It's shameful. Just look at your sister, only seventeen and already in service to the emperor. If you would dedicate yourself to excelling, there's no telling where you could be."

Marcus entered the conversation, and Kyrin grimaced. Kaden wouldn't appreciate his input.

"With an opportunity like this, you could be promoted straight to lieutenant."

Kaden glared at him. "And does it bother you that I could reach that goal without doing the work you've done?"

It was an unfair question, and Kyrin gave her twin a disapproving frown, but he didn't notice her, his eyes still boring a hole in their older brother.

"No," Marcus answered calmly. "It's just a fact."

"And he's right," the General cut in. "You could very well be promoted to such a position if you'd only apply yourself."

Kaden snorted. "What if I don't want to be promoted?"

The General's eyes grew huge as both he and Marcus looked at him aghast.

"Kaden," William said in a low warning.

The conversation fast approached dangerous territory.

"How could you not want to be promoted?" Marcus asked.

Someone as dedicated and ambitious as he was would certainly have a hard time wrapping his mind around that. "So few achieve such an honor."

Kaden sent him another smoldering look. "Maybe all I want is to live off in the woods somewhere, away from all this."

The General's face turned a fiery red. It chagrined Kyrin to know she and Kaden had inherited a measure of his temper. If not, then this argument might never have reached this point. She implored Kaden with her eyes to put an end to it, but his gaze locked with their grandfather's. She could almost see the flames flashing between them.

"What nonsense!" the General raged. "What utter foolishness. Our foremost duty is to our emperor and the gods. I'll not have one of my grandchildren waste their life away in such a manner. You will attend to your studies and training, and there will be no more undermining authority. You will work, and work hard for your promotion, do you understand me?"

Kyrin silently begged her brother not to defy him. Not daring to breathe, her gaze passed uneasily between the two of them. *Please intervene, Elôm.* She let out a huge sigh when a knock sounded at the door right as Kaden opened his mouth to reply. The footman, completely unaware of the thick cloud of tension, stepped in and announced lunch.

Before anyone else could speak, Liam stood. "Good. I'm starved."

His voice was light and eased the tension.

Kyrin rose after him. "Yes, let's eat."

She gave her brother a grateful smile for taking the first action in defusing the situation.

Kyrin and her father both made a determined effort to avoid any topics during the meal that would cause further friction between Kaden, Marcus, and the General. As much as Kyrin disliked being the center of attention, she brought the focus to herself whenever things took a bad turn. Even so, tempers remained high, and it wouldn't have taken much to turn the situation into an all-out shouting match. Kyrin barely touched her food for fear of taking her focus away from keeping the peace. Following the meal, William suggested a walk through the gardens, and Kyrin jumped at the idea. Fresh air and space would do them all good and hopefully cool their heads.

Outside, William, the General, and Marcus took the lead. Kaden followed a little behind his father, still brooding, while Kyrin and Liam walked a couple of paces back. The General dominated the conversation. After a few minutes of listening to him go on about one military thing or another, Kyrin hooked her arm around Liam's and slowed. Soon they fell several yards behind the others.

She smiled up at him. "Might be the only chance the two of us get to talk in peace."

Liam chuckled softly, his smile open and friendly. "It's always interesting when you get a group together with strong opinions."

Kyrin gave a short laugh of agreement. "So tell me about you. How have things been for you?"

Liam had always been the quiet one in the family, and so far, she hadn't learned one personal thing about him since he'd arrived.

He shrugged. "All right, I guess. Pretty boring compared to your life. Drills, marching, eating, and sleeping. That's about it."

Kyrin gave a short laugh. "Sounds kind of nice, actually. Better than being primped and polished the moment you step out of bed in the morning and having to get used to all this."

"It's a lot simpler, I'll give you that. I wouldn't want this . . . but you're a lot stronger than me."

"Not really. We all have our strengths and weaknesses."

"At least you and Marcus have made the General proud. He always feared we were a bit dim, especially me."

Kyrin's muscles bunched tight, but she said softly, "Struggling to read and write or not being socially inclined doesn't make you dim, Liam. Grandfather has a very warped idea about things."

She frowned at their grandfather's daunting figure, fighting with her ire over how he caused Liam to see himself and feel inferior. She desired to love her grandfather, she truly did. But that relationship seemed doomed to failure even before she was born, beginning the moment her mother had married her father against the General's wishes. He'd always dictated in the affairs of the upbringing of his daughter's children, his highest goal apparently never to let any of them follow the shameful path of their deceased Grandfather Altair.

Kyrin shook her head and swallowed down the bitterness working its way up her throat. She looked up into Liam's light brown eyes.

"You don't let what Grandfather thinks bother you, do you?"

He may have been the older one, but her protective instincts were always strong with him.

Liam gave another half-hearted shrug. "Not really, anymore. I am what I am. No amount of self-pity will change that."

"Well, I'm glad for who you are." Kyrin cleared her emotion-clogged throat, afraid it would reveal how close she was to angry tears. "And anyway, from what I hear, you're a heroic warrior yourself, and an excellent soldier."

Though not a natural fighter, their father had told Kyrin that Liam had become a good swordsman. He never would work his way up in rank, however. He just didn't have it in him.

Liam let out a quiet laugh, though one devoid of any mirth. "I just do as I'm told. It's not like I have much choice. The General is determined to see us all become good soldiers."

"I noticed," Kyrin murmured, beginning to understand the intensity of Kaden's feelings. She wanted to scream at their grandfather for forcing Liam to become something he obviously wasn't cut out for. He was far too gentle to live the life of a hardened soldier.

Kyrin banished these impulses and talk of their grandfather when Kaden dropped back to join them. He wouldn't have nearly as much self-restraint if he knew how she felt. They welcomed him into their little group, and from there talk was pleasant and enjoyable. Though they'd spent so little time together since childhood, their easy-going camaraderie had not suffered.

But as much as Kyrin loved the time they had together, sadness crept in. At one point, when the three of them burst into laughter at a story Kaden shared from Tarvin Hall, Marcus glanced back at them. Though it was a brief look, Kyrin caught the expression of longing that crossed his face. Always he seemed caught between having a good time with his siblings and maintaining his performance as the responsible eldest son—the man their grandfather desired him to be. It was his choice, but Kyrin determined to find a little time before he left to talk, just the two of them. She wouldn't let him leave feeling he'd missed out.

Kyrin rubbed her temples. This would be her second night in Auréa with a headache, though this one outdid the previous one. All she wanted was to scrub away the cosmetics that had begun to feel like plaster and fall into bed. But first, she walked Kaden out to the courtyard. Aertus and Vilai had risen behind them, and stars glittered in the black sky.

At the bottom of the palace steps, they stopped. Kyrin turned to Kaden and put a hand on his arm. Under her fingers, his muscles bunched as hard and tight as steel cords. The only time he'd relaxed all day was during their walk.

"Are you okay?"

Kaden shrugged and stared off at some far point beyond the palace walls.

"Wasn't much of a celebration, was it?"

His eyes, now cold after the fiery intensity she'd seen most of the day, dropped down to her. "It was good to see Father. And Liam."

Kyrin let out a heavy sigh. Her entire body felt weighted. "Don't be too hard on Marcus. I know it's difficult to understand how he idolizes Grandfather, but just imagine the intense pressure he's under. Grandfather had plans for him the moment he was born and given the same name. And don't forget, I know they serve the emperor, but there's nothing wrong with Marcus wanting to be a soldier. He's wanted that since he was little."

Kaden's face soured. "Because that's what Grandfather was always feeding us."

"True, but I don't think it's the only reason. This is what he's cut out for. Father is a soldier too, and that's not because of Grandfather."

Letting his head hang, Kaden blew out a long breath. "I know. I'm not angry with Marcus. Not really. I just don't like the way things are."

"Neither do I, but we can't do much about it. Now, you should go. The guards won't like having to open the gate for you back at Tarvin Hall as it is."

Kaden frowned. "Wish you were going back with me."

"So do I."

His brows still bent, Kaden walked away and followed the path toward the gate.

JACE'S ARMS ACHED when he lifted the saddle onto Niton's back. Even though his lungs still burned when he breathed, the coughing fits had passed, thanks in large part to Rebekah's remedy. Yet, the rest of his body only grew heavier with exhaustion. It would be their fifth day on the trail. The days were uneventful, but at night, dreams crept into his sleep. They had been a nightly plague to him for the first year after leaving slavery. Every morning he'd had to face the humiliation of coming down to breakfast knowing his anguished cries had carried through the walls. After a time, the peaceful life on the farm had ended them, and he had only suffered occasionally. But they were back now in the absence of peace and security.

Behind him, Rayad and Warin gathered their things. He had no doubt he'd kept them awake at times with his fitful tossing and mumbling. He clenched his teeth, the old humiliation rising.

Rayad's tired voice broke into the silence. "How much farther is Landale Village?"

"Only another ten miles," Warin answered.

"Good," Rayad murmured, but a wash of dread hollowed out Jace's insides. The closer they came to their destination, the harder it became to fight the urge to run. He wanted no part of any of this, but, for now, he dragged himself up every morning and followed Rayad.

Once his supplies were secure, he lifted Tyra up to her place on the packhorse and gave her head a gentle pat. She, at least, grew stronger every day.

When Rayad and Warin were ready, they all mounted and left their campsite. They'd seen nothing but thick forest since leaving Kinnim. Today didn't seem to be any different, until they broke from the trees a couple of hours later to flourishing farmland stretching out ahead of them.

"This is the southern edge of Landale," Warin announced. "Two more miles to Landale Village. We'll stop there so you can meet Baron Grey, and then I'll take you out to camp."

They rode on and followed the well-worn path, where they passed many farmers tending the fields. The people waved happily at them. Life in Landale appeared to thrive under Baron Grey.

The miles passed, and soon they rode into the village. Jace blinked away the blur of fatigue to look around. It was a sleepy little place, not much bigger than Kinnim, and Landale Castle only just earned such a title. Yet it had a certain strength to it. The gate stood open before them, and they rode into the courtyard where they dismounted and tied the horses at the hitching rail. From her place, Tyra sniffed the air with her ears perked and her alert eyes taking in the unfamiliar sights. Jace scratched her under the chin and commanded softly, "Stay, girl."

She nuzzled his face and settled in to wait. He turned to follow Rayad and Warin, who were already on their way to the castle's front entrance. He glanced back at Tyra, not completely comfortable leaving her in a strange place. Her black coat marked her as an object of fear, and people could work themselves into a frenzy far too quickly.

"She'll be all right," Warin assured him. "No one will bother her."

Jace silently took him at his word.

The butler let them inside with a familiar greeting for Warin, and instructed a footman to take them to Baron Grey's office.

Along the way, Jace scanned the interior. He'd witnessed some fine homes before, but never a castle. Everywhere was stone, and though colorful paintings and tapestries brightened the drab setting, such solid, confined surroundings brought memories of cold, barred cells. A tremor passed through him, and he fought the gnawing urge to escape to the outdoors.

Upon entering an office, they stopped. A thin, scholarly man with balding gray hair sat at a large desk. He looked up and gave Warin a broad grin.

"Welcome back, sir."

"Thank you, Morris," Warin replied. "Is Baron Grey available?"

"I believe so. Let me inform him of your arrival." The secretary rose and opened an ornate oak door at the far side of the room. Peeking in, he said, "My lord, Warin has returned. He has two other men with him."

"Send them in," came a deep voice.

Morris opened the door wider and beckoned Warin and his companions inside. The three of them stepped into the baron's private office. Jace's eyes swept the room. Rich wood pieces furnished the space, yet it was not overly lavish.

"Welcome back, Warin."

Jace's attention shifted to Baron Grey, who rose from behind a huge desk. He was silver-haired and more heavyset than Rayad. Jace measured his serious expression. The care lines in his forehead and dim shadows under his eyes gave him a tired appearance, but it softened in welcome.

"Thank you, my lord," Warin responded.

"I take it you found the man you were seeking." Baron Grey's eyes focused on Rayad, alert despite the signs of fatigue.

"I did indeed. I'd like to introduce my old friend, Rayad."

The baron came around the desk and extended his hand. "Welcome to Landale. I've heard much about you. I'm pleased to have you here."

"Thank you, my lord. Warin has told me what you and your son are doing. I hope I can be of service."

"Trask will be glad you've joined us. He's the true force behind it, and it has his full devotion. I don't think anything could dissuade him now."

"It sounds like he's doing a lot of good."

"That is his hope."

Warin introduced Jace then. Baron Grey studied him with a keen look, but he did not react to any oddities he may have noticed.

"Welcome, Jace. We're thankful for any who join our cause."

Jace gave a quick nod, but said nothing. He had followed Rayad, that was all.

"Is Trask around?" Warin asked.

"He left early this morning," Grey answered. "He mentioned stopping in Marlton to call on Lady Anne. Wanted to get there before Goler's men, I expect. But he should be at camp when you arrive. He'll be glad you've returned."

"The Korvic boys giving him trouble?"

"Not any more than usual. He has them on hunting duty to keep them away from camp. But he'll be glad of your watchful eye when he's not around."

An amused smile played on Warin's lips. "Have you received any word from Valcré since I left?"

"Nothing significant. Just the usual reports."

"I guess that's good news."

Grey gave a brief nod. "Yes, the bloodshed hasn't yet begun, and every day I pray it will be put off as long as possible. Wrong as it is, I cannot help but hope for some calamity to befall the emperor before he puts his plans in motion."

"I think we're all guilty of that," Warin replied.

Baron Grey grunted in agreement, and his gaze returned to Rayad and Jace. "I'm sure you're anxious to get to camp. You've had a long trip. I'm afraid I can't promise anything more than a tent for shelter at night, but the men are working to make it more of a home."

"As long as it provides a break from full days of riding, we'll be fine," Rayad replied.

The first hint of a smile appeared on Baron Grey's face. They bid him farewell and left the office. On the way out of the castle, Rayad asked, "So this Goler is captain of the barracks?"

Warin nodded in confirmation.

"Does he know what's going on here?"

"He has his suspicions that something is going on, he just doesn't know what. Baron Grey is careful to keep up a pretense of loyalty to the emperor. However, Trask and Goler are not on friendly terms. They're both keen on Lady Anne, the daughter of Sir John Wyland. Goler also suspects Trask's disloyalty to Daican. We fear it's only a matter of time before it's confirmed. Goler tends to keep a close watch on both Landale and Lady Anne. That's why we must be cautious and keep away from here whenever Goler's men are around."

Outside, the horses and Tyra waited quietly for them. They'd drawn interest from some of the servants, but no one ventured too close. Mounting, they rode out of the courtyard and set out to the east. After a few miles, the farmland of Landale gave way to forest once more. When they entered the cool shadow of the trees, Warin glanced over his shoulder to say, "This is it. Home."

Jace set his eyes on the surroundings. Having the word *home* assigned to this unfamiliar stretch of woods sent pain burning through his chest. Only one place had ever been home to him, and nowhere else could claim that distinction.

They followed the road for a time, but eventually Warin veered off, and they rode deeper into the woods.

"We never take a direct route," he told Rayad, who rode beside him, "just in case someone is following. Everything depends on secrecy."

The two of them fell into conversation about the camp, but

Jace followed a few strides behind and focused on the forest, so different from the wooded land surrounding the farm. There, the forest had been predominantly evergreens—tall, majestic pines that had been his companions on some of his hardest days. But here it was maple and birch with a few ancient oaks towering among them. Gentle, sloping rises and falls marked their path. Lower areas held water rippling with frogs and water striders.

It made a peaceful setting, yet none of that peace transferred to Jace. Every hoof-fall that brought them nearer to camp turned his stomach into a churning, burning cauldron. He'd made the wrong choice. He was almost certain of that now. Nearly all people considered him an outcast—a creature to avoid. Why would this situation be any different? No matter where he went, people would fear and despise him.

Consumed by this, it took him a moment to notice the large hollow that appeared ahead, cradling a handful of small tents and half-finished cabins. He pushed himself up straighter as his muscles tensed. The scent of smoke hung in the air from a central campfire, and men milled around the tents. Most eyes locked on them, and Jace battled the need to turn and hide in the woods. If he did retreat now, he probably wouldn't stop until he made it back to the farm.

The men gathered to meet them as they drew near, but parted to let one man come forward. He wasn't much older than Jace and sported short chestnut hair and a beard. His green eyes sparkled as he grinned and gave Warin an enthusiastic greeting. "Welcome back, my friend."

Warin dismounted with a satisfied smile. "Good to be back."

He was quick to introduce Jace and Rayad to the baron's son. Trask greeted them with the same enthusiasm and welcome.

In the midst of the exchange, Jace caught the eyes of one of the other men. Older than Trask, he too had short hair and a beard, but black. His intense gray eyes scrutinized every detail about Jace. The urge to look away and hide his differences nearly overwhelmed him, but he held his ground. A slow-growing hostility hardened the man's face until it transformed into a scowl.

"You're a ryrik!"

All eyes went first to the man before swinging to Jace. He drew himself up, but his mind conjured images of all the slave yards he'd ever been sent to—all the fearful or disgusted faces closing in around him, all the murmurs condemning his blood-line.

The other man's gaze snapped to Warin, his voice rough with accusation. "You brought a ryrik into camp?"

Any fighting spark of hope Jace had for this new life died in that moment and left a hollow emptiness inside him. It was just what he'd expected. And with this confirmation of all he feared, he sank that much further into himself, already re-erecting the walls Rayad spent the last three years helping him tear down.

After the initial shock of the outburst, Rayad stepped in to his defense. "He's not a ryrik."

"Of course he is." The man turned to his companions and gestured at Jace. "Just look at him."

Voice rising with the tension, Rayad said, "He's only half ryrik."

Eyes went wide and looks passed around. The hard lump in Jace's stomach worked up into his throat. Now he wasn't just something feared, but something unknown and unnatural. They all stared at him, and heat prickled up his neck.

"Half ryrik?" the dark-haired man repeated incredulously. But his face only hardened again. "What difference does it make? We can't trust him."

Trask broke in, his voice firm and authoritative, the spark of good humor gone. "Holden, that's enough. Warin is well aware of the peril of our situation. That should be enough for you." He turned to Jace. "I apologize."

Jace's eyes remained on Holden, who took a step back as he ran his hand through his hair and muttered under his breath.

Trask continued his interrupted welcome, saying to Rayad, "I hope you'll make yourselves comfortable here. It's not much yet, but we're hoping to make it a safe haven for those seeking shelter."

Rayad responded, but Jace finally gave in to the urge to turn away from all the staring eyes. Why did he always have to be a spectacle to people? He walked to the packhorse to get Tyra, one of the only things he had left to bring him any comfort. He lifted her up and set her gently on her feet, but the coiling in his gut warned of things to come.

"Stay close," he whispered.

He steeled himself before straightening and returning to his place near Rayad. Tyra followed at his side, and Jace winced at the noticeable reaction that swept through the men at the sight of her. Some reacted more than others, but none so much as Holden. His eyes grew wide, and he stepped forward again, his fierce gaze alternating between Trask and Warin.

"A black wolf? First *him*," he spat the word as he looked at Jace, "and now a black wolf? My lord, you can't agree to this."

Trask frowned. "Why not?"

Holden's jaw fell open. "We can't have a black wolf in camp."

"Surely you're not turning back to those old stories and superstitions."

"How do you know it's only superstition? That animal could very well be possessed with a demonic spirit."

Heat burst through Jace's chest and worked down his arms. He clenched his fists. To fear Tyra was one thing, to call her demonic was quite another.

"She's just a wolf," he ground out. "She's not possessed by anything."

Holden glared at him. "So says the one with ryrik blood."

Jace's muscles twitched with the instinct to hit him. Had they been alone, he likely would have, but Rayad touched his shoulder and reminded him that they weren't. The urge remained though, and his fist squeezed tighter.

"Holden, I said that was enough." Trask stepped between the two of them now and faced the other man down. "Your opinions are your own, I can't change that, but I will kindly ask you to keep them to yourself in this matter. The wolf can stay. I'm sure she won't be any trouble."

"She won't." Warin looked around to assure everyone. "She's perfectly well-behaved."

Holden sent Jace one more menacing scowl—the kind he had learned always led to future confrontation—and then stalked off to brood. Jace glared after him, and bitterness rose up to collapse his throat. *Welcome back to life.* It was just as cruel and unjust as he remembered. Once again, he would have to live every day watching his back.

With Holden gone, Trask went on to introduce the remaining men. They gave polite greetings, but the way they eyed Jace left no doubt of their mistrust. Most kept their distance. Trask nodded to one of the few who hadn't.

"Mick, you and Warin can show them your tent." He looked at Rayad. "We fit four men to a tent right now. It's not luxurious accommodations, but it's a start."

A burning coal lodged between Jace's ribs. From his first private room to a tent. Another piece of the life he'd known at the farm stripped away.

"As long as it keeps the rain out, that's all we can ask," Rayad said graciously.

With a smile, Trask motioned across camp. "I've got a few things to see to, but we'll talk later."

The group dispersed and left the three of them with the man Trask had called Mick. He was shorter than average and thin, yet strong, with a mop of dark blond hair. It was difficult to determine by his observant eyes what he might be thinking, but at least he didn't look at Jace with suspicion.

"You going to help us with these horses, Mick?" Warin asked with a smile.

"Sure." He spoke the word without much clue to his feelings in the matter.

The men grabbed the reins and led the horses deeper into camp, toward one of the far tents.

Along the way, Warin nudged Mick with his elbow. "You're not afraid of having Tyra around, are you?"

The young man glanced at the wolf, and Jace gauged his reaction.

"I'm not afraid of demonic spirits and superstitions," he answered. "Haven't seen too many wolves as pets though."

"Don't worry, she's real gentle," Warin told him. "And look at it this way. We'll have the safest tent in camp."

A bit of a smile grew on Mick's face. "Oh yes, we won't have to worry at all about being attacked by raccoons or anything like that."

Both Warin and Rayad chuckled, but Jace didn't share their humor.

At one of the pale canvas tents, Mick threw back the flap. Four straw pallets lay inside with just enough room for their belongings and not much else.

"Here it is," Mick announced. "Home sweet home."

Jace closed his eyes in a grimace. That word. If he had to hear it one more time, he just might snap.

KYRIN DREW IN deep, calming breaths, but butterflies bounced off the walls of her stomach. The moment had arrived—her first day on the job. Everyone told her it would be simple. All she had to do was observe as the emperor listened and settled disputes between the citizens of Valcré and report any pertinent information to one of his advisors. But what if she made a mistake? What if she missed something important? Something that endangered the emperor?

The butterflies transformed into bees as cramping pains darted through her abdomen. The pores on her back tickled with moisture. She tried to swallow, but her throat dried up. Afraid she would be sick before her work had even begun, she shook her head and whispered to herself. "Just relax and remember you're not alone."

Her father had reminded her of this before he'd left the previous morning.

With him in her mind, she set her eyes ahead and drew back her shoulders as she strode down the hall. At least a few days of regular use had given her more confidence in her heels.

The first order of business this morning was to meet with Daican's secretary, Henry Foss. She'd had no previous interaction with the man to prepare her. Apparently, he disliked dining with the rest of the staff. They'd called him a sour old man at the table last night. A lot of good this did for Kyrin's nerves.

She found him at his desk outside Daican's office—a hunched little figure with perfectly combed, yet thinning gray hair. A pair of spectacles perched on the end of his round nose as he scowled down at a document.

Kyrin took a couple of timid steps nearer, but even the tap of her shoes didn't gain his attention. She cleared her throat. "Mister Foss?"

His head snapped up, and he squinted at her before pushing the spectacles back up the bridge of his nose with one finger. The scowl never left his face.

"Yes, what is it?" he demanded, his voice scratchy and a bit high-pitched.

"I'm Kyrin Altair. I was told you would give me the specifics of my duties today."

Foss looked her up and down through his lenses before emitting a long-suffering sigh and grumbling something unintelligible as he slid out of his chair. He came around the desk and stood in front of Kyrin, revealing that he was actually a few inches shorter than her.

Eyes narrowed, he gave a huff. "Come along with me."

They left the room, and Foss moved at a quick pace, talking nearly as fast.

"You will be situated behind the emperor with a good view of the proceedings. Obviously, watch for anyone suspicious. Also, pay attention to the faces. After you've done this a few times, take note of any recurring individuals. If you have anything to report, Sir Richard will be present, and he will pass it along to the emperor should he deem it necessary."

Kyrin nodded at each point, though Foss didn't so much as glance back to be sure she understood.

They arrived at a side door to the throne room, but a heavy, red velvet curtain hid the view. When they emerged from behind it, Kyrin found the enormous, marble-pillared hall full of people and guards, and still more waited beyond the doors at the far end. Today was the one day a week commoners could bring their disputes and complaints before Emperor Daican. Kyrin's head went a little fuzzy at the sight of the crowd, but she had to recover quickly as Sir Richard met them. It was hard to tell which was worse—the crowd or the man. But she would have to get used to working around him. Perhaps he wouldn't seem so cold once they grew familiar with each other.

Wrinkling his nose, Foss peered up at Richard and said, "I've explained her duties. She's your problem now."

Richard's eyes narrowed, but Foss had already turned to march back out of the throne room. Now Richard's gaze slid to Kyrin. She swallowed, hoping he didn't notice the reaction, and worked mightily to hold his slicing gaze. Trying to find some of Kaden's bravery inside her, she gathered up her scattered composure. This was her job now, and she would not be intimidated. But maybe she would just forgo getting to know him.

He jerked his head and spoke in a low growl. "This way."

She followed him without delay, but concentrated on moving with as much grace as she could manage in an attempt to mimic Lady Videlle's walk. With so many eyes watching her, one misstep could lead to unimaginable humiliation. And not just for herself. What would it say of Daican's choice of her should she display such clumsiness in the public eye? How displeased would he be? Her heart became the butterfly now, fresh wings beating frantically to stay aloft.

They passed behind the tall, gold-overlaid throne. Kyrin briefly observed its magnificence, but didn't let it distract her. Richard stopped at a chair a couple of feet behind and to the left. Next to the royal splendor of the throne, this wood seat was pitifully plain. A fitting picture of her circumstances. But at least it had a cushion, and she would not have to sit on hard wood all day like the learning benches at Tarvin Hall.

"You will observe from here." Richard gestured to the chair and left her standing alone as he walked off to speak with others of Daican's staff.

Kyrin took a seat and smoothed her skirt as she thanked Elôm that she hadn't made any serious blunders yet. She rested back in her chair and glanced up at the high, arched ceiling before focusing on the crowd again. Hopefully, they would perceive her as little more than a background fixture and forget her presence.

A low buzz of murmured conversation and some back-and-forth sniping filled the chamber. Kyrin lowered her eyes from the many disgruntled faces to study the different clothing and accessories. Those closest to the front were noticeably well dressed—richly, in some cases—with brightly colored silks and velvets, and an array of jewel-encrusted gold and silver jewelry. Not just the poor sought to gain audience with the emperor on days like this, but also the rich who bore no titles. And, apparently, their money gave them preeminence.

Kyrin looked past these people to those beyond the doors. There, the more ragged commoners waited. How many would actually get a turn to speak before the day was done? She drooped in her chair, feeling sorry for them and herself. It was going to be a long day.

A sudden hush swept through the room, and Kyrin straightened. Just to her right, Sir Richard announced Emperor Daican's arrival. Dressed in splendid royal robes of Arcacia's national colors, a shining gold crown resting upon his head, Daican crossed the dais and took his seat on the throne. Davira glided in behind him. Her cool eyes slid over Kyrin once before she tipped her chin up and claimed the smaller throne to Daican's right.

"Bow before your emperor," Richard's voice boomed out.

Movement swept across the room as all bowed.

This marked the beginning of the proceedings. One or two at a time, guards issued people forward to a partitioned area at the foot of the throne to make their cases. From her position, Kyrin had a clear view of each person. Men squabbled and raised their complaints—nothing of any significant importance to anyone but themselves. Still, she dutifully studied each one, their mannerisms, expressions, and movements. Plenty of hostility came through, but only for each other—nothing to cause concern for the emperor.

This drew out through the morning. Kyrin continually had to remind herself not to slouch or let her mind wander. She drew a head-clearing breath and pressed her shoulders back against the chair as she glanced at the emperor. Only his arm was visible from her position. He spoke little, listening to the outcries of injustice and then settling each argument with a few brief words. No one argued with him, and people left either smug or sullen.

Servants brought wine and trays of delicacies to the emperor and his daughter. After a couple of hours, Kyrin's stomach grumbled. If only she'd been able to manage more of her breakfast. They did grant her a short lunch break, but it was straight back to work after that.

Midafternoon, three men came forward. One had all the trappings of a wealthy position, but the other two—an old man and one not much older than Kyrin—wore little more than rags. The rich man stepped forward first and bowed before the emperor.

"My lord, these men have borrowed a great sum of money from me and now refuse to repay it." He glanced squint-eyed at the other two men.

"That's not true." The younger man took a step forward with flashing eyes, like Kaden's when he was upset. "We—"

He fell silent when the older man touched his arm.

"Your Majesty," the man addressed Daican with a deep bow. "It's true we borrowed the money, but we have every intention of repaying. Like many here, we've fallen on hard times, and just recently, our home was robbed of everything of value. We ask for mercy and for time. We'll find a way to repay the full amount."

"Yes, you will," the wealthy man said with his lip curled like a snarling dog. "My lord, I request that they be thrown into the workhouses until the debt is paid. I've given them enough time."

"You can't do this," the young man jumped in again. "You've barely given us a chance."

The wealthy man spun to face him. They exchanged heated words, and their voices rose until Daican raised his hand. Silence fell.

The emperor had leaned forward enough for Kyrin to see the side of his face now. She watched his shrewd expression and silently pleaded with him. Surely, he could grant them just a little more time. They couldn't help their circumstances. A silent need beat inside her for him to prove himself merciful.

"Debts must be paid," Daican spoke at last, his voice contemplative at first, then hardening to a decided tone when his eyes settled on the wealthy man. "They will work off the debt."

Kyrin's elevated heartbeat slowed and sank down toward her feet.

The wealthy man gave a triumphant grin, but the older one pushed forward. A guard struck him when he came too close to the dais, and he fell to his knees. Kyrin gasped and covered her mouth with the hope that no one noticed. The younger man rushed to his side, but the old man looked up at Daican with outstretched arms.

"Please, my lord, allow the boy to go free. I will work off the debt."

"Father, no!" The young man shook his head. "You'll die in the workhouses."

But the man's eyes remained on the emperor, who considered the request for a moment.

"Very well." Daican motioned to his guards. "Have this man transported to the workhouses and escort the others out."

The guards seized them, and the son tried to resist, but they dragged him away from his father and toward the entrance.

"No! You can't do this!" He fought with all his might to break free, his eyes huge. They locked with Kyrin's.

Pain throbbed in her chest at witnessing the fullness of his desperation. Would she not feel the same watching her father hauled off to certain death? Her lungs constricted, and she clenched her fists, longing to help him, but the need to appear loyal to the emperor trapped her. Her eyes stung, and her vision watered against her attempts to blink it away. This surely wouldn't be the last time she would witness such a thing and be powerless to offer aid or comfort. The last pained look between father and son would stay in the forefront of her mind for a long time.

Struggling to breathe normally, she glanced around for a distraction. Her gaze met solidly with Davira's, and her breath fell short, frozen by the princess's cold, piercing eyes.

Kaden never realized just how much he relied on Kyrin until she was gone. He had spent his whole life to this point protecting his sister, taking for granted how she had encouraged him, supported him, and defended him just as much.

His ribs and shoulder smarted with deep bruises from sparring as he trudged toward the Hall. Training had been a disaster. He'd had enough of Tarvin Hall's activities and courses and the constant threat of disciplinary actions if he didn't take them seriously. He'd quit right here and now if only he could just walk out. But he was trapped—if not by Tarvin Hall itself, by Kyrin's position at the palace. He couldn't just abandon her there.

A mournful little sob, followed by the unmistakable snickers of taunting, halted Kaden. He marched around the corner. Little Meredith stood backed up against the building with tears trickling down her cheeks. A group of six other children surrounded her, laughing and jeering. "Crybaby."

Kaden's mind flashed back to all the times Kyrin had been

in the same position. His fingers curled into fists. "What's going on?"

The children gasped and spun around, their eyes wide. When they realized he was not one of the instructors, the fear melted away. Defiance lit in the eyes of the ringleader.

The boy crossed his arms. "It's none of your business."

Kaden snorted. Someone needed to be taught a good lesson. Without any concern for chastisement or consequences, he reached down and took hold of the boy's jerkin at the nape of the neck, lifting him up off his feet so they were looking eye to eye. The boy wriggled and complained, but when his eyes met Kaden's, he stilled.

"You won't ever bully Meredith or anyone here again, do you understand?" Kaden caught the stubbornness creeping into the boy's expression and gave him a shake. "Do you understand?"

Breathing heavily, the boy swallowed and nodded. Kaden narrowed his eyes and glared at him a moment longer. Finally, he set him back on his feet, none too gently, and resisted the urge to cuff him upside the head for good measure. Try it again, and the boy wouldn't be so lucky.

The children made a hasty retreat. Once at a safe distance, however, the boy turned back, tugging his jerkin into place and puffing out angry breaths.

"I'm telling Master Zocar, and then you'll be in trouble."

"Go ahead, snitch on me," Kaden shot back.

The boy's expression changed. He glanced warily at his friends. No one wanted to be branded the new snitch.

They moved on, and Kaden turned back to Meredith. The little girl's wide eyes still overflowed with tears, and her lip trembled.

"It's okay," he told her. "They won't bother you now."

He reached for her hand and led her over to a bench, where he sat down beside her. She tried valiantly to wipe the tears from her cheeks, but more spilled over. A little girl shouldn't have to fight to be so brave.

"It's okay to cry," Kaden said as he put his arm around her shoulders. "Don't listen to them."

Meredith looked up into his face, hiccupping. "Have you ever cried?"

"Sure I have."

"Did you cry when Kyrin left?"

"No, but I felt like it."

Meredith sniffed, and her voice wavered. "I miss her."

"So do I." Kaden released a long sigh.

"Kyrin was the nicest girl at Tarvin Hall." She clasped her hands tightly in her lap and bowed her head. "I don't have any friends here. Only you."

Kaden smiled a little and held her close, finding his own comfort in the familiar role of protector. Still, Meredith needed more than just him to make it through Tarvin Hall. His pulse quickened. This could be the worst mistake he ever made, but something compelled him to go on.

"You know, Meredith, there's a special friend who will never, ever leave you."

She looked up in question. "Who?"

Kaden glanced over his shoulder and looked around the yard, but no one lingered nearby. "Have you ever heard of King Elôm?"

Meredith's mood changed in an instant, and her body went rigid. Her eyes darted here and there before she whispered, "Mommy and Daddy used to tell me about Him."

This was not the answer Kaden expected. Outside of Kyrin, Sam, and his father, faith in Elôm seemed almost non-existent. "Did they?"

Meredith nodded and looked up at him again with eyes full of yearning. "Do you think He's real?"

"I know He is, and I believe in Him."

"You don't believe in Aertus and Vilai?"

The little girl's expression was painfully innocent. He could never suspect her of giving him away, but what if it happened by accident? He shook off the thought. It shouldn't matter—not if it might help Meredith believe.

With a silent prayer, he said, "No, I don't."

The little girl looked at him thoughtfully. "I don't think I do either." Her expression grew more serious. "But the emperor wants us to, doesn't he?"

"Yes."

"So we can't let him know?"

"No, we can't."

Meredith sighed and nestled against him as she wrapped her arms around herself. For a long moment, only silence drew out between them until Meredith murmured, "I miss my mommy and daddy."

Kaden squeezed her arm in full understanding. "I'm sure you'll get to see them again sometime."

She had to have some hope. It might be all that got her through some days.

But Meredith shook her head against him. "No," she breathed out in a sad acceptance, "they're dead."

Cold spread through Kaden, and he winced. "What happened?"

Her body tensed again, and her gaze darted around the yard before she raised her pale face to him. In a whisper Kaden could barely hear, she said, "Emperor's men."

And she would say no more.

JACE JOLTED AWAKE with a gasp, his limbs heavy and coursing with heat. Dim images of darkness and violence fogged his mind, but then Tyra's face appeared above him. She let out a low whine and the images faded. He sunk his fingers into the soft fur around her neck and breathed out a sigh.

"I'm fine," he murmured.

He peered around the tent. The other three bedrolls lay empty, and bright patches of early morning sunlight danced on the canvas above him. Outside, birds sang merrily, but Jace found no joy in it. Did he even possess such an emotion anymore? The very last of it seemed to have died upon their arrival in camp.

With another sigh, he pushed himself up and pulled on his clothes. He brushed past the tent flap and took in the sight of camp. Most of the men gathered by the fire, where a large pot steamed. They talked and some laughed, but all grew quiet as Jace drew near. A few watched him, though most focused on their breakfast bowls. He scanned the faces. Rayad wasn't among them, and after another look around, Jace spotted him near one of the tents with Warin and Trask.

The unnatural silence surrounding the men lengthened. Jace crunched his teeth together. What a fool thing to have joined them during breakfast after yesterday's reception. He turned away, but Mick's voice halted his retreat.

"Help yourself to breakfast. There's plenty."

Jace glanced from him to the extra bowls gathered on a table near the fire. Instinct drove him to forget breakfast and walk away, but that would be giving in to intimidation. Hardening his resolve, he walked to the fire, took a bowl, and served himself from the porridge in the pot. When he turned, he once again faced the silent group of men. This time he met Holden's eyes and the clear message behind their cold glint. No one wanted him around. Fine. He didn't want anything to do with them either.

He set off away from the fire with Tyra at his heels. Behind him, conversation resumed as he found a seat on a log at the edge of camp. He stared down at the bowl of pale porridge and didn't move. For the three years he had known Rayad, the man never ate without first offering thanks to Elôm. Jace had adopted this practice in the last year, but sitting here alone, no words of thanks would come.

He grimaced and shut his eyes at the questions that came instead. Where was Elôm in this? If He loved him as much as Rayad said He did, why did He leave him to face such pain and hostility? The only possible answer cut his heart like knife blades. Elôm didn't know him. He was soulless, little more than an animal, destined to struggle through life without a true purpose or an ultimate destination. Just like everyone said.

At last, it arrived—Kyrin's first day off. Her body tingled with an anticipation that added swiftness to her steps as she crossed the palace to find Trev. As grand and spacious as Auréa was, she could hardly wait to be free of its confines—away from the pressures and scrutiny of her position.

Nearing the security quarters, a female giggle caught her attention. She came through the hall doorway to find Collin standing near a pillar with one of the maids. The girl giggled again as he toyed with her hair. Kyrin rolled her eyes. He probably had a whole slew of new female admirers, and now Tarvin Hall's rules against fraternizing didn't apply.

The maid spotted her and released a light gasp. She dipped into a curtsy, cast one last shy smile at Collin, and hurried on her way. Once her footsteps faded, Kyrin looked at Collin, expression flat. He, however, wore his most charming grin.

"I hear it's your day off. Want to go for a walk?"

"And what about her?" She gestured to the doorway through which the maid had disappeared.

"Ah, that's nothing."

Kyrin lifted her brows. "Does she know that?"

A brief frown marred Collin's smile, but it regained its brightness in a moment. "It's just a little fun."

"You and I have very different ideas of fun." Kyrin shook her head and walked past him. She had better things to do today than put up with his advances. "I thought you were a gentleman."

"Hold on a minute." His footsteps echoed in the hall, and he cut around in front of her, halting her progress. "Nothing happened. Lighten up."

Kyrin drew her shoulders back and crossed her arms. If Kaden had any idea about this, he would throw a fit. She could see it now––him storming the palace to knock Collin down a peg, or twenty.

"Come on," he coaxed. "I just thought it would be nice to spend some time together now that we don't have to abide by so many rules."

Her and how many other girls? She shook her head again and tried to move on, but he backpedaled to stay in front of her.

"Why not?"

Kyrin narrowed her eyes at his persistence and worked on an answer that would make Kaden proud. Before she could use it, a third set of footsteps interrupted. She glanced around Collin to see Trev. He eyed them keenly, and his gaze rested on Kyrin.

"You were looking for me, my lady?"

"Yes, I want to go out and see my brother." She glanced pointedly at Collin as she mentioned Kaden.

As Trev closed the distance between them, Kyrin faced Collin once more and lowered her voice, but didn't bother to smooth the edge. "I'm not your entertainment."

"I never said you were," he shot back, matching her tone.

The smile had faded to reveal something more in his eyes—genuine interest and disappointment, if she read it right. A faint sting of guilt passed through her. Perhaps she hadn't needed to be so harsh, but if she didn't stop him now, he'd continue to pursue her, and she had no interest in him.

She joined Trev, who gave Collin a rather dour look as he passed. They walked in silence, and all thoughts of Collin fell away the moment Kyrin exited the courtyard gates. Her pace quickened again as she took to the streets that sloped away from the palace. They bypassed Tarvin Hall on a more direct route to the central square.

When they arrived, Kyrin scanned the crowd. Busy, as usual, but not nearly so much as it was on an execution day. She moved along the perimeter toward one particular merchant's stall. A grin leapt to her face. Kaden stood near the stall, waiting just as planned. Sharing big smiles, they hugged tightly.

"It is so good to see you!" Kyrin exclaimed.

"You too," Kaden replied.

He glanced at her clothes and was certainly more pleased with her appearance this time. She'd refused to let Holly apply more than the lightest layer of cosmetics, and she'd simply braided her hair. In a serviceable dress with slits up the sides and matching black leggings, she felt much more like her normal self.

Kaden and Trev acknowledged each other with a look, Kaden sizing up the man assigned to protect his sister. More or less satisfied, his attention returned to Kyrin.

"You hungry?"

"For pies, always."

They turned to the merchant's stall that overflowed with an array of pastries and tortes, and each selected the flaky, fruit-stuffed hand pies they enjoyed so much. It had been a special treat since they'd grown old enough to wander the city without supervision.

When it came time to pay, Kaden reached into his pocket, but Kyrin stopped him.

"This time it's my treat." She smiled at the merchant and handed him the coins. When they left the stall, she said, "Honestly, I don't know what I'll ever do with all my pay."

"I'm sure you'll think of something. You could buy a dog, or a horse . . . or a dragon."

Kyrin chuckled. "A dragon? What would I do with a dragon?"

"Fly," Kaden said in a wistful tone.

"I doubt anyone would be willing to sell their dragon these days, and I'd have to be royalty to afford that."

Kaden shrugged, but Kyrin knew him too well. The notion would never completely leave his head. He'd always dreamed about flying, though where he'd ever picked up such an idea was a mystery.

Letting him dream, Kyrin turned to Trev and offered him an extra pie she'd purchased.

"That isn't necessary, my lady," he politely declined.

"But I insist. It's the least I can do for dragging you all over the city."

"That's my job, but thank you." He smiled and accepted the pie.

Kyrin faced Kaden again, who appeared to have returned to reality. "Want to go to the shore?"

He nodded, and they headed off toward the western edge of the city. Along the way, they talked of different things, unimportant things, but none of what they really had on their minds. That would have to wait until they could talk privately.

After several blocks and an uphill climb, they came to the cliffs overlooking the spectacular Ardaluin Bay. Off to their left and below them lay the harbor filled with hundreds of magnificent tall ships, their creamy sails furled and waiting for the next voyage. Kyrin had never been on one, but it would be fascinating to see the places they traveled to. Between Valcré and her small home-town of Mernin, she hadn't seen much of Ilyon at all.

The cliffs dropped away dizzyingly and sent a thrill through Kyrin's chest. But straight out, as far as they could see, lay the brilliant Sidian Ocean. With a cloudless sky, the clear waters were a dazzling aqua and shimmered like satin in the sun. She took a deep breath of the cool, salty breeze. This was one of her favorite places in Valcré.

Before they moved on, Trev said, "I'll keep watch here."

The path leading up to this jutting area of the cliffs narrowed and made it impossible for anyone to pass by him unseen. Kyrin smiled at the arrangement. Now she and Kaden would have the perfect opportunity to speak alone.

The two of them picked their way up along the path another hundred yards and came to the ruined base of an ancient stone wall that once lined the cliffs. Disturbed seagulls screeched and scolded them as they climbed up to a formation that served as the perfect natural bench. Here they sat to enjoy their pies and the view.

When Kaden finished, he brushed his hands against his pants and settled his gaze on Kyrin. No easy humor sparkled in his eyes.

"So, tell me about the emperor."

He may not have a perfect memory like Kyrin, but he surely hadn't forgotten a word she'd said to their grandfather concerning Daican.

She shook her head. "You know I couldn't tell Grandfather everything I felt."

"Yeah, but it all sounded pretty genuine."

Kyrin hesitated. How did she explain when he hadn't witnessed everything she had? Close as they were, she didn't see him accepting this easily. He was too stubborn.

"That's because it was. What I said was true. Emperor Daican is very different from how we imagined him. You'd be just as surprised as I was by how personable he is."

Kaden frowned at her and said flatly, "So you're defending him?"

"No." Kyrin shifted and ran her fingers along her skirt. "But he's so disarming, it's hard not to like him." She stared at the ocean. Her forehead wrinkled when she returned her eyes to her brother. "Things don't add up with what we've heard. I think he's the hardest person I've ever tried to read. We've always thought of him as cruel and evil, but that's not what I see. Either we've heard exaggerations or he's better at hiding his true nature than anyone I've ever met."

Kaden's gaze never wavered and never lost its seriousness. "He's manipulating you."

Kyrin swallowed, and Kaden continued, adding to the tightness in her throat.

"He's fully aware of your abilities and what he has to do to make you like him. And why wouldn't he? You're helping to protect him. Of course he wants you to side with him and believe he's a great man."

Kyrin hung her head. Was he right? The sugary pastry in her stomach turned to a hard rock. She glanced over her shoulder and around the area to make sure no one had wandered too close. Trev still stood where they'd left him out of earshot.

"Actually, I'm more afraid of Princess Davira than the emperor," she said in a hushed tone as she swung her eyes back to her brother. "There's definitely something cold and cunning about her. She sees far more than she lets on. I have this horrible feeling she's just waiting for me to make a mistake."

Kaden's frown deepened. "You have to be careful . . . with both of them."

"I know," Kyrin murmured, but the entire thing made her head hurt. Did every day have to be such a challenge?

Kaden's eyes remained fixed on her. She wasn't sure she'd convinced him of her understanding. He appeared to wrestle with something before finally coming out with it.

"The emperor had Meredith's parents killed."

A spike of ice stabbed into Kyrin's gut.

"What?" Her breathing grew faster. "How do you know that?"

"She told me."

"But how did she know?"

Expression taut, Kaden shook his head. "I don't know. She wouldn't say, but she saw something." He paused. "They were followers of Elôm."

Kyrin wrapped her arms around her middle, afraid she'd be sick. She wanted to deny it, for both her sake and Meredith's. Between this and the instance of the father and son who owed the debt, her already frustrating and confused thoughts toward the emperor grew far more muddied.

"That's why you must *never* let your guard down," Kaden pressed.

Kyrin gave a nod, her voice choked off by an upwelling of tears that poured into her eyes.

Kaden winced. "Sorry, I didn't mean to upset you."

She shook her head, but couldn't blink away the tears. "It's just hard. It's exhausting to try to hide my feelings, watching every word I say and action I take, and always wondering what will happen if I slip up."

Two large teardrops dripped over her eyelids and rolled down her cheeks. Kaden put his arm around her shoulders, comforting her just with his presence.

"I miss you, Kaden."

He gave a short nod and cleared his throat.

"And I still wish Father were here. Marcus and Liam too." She rubbed away the tears with the palms of her hands. "I just miss home. It's been on my mind so much lately."

A short silence came.

She looked at Kaden with moist eyes, though the tears no longer fell. "How do you feel about Mother?"

Kaden frowned slightly, and then shrugged. "I'm not sure. It's hard to remember back that far. I'm not even sure I remember what she looks like. I guess I don't think about her very much."

Kyrin sagged forward under a weight she could only attribute to guilt. "I *do* remember, but . . ." She bit her lip. Would he understand? "I'm afraid I don't love her. I want to, but I just . . . don't know. I remember how she treated Father sometimes and always took Grandfather's side, and I just can't seem to find any feelings for her." Tears welled up again on her lower lids. "Am I horrible?"

"No," Kaden replied with comforting ease. "It's unfortunate you ever saw how things were between them, but you couldn't help that. It wasn't your fault."

Still, the weight remained.

"I shouldn't talk to you about this. I don't want to affect your opinion of her."

But Kaden offered immediate reassurance. "Things changed when we were taken to Tarvin Hall. We're pretty much all each other has. We've always talked about everything."

Kyrin managed a small smile, but it drooped. "I think, deep inside, I blame her for all this. I wish I didn't, but I can't help but think if she hadn't wanted it so, Father would have found a way to protect us. To keep us home."

Kaden processed this in silence, his expression thoughtful but not providing many clues to his thoughts. Kyrin waited until he was ready to speak.

"Well, what do you think Sam would say about it? Ultimately, it wasn't Mother who placed us here, but Elôm."

The words seeped into Kyrin's mind, and a little weary laugh escaped. "Of course, you're right."

JACE STOOD IN the arena again. Hundreds, thousands of people screamed down at him. His hands oozed with warmth, and his fingers gripped the sticky leather hilt of a sword. He looked down. Crimson stains glistened all the way up his forearms. The roar of the crowd died to one shouting voice, and the words pounded into his skull like physical blows.

"Murderer! Monster!"

His eyes lifted to Holden, who glared at him. He took a step back but the man pursued him and sneered in his face, "You murdered them!"

The whole scene changed. He was no longer in the arena, but at home, at the farm. Two figures lay at his feet—Kalli and Aldor. His eyes widened with horror at the sword in his hand that dripped with fresh blood. Again, Holden's accusation pierced his mind.

"You murdered them!"

No, Jace screamed inside, but he couldn't speak. Couldn't deny it.

"Murderer!"

"Monster!"

All the faces from the arena reappeared and screamed at him over and over . . .

Jace bolted upright with a hoarse cry, shaking and drenched with sweat.

"No," he gasped, unsure if the dream held any truth. He couldn't have killed them, yet hadn't he killed in the past? Hadn't the heat of his ryrik blood kicked in time after time and driven him to fight, to overcome, to kill?

Someone said his name, and a small flame flared to life. He squinted in the candlelight. It illuminated his three companions and Tyra, who stood at his side, whimpering. Rayad said his name again.

"Are you all right?"

Jace didn't answer. His cheeks flushed hot over waking his three companions and who knew who else in camp. He rose and stumbled out of the tent. Tyra followed right behind him. Even now, he shook uncontrollably. Sleep had faded enough for him to know he had no part in Kalli and Aldor's deaths, but he couldn't dismiss the others as only dreams. Their blood *was* on his hands. He tried never to let himself think of it, but the thoughts crept in now while he was too weak to stop them—what if those men had families? Wives? Children? He ground his teeth together and squeezed his eyes shut. Why hadn't he let himself die in the arena? Why hadn't he let the first man he ever faced just kill him?

His ryrik blood. Always, it willed him to fight.

A hand touched his shoulder. He recoiled and spun around to meet Rayad's gaze.

"Jace, it's all right," Rayad said. "It was just a dream."

But it wasn't. It was so much more—the haunting of his past and the things he had done.

Words stuck in his throat, and he shook his head hopelessly as he backed away.

"Come on, Jace. Come back to the tent. Try to get some more rest."

"No," the word broke free, raw and anguished. He couldn't abide the thought of sleeping again—of risking another dream. A deep shudder trembled through his body.

"Jace . . ." The lines in Rayad's forehead deepened, his eyes searching and uncertain as he tried to see Jace in the dark.

Gulping in the cool air, Jace grabbed hold of his emotions, just enough to master his expression and temper his voice. "I just . . . I'm fine." The lie stung, but the truth remained trapped inside. "Just go back to sleep."

He turned and left Rayad to watch him walk away.

Wandering off to the edge of camp, he sank down at the base of a tree and put his head in his hands. Tyra nudged him with her nose and rested her chin on his arm, but even she couldn't comfort him this time. Not when the dream so quickly replayed in his mind with such vivid detail. His pulse quickened again. Of all his nightmares, none had ever been so painful. Holden's words echoed in his ears and drove deeper and deeper into his heart. *Murderer. Monster.* He covered his ears with his hands, but couldn't make it stop.

The tantalizing smell of fresh bacon drew Mick down to the fire where the clanking of tin plates and murmur of voices signaled breakfast. Of course, Jace was not among the men. Mick looked around and spotted him at the edge of camp, where he sat hunched over near a tree. He frowned at the unhappy sight. As if in response, he caught the hushed conversation circulating around the fire of Jace's cry waking them in the night.

"About scared me to death," one of the younger men said as he darted a cautious glance at Jace. "Thought maybe he was going to come and kill us all."

It was no surprise that Holden seized on this opportunity to further his case. "I told you. That ryrik blood of his is evil. We won't have any peace or safety until he and that wolf are gone."

More than a couple of the men nodded in agreement.

Mick's mind also traveled back to last night, but contrary to his companions, fear had no part in it. "You don't know what you're talking about."

Holden's eyes flashed to him and flickered with an almost wild mix of deeply entrenched hatred and horror. "Have you ever witnessed a ryrik attack?"

Mick held the searing gaze. "No. But I did see Jace last night. A man doesn't dream like that unless he's in real pain."

Holden snorted. "Feel sorry all you want. Just remember when you find yourself at the end of his blade during a ryrik rage that I told you so. He doesn't belong here, and I aim to see that Trask understands the danger."

Mick's frown deepened. He glanced around at the other men. Most wouldn't look at him. While they were not as outspoken as Holden, it didn't appear they were willing to give Jace the benefit of the doubt. He shook his head and turned away, though he paused just long enough to look back at Holden.

"Keep in mind as you condemn Jace the courtesy and grace Trask has extended toward you."

He left the men to mull this over, dished up a plate of eggs and bacon, and poured a cup of hot coffee. Plate and cup in hand, he headed across camp. Silence had overtaken the group at the fire, and though he didn't look behind him, their eyes bored into his back.

Jace shifted restlessly as he approached and eyed him with a cool, wary look that revealed an internal preparation for either fight or flight. Mick couldn't blame him. Fierce as he may appear, it didn't hide the redness around his eyes or the dullness of their typically bright blue.

"Here, didn't want breakfast going cold on you." Mick offered him the plate and cup.

Jace stared at them as if they were objects he'd never seen before.

"Thanks," he barely murmured when he did accept them.

He glanced toward the fire, and Mick looked over his shoulder. Almost everyone stood watching. He refocused on Jace.

"Ignore them. Most are a bunch of farm boys. They haven't yet seen enough of the world. Give them time. They'll come around."

Auréa's library exceeded anything Kyrin had ever seen. Six stories of balconies, holding more books than she could imagine, edged the massive hall that stretched three hundred feet long and another two hundred wide. The library at Tarvin Hall was known as one of the largest in Valcré, but the palace held almost double that amount of books. So much knowledge to glean, if only she had the time. But even she couldn't imagine the words of so many books locked away in her mind. Her head throbbed just thinking of it.

In one corner, she browsed a shelf of history texts. Though not surprised, it still saddened her to find many of the early volumes missing—volumes that surely spoke of Arcacia's first kings and their devotion to Elôm. It was as if someone had erased that history and replaced it with whatever the emperor and his predecessors chose. History at Tarvin Hall had centered on Aertus and Vilai and how they'd brought the kings to power and prosperity to Arcacia. If not for Sam, she would never have known the truth. She took a deep breath to fight the mix of despair and ire that welled inside her.

The door at the far end of the room banged open and shattered the silence. Kyrin jumped and spun around. She froze as Prince Daniel strode in, followed immediately by his father.

"You stand and face me like a man when I'm talking to you." Daican's sharp voice echoed down the hall.

Daniel halted and spun on his heel. He threw his arms out. "What's there to talk about?"

"You, that's what," Daican snapped as he came to stand eye to eye with his son. "Your conduct is unacceptable. You're the crown prince of the greatest nation in Ilyon and will one day be emperor. It's time you acted like it."

Daniel snorted, and the emperor's face grew red.

Kyrin shrank back against the bookshelves and darted a look to both sides. How could she escape such a precarious situation without making her presence known? To witness such an angry outburst from the emperor turned her core to ice, but she had no escape. Moving now would only draw their attention. Shoulders pressed to the bookshelves, she watched and prayed they would take this argument elsewhere. But they stood their ground.

Eyes flashing, Daican declared, "You are about this close to being disowned." He gestured with barely a centimeter between his thumb and forefinger.

"Excellent," Daniel responded. "What can I do to push you over the edge and make it official?"

Daican literally shook and spoke with failing restraint. "You are of a long, proud line of kings, chosen to rule this kingdom by Aertus and Vilai—"

"Maybe I don't believe in Aertus and Vilai."

The air seemed sucked from the room. For a moment, Kyrin couldn't breathe.

Daican glared flames at his son. Very slowly, very evenly, he said, "You are treading on dangerous ground."

Daniel scoffed. "What are you going to do? Execute me?" Planting his fists on his hips, he challenged, "Go ahead. At least it will provide me escape from the throne."

Kyrin really thought Daican might hit him, but he only roared, "You are my son! You *will* learn your place, and you *will* be emperor one day!"

He ended the argument by storming out of the room.

Daniel stood motionless with his fists balled and his jaw muscles ticking as he glared after his father. But then, muttering under his breath, he reached out and snatched a book off a nearby table to hurl across the room. It sailed straight toward Kyrin. She lurched to the side, and Daniel picked her out immediately. Kyrin gulped, pinned under his still scowling gaze. Her insides trembled. What might the prince or his father do to her for having witnessed the exchange? Would it matter that it had been by accident? *Oh, Elôm, help me.*

Daniel's eyes narrowed a little. A shiver passed through her, but his expression relaxed.

"Miss Altair, isn't it?" His voice no longer held any anger.

She swallowed to loosen her tongue enough for a meek reply. "Yes, my lord."

One of Daniel's brows quirked up. "I assume you heard all that."

"Yes," Kyrin admitted reluctantly, "but . . ." But what? She had no excuse except that she'd been here before they arrived. To say so would be placing blame on them. That surely would be the wrong move. "I apologize, my lord, I—"

Daniel just waved it off. "Don't worry on my account." He stepped closer and studied her. "Not what you'd expect though, is it? A prince with no desire to be king?"

Kyrin hesitated. Did he truly expect an answer, or was he just blowing off steam? He continued to stare at her, prompting a response.

She shook her head. "No, my lord."

"Well, it's true. I don't desire to be king . . . at least not one like my father." Contempt laced his voice. He sank down in a chair near her and propped his feet up on the table. "He's a cruel man, you know."

Kyrin's gaze jumped to the door. She should not be here—shouldn't be listening to this, not even from the emperor's own son. Every sense of self-preservation screamed to flee. But how could she, little more than a servant, just walk away from the prince?

"Really, he is," Daniel insisted, recapturing her attention. "He doesn't care about people, only their submission. Me, on the other hand, I like people. He thinks I'm weak."

The prince let out a hard chuckle. Looking him in the eyes, Kyrin found an unexpected display of hurt and resentment. This was no random, rebellious outburst. This was something stronger, deeper, harbored inside him. Something only grown with time.

He stared at her, almost as if trying to read her the way she did him. Or perhaps he was searching for something.

"I heard you're close to your father." He tipped his head a little. "What's it like to have a father you love and respect, and who loves you in return?"

Again, Kyrin sensed he waited for an answer. She licked her lips. "It's a great blessing."

"I bet it is," Daniel murmured and stared off into space.

At these soft and sadly spoken words, something stirred inside Kyrin. Deep down, he was hurting and longing for what she cherished. The nurturing and loving support of a father.

"I'm sure your father loves you," she encouraged him.

Daniel snapped back to reality. "I doubt it," he said with an unhappy smile. "He loves power; he loves controlling this grand plan for his legacy. And he loves my sister."

The bitter sting in his voice was hard to miss.

"She should've been the firstborn son. She's the one who cares about all the politics and scheming. Not me." He shook his head. "That's why I find it hard to believe in Aertus and Vilai. Why would they ever have given my father me as a son? And, for pity's sake, they're moons. How are two balls of rock supposed to be gods? It's never made any sense to me."

Daniel fell into a contemplative silence, and Kyrin's heart drummed against her ribcage. Here the prince of Arcacia, heir to the throne, had admitted to not believing in his father's gods. It laid before her the opportunity of a lifetime—a chance to share with him her knowledge of Elôm. It waited on the very tip of her tongue, right there, for her to open her mouth and speak. But her jaw locked shut. What if Daniel reported her straight to his father? He himself had mentioned the possibility of execution for not believing in the gods. What if even the mention of Elôm's name brought her such a fate?

Her mind and instincts wrestled—one calling for bravery, the other fighting it. In response to her silence, Daniel released a heavy sigh and rose.

"Well, thank you for putting up with my ranting."

He turned away and walked to the door.

Her heart tripped. *Stop him! Call him back!*

But once he was out the door, it was too late. A heavy oppressiveness fell around Kyrin. She sank into the chair Daniel had just occupied and buried her face in her hands. Tears leaked from her eyes. She'd failed. Elôm had presented her with a life-changing opportunity, and she'd failed Him.

"I'm so sorry," she murmured as the tears slid through her fingers. "I'm a coward."

IT FILLED TRASK with contentment to ride into camp in the mornings and see the way his plans had come together. His father had cautioned him not to set his hopes too high. After all, he'd started out with only two men, whom most considered to be fugitives, and an empty clearing deep in the forest. Now, a little less than a year later, he had over a dozen men and an organized camp. The way things were going, that number was sure to increase.

He rode up to the edge of the corral, where Holden met him before he even had a chance to dismount. The man's unpleasant half scowl would repel just about anyone who didn't know him well, but he was given to brooding, so Trask just smiled and greeted him cheerfully.

"Morning. What's going on?"

"We need to talk."

The sharp, immovable tone replaced Trask's smile with a frown. He went to great lengths to make camp a comfortable and satisfactory place for the men to live, and therefore he took all problems seriously. "All right."

He dismounted and secured his horse at the rail, and then turned his full attention to Holden. "What's on your mind?"

"Jace."

Trask held back a sigh. He should have guessed, though he'd thought the matter settled. It wasn't often that anyone questioned him.

"What about Jace?"

"You, Mick, and Warin might not be able to see it, but he's dangerous. You're risking the entire camp by allowing him to remain here."

Trask gave a quick shake of his head. He might not know Jace yet, but he did know Warin and trusted his judgment. "He's not dangerous."

"With respect, my lord," Holden said, voice taut, "you don't understand what ryriks are capable of, and don't think because he's only half ryrik he isn't just as capable. All you have to do is look at his eyes. They're the eyes of a killer."

Trask crossed his arms and drew a deep breath to prevent his shoulders from tightening. A man like Holden required much patience and tact. "What would you have me do?"

"Send him away before he can snap and kill us all."

"I won't do that," Trask said calmly. "I set up this camp as a refuge for those in need, and if you can look past your hatred for ryriks, I think you'll see he's in need. He's no killer, Holden. I'm not sending him away."

He turned to unsaddle his horse. Holden didn't move at first, and Trask anticipated further discussion, but eventually, the man stalked off. Now Trask did release a sigh and murmured to Elôm for wisdom and strength in these situations. He couldn't expect all of the men to get along all the time, especially when new faces came in. But that was part of being a leader, and thanks to his father, he'd grown up preparing for just such a position. One day he'd have more than just this camp to oversee.

He turned his horse free in the corral and caught a glimpse of movement. This time Rayad approached him. The man had only been in camp a few days, but Trask liked what he saw. He valued men of experience and wisdom like Rayad and Warin. It was one reason he wouldn't consider sending Jace away. If Jace left, Rayad surely would too.

"Is there a problem?" Rayad cast a pointed glance at Holden down at the fire.

Trask latched the gate and then leaned back against it.

"Holden would like me to send Jace away."

"What has him so set against Jace?" Rayad asked with a hard, protective tone.

"He does have his reasons. When he was young, ryriks tortured and killed his parents right in front of him. You can imagine what that did to him. He hates ryriks, and to see Jace just brings it all back. It's preventing him from thinking logically. All he sees in Jace is what happened to his family and the possibility of it happening here."

"Jace isn't like that," Rayad assured him.

Trask nodded, willing to believe that was true. "I know, but Holden doesn't—or rather, he can't accept it. And I believe there's more behind this than is apparent." He glanced at Holden. Everyone knew his story. The newest camp members should too. Perhaps it would help bring understanding.

"He has his own past he's dealing with. He was an informant for the emperor before coming to know Elôm. The information he collected led to many lost lives, and he despises himself. He's driven now to protect people and make up for what he did. Between the fear and the condemnation, I think he's turned Jace into a threat he feels the need to protect everyone from."

Rayad looked over his shoulder as his expression softened. He shook his head and spoke quietly. "Those two have more in common than they realize."

Holden stared into the smoldering logs of the fire. His mood matched the crackling heat. He gave Jace, who still sat at the edge of camp, a brief glance and ground his teeth together. Every time he looked at him, he saw it again—the scene of his parents' brutal murders. And he'd been helpless—utterly helpless to stop it. Had the neighbors not shown up, he would have been tortured and killed too. But he wasn't helpless now. He wouldn't risk seeing such senseless bloodshed again. Jace was dangerous. He was one-hundred percent convinced of that. Why couldn't Trask see it?

"How did that go?"

Holden looked up, and one of the men nodded toward Trask. He swallowed down the acidic burn in his throat.

"Not well. He refuses to send Jace away."

"Well, maybe everything will be fine," another man said.

"No," Holden snapped. The bloody images ever lurking at the edges of his mind wouldn't allow him to believe that. Not for a moment. "As much as I respect him, Trask just doesn't understand the risk. He hasn't seen what I've seen. None of us will be safe as long as Jace is around, do you understand? *None* of us. And I'm afraid if someone doesn't do what needs to be done, we'll all suffer for it."

Across the fire, his eyes caught the three Korvic brothers exchanging a glance. They were just crazy enough to try something stupid, and Holden didn't mind letting them.

Kyrin wasn't sure what she hated more—observing during Daican's meetings or sitting with Mister Foss for hours as he grudgingly shared mounds of information about all the prominent lords in Arcacia. She understood it would aid her in her job, but even she could only take so much at a time. Especially when her mind kept wandering back to the incident in the library earlier that morning and her failure. Every thought of it made her miserable.

Mister Foss, on the other hand, just wanted to get it over with and didn't appreciate her lack of attention. She often caught him grumbling about already having enough work to do without needing to instruct her on top of it. Kyrin tried not to take offense, but every comment wrung the muscles in her neck and back tighter and tighter. After all, she didn't want to do this either.

Still trying to absorb the overload of information, Kyrin walked wearily toward her room for a little alone time before returning to work for the remainder of the afternoon. If only it were closer to bedtime. To lie down for even just a few moments and close her eyes would be heavenly, but she wouldn't dare for fear of drifting off.

"Miss Altair."

The icy female voice stopped Kyrin in her tracks. Her stomach squeezed like a fist, and she had to battle all her nerves to turn and face the princess.

"Yes, my lady?"

Davira strode toward her and tipped her head a little as she peered at Kyrin. "I thought it was time for the staff to pray and worship."

Kyrin hesitated for the briefest moment to calculate the time. "It is, my lady. I was just going to my room. That's where I always pray. It's quiet, and there are no distractions."

Davira's unblinking eyes bored into hers as if sifting for information. Kyrin's heartbeat echoed in her ears, and a tremor passed down her back. Afraid it would visibly work its way through the rest of her body, she asked in as steady a voice as possible, "Is there anything you need, my lady?"

But it rasped at the end, and she swallowed.

"No," Davira replied a little too slowly. She tipped her chin up. "I won't keep you."

With a brief curtsy, Kyrin turned. Davira's eyes scorched her all the way down the hall. Fighting every impulse, she forced herself to walk casually. The moment she stepped into the solitude of her room, she sagged back against the closed door and dragged in a breath. She thought she might be sick. Two perilous confrontations in one day. She closed her eyes and tried to swallow, but her mouth turned to chalk. Had she been convincing enough? Or did the princess suspect her of disloyalty? *Oh, Elôm, I don't know if I can do this. Protect me, please.*

In the days following his rescue from slavery, the forest had always provided Jace with the solitude he needed. Now, once again, he sought such solitude. Even when Holden wasn't nearby, camp was unbearable. The men, influenced by Holden's warnings, still kept their distance, casting suspicious looks, or speaking quietly in small groups. Exactly what people always did around him.

So he took to the woods and spent long hours with no one but Tyra while he contemplated his future. It couldn't go on like this. But what future did he have anywhere? People like Kalli and Aldor just didn't exist. He'd never find anyone like them again. Never find a home like that. It didn't leave him with much choice other than a solitary life somewhere civilization could not find him.

Tyra broke him out of these thoughts and put a pause to his aimless wandering. Her growl warned him they were no longer alone. He followed her intense stare and spotted three young men weaving through the trees. The Korvic brothers. Out of everyone in camp, he disliked them the most right after Holden. They were loud, obnoxious, and had little respect for anyone. Much like Morden.

He knew the moment they spotted him. They stopped abruptly, muttering in hushed tones, and adjusted their course straight for him. Tyra released another low rumble in her throat. Even she knew they were up to no good.

"Easy, Tyra," Jace murmured. He wasn't about to let her do something Holden could use against her. The brothers drew nearer, and he commanded her, "Back."

She looked up at him, eyes questioning, and he repeated his command. Obediently, she turned and trotted a few yards away, but her gaze remained fixed on him. By now, the Korvic brothers were drawing into his personal space. A shiver of warning needled Jace's skin, but he stood his ground.

"What do you want?" he asked in a low voice as Brody, the oldest, came face to face with him. The two younger ones spread out on either side. He gave them each a cold glance.

"What do we want?" Brody's lips curled in an insolent smirk as he glanced at one of his brothers. "What we want is for you to leave. You're not welcome in camp, *half-blood.*"

Jace fought the spark of heat in his chest, clenching and un-clenching his fists

"Do you hear me?" Brody demanded, getting in his face, though he was shorter. "You're to leave camp and never come back. Nobody wants you here."

That might be true, but Jace would leave on his own terms. He wouldn't be ordered out like some animal by these three. Looking Brody straight on, he said, "No."

Brody's eyes narrowed. "You will go. It just depends on what condition you want to go in."

Jace glanced down to Brody's balled fists. The brothers aimed to fight him. He ground his teeth together as his fighting instinct kicked in. It would be a pleasure to knock all three of them senseless, yet this thought carried a warning. If he gave them the beating they deserved, it would only confirm everything the men in camp believed about him. It would prove him dangerous. But did he care?

Somewhere, buried deep inside, the answer was yes. Wasn't that why he had purposely gone without a single weapon so there would be less chance of ever hurting or killing anyone again? He breathed out and turned away from Brody. For the briefest moment, a confirming sensation that he'd done the right thing brought a hint of peace to his mind, but a hand latched onto his arm and yanked him back around. Before he could react, Brody's knuckles plowed into his jaw.

Fire burst through Jace's body like molten metal. Brody didn't even regain his balance from the swing before Jace's hard fist caught him in the cheekbone. The young man staggered and almost went to the ground. His two brothers jumped in to help and each grabbed one of Jace's arms. He wrenched away from them, and nearly broke their hold. In a second attempt, he would have succeeded, but it struck him what was happening. His ryrik blood was taking over and driving him to fight, just as it always did. Maybe the accusations were right; maybe he was a monster. *Just let them win,* the thought whispered in his mind. *Do what you should have done in the arena.*

Giving in to the voice of condemnation and surrender, Jace stopped fighting. Caught between the brothers, he took the full impact of Brody's next blow just under the ribs. He doubled over with a gasp. Behind him, Tyra snarled and charged toward them.

"No, Tyra, back," he ground out. "Stay back!"

All his bulky weight behind the swing, Brody delivered another blow to Jace's jaw. Pain lanced through his skull and his blood burned hotter, but he refused to act on it this time.

Brody took full advantage of the lack of struggle. Jace's breaths soon came in short pants as the air was forced from his lungs by fist blows. Blood flowed down his chin from his nose and lips. Despite his surrender to the unrelenting attack, some small seed of stubbornness remained, and he stayed on his feet longer than most would have. But, eventually, his legs buckled underneath him, and he found himself on his back in the leaves, mind foggy, squinting up at the hazy figures.

Brody's face appeared only a foot away from his own, and the young man's knee pressed hard into his battered chest. Jace gasped, unable to draw more than small, painful breaths. Brody grabbed his collar.

"You don't come back, half-blood. Understand?"

He pushed up and away. Searing pain knifed through Jace's chest as Brody gave him one final kick in the ribs. He grasped at his side and a small groan escaped him. With sneers and cruel laughter echoing in their wake, the Korvic brothers wandered off. Jace lay still as his mind faded in and out. The burning in his blood abandoned him now to pulsing waves of pain. He struggled for air and choked on the blood trickling down the back of his throat. Why couldn't his body just die?

Leaves crunched near his head. He forced his eyes open. A black shape filled his vision, and a wet nose nudged his chin.

"Tyra," he breathed, though his lips barely moved.

She faded away again, and he lost all sense. He had no knowledge of how much time passed or if he even remained conscious, but sometime later, he opened his eyes and things cleared. Life still clung to him, though he didn't welcome it. Every breath came with a protest from his throbbing ribs. He winced, his face tight and swollen, and tipped his head to his left and right. The area was abandoned. Only the trees witnessed his struggle.

Slowly, he pushed himself upright and locked his teeth together to keep from groaning. He wrapped his arms around his bruised ribs and took another look around.

"Tyra," he called, but his voice only croaked.

He grimaced at the unpleasant thickness of blood in his mouth. He spit into the leaves, which caused his lip to bleed again. The faint trickling of water whispered to him from somewhere nearby.

He gathered his strength and pushed to his feet. His legs wobbled at first, and he almost went back to his knees, head swimming. But the dizziness cleared, and he staggered toward the sound of water. After stumbling a few yards, he reached a small stream and collapsed to his knees on the mossy bank. In his quivering reflection, he took in his bloodied face and the bruises darkening under his eyes. He reached into the stream and brought cold water to his face. It ignited pain in his nerves, and he sucked in his breath, but once it died away, the water soothed the pulsating cuts and swelling.

"Jace!"

He looked over his shoulder. Rayad, Warin, and Trask rushed toward him. Tyra led the way. She arrived first and nosed his dripping face. He lifted his hand to pet her head wearily.

Rayad reached him a moment later and knelt on his other side. At first, Jace tried to hide his face, but one glance at Rayad provided enough for the older man to see everything.

"What happened?"

Jace shook his head. "Nothing."

Rayad's voice was rough, just as it had been that day in Kinnim's jailhouse. "Don't tell me 'nothing.'"

Jace pushed back to his feet, though his legs wobbled. Rayad gripped his arm to steady him, but Jace pulled away and came face to face with Warin and Trask. They both winced at the sight of his injuries, and Trask asked, "Who did this?"

Jace moved away from them. What did it matter who did it? There were an endless number of men who would have liked to do the same thing. There always would be.

"Was it Holden?"

Jace glanced over his shoulder. "No."

Silence fell behind him. Rayad was the first to move as he came to his side.

"Let's get you back to camp and make sure you're all right."

"I'm fine."

"You could have broken ribs or something."

"I don't," Jace said through his teeth. He didn't want to be fussed over, or pitied, or pressed for answers. He could take care of himself and his own affairs. But Rayad's frustrated sigh made him pause.

"Let's at least get you cleaned up."

Jace touched his still-bleeding lip and reluctantly followed him to camp. It was the last place he wanted to be, but he couldn't refuse Rayad completely. When they arrived, whispers and murmurs of his condition spread ahead of them, though it was hard to tell if they held more than surprise.

Warin went to get water, and Rayad set up a small stool just outside their tent. Jace sank down slowly and let his breath seep out. He glanced around camp at the many eyes watching him and turned his face away. It had been a mistake to come back. He'd been the object of an audience enough times already. He almost pushed up to walk away, but Rayad spoke first.

"Jace, we need to know what happened."

Jace looked up at him, setting his teeth stubbornly, and winced at the pain that shot through his jaw. Why couldn't they just leave him alone? What would it change to talk about it?

"It doesn't matter."

"It does matter," Trask stressed. "I will not tolerate this sort of thing in camp."

But Jace remained silent.

Trask clenched his fists, and a tremor passed through his forearm. So much for his sense of pride this morning. He'd expected his men to see the error in their ways, but they'd only let him down further, and enough was enough. To have them beat a man under his protection was unacceptable, and he would get to the bottom of it one way or another.

He turned and strode into the center of camp, his voice rising with his tension. "Everyone gather up, now."

The men assembled around him and passed looks back and forth. In all these months, he'd never had reason to address them like this, and he loathed the need. They were good men who had let preconceived notions and fears get the best of them. But this couldn't continue or happen again if they were going to succeed here. He turned slowly in a circle and let silence reign for a moment as the men fidgeted under his gaze.

"One or more of you is responsible for beating up Jace. I don't know who yet, but I will find out, I guarantee it." He shook his head. "I'm ashamed this has happened. This isn't who we are, men," he said, hoarse with disappointment, "or what we stand for. This isn't what we believe. What I've witnessed here in the last few days is shameful. This camp is supposed to be a refuge. A place of safety and aid. I thought you all agreed with me, but here you are shunning and bullying one of our own. Well, I'll have no more of it. If any of you still wishes harm on Jace or anyone else who comes into this camp . . . you can leave."

He paused to let the weight of these words sink in and make sure every man fully understood his position. Most had their heads bowed in shame. He caught Mick's eye, and the other man jerked his head to the right. Trask's gaze landed on Brody. The young man faced slightly away from him, but not enough to conceal the redness under one eye.

"Brody!"

The young man glanced up and confirmed Trask's observations. He marched up to him and demanded, "What happened to your eye?"

Brody opened his mouth. "I . . ." He glanced at his brothers.

"That's what I thought," Trask said in a low voice before Brody could come up with an excuse. "I'm ashamed of you three. Obviously, you're bored. Very bored."

Brody tried to protest, but Trask spoke over him.

"Fortunately, I know just how to counter that. We need a well. I want you to dig one. And after that, we need cabins. Lots of cabins. You will help with the one going up now. Then you will get to work on the next one, and after that, the next one, and the next one, until I decide we have enough. Do you understand?"

"But what about hunting?" Brody scrambled for a way out. "The men need to eat."

Of course they would want to avoid manual labor and spend all day in the woods. He wondered how much time they had actually spent in search of game.

"I'll worry about the hunting. Now get to work on that well."

Brody hesitated. The rebellious light in his eyes warned of an argument, but Trask wouldn't have it.

"You will follow my orders or you will leave camp."

Grumbling, Brody turned with his brothers and trudged off to get to work. Trask glared after them with no intention of letting them off easily for what they'd done. Not them or anyone else. He turned and his gaze encompassed the rest of the men.

"Remember what I've said."

With a nod to Mick, he walked back to Jace and Rayad as the group dispersed behind him.

"I'm sorry about Brody and his brothers," he told them, though Jace didn't look up. "They've always been trouble. Personally, I'd rather not have them in camp, but I allow it for their mother's sake. In the village, it would only be a matter of time before Goler arrested them for one reason or another."

However, if they continued to act up, he might have no choice but to send them away. Such maliciousness would only poison camp and destroy his vision for providing a place of refuge.

By evening, Jace's whole body ached as though a herd of horses had trampled over him. He hadn't taken such a beating in years. He passed the afternoon on the outskirts of camp, resting, but never able to relax. No matter where he went, he sensed someone watching him. It seemed he'd become even more of a spectacle now that he was injured. When night fell and he'd forced down the supper Rayad offered him, he ducked into the tent. He hissed out a breath as he bent over and gathered up his bedroll. Just outside, Rayad met him with a questioning look.

"What are you doing?"

"I'm going to sleep in the forest. I'll just wake everyone up again if I stay here." The dreams were escalating, and he wouldn't risk waking camp with another outcry. He'd suffered enough humiliation for one day.

"You don't know that."

Jace just stared at him. He had no reason to hope for the best.

"Then I'll go with you," Rayad decided. "There's probably an extra tent we can use."

"No," Jace said abruptly, but winced at the harshness of his own voice. He softened his tone. "I'll be fine."

He set off into the trees before Rayad could respond.

The shadowed forest engulfed him until the light from camp had disappeared and he came to the stream he'd found earlier. On the bank, he dropped his bedroll, but did not spread it out. He sank down next to it, and Tyra lay beside him. He glanced at his reflection in the water. His dark features were shadowed except for his eyes. They shone bright blue, absorbing the moonlight. *Unnatural.* They were animal eyes.

He turned away from the stream with a scowl and settled in to wait out the long night.

KYRIN PRESSED HER palms into her eyes with a groan and then pulled her blankets up over her head. If only she could hide in their folds for the rest of the day. The tension that squeezed her neck and shoulders before bed had grown into a full-blown stress headache and made her a little nauseous. She had barely slept, though the headache wasn't entirely to blame. Thoughts of Davira, the emperor, and Daniel would not allow her any peace. That last look of suspicion in the princess's cold, penetrating eyes still made her heart seize. She tried to convince herself she was just hypersensitive and overreacting, but it did little good.

She sighed in the warm darkness under the blankets. Secure though it seemed, she couldn't hide. The day awaited, and she must face it. Holly would be along anytime now to help her dress. In desperate need of strength, Kyrin slipped out of bed, dropped to her knees, and rested her heavy head against the mattress.

"I'm surrounded, Elôm," she murmured. "I'm surrounded by those who don't know You and would harm me if they learned of my trust in You. I'm afraid they already might suspect me. I don't want to be afraid . . . but I am. Oh, please give me courage. I want to live bravely for You, but I'm weak. I cower under the threat of discovery." She bit her lip, stung by the memories of what happened in the library. "I'm sorry I keep failing. Please help me better serve You."

The doorknob turned, and Kyrin jumped up. Holly entered the room.

"Good morning, my lady," she said sweetly.

Her kindness brought a smile to Kyrin's face, yet it died with one thought. How many opportunities had she wasted to speak with her maid about Elôm?

"Good morning," she murmured, though distracted by her shortcomings.

Holly paused on her way to the wardrobe. "Are you all right, my lady?"

Kyrin shrugged and scolded the tightness at the back of her throat. "I'm afraid I have a rather painful headache."

"Oh, I'm sorry. Let me help you dress and then I'll get you some tea for that."

Kyrin managed another smile in thanks.

Holly helped her into one of her dresses and then excused herself for a few minutes to fetch a cup of tea. Kyrin used this time to pull herself together. She had no such luxury as to break down whenever something went wrong. Not here.

When Holly returned with the pleasantly fragrant brew, she said, "This always helps me."

"Thank you."

Kyrin took the cup and sat down at the dressing table to sip it while Holly worked on her hair. The silence hummed in Kyrin's ears. She raised her cup to her lips, dismayed at how her hand trembled. *Help me.* She took a shallow breath and set the cup down.

"Holly?"

"Yes, my lady?"

"Do you ever . . . think much about . . . faith?"

The space between Holly's brows scrunched up in a delicate frown. "Faith? I'm not sure, my lady. I mean, I go to the temple every day to pray just like we're supposed to, but . . ."

Kyrin waited and watched her reflection.

"I'm afraid I can't say too many of my prayers have been answered." Holly shrugged. "I suppose I'm pretty insignificant to Aertus and Vilai."

But not to the real God. Kyrin closed her eyes a moment to pray again. Dare she say it? Should she make known exactly what she believed?

Right as she opened her mouth to speak, the door swung open, and Lady Videlle bustled in. Kyrin snapped her mouth shut and swallowed her disappointment.

"Well, you have a big day," Videlle announced without so much as a *good morning*. "The emperor has requested your presence at his dinner tonight."

Kyrin looked up at her as best she could without bothering Holly's work. "Dinner?"

"Yes, yes, his dinner with the surrounding lords and governors."

Kyrin fought a groan. Her head pounded harder already.

The sky hung low with gray clouds and sent a damp chill through the forest. Jace pulled his blanket tighter around his shoulders, but his bedroll still lay beside him, unused. Tyra yawned and stretched before gazing up at him. She was probably hungry. He hung his head and sat still for another few minutes. His eyes slid closed a number of times before he jerked back to full awareness.

Enough of this. He pushed stiffly to his feet and hissed out a breath through his teeth at the pain that stabbed his chest. He lifted his shirt and touched cool fingers to the dark, mottled bruising across his ribs. Even a light touch burned, but he didn't think they were broken. He tugged his shirt back into place and motioned to Tyra. Together, they trudged back to camp.

The campfire crackled and glowed ahead of them, a welcome

sight on a chilly morning, but the men around it created a barrier he had no desire to overcome. Whenever they caught his eye, they looked down, their faces somber. The usual silence surrounded them.

Hardened against it, Jace took a small helping of breakfast and moved off to sit near the tent, where he ate without tasting. He spared only a brief glance when Rayad joined him with breakfast plate in hand.

"How are you this morning?"

Jace shrugged. Pain was pain. He was used to it. He brought a small bite of fried potatoes to his mouth, but his tender and swollen jaw worked slowly. After only a few more bites, he lost interest and gave the rest of his food to Tyra.

"You should eat more," Rayad said in a conversational tone.

"I'm not hungry," Jace muttered. He had no appetite these days. What was the point?

Rayad stared down at his own food and didn't eat much either. The silence drew out between them and grew uncomfortable.

"I think I should leave."

Rayad's eyes flashed to him. "What?"

Jace stared down at his hands. It was too difficult to speak while looking him in the eyes. "Why stay? I'm not doing any good here."

"Just give it more time. We've been here less than a week. Things just need time to settle."

Jace shook his head. What would time do? Maybe the men would grow accustomed to his presence, but would they ever fully trust him? No. He'd live on the edge of their group, not a stranger, but never truly a member. He couldn't live like that.

Rayad breathed out slowly, voice tired and ragged. "Jace, you're a man now. If what you want is to set out on your own, then I'll let you go. But if it's grief and this camp driving you away, then I'm going with you."

"No," Jace replied firmly and managed to look at him. "You're needed here."

"So are you."

Jace let out a short, hollow laugh. He wasn't needed anywhere. "No, I'm not."

The pained look in Rayad's eyes forced him to turn away again.

"You're valuable to this group. The men just have to come to realize it."

"Not if Holden has anything to say about it."

Jace rose to his feet to fight the heaviness building inside him. Emotions brought nothing but more pain. He needed to be alone, to harden, to protect himself.

"I think we have to cut him a little slack," Rayad told him. "He's been through more than you know."

Jace looked down and let his voice flow from behind the cold walls inside him. "I don't blame Holden. I do have the blood of a monster."

Rayad pushed to his feet, determined to make Jace see it wasn't true, but the young man turned away and headed for the trees. Rayad called to him, twice, but he would not turn back. When he disappeared into the forest, Rayad sank down with a groan and scrubbed his hands over his face, tired of the whole sorry situation.

"What can I do, Lord?"

If only the clouds would open with an answer to that. But they remained gray and dark, just like his mood. He didn't like powerlessness any more than Jace did.

"Are you all right?"

Rayad lifted his eyes to Warin as his friend came and sat across from him. He released a broken sigh. "What do you do when someone is giving up? How are you supposed to help when they just won't listen?"

Warin slowly shook his head, unable to provide an answer either. "It's my fault. I shouldn't have pushed you to join us."

"No," Rayad murmured. The true guilt rested inside him. "If anyone is to blame, it's me. I know Jace. I should've known better than to drag him into this."

He grimaced, reluctant to voice his fears, though he knew them to be true. "I'm afraid one of these days he'll go off and won't come back. Then I'll lose him for good. He only stays because of me, but soon, I don't think even that will be enough."

Kyrin scrutinized herself in the mirror. Instead of her usual gold dress and black vest, Lady Videlle had chosen something more elaborate for tonight—a deep scarlet, off-the-shoulder gown of shimmering satin and black lace. Certainly the most elegant dress she'd ever worn, but she made a face when no one was looking. The neckline dropped much too low for her comfort. Collin had better not catch a glimpse of her. Yet, even at this, Lady Videlle wasn't satisfied. She chattered again about needing to have the dresses altered.

Kyrin ignored her and continued to ponder her reflection. Her cosmetics were different tonight as well. Holly had replaced the normal blue on her eyelids with a thick layer of rich, cherry brown and painted her lips deep red like her dress. Combined with the exquisite hairstyle accented by a couple of red roses, she looked nothing like herself.

"Well then, let's get you to the drawing room," Videlle said. "Dinner will be served shortly."

Kyrin surrendered without a word. This was her life now, and she couldn't fight it despite how her mind cried out to do so.

Though she had resigned herself to what was expected of her tonight, upon entering the drawing room, her heart jumped into her throat. Daican stood as regal as ever in the midst of several other well-dressed men, all strangers except for Sir Richard. Her palms prickled. She willed them not to sweat and bit the inside of her lip. Observing people she'd likely never see again was one thing. Finding herself at the center of the emperor's lordly acquaintances was quite another. If she made a bad impression now, she would no doubt have to face them again in the future.

She glanced to the perimeter of the room and barely stifled a groan. Collin stood stationed with a handful of other security personnel. The half-hidden smile on his face said he'd noticed the moment she stepped through the door. She had to battle the urge to tug the front of her dress up higher. She could just shake Videlle for making her wear it and insisting on modifications that would further mortify her.

Rattled, she looked down and lightly smoothed her skirt in an attempt to fortify herself. *I don't want to do this, Elôm.*

"Miss Altair."

Her eyes lifted to Daican's grand smile. At least it caused fewer jitters than Collin's did. The emperor motioned her closer.

"Gentlemen," he said as he swept his hand toward her. "My newest assistant, Kyrin Altair."

He introduced her to each of the men—lords and governors of Valcré's neighboring cities and provinces. Working both to display poise and do her job, Kyrin took note of their particular responses and mannerisms so she would have something to build on later in the evening. The men greeted her courteously, though a few fell on the cold side, their eyes narrowed in suspicion. She understood the discomfort of such close examination. Even now, the princess's face flitted through her mind like a ghostly presence.

Once the greeting concluded, the men promptly forgot about her and went on discussing a variety of subjects. Kyrin welcomed this chance to fade into the background and re-gather herself.

She stayed on the outside, but listened for anything she might need to know. Just when her heartbeat had begun to normalize, a whisper came from over her shoulder.

"You look stunning."

She looked back into Collin's twinkling grin. However, it wasn't quite as overflowing with confidence as usual. It held contrition, an unspoken apology for the other day. Still, he couldn't fully mask his appreciation for her appearance.

Kyrin looked away, heat rising up her neck and into her cheeks. Could she just ignore him? If someone noticed, they would probably consider her extremely rude. She cleared her throat, though her words scratched it. "Thank you."

Out of the corner of her eye, she saw his grin intensify, but he stepped back before anyone could catch him distracting her from her duty or neglecting his. She set her eyes on the emperor's gathering but couldn't shake the sense that Collin still watched her. No doubt this would continue all evening. The muscles at the back of her neck drew tight again. What she wouldn't give to have Kaden here to send him one of his "touch my sister and you're dead" looks. Not that she truly wished him harm, but his attention added one more level of difficulty to her life. How was she supposed to focus on her job when he watched her constantly, especially in this hateful dress? If only Trev had been assigned to security tonight.

Twenty agonizing minutes passed. Why did the air have to feel so close and stifling in such a large room? It was as if an invisible hand slowly squeezed the back of her skull. Never would she be glad to see Davira, but the arrival of the queen and her daughter brought just the distraction Kyrin needed to refocus her fuzzy thoughts.

The women swept in amongst much flattery and admiration. Kyrin's gaze followed Davira as the princess appeared to drink it all in, but it was only a mask for the underlying disdain lurking in her eyes. A blast of wintery cold froze Kyrin's insides when Davira cast her a cruel little smile.

With the queen at his side, Daican led everyone into the dining room. Once again, Daniel was absent. Kyrin hadn't seen him at all since yesterday afternoon. Of course, there were any number of places in the palace he could hide out. Or perhaps he was off "dispatching bandits" again. Whether his absence angered Daican or not, tonight he did not show it. Instead, he told humorous little anecdotes and soon had the nobles chuckling.

A footman seated Kyrin in the middle of the table. A sigh leaked past her lips when Collin stationed himself right across from her. He winked, and Kyrin looked down at her plate before casting a glance at each of the two lords on either side of her. Though both advanced in age, they were complete opposites. The man to her right had a portly frame and a thick gray beard, while the other was very slight with a long hooknose and not a hint of facial hair. Neither came across as particularly sociable, and they paid her little attention. They chose, instead, to devote their time to complaining about ryrik attacks—a constant problem in the Southeast near Wildmor, the ryriks' home territory.

These grumblings set everyone else to complaining about their own respective difficulties. However, the more the footmen filled their wine goblets, the lighter the mood became. Laughter returned, outweighing the complaints—that is until Daican fixed his eyes on a baron from a province southeast of Valcré near Kyrin's hometown of Mernin.

"Arther, I've heard rumor of individuals turning up near Keaton who are rejecting the worship of Aertus and Vilai."

Though the emperor spoke in a pleasant tone, quiet spread across the table. Arther, a large man with gray-streaked black hair, paused for the briefest moment before looking at Daican.

"I'm sure it's just a few random people, my lord. Nothing to be concerned about."

His voice trembled slightly. Kyrin paused with her wine glass halfway to her mouth when Daican glanced at her. For the first time, his warm eyes chilled her. Their cunning glint matched the very same she had seen in Davira's eyes. Hand shaking, she set her glass down. He wanted her to pay attention.

"That's not what I'm told," Daican responded smoothly. No one probably even noticed his look in her direction. "Aertus and Vilai have placed me in authority over our kingdom. When people begin to reject the gods, they also begin to question my divine authority. So, it is something to be concerned with."

"Yes, my lord, forgive me. You're right," Arther hastened to agree.

"And I'm sure you have no part in this, Arther. You would never hold with rebellion toward your emperor."

"Of course not, my lord." He spoke with conviction, but his gaze faltered.

"You will take necessary steps to end this once you return to Keaton, won't you? We don't want to see this get out of hand."

"Yes, my lord, I will do everything I can."

He swallowed, briefly rubbing his chin, and perspiration glittered on his forehead. Kyrin's own skin tickled with dampness despite the cold flow of her blood. She didn't miss the baron's exhale when the emperor directed the conversation toward someone else.

Kyrin rested back in her chair, done with her meal though her plate remained half-full, and contemplated what she had just witnessed. Why did it leave her stomach in such a jumble of knots? That look Daican gave her. She'd seen him angry, but this was something different. Something cruel. Daniel's words echoed in her mind. *"He's a cruel man, you know."* Deep down, she hadn't wanted to believe it. It was easier to live here thinking that just maybe they'd all been wrong about him.

Remembering her job, her attention snapped back to the dinner table, where she found Davira watching her. Their eyes locked, and Kyrin's air remained trapped in her lungs until the princess looked away. It then seeped out in a trembling stream. Her eyes flicked to the door, and her heart beat against her breastbone. The urge to escape gnawed at her will, but she forced herself to remain seated and prayed for the night to end soon.

But it wasn't to be. Dessert arrived some time later, and the men continued to talk late into the evening. Kyrin's grip on her nerves frayed. Even avoiding Collin's glances didn't offer a distraction anymore. Images of panicking and making an utter fool of herself tiptoed on the edges of her thoughts. She truly feared giving in to them, but finally, the dinner wound down. Solora and Davira excused themselves, and Daican granted Kyrin permission to leave.

With wobbly legs, she pushed to her feet, gave the lords a weak smile, and stepped cautiously around the table while conversation resumed. At the door, Collin met her. He'd never looked so serious.

He bent down just a little to ask quietly, "What's wrong?"

She swallowed, though none of the wine she drank had kept her mouth from going dry. "Nothing. I just need rest."

"Would you like me to walk you to your room?"

She flashed him a vexed look, and he held up a hand. "It's an innocent offer, I swear. I just want to make sure you're all right."

Kyrin shook her head. What she needed more than anything was to be alone, and the sooner the better. "I'll be fine."

"All right," he murmured, his eyes lingering on her face as if to make sure.

Taking a deep breath, she walked out and left the dining room and its hum of voices behind. The silent, shadowed halls engulfed her, drawing her toward her room and bed. Good thing Holly would be there to help her. After this, she had little strength left to wash up and change into her nightclothes.

Something black flashed to her right. She spun around to face

Sir Richard. The flesh along her arms crawled as she stared wide-eyed up into his dark face.

"The emperor wishes to speak with you." His low voice rumbled ominously in the dim hall. "Come with me."

Kyrin's heart almost thrashed itself to death, and her head felt too airy. Ironic that she now almost wished she had accepted Collin's offer, foolish as it would've been.

Richard's black brows inched downward, his gray eyes like thunderclouds, when she didn't move. With a dry gulp, she nodded, and he strode off without another word. She had to hurry to keep up, but her legs threatened to give out. Her thoughts jumbled so badly, she couldn't figure out exactly where in the palace they were until they arrived in Daican's office. Richard gestured to a chair near the desk.

"Sit."

Kyrin obeyed the terse command and rubbed her palms against her skirt. She took a quick glance around to confirm they were the only two present before lifting her eyes to Richard.

"The emperor will be here when he is finished."

These were the only words he left her with before he walked out and pulled the door closed. The thudding sound of Kyrin's pulse filled the silence, and her eyes wandered the room. Only a few candles burned, yet they illuminated a fascinating array of art on the walls, and the desk covered in books and parchment begged for further inspection. But she would never leave her seat.

Minutes ticked by. Kyrin's heart continued to pound and the rich colors around her slowly turned to a more grayish hue. She started when the door finally opened. Emperor Daican strode in first, followed by Richard and Davira. Kyrin rose as they approached her.

"Miss Altair, I apologize for keeping you so late." Daican's voice was calm, and he even smiled a little. It would be easy to let it soothe her, but the probing look in his eyes prevented any such comfort. "I was glad of your presence tonight. Tell me, what did you gather?"

Kyrin licked her lips and strained to let her voice break free. "Nothing of much interest, my lord . . . but . . ."

That's when it occurred to her. They were using her exactly as they had at Tarvin Hall—as a snitch—yet this wasn't the harmless disobedience of children. This carried far more dire consequences.

"But for Baron Arther?" Daican prompted.

Expectation saturated the silence as three pairs of eyes bored into her. She had to speak up. She had no choice.

"Yes, my lord."

"And what are your thoughts on him?"

Don't do it. Every sense warned her it was a mistake, but how could she withhold information from the emperor? He might think that she was an enemy—that she sided with Arther. She almost choked on the thick, black fear that rushed up inside her.

"He was nervous. He held himself rigidly when you spoke to him and would not maintain eye contact."

Daican gave a slow nod. The smile faded. "Tell me, was he truthful in answering my questions?"

Kyrin swallowed, but she had no strength to resist his questioning. "No, my lord. His manner didn't indicate so."

Daican glanced briefly at Richard before his gaze settled back on Kyrin.

"That will be all, Miss Altair."

THE NIGHT OF the dinner lingered in Kyrin's mind like dark storm clouds threatening to burst open with rain and deadly lightning. Both Lady Videlle and Holly commented on how jumpy and distracted she was. It took a great deal of prayer and two full days before she could push the overshadowing unease to the back of her mind and focus on her daily tasks.

Until Davira came upon her in the library. Kyrin sat at one of the tables, engrossed in a book when the princess walked in. At first, she gave no sign that she was aware of Kyrin's presence. Kyrin peered at her out of the corner of her eye while her stomach heaved and churned. She avoided Davira at all costs these days. She looked to the door with a longing to run. But Davira would see it for what it was. *Elôm, help me.* She set her eyes on her book and forced herself to concentrate. Maybe the princess would just leave her alone.

Wishful thinking.

Davira's voice cut into the silence, as silky and smooth as poisoned wine. "Oh, Miss Altair, did you hear about Baron Arther?"

Kyrin looked up with an internal flinch at the almost inhuman gleam of the princess's deep green eyes. Slowly, she shook her head.

"Everyone's been talking about it," Davira said as if Kyrin should have known. "Apparently, he had a terrible accident on the way back to Keaton. He's dead."

Kyrin's fingers turned to ice, the cold threading up through the veins in her arms until it reached her heart and lungs.

"Dead?" she gasped.

"Yes, dead." Davira casually flipped through the pages of the book in her hands.

The ice seeped into Kyrin's stomach now, then to her legs, and finally to her toes. She couldn't draw a full breath. This was no accident. She knew it as surely as she knew her own existence. Arther had been killed, and she'd been the one to report him to the emperor. *What have I done?* The world and everything tangible floated away from her.

"Miss Altair."

Kyrin started, her eyes jumping back to the princess.

"You're awfully pale," Davira said. "Are you ill?"

Not a trace of true concern warmed her tone.

"I . . . I'm surprised." Kyrin gripped her skirt under the table to keep from shaking. "It's just unexpected."

Davira tipped her head as she peered at Kyrin. "Yes, quite." Her tone was now condescending. She shrugged. "Though, I suppose, in the end, it's for the best. After all, he did lie to my father, as *you* pointed out, and therefore lacked true loyalty."

Kyrin's throat seized up and wouldn't allow her to swallow. She almost gagged. Her stomach's contents wouldn't have been far behind.

"You don't agree?"

The dare in Davira's voice was as plain as the evil in her eyes.

Kyrin licked her stone-dry lips. "I . . . I've always viewed death as a tragedy."

Davira's eyes narrowed, almost snake-like, and she sidled over to Kyrin's table. Kyrin's head grew dizzy as if the princess could suck the life right out of her.

"Well," Davira said, and though she smiled, it didn't come close to reaching her eyes, "you'd best be cautious about these things. You wouldn't want anyone to question *your* loyalty."

She set her book on the table and left without another word.

Kyrin couldn't move for a full five minutes, paralyzed like the aftereffects of a nightmare, but worse. This wasn't just a dream that would disappear with time. Once some warmth returned to her body, her eyes dropped to the book Davira had left behind—a scientific volume on torture and execution. Black dots floated in front of her vision. She gripped the table and pushed herself up, though her legs were like water. They gained just enough strength to rush back to her room.

Safely behind the closed door, she slid to the floor. She pulled her knees up to her chest and shook violently as hot tears poured down her cheeks. She couldn't take it. Because of her, a man was dead, and now Davira surely suspected her of disloyalty. It was only a matter of time before she told Daican, if she hadn't already. Would they kill her too?

She clamped both hands over her mouth to stifle the sobs that ripped through her chest. Her flailing heart beat with one delirious thought—*run*. It filled her mind and flooded her system with nearly uncontrollable desperation. But that would seal her fate. They'd just hunt her down, and then she would die. Like a rabbit caught in a trap, she had no choice but to wait and discover her fate.

Rayad stared into the forest, searching every tree and shadow for some sign. Jace had come by twice in the last couple of days, but even then, they traded only a brief handful of words. He usually showed up in the mornings, yet midday had arrived without an appearance. He'd had the habit of spending long hours in the forest back at the farm too, but that fact didn't help the uncomfortable twisting in the pit of Rayad's stomach as he considered what he'd discussed with Warin. It was all he could do not to go looking for Jace. But if he had left, he'd be long gone by now without a clue as to where he went. In silence, Rayad whispered a plea to Elôm to bring Jace back.

Sighing, he entered the tent to replace a knife he'd used. When he ducked back out, the tension released from his body and allowed him to breathe more easily. He glanced toward the treetops and whispered a thanks before dropping his eyes back to Jace and Tyra. But his elation faded as he crossed the distance to meet them. Jace's shadowed eyes hinted at yet another sleepless night.

"I was afraid you'd gone."

Jace just stared past him, and his silence confirmed Rayad's fears. He'd considered it.

"Jace, all I ask is that you never go without a goodbye at least."

Jace finally looked at him with eyes disturbingly dull and void of any sort of will. "So you can try to talk me out of it?"

Rayad gave a sad shrug. Of course he would. "The King knows I'll try." He gripped Jace's shoulder, willing him to listen. "You're my son, Jace, by all accounts. I can't see it end that way."

Jace stood as if numbed to the world, but at last, he gave a little nod.

"Good," Rayad breathed. "Now, let's get something to eat."

Jace put up no protest, and soon the two sat near the tent with their lunch. Rayad picked at his meat, but his eyes always returned to Jace. The blank stare on his face disturbed him like nothing he'd seen before. In the years prior to now, he thought he'd seen Jace at his lowest, but this was different. Jace always had fight in him—too much at times—but the fight had gone out, replaced by a dangerous surrender. He didn't believe Jace would go so far as to take his own life, but letting it just deteriorate and slip away . . . that he might do. Especially if he refused to eat.

Rayad shook away these thoughts. He couldn't give up hope. He might be the only one still fighting for it.

Footsteps signaled Trask's approach. He looked at Rayad, a question in his eyes, and Rayad nodded. He wouldn't have discussed Jace with others under normal circumstances, but they needed a plan to set him on the right path again, and Trask had just the thing—a specific duty around camp that might help him settle in and give him a reason to stay. A reason to live.

Trask stopped and waited a moment, but Jace only acknowledged him with a glance.

"I'm glad you're back. I have a proposition for you."

Jace looked up more fully now, though his eyes were shielded.

"I'd like you to take over hunting duty. The men rely on game for meals, and what we don't use here we give out to the poorer families around the area. We haven't had any fresh game for a couple of days now."

Jace absorbed this with the same lack of reaction reminiscent of their earlier days. Rayad traded a glance with Trask. Would Jace see through their motives and refuse? The longer the silence stretched on, the more likely it seemed, but then he gave a nod.

"All right."

His voice lacked enthusiasm, but it was a start.

Jace didn't wait to finish his lunch. He gave it to Tyra and went into the tent. When he emerged with his bow and hunting supplies and started off, Rayad set his own plate aside and followed him.

"Can we talk?"

They'd had little enough time to speak as it was. With Jace on hunting duty now, he would have to take advantage of every opportunity. Jace, however, just trudged on as if he hadn't heard. When they were far enough from camp to speak in private, Rayad reached out to stop him.

"Would you just stop and listen, please? I'm trying to help you."

Jace's throat moved as he swallowed, and his jaw clamped tightly. He shook his head, not looking at Rayad. "You can't."

And that was at the very heart of Rayad's frustration.

"You're right, maybe I can't, but you and I both know who can. Jace, look at me." When he did, Rayad read the doubt in his eyes. "Elôm can and will help you through this."

But Jace was already shaking his head again.

"Yes, He will," Rayad insisted.

"No," Jace snapped. He grimaced. "I . . . can't . . . be helped." Rayad opened his mouth to convince him, but Jace held up his hand. "I have the blood of a ryrik. I *am* a monster. I'm reminded of it every time I close my eyes."

"No, Jace. No," Rayad said with conviction. "You once believed you have a soul and Elôm saved you. Deep down, you must still believe that. Don't let the lies of the world rob you of peace and assurance. King Elôm loves you, and He wants to help you, but you need to let Him. Turn back to Him. Then you'll find comfort."

Jace's chest rose and fell as if it was the last breath he would ever take, and his eyes glittered. With a weak, defeated shake of his head, he whispered, "I don't think so."

With those words, Rayad was able to see right into the broken and vulnerable soul he knew was there, and Jace came as close to crying as he had ever seen. But, in the next moment, he rebuilt the walls that both protected him and harmed him, and steeled himself against the pain. Unwilling to talk any further, he walked off.

Rayad could only watch, but before he disappeared, he called out to him, voice husky. "I won't ever stop praying for you, Jace."

The next day's overcast sky and on and off drizzle matched Kyrin's mood. Wrapped in a black velvet cloak, she stood at the center of the nearly empty square and waited. Trev stood behind her, but they said little this morning. Could she trust him? Could she trust anyone from the palace? What if every word she spoke condemned her further? Tears burned her already sore eyes. She must look a sight. Videlle had been convinced she was ill and couldn't understand her going out in this weather.

She blinked hard, desperately watching the street. Maybe Tarvin Hall's instructors wouldn't allow Kaden to meet her today. Then again, if he'd received her hastily sent message, he'd come with or without permission. She almost smiled, but the effort was too much.

After more than twenty minutes, her spirits sank into the cold puddles around her feet. If he didn't show up soon, she would have to return to the palace, alone . . . scared. She bunched her fists in her cloak and closed her eyes. *I need to see him, please.* Her heart beat sluggishly, and her body ached. Maybe she had made herself ill.

"My lady."

She opened her eyes to Trev's voice, and her gaze locked on the tall figure entering the square. She rushed to meet her brother.

"Kaden," she gasped, and latched onto him.

Safety. For the first time in days, she could breathe without drowning in uncertainty. She didn't relinquish her hold for a good long moment. When they did part, he studied her face and his eyes darkened.

"Are you all right? You don't look well."

"I couldn't sleep last night." She glanced back at Trev and bit her lip.

The shadows around Kaden's eyes deepened, and he stood up a bit taller, with his shoulders squared as if prepared to take on any enemy, no matter how big or ferocious. "What's going on?"

She lowered her voice. "We need to go somewhere to talk."

With a nod, Kaden guided her along with him. She had probably worried him, but he had good reason to be concerned.

Though she'd tried her best to do her job like Sam said, every-thing she'd feared was manifesting itself.

They moved through familiar streets and didn't say a word. It had begun to mist again when they came to a less populated area of the city filled with abandoned, dilapidated buildings. Here rose an old bell tower they had discovered a couple of years earlier. They stepped inside the dim, musty interior, and Kyrin turned to Trev.

"Will you stand guard here?"

His watchful eyes scanned the dark, cobweb-infested corners before he nodded. "Yes, my lady."

Kyrin managed a bit of a smile. Maybe he wasn't a spy. "Thank you."

She and Kaden took the spiraling staircase up forty feet to the top of the stone tower. Though some areas had begun to crumble, the structure was still solid. Near the top, Kaden pushed open a heavy trapdoor, and they emerged into the space where the bell once hung. The sides were open to the elements, but the roof protected them from the rain. From this vantage point, they had a perfect view over the city. Kaden let the door down with a thump.

Now that they were well and truly alone, he faced her. "What happened?"

Like a dam letting loose, Kyrin poured out everything—all about the dinner, Baron Arther, and Davira. Kaden listened intently, but the creases in his forehead sunk deeper and deeper, and his jaw tensed.

"I don't know what I'm going to do." Kyrin let her arms fall helplessly to her sides, all her strength spent. "How can I keep doing this if people might die because of me? And what about Davira? If she suspects me . . ." She shivered and battled tears again. "I'm scared, Kaden. If Baron Arther was killed, what will happen to me?"

"Nothing." Kaden looked off in the direction of the palace as if just his threatening glare alone could stop them. "We won't let anything happen."

"But how?"

He looked down at her, the fight growing in his eyes. "We leave. I know we said we couldn't before, but now, what choice do we have? You can't stay at the palace."

Kyrin's heart collided with her ribs. She'd wanted to run, but could they really do it and survive? Her throat tightened and strangled her voice. "What if we get caught?"

"We won't."

He might be confident, but it would take more than just his word to assure her. "We can't just run off. *If* we do this, we have to prepare. We'll need food, and supplies, and we'll need to know where we're going." She paused as a wave of nausea and faintness overwhelmed her. Cold spread all over. "Oh, Kaden, this is crazy. How could we do this?"

"Don't worry, I'll take care of it." Kaden reached out and squeezed her shoulders. "I'll gather supplies and find somewhere to stash them until we're ready. I'll figure out how to get out of the city. As for where we'll go, I'll talk to Sam. He'll help us."

Kyrin closed her eyes and drew in air through her cold lips. The tower seemed to spin in a circle. What was worse? Remaining at the palace near Davira, or the risk of being caught trying to escape? Either way, she could face death.

Slowly, she opened her eyes. "We have to pray about this. We can't just charge forward with our plans."

Though fired up to take action, they couldn't foolishly rush into something of this magnitude and consequence without Elôm's guidance. She shivered again and rubbed her arms as she looked out toward the palace. It stood like a menacing guard over the whole city—one that wouldn't release them willingly.

"Can we really do this?"

"Sure we can."

She looked up into his eyes again—eyes that were so strong

and determined. Of course, if he had his own doubts, he wouldn't let her see them. It would only be after they were safe that he might admit his fears.

"What's the alternative?" he asked. "And just think about it. We'll be away from the emperor's influence. We'll be able to make our own choices, live the way we want. We'll be free."

At the exhilarating ring in his voice, Kyrin truly considered life outside of Valcré. It would be dangerous, but they would have their freedom. Perhaps they could even sneak in visits with their family and see their younger brothers. Warmth surged back into her veins. They could be normal.

"All right, but make sure you talk to Sam."

"I will."

A slow grin took hold of Kaden's face. Knowing him, he'd been prepared for this moment for the last ten years.

"We'll make it," he assured her, and she trusted him.

In the quiet, they shared their ideas about where they might go and how they would make a living after this. They would have to disguise themselves and certainly use a different family name. They'd lived for so long under the emperor's control. What would it be like to be on their own? The first bit of giddiness tingled through her, but she cautioned herself against getting too excited just yet. They still had to pull off their escape.

When Kyrin's stomach growled, she looked out at the dark sky. Though the sun hid behind the clouds, it must be close to noon. "I should get back. I'm not sure yet if the emperor or Lady Videlle have plans for me this afternoon."

But she gulped at the thought of returning. How could she face the emperor, how could she face Davira, without feeling as if they could see right through her? This fear must have played over her face.

"Listen," Kaden said, "just lie low and act normal. Try not to let them see you're nervous. I'll get everything ready as quickly as I can. It should only be a few days."

Kyrin nodded, drawing from his strength and shoring up her own. For a few more days, she could do this.

Kaden lifted the trapdoor. Back on ground level, Trev stood at the entrance of the tower. He stepped back as they passed through.

"I'll walk you back to the palace," Kaden said.

"What about lunch? You'll be late."

He shrugged. "I'll find something to eat."

At last, Kyrin smiled.

They walked in silence from there. Kaden's forehead wrinkled in concentration. He was brave—certainly braver than she was. Without him, she would never do this. But then, without Elôm, neither of them could. *We need You to guide us in this, Elôm. Show us if this is the right decision. We—*

"Look out!"

The shout came from Trev just a moment before light caught on the sharp edge of the blade plunging straight for Kyrin's chest. She flinched, tensing in in anticipation of the blow. But Kaden shoved her to the side. She stumbled, and someone grunted. Regaining her balance, she locked wide eyes on a struggle between Kaden and the attacker. She took an instinctive step forward to aid him, but Trev grabbed her shoulders.

"Stay back!"

He rushed toward the struggle. The dagger clattered at their feet, and the attacker gave a hoarse cry as Kaden and Trev wrestled him to the ground and pinned him. Once Trev had a secure grip on his arms, they pulled him up again.

"No!" the man cried out as he fought against them. "She has to die! The emperor has to know he can't do this!"

Kyrin's face went cold and slack. *Him.* The same young man whose father Daican had sent to the workhouses. But his clothes were more ragged now, and his hair and eyes wild.

"She has to die," he said again, his face twisting in anguish. "The emperor must pay!"

Kyrin couldn't move. His words echoed inside her head and drowned out all thought. She stared down at the long, slender dagger that had nearly taken her life. She couldn't draw a full breath. She'd almost died. Not at the palace, but right here on the street.

Kaden grabbed her arm, and she flinched. She looked up into his face, but then her eyes dropped to the dark red stain seeping through his sleeve.

"You're hurt!"

"I'm fine."

He wrapped his arm protectively around her shoulders and prompted her forward. Trev led the way, guiding the prisoner in front of him. The man's head hung in defeat, the fight having gone out of him. His shoulders shook with audible sobs. Kyrin moved numbly, and only at Trev's voice did she realize they'd reached the palace.

"Bring her inside," he told Kaden. "She can send for a physician."

Kaden guided Kyrin up the front steps, but she paused to look back as Trev led the young man away. This was probably the last she would ever see of him. Slowly, her eyes rose to the palace. Numbness warmed into a heavy ache in her limbs. She would do anything to return to the bell tower—to hide and never enter this place again. She shook under Kaden's arm, and he held her more tightly.

"It'll be all right," he murmured.

Kyrin offered a quick nod and fought back every cry to the contrary.

Inside, she sent a passing servant for one of the palace physicians and took Kaden to her room. She cast her cloak aside and turned to her brother. Her eyes latched onto his sleeve and the stain that had grown.

"I'm all right," he assured her.

She locked eyes with him, and the hoarseness welling up in her throat distorted her voice. "You could've been killed." What if the dagger had found his heart instead?

Tears tore viciously at her eyes. Trying to swallow them down, she carefully rolled back Kaden's sleeve. A long gash ran from the middle of his forearm up to his elbow. Now that the sleeve no longer soaked in the blood, it welled up on the wound. She grabbed a towel from the dressing table and pressed it over the cut, but her fingers trembled in an effort to keep herself together.

A moment later, Lady Videlle bustled into the room, followed by the physician.

The woman gasped at the sight of blood. "What happened?"

"A man tried to kill me," Kyrin murmured.

"Where is Trev?"

"I think he's taking the man to Sir Aric."

Videlle pressed her hand to her throat. "Oh, this is just terrible! I must inform the emperor at once."

She rushed out again, and Kyrin moved aside to let the physician tend Kaden, though she hovered close by to watch as he cleaned the wound. It would heal quickly, but Kyrin couldn't think past what could have been. Inwardly, she cried out thanks to Elôm that she still had her brother.

As the physician was applying bandages, Trev stepped into the room.

"Is everything all right?"

Kyrin raised her watery eyes to his face and the expression of true concern he bore, but let the physician answer.

"He'll be as good as new in a couple of weeks."

"Good." Trev's attention returned to Kyrin. "Are you all right?"

She gave him a slow nod, though her heart said no. She wouldn't be all right until she escaped this place and all the dangers it brought.

When the physician gathered up his supplies and left, Trev turned to follow him, but Kyrin held him back. She licked her lips and fought for the courage to question him.

"What will happen to the man who tried to kill me?"

"He'll be punished. Imprisoned, maybe."

Kyrin's throat ached and constricted around her words. "Will he be executed?"

Trev didn't answer for a moment, his eyes sympathetic. "It's possible."

Kyrin stared down at the floor. It was surely more than possible.

"I'm sorry, my lady, if this upsets you."

Kyrin worked hard to conceal her distress. What might he think to find her so distraught over an enemy of the emperor? She looked up at him and forced a weak smile.

"Thank you for shouting the warning."

"I'm glad I saw him and that Kaden reached him in time." He winced, no doubt remembering back as she was. "It was close."

Kyrin raised her hand to her chest where the dagger would have plunged, and a shudder ran through her.

"If you need anything else, my lady, let me know," Trev said quietly. He stepped out and closed the door behind him.

Kyrin stared at it a moment, and then turned to Kaden. She swallowed against the pressure rising up toward her eyes.

"That's two people now," she whispered. "Two people who will be dead because of me."

Kaden shook his head. "It's not your fault. You can't blame yourself."

She pressed her palms against her eyes, but when she pulled them away, the tears spilled over. "But I had a part in it."

Kaden rose to stand before her. "This just gives us more reason to go through with our plans. We will get out of here."

Kyrin brushed her fingers across her cheeks and gave a shaky nod. She begged Elôm that escape would come quickly.

Kaden remained with her for most of the afternoon—long enough for her to gain some hold over her emotions. Still, when he left, a cold descended on the room. Kyrin huddled in her chair as her mind replayed the events of the day more times than they were welcome. She rubbed the ache between her eyes and prayed for peace in all this. Or perhaps it was more answers she sought—answers for why Elôm had placed her in this position and what she could have done differently to change the outcome.

She contemplated skipping supper and going straight to bed when Holly arrived to announce that Daican wished to see her. Spasms shot through Kyrin's middle. To face him now after the trauma of the day and after discussing escape plans with Kaden right inside the palace left her weak.

But she let Holly help her clean her tear-stained face in an attempt to look more presentable, though a glance in the mirror at the drawn, pale, and red-eyed girl in her reflection destroyed any hopes she had for her appearance. The emperor would just have to see her as she was, without masked emotions or layers of cosmetics to help conceal them.

The cold hollow in her chest spread through her limbs as she walked alone to the emperor's office. She paused just long enough for Mister Foss to let her inside. The usually grumbling little man didn't say anything this time. Despite a grim expression, something akin to sympathy flickered in his eyes. Maybe he wasn't completely sour after all.

Bracing herself, Kyrin stepped into the office. Daican sat at his desk, but rose the moment he spotted her.

"Miss Altair, I was told you were unharmed, but it is good to see it for myself."

She swallowed, her throat still sore from her earlier tears, and forced herself to hold his eyes. They were warm, as usual, but her plans with Kaden put her on edge.

"I wouldn't be if not for Trev and my brother."

Daican stepped around the desk and closed a little of the

distance between them. Kyrin fought the discomfort of his nearness and worked to recall her former ease in his presence.

"Yes, Trev informed me of the details. You're lucky to be alive."

Kyrin dropped her eyes. How long would it take before the vision of that dagger wouldn't keep flashing in her mind? Cold like melting snow slid through her veins, and she suppressed a shiver.

"I assure you, I will not allow this attempt on your life to go unpunished."

Kyrin's eyes rose back to the emperor, and her stomach convulsed. She breathed out slowly, convincing herself not to be sick. Her first instinct was to plead for mercy for the young man and avoid another death on her conscience, but how could she do that? It had not just been an attack on her, but on the emperor. The desire for such mercy would no doubt reflect poorly on her mask of loyalty.

She wavered under the pressure of what to say as she endured the emperor's scrutiny. Maybe it was only her nerves, but a little of the light seemed to have gone out of his eyes. Her tongue grew thick and useless despite her mind's outcry to say *something*. But, as the silence lengthened, Daican beat her to it.

"I can see you've had a trying day. I'll not keep you."

Kyrin swallowed down any drop of moisture she could find, but her voice was as thick as her tongue. "I'm sorry, my lord. You're right. It has been very trying."

"Go and rest then. I shall see that you're not summoned for the next couple of days unless it's absolutely necessary."

Kyrin's breath seeped out in a release of tension. To have a couple of days to herself was more than she could have hoped for. "Thank you, my lord. I'm most grateful."

Daican gave her a nod and a smile.

Kyrin backed toward the door and let herself out. She glanced at Mister Foss sitting at his desk and hurried past to her room.

But she couldn't shake the nagging sensation that, like Daican's eyes, something had been off about the emperor's smile.

Aertus and Vilai hid behind the lingering clouds when Kaden stepped out of Tarvin Hall. The courtyard lay in deep shadow except for the glow from the library. He strode toward it, but slowed when he came near. This would be the first time he visited Sam since Kyrin had left. He winced. He hadn't handled her absence well, and Sam would be disappointed.

Preparing himself to face up to Sam for his behavior, Kaden stepped into the library. Quiet loomed around him. Never once had he found anyone but Kyrin here in the evenings. He walked deeper, and his footsteps echoed faintly.

"Kaden."

The deep voice drew his focus to the right. With a warm smile, Sam approached him. "I was hoping I'd find you here one night."

And that was the great thing about Sam. Even if he was disappointed, he never showed it.

"How are you doing?" His gold eyes held Kaden's, open and inviting.

"It depends. We really need to talk."

Sam motioned to the nearby couches. "Come, sit. There's no one else here."

Kaden dropped down into the same seat he and Kyrin had occupied just before the promotion ceremony. Had it only been a couple of weeks ago?

"A man tried to kill Kyrin today," Kaden said. Though they'd instructed him not to speak of it because it might embolden others to try the same thing, Sam needed to know. "He came at her with a knife."

"Is she all right?"

"Yeah, but it was close. Her bodyguard spotted him coming, and I stopped him before he reached her."

Kaden shook his head. He still saw it perfectly in his mind. Thank Elôm for the quick reflexes he had developed in training. Had he been one second slower, his sister might be dead right now.

Sam sighed in relief. "Do you know why he tried to kill her?"

"The emperor threw his father into the workhouses. This was the best way he could find to hurt Daican."

Silence followed for a long moment.

"Things aren't going well for her," Kaden said at last.

Sam leaned forward to listen as Kaden relayed all of Kyrin's troubles at the palace.

"She blames herself for what's happened to these two men, and she's afraid Davira will discover she's a follower of Elôm, if she hasn't already."

"I was afraid this would happen," Sam murmured, his eyes troubled.

"We're planning to leave," Kaden said, and before Sam could speak, he continued firmly, "I won't leave her there to face this."

To his surprise, Sam did not speak against these plans. He only sat in contemplation for a moment and then said, "You do know what you'll be risking if you go?"

"It's not any more risky than Kyrin staying at the palace and being found out."

"It will be a dangerous life," Sam warned gently. "I don't know how far the emperor will go to find you, but he'll try. You'll need to find shelter and work. It won't be easy."

"I know." He wasn't naïve. He would have to work hard to keep them fed, sheltered, and protected. Harder than he'd ever worked in his life. He knew that, but he was willing. "I'll do whatever I have to do. We just have to get out of here."

"When do you plan to go?"

"As soon as we can. We'll have to gather supplies and figure out how to get out of the city and where to go." Kaden held Sam's gaze. "Will you help us?"

"Of course." The talcrin paused, thinking. "If you can give me a little time, I know a few people. I have an idea of where you'll be safe."

THE OPPRESSIVE CLOUDS that gathered in Kyrin's head the night of the dinner followed her everywhere and only grew darker with the strengthening sense of paranoia that plagued her waking hours. The only ray of hope came in the prospect of escape. Just enough to cut through the heavy gloom and give her strength each day. She had only seen Kaden once since their talk in the bell tower, but every day he prepared for them to leave. Kyrin held onto these plans and hopes for the future like a lifeline keeping her afloat.

In the quiet of the early afternoon on the fifth day, she rested on the couch at the foot of her bed with her eyes closed in prayer. The next day she would be required in the throne room as the emperor met with another round of Valcré's citizens. But if all went well, it would be the last time.

A rap at the door broke the stillness. Light but insistent, it no doubt belonged to Lady Videlle. Holly's knock was much softer, almost timid. Kyrin breathed out hard in frustration. It seemed her quiet afternoon had ended. Clearing her expression, she crossed the room and opened the door to Auréa's head mistress. Whatever she had to do, she would do it to the best of her ability, as always. However, the woman's pinched face and the lack of sparkle in her eyes gave Kyrin pause.

Videlle spoke no greeting, saying only, "His Majesty wishes to see you."

Invisible spiders crept up Kyrin's arms. She waited a moment for Videlle to say more. Surely, Daican only wanted her presence at a meeting, but the woman just stared at her. Her thoughts dangerously close to running off in directions she didn't want to contemplate, Kyrin stepped out to follow Videlle. The silence between them was unnatural for a woman who rarely stopped talking.

At the tickle of sweat, Kyrin brushed her hands against her skirt. Her eyes darted to each hall they passed as if to find an escape. She shook her head. She had to get a grip and stop this constant panic always creeping just beneath the surface. Daican had any number of reasons to summon her.

At the emperor's office, Lady Videlle motioned her inside without a word. Kyrin looked at her, but the woman wouldn't meet her eyes. A warning chill snaked down Kyrin's back. With no recourse, she stepped into the office. The waiting group did nothing to aid her waning confidence. Daican, Davira, Sir Richard, and Sir Aric all stood around the desk. The door closed behind her, and she looked back. Videlle had not joined them. Kyrin's gaze returned to the emperor. His expression was controlled and difficult to read.

"You wished to see me, my lord?" Every effort went into keeping her voice as even and normal as possible. How despicable, this dangerous game of deception. She glanced at Davira and regretted it. Such cold, pitiless eyes. She'd falter if she held them long.

"It's time for the staff to worship, is it not?"

Kyrin's insides lurched, and her eyes slid back to Daican. Her only answer stuck on her tongue with the taste of their condemnation. "Yes, my lord."

"And what were you doing?" His eyes pierced hers, his voice as controlled as his expression. Where was the man with the charming smile who almost lulled her into a sense of security?

Kyrin made an unsuccessful attempt to swallow, almost choking herself, and her lips moved clumsily. "I was . . . in my room . . . praying."

Her cheek twitched, barely hiding a wince. Of all questions, she needed to have answered this one without stammering or hesitation.

"So far, no one has seen you at the temple."

This statement carried more than a hint of accusation, but the throbbing rush of Kyrin's blood almost drowned it out. *Please, not this.* Like mice fleeing sudden light, her thoughts raced in all directions. She needed more time. Kaden needed more time. She needed to get out of here.

Only one small hole of escape settled before her, but would it work here as it had at Tarvin Hall? "I find it hard to concentrate with the distraction of so many people."

Daican stared at her for a long moment, and it took sheer willpower not to fidget or tremble. He had to believe her. Just for a few more days. *Please.*

"Come."

She flinched at his command, and he strode past her for the door. Kyrin froze to the tile, but one menacing look from Richard sent her following the emperor. In silence, they marched through the palace. Kyrin's breath came in short pants. Her thoughts rushed ahead, creating all the worst possible scenarios, but she battled them with all her strength. She would get through this, she and Kaden would escape, and they would have the free life they'd always dreamed of and planned for. *Elôm, please, let it be!* They were too close to fail now.

When they passed through a door and entered the courtyard behind the palace, everything inside her tumbled to a tangled halt. Just ahead loomed the temple, and Daican set their course straight for it. A violent tremor raced through Kyrin and stalled her feet. The end had come. The deception was over. Paralyzing certainty of this rushed over her and stole the breath from her lungs.

A strong shove from behind forced her onward, but heavy weights dragged from her ankles. *Elôm, no, please, I can't do this.* The temple's tall, wide doors drew near like the gaping mouth of some giant beast. Kyrin darted a look left and right—to the gardens, to the outbuildings—anywhere to escape. But they would find her. She would never slip past the wall. Not alive. And then, a numbing clarity settled over her. The time had come to take her stand. There would be no going back now. No escape.

But what if she failed? Blood beat her eardrums, and she gulped for air. She was a coward. What if she gave in to her fear? What if she didn't stand? Her chest shuddered and fiery spasms shot through it as if her heart just might stop. Such a thing might be preferable to facing what would come when they reached the temple. She slowed again at the doorway, but this time, Richard's rough hand clamped around her arm to drag her inside. Her heart rate spiked and her vision clouded. *Help me, Elôm! Please!*

The shadows of the interior engulfed them. Struggling to get enough air, Kyrin stumbled through the short hall that opened up into a cavernous chamber in the belly of the temple. Hundreds of candles gave off an eerie, reddish light. Incense hung thick in the air. It coated Kyrin's tongue and throat with a bitter film that choked her and accelerated her dizziness. Richard yanked her to a halt, and Kyrin raised her eyes. There they stood—the two towering gold idols of a man and woman that were more ornate and larger than the ones she'd once bowed before at Tarvin Hall. Her knees trembled.

Dead silence hung over the chamber. Most of Auréa's staff was present, and all eyes fixed on the group. Here, Daican turned. He grabbed Kyrin and pushed her forward. She winced in his tight grip. In a low, forbidding voice, amplified by the open space, he commanded, "Bow before your gods."

Wide eyes locked on the glittering idols, Kyrin shook from her fingers right down into her core. Her thoughts scrambled in every direction, chased by fear and the pounding, overpowering cry to give in to the emperor's demand. All she had to do was bow. She didn't even have to mean it, did she? She only had to convince him long enough to get away. Strength faded from her knees. But then, it was as if some force stepped in, melting the terror, casting it from her body, and wrapping her mind in a protective shield. An upwelling of strength and confidence she had never known before took its place. Her racing thoughts ceased and her mind stilled. Clarity came again, though not with a wash of dread, but assurance.

"Bow before your gods," the emperor repeated with more force this time. The words resonated against the walls.

Kyrin drew in a slow breath and filled her lungs. No longer did her pulse thunder in her head. She slid her eyes over to meet the emperor's, and her voice came out soft, yet strong with words never before uttered in the palace temple.

"They are not my gods . . . Elôm is my God."

With this declaration, warmth burst through Kyrin's chest with a giddiness that almost trickled into laughter. She'd done it. No more hiding, no more pretending. The truth was out, and it cloaked her like a soothing blanket.

The world seemed to rest at a standstill for several seconds, but then came a collective gasp. Murmurs rose up and filled the hollow space with sharp hisses, but Kyrin's gaze remained locked with Daican's. In that moment, his true nature revealed itself— the ice, the darkness in his eyes she expected from the beginning. Though his expression barely changed, it hardened to iron.

"Aric," he snapped. His eyes never left Kyrin. "Take her away."

The man's strong hands closed around her arms, and only then did Kyrin withdraw her eyes from Daican's piercing gaze. Amidst the murmurings and whispers, Aric escorted her out of the temple. Leaving the dark interior, they stepped out into fresh air and sunshine. Kyrin looked up as the light hit her face. She soaked in the heat and radiance, so pure compared to the eerie gloom of the temple, resting like a comforting hand against her cheek.

She would need that comfort. This was only the beginning. There would be more to endure. There would be pain. She didn't try to fool herself into thinking otherwise. It just didn't matter now. She had proclaimed her belief in Elôm, and her life was entirely His. The same divine peace that surrounded her in the temple still stirred inside her, carrying her.

Her eyes caught on someone to her right. Daniel. The prince watched them pass with a frown. Kyrin held his confused gaze for a moment. Oh, why hadn't she spoken to him when she had the chance? But it was far too late now.

The prince fell behind them as Aric guided Kyrin through a door that led down a deep, stone staircase. Torches lit the way as they descended. The temperature dropped and the air dampened, raising goose bumps along Kyrin's arms. A thick, musty odor drifted from down a long hall, and the heaviness of it pressed on her lungs. She hadn't thought, as she walked the gilded palace halls, what lay beneath it. A shiver prickled up her spine.

Aric led her on a ways before stopping at a thick door where he pushed her inside a small room. It stood empty save for one burning torch and a solitary chair in the center. Aric ordered her to sit. She did so, looking up at him, and detected some unreadable shadow in his eyes. But he said nothing as he turned his back on her and left the room. The door closed loudly behind him, and the lock clicked.

Alone in the silence, Kyrin rubbed her chilled arms. She gazed about the room and found only dark stone until she paused on the darker patches on the floor around her feet. She frowned, but her stomach roiled with understanding. Dried blood. Stains spattered the chair too. She jumped up from her seat as her mouth turned to dust. With slow but shuddering breaths, she sank back into the chair.

"Elôm." The hollow space swallowed her voice, but she went

on, "I need You to continue strengthening me to endure whatever is coming. I'm not strong enough or brave enough on my own." She worked her throat to loosen the painful tightness. "I don't know what's going to happen, and I'm afraid, but You gave me courage in the temple. Please, I still need that courage."

The seconds drew into long minutes. Everything was still. Kyrin had never experienced such silence before. Even the burning torch barely made a sound. Before long, claustrophobia rose up around her like floodwaters, and she tried to moderate her breathing. She wobbled with lightheadedness and gripped the chair until her fingers hurt. Squeezing her eyes closed, she whispered prayers to fill the quiet.

"I am a child of Elôm," she murmured to herself, drawing from all Sam had taught her. "My life is in His hands. I live for Him and Him alone. He controls my future. Nothing happens without His knowledge."

The thump of footsteps interrupted her steady flow of words. She raised her head as the lock worked and licked her dried-out lips, but her tongue wasn't much better. The door swung open, and Daican entered. Though Kyrin's body reacted with a flush of cold, somehow a quiet assurance maintained control over her mind. Richard and Aric stepped in next, but Aric remained at the door. Kyrin's gaze shifted from him to the emperor, who peered down at her with his fists on his hips. Even Master Zocar's most withering stare couldn't compare to the intimidation behind Daican's.

"How long have you believed such lies?"

Kyrin sat in silence, but inside she begged Elôm for strength not to give up any information. Daican narrowed his eyes and then nodded to Richard. The man stepped forward and dragged Kyrin up off the chair. She tensed in his grip, but didn't take her gaze from the emperor. What a fool she'd been to think and hope he would prove himself to be more than the man she believed he was at Tarvin Hall. He'd actually had her convinced at times, but Kaden had been right.

"Who taught you?" Daican demanded.

Sam's face flashed in her mind. This answer above all else must be guarded with her life. She clamped her teeth down hard. Grasping her wrist, Richard twisted her arm up behind her back. Pain shot through her shoulder, and she gasped out a small cry.

"Who taught you about Elôm?" Daican repeated his question calmly, but with a sharp edge to his voice.

Kyrin just shook her head, not trusting herself to speak. Elôm help her, she would never give Sam up.

Richard yanked her arm farther. Another wave of pain seared through her shoulder muscles as her tendons stretched taut. She ground her teeth together to stifle a groan. Tears stung her eyes.

"Tell me who taught you." Daican's voice rose. "Was it someone at Tarvin Hall? Or someone in the city?"

Kyrin met each subsequent question without answering. They varied, but always returned to who had taught her of Elôm. With each refusal to speak, Richard twisted her arm up a little higher. Surely, at some point, a joint would pop or a bone would snap. It was only a matter of time. Beads of sweat rolled down her face, mixed in with leaking tears. Dizzy with pain, another whimpered cry broke free. Panting, she looked at Daican's blurred face through her tears and a surge of defiance built up in her.

"No," she declared. "I'll never tell you anything. No matter what you do, I'll never speak."

After the prolonged silence, the release of such words brought relief, but only for a moment. Sheer agony ripped through her shoulder, and she cried out. Her legs buckled, and she crumpled at Richard's feet. Slumped over, she cradled her arm. Her shoulder pulsed and burned, the muscles throbbing down to her fingertips. She held her arm close to her middle.

Footsteps drew close, and Daican's boots appeared in front of her. She raised her head as he bent closer. In a low, dangerous tone, he said, "Whether you tell me anything or not is of no consequence. Your life is forfeit."

Tears bit her eyes, but the small, flickering flame that had kept her fighting all these years still burned, even here in this dungeon. "Then I die knowing I have a better life waiting for me."

Daican's blow landed hard on her right cheek and snapped her head to the side. Her ears rang, and she almost toppled over. By the time her senses cleared, the emperor was at the door. He paused and glanced back at her, true regret in his tone. "It's a shame, Miss Altair. I liked you." The regret vanished when he yanked the door open and ordered, "Take her."

Two guards strode into the room. Before Kyrin could move, they grabbed her arms and hauled her to her feet. She moaned a little, but neither man showed concern for her injuries. Out in the hall, they marched her along, deeper into the dungeon. Kyrin couldn't focus past her shoulder and the pain robbing her of breath. When they did stop, a corridor of cells stretched before them. They shoved her into one. Only then did Kyrin take notice of Aric. He stepped to the door.

"You will need to give me your dress."

Kyrin glanced at her clothing and then back to him. "What?"

"Your dress, you need to give it to me."

Kyrin gripped her vest and inched back in the cell.

Aric breathed out audibly and spoke in a quiet tone. "Don't make me have to take it from you."

Kyrin looked around, but the dark cell offered no solution or alternative. Moving slowly, she tried not to think, just act. With shaky fingers, she unlaced her vest. Her left arm wasn't much use, and she had to blink to keep her eyes clear. Carefully, she worked the vest off and handed it to Aric. Looking down at her dress, she hesitated again. How far would they make her go? She shuddered.

Crying out to Elôm, she loosened the laces as best she could and glanced up. Aric stared at the floor, but the two other guards peered in at her with no attempt to conceal their fiendish satisfaction. She fumbled with the laces. Once she was able, she slipped the dress off and handed it over, too. Wearing only her shift, she felt utterly exposed and wrapped her good arm around herself.

"The shoes."

Kyrin slipped them off and pushed them toward Aric. The cold, damp cell floor leaked up through her thin stockings and chilled her toes.

Clothing under his arm, Aric stepped out of the cell. The door shrieked shut and locked with a finalizing clank. With one last look at her through the bars, Aric strode away with the guards. For several long seconds, Kyrin just stood in the dark, her uneven breaths all that broke the stillness. Nothing moved, but the thick air settled cold on her exposed skin and sent a shiver up her arms and across her back. She looked around. The darkness hid even her own hands. Reaching out, she felt her way to the back of the cell and sank to the floor.

For the first couple of minutes, a cool numbness encased her, her mind sorting through everything she'd just faced, but then the trembling took hold and tears spilled from her eyes. It hardly seemed real, yet as reality fully settled in, small choking sobs tore at her chest.

"Kaden," she cried. She would probably never see him again, at least not in Ilyon. Neither him nor her father. If only she could see them, just once, and explain what happened. What would they do when they found out? What would Kaden do? This question ripped through her.

"Please, Elôm, don't let him do anything foolish."

She wept until her tears dried up and leaned her head back against the wall. So, this was it. Less than three weeks at the palace and she faced execution. Just how would her death come? Would Daican have her killed in secret or publically? Scenes from the ryrik executions flashed before her, and she put her hand to her throat. What a gruesome way to die. She closed her sore eyes.

"Elôm, if there's a way out of this, please provide it. But . . . if not, please help me stand strong . . . right to the end."

Supper would start any minute. Kaden was cutting it close tonight, but he'd made good progress in ensuring their escape route from the city. It was almost time. All they needed was the information about the group Sam had mentioned. Only another day or two. Then they would run and never look back.

When he reached Tarvin Hall, he hurried up the steps and let himself inside. A few groups of students lingered in the halls. Maybe it wasn't so late after all. At least he wouldn't have to sneak down to the kitchen. Like he'd told Kyrin, it was best to lie low these days and avoid unnecessary trouble and attention.

He passed a couple of his classmates, who just stared at him. Nothing so strange about that. With Kyrin gone, it was starkly evident just how few people even acknowledged his existence. But with every blank stare he passed, a warning tickled the back of his mind. What were they all looking at? Usually they just ignored him. He glanced down at his uniform. Nothing wrong with it. He frowned at them, but by the time he reached the dining room, his stomach clenched, and it had nothing to do with hunger.

The first person he spotted was Sam. The talcrin's tense expression clamped a slowly tightening vice around Kaden's gut. He questioned him with his eyes, but his attention shifted to Master Zocar, who approached. Two very alert-looking guards trailed him. Kaden's heart punched his ribs.

"What's going on?" he asked, his voice not as strong as he intended.

Master Zocar grimaced. "I regret having to tell you this, Kaden, but . . . your sister has been arrested."

Kaden took a step back as if he'd been struck. Arrested? No, not yet. She couldn't be. His mind nearly fuzzed out Zocar's next words.

"She renounced Aertus and Vilai and tried to attack the emperor."

"What?" he gasped. "No . . . she can't . . . she wouldn't . . ."

Kyrin wouldn't attack anyone. Certainly not the emperor, and not just before their escape.

"Kaden." Master Zocar's voice reached out to him gently and with as much sympathy as he'd ever heard it. "I know this is difficult, but you must be calm about it."

Kaden shook his head. Forget calm. He had to get to Kyrin. He had to do something to get her away from the emperor. The man would surely kill her, given the chance. He backed toward the door, but the guards rushed in and grabbed his arms.

"No!" He jerked against them.

"This is for your own good," Zocar told him. "You're not thinking clearly. You need time to calm down."

But Kaden fought to get away, yanking his arms against the guards' strong grips. Between the two of them, they were able to restrain and drag him out of the dining room. Master Zocar followed along and tried to calm him, but he didn't hear a word of it through his struggles. They couldn't do this to him. His sister was a prisoner somewhere, and he should be with her.

Despite his resistance, they managed to take him to one of the studies. After pushing him farther inside, they closed the doors behind him. Spinning around, he slammed his fists against the doors.

"Let me out!"

He hit them again to no avail. Finally, he turned around and ran his hands through his hair. This couldn't be happening. Everything was nearly ready. Their escape, their new life . . . He paced the room, and his mind raced. He had to get to Kyrin. But how? Could he even find out where the emperor was holding her?

Chest heaving, he balled his fists and let out a strangled groan. "What do I do, Elôm? I have to help her."

For a very long time, he wrestled with the image of Kyrin as a prisoner and the fire burning inside him to do something about it. Hours passed before the doors unlocked. He jumped up, prepared to do anything to get out, even if he had to face every guard at Tarvin Hall. This time he'd be ready for them.

The door swung open. Master Zocar entered first, followed by Sam, but Kaden set his eyes on the two guards who stood firmly in the doorway. If only he had a sword from the training building.

"Kaden," Zocar drew his attention. "I know how difficult this must be for you, but you're going to have to accept it."

Tensing all over, Kaden's eyes jumped back to the guards. He would never just accept this. Sam's voice was the only thing that kept him from acting.

"Kyrin made her choice, Kaden. Don't do anything foolish because of it."

His gaze swung around to the talcrin. In those gold eyes, he found both a warning and a plea. "Just be calm and get through tonight. Things will get better."

Kaden stood, torn. Kyrin needed him. Even if it meant being arrested himself, he had to find her. But what good would it do in the end? They'd both be dead with no one to rescue either of them. At least if he played along, he still had a chance to save her. Yet how could he just leave her, even for one night, at the mercy of the emperor? The heavy weight of the situation pressed down. He hung his head and let his tense arms fall limp. For now, he had no choice.

KYRIN AWOKE SHIVERING. Darkness still surrounded her, and the cold stones had drained the heat out of her body. She wrapped her arms around her chest, but her left shoulder was stiff and burned with the slightest movement. Tremors ran through her muscles. Head drooping on her chest, she'd drifted in and out of sleep, though for how long was impossible to guess. The empty squeezing of her stomach suggested hours. She hadn't eaten much for breakfast or lunch. Certainly a mistake now, looking back. They had probably been the last meals she would ever have. Her stomach pinched more painfully, and she forced that thought away.

When her teeth began to chatter, she couldn't stand it anymore. How could they just leave her down here like this? Couldn't they, at least, have left her properly clothed? None of the warmth of spring penetrated this stone prison. In desperation, she groped about for anything she might use to get warm. Her fingers found only grimy, rough stone, but then, in the opposite corner, they came upon something softer. She felt around the crumpled heap and discovered it was a large piece of cloth, perhaps an old blanket. Grabbing one edge, she lifted it from the floor. The reek of mold overwhelmed her. Gagging, she turned her head away. The damp cloth hung heavy in her hands, most likely covered in mildew and who knew what else.

Tears poured into her eyes. She was desperate to get warm, but this? The hot teardrops rolled down her cold cheeks. She had to do it. With a grimace, she pulled the cloth over her shoulders and wrapped it around herself. The smell of rot burned her nose, choking her, and the cloth clung to her like a filthy rag, but she forced herself to endure it. At first, it brought no comfort, but slowly, she warmed up and the shivering ceased. In time, she drifted back into another uneasy sleep.

Kyrin rocked slowly and squeezed her eyes shut. The darkness in her head somehow felt better than the smothering darkness of the cell. At least in her head she could lose herself in memories of the past—good memories. Anything to keep the chilling, claustrophobic tide from drowning her. It was as if she were trapped in an empty, black void and cut off from any other living being. She craved contact with her brother, if only for a moment.

Hunger pains gnawed at her stomach, and her mouth barely produced the moisture to swallow. Lack of nourishment encumbered her limbs. Any attempt at movement grew harder, slower, and her head pounded to match the rhythm of her heart. What if they just left her here to die? To just fade away? She shuddered, and tears leaked out from beneath her eyelids.

"Elôm." The weak whisper broke the silence. She couldn't force any more words through her throat, but they flowed from her mind, desperate and reaching. And the more her cries flowed out, the more comfort flowed in. Sam had once told her Elôm was a shield for His children. She imagined a shield of protection around her in the midst of the darkness. She clung to it, trusting it, refusing to let fear push it away.

The inability to tell time frayed at her mental grip, but through prayer, she prepared to let it just slip by until it simply ran out for her. After all, Elôm would be waiting for her at the end of it. Maybe one of these times she would fall asleep and it would be done. That didn't seem so bad. There were plenty of worse ways to die.

The distant echo of footsteps startled Kyrin. A flickering glow appeared and rolled away the darkness. She squinted as it grew in strength and illuminated the shapes of men. She pulled the tattered old blanket more tightly around herself, not sure whether to feel relief or the desire to be left alone.

Aric reached the cell first and opened the door. Two other guards walked in. Kyrin moved away, a useless act, but instinctual. They grabbed her by the arms and pulled her up. She bit her lip to keep from crying out. Her legs wobbled, and her head spun even as she fought to strengthen her mind to face whatever was coming. Metal clamped around her wrists, securing them behind her back, and the guards led her out of the cell and through the underground dungeon. They did not stop at any of the rooms along the way. Instead, they came to the stairs leading out of the dungeon and climbed them.

Though clouds blanketed the sky, it took Kyrin several moments to be able to see when they emerged in the courtyard. She pulled in the clean, warm air and focused straight ahead, but her breath was cut short. Six extra guards stood waiting. She had witnessed gatherings of guards like this before, at executions. Her legs grew weak again, and dim shadows closed in around her vision, followed by a sensation of sinking. But the stab of pain through her shoulder snapped her out of the near faint.

The guards dragged her toward the company, two of whom were Trev and Collin. Kyrin met Trev's gaze first. His eyes held sadness, though he kept his face blank. At least one person seemed to have pity for her. She looked next at Collin's stormy expression. It was hard to tell if he was angry, hurt, or concerned about her. Strange to see him so bothered. He stared hard at her until she was just close enough for him to whisper, "How could you do this?"

Kyrin breathed out, but struggled to draw in more air. It was too late to try to explain. If her throat would barely allow a breath, how could she manage words? She shook her head, eyes stinging, and looked away. He'd never understand.

The guards closed around her. Collin took his spot to her left and stared straight ahead, his bunched jaw muscles twitching. With Aric in the lead, they marched silently through the courtyard. Kyrin struggled with the pace, her legs sluggish, but they forced her to keep moving. It must have rained recently. Puddles checkered the stone. In one, she caught a glimpse of her reflection. What a dreadful sight she made—cosmetics streaked grotesquely, hair falling in limp, matted tangles, white shift stained, and her eyes shadowed, with one side of her face bruised.

They passed through the gate and headed straight for the square. A jolt of heat passed through her nerves. Her whole body pulsed with urges to fight and flee, but when she lagged, the guards tugged her forward. This time she couldn't hold back a groan. Collin glanced at her, but his face blurred behind the welling of tears. She stumbled along as her unprotected feet bruised on pebbles and jagged cobblestone.

Only another block to go. Kyrin trembled. She glanced to her right and caught Trev's eyes again. He didn't hold her gaze this time. *Please, help me!* She wanted to beg aloud, to fall at their feet and plead for mercy, but a new, clearer thought took over. She could either be overtaken by fear or fight it. No, she wouldn't die a coward, sniveling at the feet of men who really had no power over her future anyway. If she were going to die, she would do it serving her God. Her waning strength flared back to life. She held her head higher and her steps gained confidence.

When they drew near the square, a roar of voices rose up. What would cause such commotion? She hadn't even arrived yet. And even at the ryrik executions, she'd never heard anything like this. A moment later, it came again, even louder, before ebbing away once more like the rushing of waves at the shore. Then the square came into view, and Kyrin sucked in her breath. Thousands had gathered.

A murmur rippled through the mass of bodies as the guards, with Kyrin between them, moved toward the platform in the center of the square. Kyrin looked to her left and right. Hundreds of cold, hard expressions glared at her. Some broke into scowls and jeers. How could they hold such hostility against her? She was just a girl—not some murdering ryrik or depraved criminal. They didn't even know her.

Then they reached it—the steps leading up to the platform. Kyrin had to swallow down a reaction of fear. These steps led to death. Her heart stopped for a paralyzing moment. And to think, this had all begun with another climb, up the steps to the stage at Tarvin Hall.

The guards shoved her forward. One step at a time, she climbed up to the platform. Her eyes met squarely with Emperor Daican's, and their gazes held until she reached the top. Here, she looked out over the square. The size of the crowd from this vantage point dizzied her. She'd never witnessed one so large. People packed in without an inch to spare, even spilling out into the side streets as far as she could see. Thousands upon thousands of people with eyes on her. A cold chill twisted through her body.

Her sweeping gaze snagged on one figure. Emotion exploded inside her chest, biting her eyes, and she had to blink to see.

"Kaden."

Amidst the sea of people, he stood, tense and pale, his blue eyes more pained than Kyrin had ever seen them. Their gazes locked. Kyrin strained against the iron grip of the guards. She would do anything, *anything* to get to him. If only they'd had a little more time to escape, but the dream was dead now—so utterly crushed she had to bite back a sob. Her throat ached to call out to her brother and tell him to go, to escape, to live. She wanted to convey hope to him, but there was only pain.

The emperor's voice echoed out across the square and broke

Kyrin's focus. "Here she stands, the girl I bestowed with honor and great generosity, only to have her profane our gods and viciously attack me."

Kyrin's eyes snapped to Daican. *What?*

"No." Her voice cracked. She gathered her voice to defend herself more loudly from the emperor's lies, but all that came was a strangled cry as one of the guards twisted her arm. She shook her head desperately. The emperor, however, already held sway over the crowd. Their grumbling and murmuring rose up from all sides of the platform.

"She has shamed us all, following in the footsteps of her grandfather, Jonavan Altair, betraying her emperor and her country, and blaspheming the gods." Reaching out, Daican grabbed her by the arm. She fought him at first, but she didn't have the strength to resist for more than a moment. He dragged her near the edge of the platform, where the people could see her clearly. "And what do you, citizens of Arcacia, believe should be the punishment for such a blatant crime as this?"

In one massive roar, they gave their answer. *"Death!"*

The sheer volume of it stole Kyrin's breath.

Over and over they screamed it at the platform. At her. Fists shook in the air. Courage fleeing her, Kyrin sought Kaden again. This time, Sam was with him, the only thing keeping her brother from fighting through the crowd to come to her defense. She could see it burning in his eyes—the desperation, the anger, the hurt. In her fear, she wanted him to help her and to protect her like he always did, but she knew better. He would be killed right there with her, and the threat of that outweighed the terror of the moment. She pulled in a shaky breath and set her expression. She must be strong now, to show him she accepted this as Elôm's will, and that he must too. She wanted to show all these people she would not cower at death—that Elôm was in control, and she was prepared to give the greatest sacrifice of service to Him. She straightened in the face of their uproar.

Daican raised a hand and silenced the outcry.

"It shall be as you say," he announced. "Tomorrow, here, she will die for her treason."

The air in Kyrin's lungs rushed out. She wasn't going to die, not quite yet. She had one more day.

"But," Daican continued in response to the crowd's murmur of disappointment, "today she will bear the shame of her betrayal and be remembered always as her grandfather is—a traitor!"

The crowd erupted again. One of the guards moved behind Kyrin. He grabbed a fistful of her hair and yanked her head back. At a scraping noise, the tension released. Bit by bit, he cut through her hair. The crowd whooped and cheered as long pieces of it fell around her feet. She closed her eyes and tried to shut them out. Tears gathered against her eyelids, but she would not let them fall. Her weakness would only satisfy the onlookers. She pressed her lips together until the man finished. Her head slumped forward.

"Look at her, the traitor!" Daican encouraged the people's jeering.

Kyrin stood before them, as good as naked in her shift, with her hair cut off—a vile object of scorn. She peered at them through strands of hair and cried to Elôm for strength to bear their hatred. Where did it all come from? How could one man hold so much influence over them? Did they even see her as a girl?

Curses and insults flew at her. Then came the garbage. All manner of rotted food and waste bombarded her as she stood alone and unprotected at the edge of the platform. She tried to duck away, but something hard struck her forehead. Light flashed in her vision, and everything went dim. She pitched sideways, almost numb to the hands that grabbed her and kept her from toppling into the crowd. Kaden's agonized cry echoed faintly in her head, and a sensation of warmth flowed down her face. Her head lolled to the side, but she forced it up again to look out at the crowd. Though her vision blurred, she found her brother's wide, desperate eyes. Sam had his powerful arms wrapped around Kaden's chest to hold him back.

And that was the last glimpse she caught of him. Someone lifted her up from her knees and held her upright until strength returned to her legs. Even then, the ground rolled beneath her, and she couldn't form any solid thought. Her head drooped forward. Red spattered the front of her shift, spreading.

It wasn't until they reached the bottom of the steps that her head cleared and clarity returned. Her guards surrounded her again, and someone had an arm around her. She looked up to find it was Trev. His face was set in a determined frown. Collin must be somewhere behind her, but trying to look back made her dizzy. The crowd pressed in around them and forced the guards to push their way through. Shouting continued and garbage still flew at Kyrin, but Trev held her close to keep her shielded between himself and Aric.

They inched forward. The tight quarters made it hard to breathe. People reached out to grab her. Someone caught her sleeve and it started to rip, but Trev yanked the man's hand away. Kyrin's heart thrashed her chest. Would she make it through the crush of thousands of people with just a few guards? Would her guards even try to protect her if the crowd grew more fierce? Why would they?

The people pressed harder, their hands reaching closer and closer. A sob pushed up in Kyrin's throat, and she shut her eyes. They would kill her. She just knew they would kill her. But Trev held her more tightly and kept guiding her forward. Kyrin almost screamed, but that's when they broke out of the square and the tangled crowd. Aric immediately increased their pace. The houses and shops passed by in a rushed blur, and footsteps and jeering followed them. Kyrin shook all over, wanting to run, but she was hardly able to walk. Eventually, once they reached the palace, the pursuers faded away. Inside the courtyard, the last of Kyrin's strength abandoned her. She collapsed, but Trev caught her before she hit the ground and lifted her up into his arms. Even now, he was protecting her—his last act as her bodyguard. Why did it have to end like this? If only she could thank him, but her voice failed her.

He carried her all the way down to her cell, where he set her carefully on her feet and let Aric remove the chains from her wrists. Kyrin struggled to remain standing, but dizziness overtook her. Again, Trev broke her fall and lowered her to her knees. With the dizziness came a wave of nausea, and her stomach heaved. She barely noticed Trev back away and join the others outside the cell as the door shut.

The torchlight faded, and Kyrin crawled to the corner and grabbed her blanket. She lay down on her side and pulled her knees up, curling into a little ball. Her forehead throbbed and sharp pains shot to the back of her skull as blood oozed down around her left eye, mixing with tears. Once again enclosed in darkness, she let her lonely sobs echo through the dungeon.

THE DEEP, SPLITTING pain in Kyrin's skull prodded her toward consciousness. She let out a weak groan. Though she tried to open her eyes, her heavy lids parted only a crack. She forced them open again, and this time she caught sight of a faint glow. It didn't register at first, but then she jolted to full awareness. She pushed herself up and rocked dizzily. Dread clamped a hand around her throat and drove a fist into her stomach. Footsteps and torchlight approached her cell. That could only mean one thing.

She scrambled to gather whatever bit of strength she hadn't already spent as she thought of facing the mob again, this time to die. Trembling seized her, and tears followed along with the urge to beg for her life. She was just a girl. Couldn't they let her live? *Don't go out like this,* a quiet, but stronger part of herself admonished. *Elôm, please.* She let out a small cry, but then forced herself to stand up and meet her enemies with courage.

She surely presented quite an image—covered in filth and blood. But a spark burned inside her—a spark of strength that was deeper than herself and wouldn't die even if she did. Tears choked her, but she wouldn't be overcome. She refused.

Aric and Trev arrived at the cell. They glanced at each other, and Aric opened the door. "Come."

She waited a moment, expecting them to replace her shackles, but they did not. In this state, she didn't present a threat anyway.

She gave a resigned nod and stepped out of the cell. Trev took her firmly but gently by her good arm. As much as she wanted to be strong, she shivered in his grip and ached all over. One last meal would have been helpful in facing this fate.

Aric took the lead, with Trev still at Kyrin's side. They moved rather quickly, which made it difficult for Kyrin to maintain her footing. Her bruised feet ached with every step. Twice, she almost tripped, but Trev caught her.

"Not too much farther," he murmured.

Kyrin glanced ahead. Nothing looked familiar. Had they even gone the same way? No, they'd turned left instead of right . . . hadn't they? Her voice cracked when she spoke. "Where are we going?"

She shook her head. What a ridiculous question, considering, but something didn't add up. Or maybe she was just too hungry to think straight. She must look delirious.

But a smile appeared on Trev's face and lit his eyes. "We're getting you out of here."

All the breath went out of Kyrin's lungs, and they had to stop or she would have gone to the ground. She held on tight to Trev as she looked between him and Aric with wide eyes.

"You're . . . you're helping me?"

This time, Aric smiled. "We don't believe it's Elôm's time for you yet."

At the sound of Elôm's name from his lips, Kyrin nearly buckled again. She clung to Trev, her head a little too light.

"I know, it's a lot to take in," Aric said, "but we must hurry."

Warmth tingled through Kyrin's limbs and added stability to her body. They moved on and shortly came to a door at the end of the long hall. Here, they stopped. Aric doused the torch in a barrel of water and engulfed them in pure darkness. The door latch creaked, and light returned, only this was the pale light of Aertus and Vilai. Nighttime bugs chirped around them as they stepped outside. Kyrin looked up to find a wall towering above them. The tunnel had led them secretly and safely outside the grounds of Auréa.

Her eyes dropped down again and landed on a tall figure. "Sam!"

She put her one good arm around him, and he enveloped her in his strong embrace. Tears gushed into Kyrin's eyes and burned her nose as the truth sank in. She was safe. She wasn't going to die.

"Are you all right?" Sam asked in a low, thick voice.

Kyrin pulled away from him. "I think so." But her own safety flew from her mind, and her eyes did a quick sweep of the area. "Where's Kaden?"

"He's all right for now," Sam assured her. "Believe me, I wanted to bring him, but he's being watched at Tarvin Hall. There was no way I could get him out. Not tonight." He glanced at Aric. "Kyrin, I know you're tired, but we have to get you out of the city before someone discovers you're gone."

Kyrin shook her head before he could even finish. "I can't go without Kaden."

"You must."

"No." Tears welled again. She couldn't leave her brother behind. What if the emperor went after him next? He'd kill him for sure—just to spite her if nothing else.

"Listen to me," Sam said gently as he looked into her eyes. "I'll do everything I can to get Kaden out, I promise. But you can't stay here. There's nothing you can do to help him. Trust me, he wants you to go."

A small sob caught in Kyrin's throat, but she swallowed it down. It didn't take much to imagine Kaden standing there and telling her to leave. Of course, he would want her to. But what if she never saw him again? Biting her lip, she nodded. She had to do what he wanted and trust Sam to help him escape.

Sam turned to guide her along with him. Two horses and another man stood under a tree nearby, dappled by the moonlight filtering through the branches. A closer look at his dark skin marked him as another talcrin. His silver-blue eyes shone as they neared.

"Kyrin, this is my nephew, Tane," Sam said. "He'll take you to safety."

She looked up at the only other talcrin she had ever met. His face was younger than Sam's, but just as kind.

Sam grabbed something from the saddle of one of the horses and turned back to her. "Put this on."

He helped her slip a woolen overdress over her head. It was a bit big, but the thick material warded off the nighttime chill and remnants of the dungeon. He also wrapped a light cloak around her shoulders and handed her a pair of boots to slip on.

"There are more clothes in the saddlebags. You can change once you're well away from the city." Sam waited for her to look up at him before continuing. "You'll have to ride hard and fast. Do you think you can do that?"

Kyrin nodded. It wouldn't be easy, but for now, the warm coursing of adrenaline chased away the weariness.

"Good," Sam said.

A silence fell between them. Kyrin stared up into the gold eyes she'd sought so many times for counsel and encouragement. Was this goodbye? Would they ever meet again? She fought tears, but they came too readily tonight.

"Thank you so much, Sam." Her voice wavered. "I'd still be lost without you."

She gave him another tight hug.

"You're the bravest person I know," Sam told her. "I've never seen the kind of bravery you displayed on that platform."

Kyrin just shook her head. "It wasn't me."

Sam smiled, squeezing her arms, and then helped her mount one of the horses. Tane mounted up beside her. From the saddle, Kyrin's eyes caught on Aric and Trev. They had risked everything to provide this escape.

"Thank you," she told them, hoping her voice carried the depth of gratitude in her heart. They nodded, and she added, "Thank you for protecting me, Trev."

"It was my pleasure, my lady," he said with a smile hinting of admiration.

Kyrin's gaze dropped back to Sam. "Goodbye. Please be careful, and please watch over Kaden as best you can."

"You have my word."

Kyrin's raw throat constricted with a fierce sting and reduced her voice to a hoarse whisper. "Tell him how much I love him."

Sam gave a solemn nod. "I will."

He then motioned for Tane to go. The other talcrin turned his horse around, and Kyrin's followed. As they trotted away, she looked back at the three men who'd saved her life and breathed a prayer for their protection.

They maintained a steady trot through the city, heading north, the horses' shod hooves clacking sharply on the stone. Kyrin's pulse matched the rhythm and throbbed in her head. Even in the darkness, she felt so exposed on the empty streets. She eyed the shadows ahead, just waiting for them to produce a swarm of gold and black that would drag her back to the dungeon.

Twenty minutes of tense travel passed as they navigated the winding, sometimes narrow, city streets. Kyrin's chest started to ache from the constant, heavy battering of her heart, but they reached the outskirts without incident and slowed. With quieter hoof beats, they passed through one of the gates, and Tane motioned her to halt just beyond the wall. They sat still and listened for a moment before Tane murmured, "This is the last you'll see of Valcré."

Kyrin peered through the gate. The entire city lay on the other side, illuminated by the moons. The palace rose above it all—a pale, gold structure. Her eyes dropped to where Tarvin Hall lay, and a stone formed in her throat. For the first time in ten years, she was leaving Valcré, but she did so without her brother.

It was so very wrong. They'd arrived here together—scared little children who only had each other—and now they should be leaving and facing yet another new life together. Her breath hitched.

"Are you ready?" Tane asked.

Kyrin's eyes swept the city one last time. She had spent most of her life in Valcré. Just what kind of life awaited her outside of it? One she had no choice but to face without someone familiar at her side. It took effort, but she cleared her swollen throat.

"Yes, I'm ready."

Tane turned his horse to the east, and the two of them rode off again at a faster, more urgent pace.

The sun rose and beamed warm on Kyrin's face. It held a certain beauty this morning, but failed to penetrate the over-whelming pain and weariness she fought to keep at bay. She gripped both the reins and the saddle with her right hand and struggled to breathe through every burning jolt the horse's gait shot through her shoulder. For more than an hour, she'd resisted the need to call for a break. She wouldn't be able to go on much longer, but she didn't have to. Her talcrin companion pulled his brown horse to a halt, and Kyrin's sorrel stopped beside him. Both mounts panted, with foamy white sweat lathering their chests. Tane patted his horse's neck.

"We'll rest here for a while."

He swung down from his saddle. Kyrin moved much more slowly and held her left arm close. Every part of her body ached. When her sore feet touched the ground, her legs almost gave out. Fortunately, Tane reached out to steady her.

"Come, sit over by this tree," he said.

With him supporting her arm, Kyrin took wobbly steps to a large maple growing alongside the road and sank into the soft grass at the base of its trunk. The last time she'd rested comfortably was back in her room before Lady Videlle came for her. How many days ago was that?

Tane returned to the horses, dug in his saddlebags, and brought Kyrin a waterskin, a bag of jerky, and some dried apples.

"Take it slow at first," he cautioned.

Kyrin lifted the waterskin to her lips and sipped slowly, letting the water wash around in her mouth before trickling down her parched throat.

"There you go," Tane said with a smile.

While Kyrin dug into the jerky bag, Tane turned to unsaddle and brush the horses before letting them graze on the lush grass beside the road. The jerky and apples were not palace food, but none of the emperor's dinners had ever been as satisfying. With the nourishment, physical strength returned to her.

"How do you feel?" Tane asked after she'd taken another long drink.

Kyrin wiped a little water from her chin, noting how her hand came away smeared with red, and looked at the talcrin. "All right, I guess."

"How about since you were hit with the rock?"

Kyrin grimaced. "I've had a headache ever since I woke up in the cell. And I feel sick once in a while." Three times she'd nearly thrown up during the ride.

"You probably have a concussion. It would be best if you could take it easy the next few days, but we'll have to keep riding. What about your arm? I heard what happened with Richard."

Kyrin wrapped her hand around her left shoulder. "It hurts quite a bit, especially when I'm riding, but I can move it."

"Doesn't sound like it's dislocated, fortunately. We'll put it in a sling and that will help."

Tane reached into one of the supply packs and pulled out a wooden bowl, cloth, and a small looking glass. He filled the bowl with water and handed the three items to Kyrin.

"First things first, we'll get you cleaned up and prepared for the rest of our journey."

Kyrin held up the looking glass to see her reflection. Dried blood stained half her face, originating from a surprisingly small wound just above her left brow. "I look awful," she murmured.

"Thankfully, it's not as bad as it looks," Tane told her. "Everyone was worried."

"Were you there when it happened?"

He nodded. "I think almost everyone was."

Kyrin shuddered at the memory. It would surely haunt her for some time to come. "I've never seen anything like it."

"Neither have I."

Putting it out of her mind, she soaked the cloth and wiped the blood and leftover cosmetics from her face. She frowned at the jagged strands of hair that fell just to her shoulders or shorter. She always had been different from everyone else. Now her appearance reflected that, and it wouldn't be easy to hide.

Glancing up from the looking glass, she asked, "Where are you taking me?"

"Marlton first, but from there you'll likely go on to Landale."

Kyrin pictured a map of Arcacia. Landale wasn't far from Valcré. Only about two days' ride. Not as far as she'd expected to have to go to escape the emperor. "What's in Landale?"

"Baron Grey's son has set up a secret camp in the forest for people exactly like you who will be fleeing the emperor. As far as I know, you'll be the first one to come under these circumstances." Tane sighed, his eyes a solemn, shadowed gray. "But, after this, there will be more."

"What do you mean?"

"What happened, or what was going to happen to you, is something we've feared for years."

Kyrin set aside the looking glass to listen more closely.

"Had you been killed, it would've been the first public execution for believing in Elôm in the history of Ilyon. It was the first step in plans Daican's been preparing since before you were born. Yesterday was only the beginning. Arcacia is about to change dramatically."

These last words drew goose bumps from Kyrin's skin. What terrible scheme had she somehow found herself caught up in?

"What will change? What are his plans?"

"For years he's increased his power, preparing, but it didn't just start with him. It started with his father. That's why Tarvin Hall was established. It's all for control. And now that Daican has publically declared the worship of Elôm to be a crime punishable by death, and the people have accepted it, there will be many others just like you."

Bits of memories collected in Kyrin's mind—Daniel's words, and even things the emperor himself had said—fitting together to form a clear picture. "He's building the legacy his father was working toward."

Tane nodded slowly. "Neither one of them ever looked kindly on the followers of Elôm."

Kyrin rubbed her eyes with her fingertips. If only she could sleep and forget the emperor for at least a brief couple of hours. How had she not seen this happening? This quest for control and power brewing around her. But how could she? She'd grown up at Tarvin Hall surrounded by the emperor's lies. *Lies.*

Her gaze lifted back to Tane. "I never attacked the emperor. He lied."

"Ah, I was going to ask you about that. We suspected it was a lie. No doubt it was to paint a picture of the followers of Elôm as dangerous and violent enemies. It was all in how he wanted the people to perceive you. The whole day from the moment of your arrest until you were brought to the square, he had men spreading the lies, firing up the city, and turning everyone against you.

That's why he presented you to them the way he did. He wanted them to see you as more than just a common criminal, and leave an image in their minds that would prevent them from questioning what's coming."

No wonder they had so passionately screamed for her death. Kyrin gulped. They would want it just as much now as yesterday. "Daican will do everything he can to find me."

"Don't worry," Tane reassured her. "I'll make sure you get to Landale. You'll be safe there."

"Thank you."

Tane smiled, reminding her comfortingly of Sam.

Letting talk of the emperor rest for now, Kyrin finished cleaning her face, and Tane applied a salve to the cut. He rummaged through the supply packs again, and after stringing a bit of rope and a blanket between two trees, he handed Kyrin a bundle of clothing.

"You can finish cleaning up and change if you'd like."

Eager, Kyrin took the clothing and cleaning supplies behind the hanging blanket. Careful of her arm, she changed out of her filth-covered shift and cast it aside. Only now did she notice how badly it reeked of garbage and mildew. Once she'd cleaned up, she slipped into the fresh clothing—a pair of sturdy linen pants, a soft blue shirt, and a dark gray overdress better suited for riding. She ran her hand down the front. What a strange thing not to see herself in black and gold. They were colors she'd worn every single day for ten years, but she never wanted to see her wretched uniforms again. If she'd still had her gold dress, she would have burned it. She checked her feet for cuts, but found only bruises, and pulled on her boots again.

Brushing her fingers through her tangled hair, she stepped out from behind the blanket. Tane had gathered up the horses and changed as well. In contrast to the dark brown clothing he'd worn before, he now donned a distinct black and gold uniform.

"You're a courier?"

The talcrin shook his head with a smile. "Yes and no. It's more a cover than an actual job. I do take some messages to and from Valcré to keep up appearances, but my main objective is delivering news from Valcré to Landale and other groups of believers. I keep them informed of the progress of the emperor's plans."

"And you get that information from Sir Aric," Kyrin guessed. Being head of Daican's security, he must hear a lot.

"Him and Mister Foss, mostly."

Kyrin's mouth fell open. "Mister Foss? Daican's secretary?"

"Yes," Tane said slowly. "Why?"

Kyrin shook her head in surprise. All those times she'd worked miserably with him, they'd been on the same side. Out of everyone in the palace, he'd certainly fooled her the most. "I never would've guessed Mister Foss. He was always so . . . bad-tempered. Everyone hated him."

Tane chuckled. "It's a perfect cover."

"So he's a believer in Elôm?"

"Actually, no, but he holds no love for the emperor either. I believe it has something to do with his wife's death, but whatever reason, he's been one of our main suppliers of information, being privy to nearly all the emperor's most sensitive documents."

Kyrin stood for a long moment to let this sink in. She'd had more allies at Auréa than she ever imagined.

"I hate to ask this of you," Tane said, breaking into her thoughts, "but can you keep riding? It's important that we keep our lead on Daican's men."

Kyrin gave a firm nod. All she truly wanted was to drop down with a blanket and sleep, but eating had provided the strength to move on. Once Tane had the horses re-saddled, he tied her arm up in a sling and wrapped a bandage around it and her middle to keep her arm in place while they rode. He helped her up into the saddle, and they took to the road again with a prayer to stay well ahead of any pursuers.

KYRIN LET OUT a wide yawn and rubbed the sleep from her eyes. A full day of riding left her stiff and sore, but the night's sleep had done wonders in restoring her energy. Stretching, she sat up and carefully maneuvered her injured arm. Still tender. She slipped her sling over her head and crawled out of the little tent Tane had set up for her. The talcrin knelt at the fire, cooking a pot of bubbling porridge.

His flashing white smile greeted her. "Good morning."

She echoed him and smiled in return. If she'd learned one thing about him in the last day together, it was that he always found something to take joy in, no matter what the situation was. Such an attitude was contagious.

"How's your head?" he asked.

Kyrin shrugged her good shoulder and joined him at the fire. "The cut stings, but the headache's gone." It would certainly make riding easier not to have her head pounding along with the horses' hooves. Maybe the nausea wouldn't return either.

Tane dished up a bowl of porridge for her. Balancing the bowl on her knees, she took a bite before saying, "I don't know your full name."

He looked at her appreciatively. "Most people don't even realize we have longer names. It's Imhonriltane. It means 'little

293

warrior.'" He shrugged and chuckled deeply. "I was born unusually small for a talcrin. But I've grown some."

Kyrin laughed with him. Tane was every bit as tall and powerful as Sam.

"So, what does Endathlorsam mean? I never thought to ask him."

"Oak tree," Tane replied. "Well-suited, I'd say."

Kyrin agreed. "Very well."

They talked a little of Tane's family—his parents and Sam being the only ones who lived outside of Arda—but hurried through breakfast in order to be on their way. Kyrin had just finished her last bite when Tane's attention jumped to the road. Kyrin stiffened, and her skin turned icy. She prayed it would be nothing, but Tane exclaimed, "Someone's coming! Grab your things and hide, quick."

Kyrin scrambled to her feet, bowl still in hand, as a terror threaded through her that she hadn't felt since the walk to the square. Tane reached for the extra saddle and glanced back at her, his voice calm despite the urgency in his eyes.

"Remember, if anything happens, follow the road straight east. It will take you right to Marlton."

Her heart surely matched the pace of a fleeing rabbit as she dashed into the tent and grabbed anything that would give them away. Ducking out the back, she pushed into the thick brush lining the road. Branches snapped to her left as Tane concealed her saddle and the extra supplies. By now, fast-approaching hoof beats rumbled just up the road. Kyrin dropped to the ground and lay still. She clutched her pack, and her breath trembled in and out. Through the brush, she had a small view of camp. Tane had returned to sit by the fire.

A few seconds later, five horses galloped into camp, scattering dirt as they skidded to a halt. Kyrin only had a view of their legs, but their panting and snorting rattled toward the bushes. A couple of the riders dismounted, boots stomping to the ground, and Tane rose.

"Can I help you?"

"We're searching for an escaped prisoner," a deep, rough voice said. "She's a dangerous fugitive and a traitor to Arcacia."

"She?" Tane feigned surprise.

"Yes, a young woman, seventeen years old. She's the granddaughter of Jonavan Altair." He ground out the name like a curse. "She'll be easy to recognize. Her hair has been cut, and she has a wound on her forehead."

The man turned, apparently surveying their camp. "Are you the only one here?"

"Looks that way."

Though Kyrin could not see their faces, the other man's voice lowered in suspicion. "There are two horses."

"Never know when one might turn up lame while delivering an important message. I like to be prepared."

After a brief pause, the other man turned again. "Search the camp."

His men obeyed, and Kyrin sucked in her breath. What if she'd left something behind? Her heart thumped like a fist into the ground, and her lips moved in a silent prayer.

The leader turned back to Tane. "Let me see your papers."

Tane produced the official documents confirming his status as a courier in the emperor's service. The man examined them thoroughly. Meanwhile, one of the other men looked in the tent. After a long moment, the soldier seemed satisfied, though he now faced the bushes. Kyrin held her breath, but resisted the urge to shrink back. Any movement could give her away. When the leader spoke again, the soldier turned, and Kyrin let her eyes slide closed as she breathed out slowly.

"What areas do you cover?" the leader asked Tane.

"Around Landale mostly."

"I want you to bring word of the Altair girl's escape to all the villages in the vicinity. Anyone who can bring her in to Valcré either alive or dead will receive one thousand gold pieces, and anyone with useful information will receive five hundred."

Tane gave a low whistle. "That's quite an incentive."

"As I said, she is a dangerous fugitive. Make sure all are aware of this, and the reward."

Tane must have nodded because he said nothing. Satisfied, the men returned to their horses. In another minute, they galloped on down the road. Kyrin didn't move until several minutes later when Tane called her out. Crawling from the bushes, she stood with shaky legs.

"That was close."

"Too close," Tane murmured. "It's probably best we take to the forest from here. It will slow us down, but we don't want to run into them again."

Full darkness had fallen nearly two hours before. Tane scanned the grounds of Marlton Hall, the home of a retired knight, before he motioned for Kyrin to follow him from the shelter of the forest. All lay still and quiet except for the nighttime bugs and frogs from a nearby pond. Nothing stirred, but warm light glowed from one window of the large house.

They moved in silence through the yard and up to the back door. Glancing over his shoulder once, Tane tapped lightly on the door, and they waited a moment. Before he had to try again, the latch lifted. The door opened a little, and a thin stream of light speared across the threshold, landing on Tane's face.

"Tane," a deep male voice murmured in surprise. "I thought it might be Trask." The door opened wider. "Come in."

Tane stepped inside. "No, not Trask, but we'll need to speak with him. I've brought the first refugee for his camp."

He motioned to Kyrin, and she walked into a warm living area. Her eyes landed first on the strong-bodied man who had let them in, and then on a woman nearby. Both were in their late fifties and looked on her with curiosity.

"This is Kyrin Altair," Tane said, laying his hands on her shoulders. "Kyrin, this is Sir John Wyland and his wife, Lady Catherine."

Kyrin gave them a smile and clasped her hands to keep from fidgeting. "Pleased to meet you."

Sir John repeated her name. "Are you related to Jonavan Altair?"

"Yes, he was my grandfather," Kyrin answered, uncertain as to whether she should feel apprehensive or not. His voice lacked the scorn the name typically evoked.

Sir John's eyes shifted back to Tane. "What brings you here?"

"Father?"

The voice drew their attention to the stairs, where a young woman descended as she wrapped a robe around her nightgown. Dark hair fell in large curls around her shoulders and down her back.

"Annie, I thought you were asleep," John said.

"Not quite." She looked at the talcrin. "Hello, Tane."

"Anne," he replied.

Her eyes rested on Kyrin, deep blue and kind, yet hinting of strength. She couldn't be more than a few years older than Kyrin. Tane promptly introduced her as John and Catherine's daughter, Lady Anne. They traded smiles before Tane returned to the matter at hand.

His expression more serious than usual, he looked at Sir John and said, "I'm afraid it's starting. Kyrin was scheduled for execution at dawn yesterday in Valcré for refusing to worship Aertus and Vilai."

Lady Catherine's hand fluttered to her throat, and Sir John

closed his eyes for a moment. A shiver still passed through Kyrin at the mention of it. She'd be dead now if not for secret friends at the palace.

"How awful," Anne murmured as her gaze fell on Kyrin again. "Are you all right?"

"Thankfully, yes."

With a deep sigh, John said to Tane, "So it has begun, as you say. But thank the King it didn't go according to the emperor's plans."

"Indeed," Tane replied. "Sam and Aric suggested I bring her here. They thought Anne could help her prepare to go out to the camp."

"Of course," Anne said. "I'd be glad to help." She gave Kyrin a warm smile.

"Have you ridden all day?" Sir John asked.

Tane nodded. "We had to cut through the forest. We met some of the emperor's men this morning and didn't want to risk running into them again."

"Come, both of you, and sit down," Catherine invited and motioned to the couch and chairs near a large, dark fireplace. "I'll get you something warm to drink. You must be exhausted."

In a short time, everyone was seated with mugs of tea, and Kyrin and Tane relayed all the events back in Valcré. Once they'd discussed it in full, Tane focused on Anne. "Is Trask ready to receive anyone?"

"I haven't seen him in a few days, but last I heard, progress on the cabins was going smoothly. He should be about ready. If not, I'm sure it'll be no trouble for Kyrin to stay here." She looked to her parents for affirmation.

"Of course," John replied, facing Kyrin. "You may remain here as long as you need. We'll just have to keep you out of sight from Goler's men."

"We'll manage," Anne said. "They haven't been hanging around quite so much lately."

"Thank you," Kyrin replied, unsure how to express her full gratitude.

Sir John nodded and said to his daughter, "Annie, why don't you show Kyrin to a room?" He rose from his chair. "Tane, I can help you with the horses and then we'll see about getting you a comfortable bed for the night."

Tane smiled his appreciation, and the rest of them stood. Kyrin followed Anne upstairs into a spare bedroom where the young woman lit a couple of candles that cast a warm light.

"I'll get you a nightgown and something to change into in the morning."

She disappeared across the hall, and Kyrin's eyes wandered over the room. A pang of longing stabbed her. Something about it reminded her very much of home—of her own room, simple, but filled with her dolls and toys and everything she'd ever loved. Kaden used to come in and run off with them, but he always gave them back if she started to cry. A quiet laugh broke from her squeezing throat.

Anne returned and draped a nightgown across the bed and laid an extra set of clothes over a chair. She turned to Kyrin. "My room is just across the hall. If there's anything at all you need, please ask."

Kyrin worked out a smile, though her cheeks were heavy. "Thank you."

She just stood after that, not quite sure what to say or do. The thickness in her throat pushed up toward her nose and forced moisture to her eyes. She blinked against the stinging pressure.

Anne placed her hand gently on Kyrin's arm. "It's all right to cry."

With that permission, the tears dribbled over Kyrin's eyelids.

"I don't know why I'm crying," she murmured. "I'm so thankful to be safe, it's just . . ."

"Overwhelming?" Anne supplied. She rubbed Kyrin's arm. "I can't imagine."

Kyrin wiped trembling fingers across her cheeks. "I just wish my brother were here. We're twins, and we were brought to Tarvin Hall when we were very young. We've faced everything together except for what has happened recently. I just want to know he's safe."

"It's always difficult when we fear for our loved ones. I'm sure your friends in Valcré will do whatever they can to protect your brother, just as they did you. The best thing we can do is pray and trust Elôm to bring him out."

Sniffing, Kyrin nodded. Trust was the only thing she had.

RAYAD LEFT THE tent and stretched. A still and quiet mist shrouded the forest. He scanned the campsite, but Jace was nowhere in sight. He barely saw him these days, but he still showed up in camp every night. For now, that was all Rayad could ask.

His eyes drifted to one of the recently completed cabins. A little smoke curled from the chimney. Camp had gained its first female member the day before—Lenae, the mother of one of the young men. Widowed, she'd been living in Landale Village alone, but Trask had asked her to move out to the forest with her son.

Rayad smiled in spite of his estrangement with Jace. Lenae's presence was good for camp life. Everyone enjoyed her kindness and mothering. She'd even cooked up a delicious supper for everyone the night before. Some of the men were a bit jealous that Jeremy, her son, would get to enjoy her cooking regularly. Rayad chuckled. He wouldn't mind that himself. He could cook up a good meal, but it just never tasted quite the same as a woman's cooking.

The soft, muffled sound of hooves drew Rayad's attention to the trees. It couldn't be Trask, since he'd spent the night in camp. Warin joined Rayad just as a tall, brown horse appeared through the fog. The sight of the rider's dark skin surprised Rayad. He hadn't seen a talcrin in years. Most who still lived outside of Arda kept to the big cities where the universities and libraries were plentiful.

"It's Tane," Warin said with his own tone of surprise.

Rayad looked at him in question.

"He brings most of the news from Valcré," Warin explained. "He must be here to see Trask. I wonder why he didn't wait at Landale Castle."

Drawn by the growing commotion, Trask emerged from one of the tents and met the talcrin rider. Rayad and Warin both moved to join them, curious what news he brought. They reached the pair just as they concluded their greetings.

"You must have important news," Trask said.

"Unfortunately, yes." Tane paused with a glance at Rayad and Warin before refocusing on Trask's intent expression. "The emperor has made his stand public. It's now a crime punishable by death to worship any god other than Aertus and Vilai."

Rayad's stomach sank like a bag of rocks. Of course, they all knew it was coming, but part of him hoped it wouldn't be within his lifetime.

Trask's head dropped as he let out a sigh, but then he looked back up at Tane. "Was someone executed?"

"Nearly. We got her out the night before her execution."

Trask's brows rose. "*Her?*"

Tane nodded. "A young woman from Tarvin Hall. Kyrin Altair."

"Altair," Rayad repeated.

The talcrin's silver-blue eyes came to him. "Yes, the grand-daughter of Jonavan Altair. She has very unique abilities. The emperor requested her specifically to serve him, but my uncle led her and her brother to knowledge of Elôm while at Tarvin Hall. Daican must have suspected her and tried to force her to bow before the idols in the palace temple. She refused."

"Brave girl," Trask said.

"Very brave," Tane replied. "And your first refugee. I don't know if you're ready to take her. She's at Marlton Hall right now."

"Lenae, Jeremy's mother, just moved into the finished cabin. I'm sure she'd be happy to have Miss Altair stay with her once she's ready."

"Good. My uncle will be glad to know she's well looked after."

Kyrin awoke to a sound she had not heard in the morning for years—birds singing. Robins warbled, and somewhere a sparrow gave an exuberant trill. For a long moment, she didn't move, relishing the beauty of it. Anne had told her to remain in bed as long as she needed. A novel thought that was. There had been no sleeping in at Tarvin Hall or the palace. She lifted her head to peek out the window. Judging by the brightness of the sun, it must be well past when she usually rose.

She ducked her chin back under the warm covers, but the new surroundings beckoned her to get up and look around. After all, this was the first stop in establishing her new life. Her insides fluttered, and she pushed away the blanket. The cool air sent a tingle through her exposed arms and feet. She slipped out of bed to wash up and change into the clothing Anne had left. At the mirror, she brushed through her short hair, frowning at the chopped, uneven pieces. Still, the important thing was she had escaped with her life.

The savory smell of bacon set Kyrin's stomach to rumbling as she descended the stairs. She would never complain about food after her time in the dungeon, but something other than porridge and simple trail meals would be wonderful. Kaden would agree . . . if he were here.

At the bottom of the steps, she came upon a servant girl bent over a broom and dustpan. The young woman straightened as her bright eyes rose. Kyrin paused. Did the girl know the Wylands had a guest? One that so happened to be considered a traitor by the Arcacian government? Thankfully, Anne walked in.

"Good morning, Kyrin," she greeted. She then smiled at the maid. "Sara, this is the guest I told you about, Kyrin Altair."

"Pleased to meet you, Miss Altair," the young woman said sweetly.

Kyrin smiled, and Anne asked, "Sara, will you please get Kyrin's breakfast?"

"Right away, my lady."

She hurried out of the room, and Anne led Kyrin to the table.

"You don't have to worry about the servants," she told her. "They're aware of the situation, but would never give you away."

Kyrin breathed freer with this knowledge.

"How did you sleep?" Anne asked as they each took a seat.

"Very well," Kyrin was happy to answer. Better than her nights at Auréa. "It was just what I needed." She looked around. She and Anne were the only two present. "Where's Tane?"

"He left around dawn for Landale. He wanted to talk to Trask and see if he has a place ready for you in camp."

"So, it's in the forest?"

Anne nodded, and Kyrin considered this. Living in the forest would be a different world compared to life in Arcacia's largest city. But it sounded peaceful. Not too many people, and no need to pretend to be someone she wasn't. Exactly what she and Kaden had dreamed of.

"I'm sure they'll have you living comfortably in a cabin." Anne smiled mischievously. "In fact, I'll make sure they do."

A wide smile broke across Kyrin's face. She liked Anne a lot. She liked her strength and spirit.

Through a delicious meal of fresh eggs and bacon, Anne remained with Kyrin at the table to talk. Lady Catherine joined them as well. The three of them were deep in a conversation about Tarvin Hall when a gentle knock came at the back door. Anne rose to answer it.

"Well, look who decided to show," she said with a smile in her voice.

She opened the door wider. A man in his late twenties with chestnut-brown hair stepped inside. He wore a grin, his eyes twinkling down at Anne. Tane walked in behind him.

"So, you finally came to say hello?" Anne asked as she raised an eyebrow.

"Actually, I came to meet Miss Altair," the man answered.

"Oh, so it wasn't for me?"

"I didn't say that."

He bent a little closer as if to kiss her, but Anne just grinned and turned away from him. "Kyrin, this is Baron Grey's son, Trask."

Kyrin rose to meet him, and he greeted her with a kind smile. An endearing air of mischief and good humor sparkled in his eyes. Any fears she had about meeting new people without the support of her brother were quickly vanishing.

"Tane told me about your ordeal in Valcré," Trask said. "We don't often see bravery like that these days. You'll be very welcome in camp. The mother of one of my men just moved out there. She was delighted when I asked if she would share her cabin."

"It sounds very nice," Kyrin replied, and she meant it. It would take some getting used to on her part, but if the woman was as kind and accommodating as the Wylands and Trask, it wouldn't be hard. She'd never had a good relationship with any of the female instructors at Tarvin Hall. In fact, she had never had a good relationship with any older woman. Hopefully this would be the first.

"Then, whenever you're ready, I'll come and take you to camp," Trask said.

"You can give us a couple of days," Anne told him. "I'll get her clothes and see she has anything else she needs."

"Sounds good. I'm sure Lenae will have the cabin ready for two people by then."

Before they could go on, the sound of hoof beats came from out front. Lady Catherine hurried to the window.

"It's Goler and his men," she said in a hushed but urgent voice.

Kyrin's heart took a hard stumble. If the emperor found her here, she wouldn't be the only one to pay the price.

"Not again," Anne muttered. She faced Trask. "All of you, in the kitchen, quick. He won't go in there."

Tane motioned for Kyrin to follow, and they hurried toward the kitchen. Trask, however, lingered behind.

"Go," Anne urged him. "It won't do any good for him to find you here."

Kyrin glanced back. Trask's relaxed expression had gone hard, but he followed them into the kitchen. The servants there just looked at them and quietly went back to work. Tane started to close the door, but Trask held it open a little so he could see out into the dining room. Loud footsteps sounded on the porch outside, followed by a forceful knock. A moment later, the door opened.

"Captain Goler," Catherine's voice filtered into the kitchen, "what brings you here this morning?"

A deep, yet smooth voice replied, "Is Lady Anne in?"

Following a brief silence, Anne answered, "Yes, I'm here."

Boots clomped on the floorboards with the faint jingle of spurs. Kyrin leaned forward to peek through a small crack in the door planks. A man stood near the table facing Anne. The sight of his gold and black uniform wound Kyrin's insides into a tight coil. He was average height, a little on the heavy side, and had long, dirty-blond hair. Though she didn't have a view of his whole face, she caught sight of a long scar starting at the bridge of his crooked nose and trailing down his right cheek. He certainly wasn't a handsome man, though the way he held himself suggested he believed he was.

"How are you this fine morning, Anne?" he asked with a wolfish smile, displaying surprisingly white teeth.

"*Lady* Anne," Trask muttered to himself.

"Very well, thank you," Anne answered primly.

A pause followed in which Goler clearly took pleasure in the sight of her. Trask tensed and his fists clenched, but Tane put his hand on Trask's shoulder and shook his head.

"Is there something I can do for you?" Anne asked. She had a definite edge to her voice now.

With a smug smile still perched on his damp lips, Goler said, "I just came from Landale Village. I'm looking for Trask. He wasn't around, so I thought I'd come by and see if you've seen him."

Anne shrugged. "Trask always has something keeping him busy these days. He hasn't been around here regularly." Her prim tone had returned, no doubt with full knowledge that Trask could hear every word.

"I see," Goler replied, though he didn't sound convinced.

"What is it you wish to speak with him about?"

"I received news about an escaped prisoner from Valcré. I wondered if Trask might know something."

"And why would that be?"

Goler's smile stretched into a vicious grin. "Just a guess. Perhaps I'll stop by Landale again later this evening and see if he's around. And, when time permits, I'll come call on you again. Maybe you would join me for an afternoon ride one of these days before the weather turns too hot."

"My days are usually pretty full. I've got new gowns to make, needlework to finish—you know, those sorts of things." She smiled sweetly, but it didn't reach her eyes. "Always something more to do."

Goler's grin cooled. "Of course. Nevertheless, keep it in mind. I will ask again." He nodded to Lady Catherine before his gaze swung back to Anne. "Good day, my ladies."

Spurs jingled again and signaled his exit. Kyrin, Trask, and Tane waited for the sound of hoof beats to die away before leaving the kitchen. Trask glared at the door where Goler had left as if to send fire after the man.

"I don't like him coming out here," he told Anne.

She shrugged and appeared less bothered than Kyrin would be in her position. "Neither do I, but there's nothing we can do about it. Usually, Father is around, and that helps."

"You won't accept his invitation to a ride, will you?"

"Not unless I have to."

Trask's frown deepened. "That could be dangerous. I could throw him farther than I trust him."

"If he pushes, I may have no choice but to go, or he'll start to grow more suspicious."

"Well, if you must, set a time and let me know. I can follow from cover. He'll never know I'm there . . . unless, of course, I have to beat him senseless."

Anne laughed. "I would hope it doesn't come to that, but I'll let you know."

"Good," Trask said with a nod. "Now, I better get back to camp and see that everything's taken care of there. I want to be home if Goler shows up tonight." His smile resurfaced when he turned to Kyrin. "I look forward to showing you out to camp."

She thanked him, and Anne followed him to the door.

"Be careful," she cautioned. "I don't trust Goler around you either."

WILLIAM ALTAIR EASED down into the canvas folding chair at the desk in his officer's tent and absently flipped through a stack of reports. It was a slow time at Fort Rivor, where many of the kingdom's battalions were stationed. Aside from drills and training new recruits, his day mainly consisted of paperwork. It was not quite the adventurous life he thought he'd signed up for in his youth, but he was old enough now to appreciate the quiet moments, dull as they might be.

He'd just settled in for the long afternoon of sifting through endless figures when someone threw back the tent flap. A fellow captain stepped inside. William peered at him over the papers. Though the man saluted with his right fist to his chest, they had never been on particularly friendly terms. Bearing the name of Altair saw to that, but he rose and did the same.

"An urgent message from Valcré, Captain," the man announced.

Whether it was the look in the other captain's eyes or simply intuition, William's heart stopped. It could be anything, but somehow, by instinct, Kyrin's face appeared in his mind.

A courier stepped into the tent at the other captain's bidding. The man looked to have been riding hard.

"Captain Altair, I bring unfortunate news from the emperor. Your daughter has denied the gods . . ."

In that heartbeat of frozen time, William leaned forward and braced himself against the desk. She'd done it. His brave daughter had stood for her faith. But at what price? The weight of these thoughts nearly drowned out the courier's next words.

". . . and attacked His Majesty."

William's eyes snapped back to the courier. "Attacked the emperor?"

"Yes, sir," the courier confirmed.

William frowned deeply, but he became aware of the intense way in which the other captain watched him. He licked his lips and struggled to find his voice as he prepared for the worst. Already his heart had begun to rip in two, burning through his chest.

"And what . . . has been done with her?"

"She was scheduled for execution, but somehow disappeared three nights ago. We believe other traitors were involved."

William barely caught himself from blowing out a great sigh. Careful to keep his face neutral, he asked, "Is the emperor taking strides to find her?"

"He is, sir. He has set a generous reward for her capture or information on her location. Every effort will be made to locate her."

William gave a slow nod. "Thank you for bringing word."

The courier nodded and left the tent. William's eyes shifted to the other captain, who said, "You must be devastated. I can't imagine the pain of one of your children bringing such dishonor to the family."

Smugness tainted every word.

"This certainly will be a great blow to us," William responded quietly. Though it mattered little to him, it would further sully the Altair name and be difficult for the rest of the family. The captain watched him intently, as if waiting for him to slip up, so he continued, "Thank you for your concern. Will you please send word to my sons that I wish to see them? I would like the news to come from me."

"Of course," the man responded coolly.

Saluting again, he backed out of the tent. When the flap had fallen into place, William sank into his chair and rubbed his hands over his face.

"Oh, Lord, thank You for sparing my daughter," he breathed.

Not more than a few minutes later, footsteps approached the tent. Marcus ducked in first, Liam on his heels. Marcus's brows were furrowed, while Liam wore a wide-eyed look of worry as they faced their father.

"You have bad news?" Marcus asked.

"Yes." Though Kyrin lived, it was hard news to deliver because, unlike him, they would not understand it, and they would surely have questions he could not easily answer. "I've just received word from Valcré. Apparently, Kyrin has renounced Aertus and Vilai and . . ." He hesitated. This part was all wrong. "She attacked the emperor."

"What?" Marcus's eyes grew wide as he glanced at Liam. "It can't be."

"I'm afraid it is."

Marcus shook his head. "But . . . how could she do that?"

William winced at the confusion in his son's eyes. *Let this provide an opening for the truth.* "It's what she believes."

It's what I believe, wanted to come out with it, but he couldn't shock them further. There were better times and ways.

Marcus stood processing it for a long moment. He shook his head and murmured, "I can't believe she would do that." Then something seemed to occur to him. When his eyes returned to his father, pain had taken the place of confusion, but his expression was one of acceptance. "What's been done with her?"

William glanced at Liam. He had yet to say a word, but he didn't appear nearly as accepting as his brother. Fear made him look more like an uncertain young boy than the tall man he'd grown to be.

"She was scheduled for execution," he told them, "but managed to escape."

He watched both their reactions. Liam didn't hide his relief, letting go a pent-up breath, but Marcus hesitated. Certainly, there was relief, but his strong sense of duty was winning the struggle. This hurt William almost as much as Liam's fear. He couldn't be more proud of his son's work and dedication, but why must it be so misplaced?

"I'm sure the emperor will do whatever he can to find her," Marcus said, though his voice wasn't as strong as usual.

Liam gave him a disbelieving look but said nothing. Marcus didn't seem to notice, asking, "What about Kaden?"

William shook his head. "I didn't hear anything about him." But how he ached for his middle son. How was he coping with this? He'd never known closer siblings than Kyrin and Kaden. And how much longer until he too was found out? Surely, the emperor would have suspicions about him.

Marcus gave a slow nod. "Has word been sent to the General?"

"I don't know."

"I'll go find out," Marcus said in a calm and controlled voice.

William watched his son leave. He didn't have to be there to know how his father-in-law would explode in fury and surely blame him for passing on the traitorous bloodline of his father.

Left alone, he and Liam just looked at each other. Oh, to know what his son was thinking. He appeared to be fighting for understanding, as William knew he would. He and Kyrin had always been close, too. Of everyone, it would probably be the hardest for him to accept.

"Do you really think she attacked the emperor?" Liam spoke at last.

The entire barracks might believe him to be slow, but Liam had plenty of smarts and knew his sister well enough to see the lie right in from of them. William glanced at the tent flap.

"No," he murmured.

"Neither do I," Liam said, bringing a hint of a smile to William's lips. With hope in his eyes, he asked, "So . . . she's safe?"

"As far as I know."

Liam nodded with a glance over his shoulder. "Good."

Kaden wouldn't do it. He was done with Tarvin Hall. Done with the emperor. Done with everything. Now that Daican had nearly murdered his sister, he wanted nothing to do with anything the man stood for.

He'd refused to attend any of his classes since the day of Kyrin's arrest. Hour after hour, he sat alone near the outer wall of Tarvin Hall. Sometimes he didn't even come in for meals. Two guards stood nearby, always watching to make sure he didn't do anything "foolish." Different men rotated through this position, but Kaden never took much notice. Whatever happened now, he didn't care.

Midday and lunch hour had already passed when he glanced up to see Sam crossing the courtyard. But even the sight of a friend couldn't lift his dark mood. The talcrin paused to speak with the guards and then approached him, saying openly, "Kaden, it's been five days. You're just going to have to accept this and move on."

Though said purely for the benefit of the guards, Kaden still didn't like to hear it and scowled. Sam knelt in front of him.

"Listen to me," he said in a much lower yet deathly serious tone. "You really do need to stop sulking around and get back to your studies."

Kaden glared toward the Hall, but had enough sense to keep his voice down. "I won't do anything that serves the emperor."

"If you want to see Kyrin again, you'll have to," Sam said firmly. "Those guards over there are watching you for one reason— to see if you believe the same as your sister, and you're well on your way to convincing them you do."

"So why don't they just arrest me?"

Sam shook his head. "Either you're fortunate enough for them to think Kyrin's beliefs were exclusively her own, or they're biding their time. Kyrin's near execution was a turning point in this country. Things are beginning to happen that I've feared for years. The emperor is focused on his plans, but don't think he won't eventually remember you exist. That's why your situation is so dangerous. You're running out of time. You must convince them, Kaden. Convince them you don't need to be watched so closely. We can't get you out of here unless the emperor calls off his men. Do you understand that?"

Still stewing over Goler's visit to Marlton and his own inability to prevent such visits, Trask returned home to the castle in Landale and went straight for his father's office. He acknowledged Morris with a friendly greeting and then stepped inside.

"Trask," Grey said as he rose from his desk. "Goler was here to see you this morning. He brought word of a young woman who escaped execution in Valcré after refusing to worship the emperor's gods."

"I heard. I was at Marlton Hall when he showed up there looking for me. I hid in the kitchen while he talked with Anne." He scowled at the memory. He should have just faced the man there.

"He mentioned stopping by again this evening. You should go before he returns."

Trask shook his head. "I'm not going to hide from him. This is my home, and I have a thing or two to say to him anyway."

Grey sighed and rubbed his red-rimmed eyes with his fingers. "I just think it would be better to avoid the confrontation. I don't want to see you arrested."

"He doesn't have anything on me . . . yet. Nothing he can prove."

Grey put his hands out, his voice strained. "But how long until he does?"

Trask released a sigh of his own. He did hate to cause his father such concern and didn't like the way it weighed on his health, but he felt too strongly about his work to back out now. Before he could reassure him, Morris's gray head poked into the room.

"Excuse me, my lords. One of the servants has just informed me that Captain Goler is here to see Lord Trask."

"Guess that settles it," Trask muttered. He cast a glance at his father's tense face and strode out of the room. His father followed just behind. When they stepped into the grand parlor, Goler stood in the center of the room with his hands clasped behind his back and his jutting chin tipped up as if he were the baron. It was tempting to punch it back into place. Trask flexed his fist.

"Captain Goler, what a surprise," he said in a tone dripping with sarcasm. "To what do I owe the pleasure?"

Goler snorted. "I stopped by earlier."

"So I heard."

"Where were you this morning?"

Trask folded his arms and leaned casually against an armchair near the giant stone fireplace. "Out."

"Obviously, since you weren't here when I called," Goler replied tightly. "So again, I ask, where were you?"

Trask shrugged and studied the designs in the rug. "I have people to see, places to be." A cold smile grew on his face as he lifted his gaze. "Running Landale takes work, after all."

Goler's eyes darkened, matching the walls. "You're avoiding the question. I want to know specifics."

"And I, *Captain*, have no obligation to report my activities to you."

At this reminder of his low status compared to Trask's, Goler's face turned as red as an ember. Catching the way he gripped his sword scabbard with whitened knuckles, Trask had no doubt the man wished to run him through where he stood. He almost dared him to try.

His voice taut, Goler said, "You won't tell me because you're hiding something."

"What, pray tell, might I be hiding?"

A little of Goler's fury finally slipped, and he snapped, "An escaped prisoner, for one thing!"

Trask straightened. He was quite tired of this captain coming onto his father's estate and accusing him, whether or not the accusations held any truth. Like he'd told his father, the man had no proof to base such accusations on. "What would make you think I'd hide an escaped prisoner?"

Goler stepped up to Trask, their faces only inches apart. Trask's fist closed again. Any closer and he'd hit him.

"Because that's just the sort of thing you would do."

"And you know me that well, do you?"

"Well enough."

"You're wrong," Trask responded evenly. "*I* am not hiding any escaped prisoner." *Yet.*

Goler scowled. "I don't believe you."

Trask leaned a little closer. "Suit yourself."

The tension built between them, but Trask wouldn't back down. Not here in his own castle. Fortunately, his father stepped in before things could escalate to the point of violence.

"Captain Goler, I'm quite certain my son isn't hiding the girl. I would be aware of such a thing."

Goler just glared past the baron at Trask with a look that clearly spelled murder. One of these days, they'd have it out, and it would probably end with one or both of them in the ground.

"Very well," Goler conceded through clenched teeth. "I'll expect you to report any information or suspicious activity you might come across."

"Of course," Baron Grey said, and Goler took his leave, stomping out of the room.

Silence settled, and Grey turned. "You shouldn't provoke him."

Trask frowned deeply. "He shouldn't be coming in here making accusations. He's a despicable individual."

Baron Grey just shook his head and released a wearied breath, but his eyes sparked keenly. "You're not hiding the girl, are you?"

"No," Trask answered. "Not yet anyway. She's in Marlton with Anne. She's going to stay there a couple of days before coming out to camp."

"Do you know about the reward on her head?"

"Tane told me."

"Then you'll understand why Goler is so determined to find her."

Trask narrowed his eyes. "He's after the reward."

"Yes, and it will make him especially dangerous. You, Anne, and the girl need to be very careful. He'll stop at nothing if he thinks you're harboring her."

KYRIN SAT STILL as Anne moved around her, snipping off bits of hair to even it out.

"I'll show you how to put it up in a hairnet," Anne told her. "Then, unless they look closely, no one will be able to tell it's so short."

Kyrin smiled appreciatively. Anne's advice and help the last two days had been invaluable in preparing her to move out to the forest. She'd even gone to the market in Landale to purchase Kyrin several pairs of clothing that would suit her new life. It would be hard to leave Marlton after all this. Kyrin would miss Anne's companionship, but with Goler snooping around, it was time to go. Trask was set to come by to get her shortly. After all their kindness, she didn't want to endanger Anne and her parents any more than she had already.

"There, I think that will do," Anne announced. "You can have a look if you want."

Kyrin stood and stepped in front of the mirror. Her brown hair hung as straight as ever, right above her shoulders.

"I think it looks quite nice for what's there," Anne said.

Kyrin turned her head from side to side. "Thank you." Evened out, it did look significantly better than her previous hacked-off locks. At least for now it would be easier to manage.

She turned with Anne and followed her downstairs, sharing breakfast with Anne and her parents just before Trask showed up. His arrival brought yet another round of goodbyes. She'd already had to say goodbye to Tane when he'd left at dawn. This would be equally hard. She'd become so fond of the Wylands.

She said her goodbyes to Sir John and Lady Catherine inside the house. Both wished her the best and expressed their hope to see her again soon. She and Anne then joined Trask outside where he attached Kyrin's newly acquired possessions to the saddle of a beautiful dappled buckskin with three white socks and a wide blaze.

"This is Maera," he said as he stroked the horse's neck under her thick black mane. "If you find she suits you, she's yours."

Kyrin's eyes grew wide. "I can have her?"

"If you like her."

With a big smile, Kyrin rubbed her hand down the horse's nose. These people were more generous than any she'd ever known. "I'm sure I will."

When it came time for the final goodbye, Kyrin turned to Anne. "I wish I knew how to thank you. You've done so much for me and risked so much." She cleared her clogged throat. She wouldn't cry. That just made it too hard. "I'm going to miss it here. I'm so thankful for how you've helped me adjust and get through all this. I've had so very few friends in my life."

Anne smiled, her eyes bright and kind. "I've enjoyed getting to know you. You're quite an inspiration. I'll miss having you here." She looked at Trask. "You make sure she's comfortable out at camp, and see that those boys of yours treat her well."

"You have my word," Trask promised.

Anne's smile returned to Kyrin. "Don't worry. I'll come out to visit and see how you are. We aren't far apart." Following this statement, her eyes shifted past Kyrin once more. "What?"

Kyrin looked over her shoulder to catch the funny look on Trask's face.

He shrugged. "You've hardly ever come out to visit me."

"That's because you used to come around here more often."

"Ah, I guess it's my fault then."

Anne shook her head. "Whatever will I do with you?"

Again, Trask gave a little shrug as he eyed the reins he fiddled with. "Well, you could always marry me." He peeked up at her.

Anne fought to hide a smile, but it crept out anyway and dusted her cheeks with pink. "That's something we'll have to discuss another time. You two really should be going before Goler or his men show up. They have a habit of doing that at the worst times, you know."

Trask let out a great sigh. "As you wish, my lady."

He turned and swung up into his horse's saddle.

Kyrin and Anne shared a quick grin before Anne said, "Good-bye, Kyrin. I'll see you soon."

"I look forward to it," Kyrin replied as she, too, mounted.

"Be careful along the way," Anne warned, her seriousness returning. "You never know where Goler might turn up."

"We will," Trask assured her.

He gave her a charming smile and turned his horse. Kyrin followed him out of the yard and into the forest. He kept them in the trees and out of sight as a safety measure. Since Maera followed Trask's horse without much guidance, Kyrin took in the scenery—so green and lovely with the wildflowers in full bloom. Tiny, delicate white flowers blanketed the ground like snow in some areas. Deep purple violets peeked up through the grass, and vivid buttercups grew in the marshy areas. Meredith would have loved to be here to pick them. Pain needled Kyrin's ribs. If Kaden ever managed to get free, the little girl would be all alone, but Kyrin prayed Meredith would somehow find freedom too.

Not wanting to arrive at her new home in such low spirits, Kyrin looked over at Trask and her curiosity took over. Hopefully her question wouldn't upset him or invade his privacy.

"Why won't she say yes?"

Trask swung his alert eyes from the forest ahead over to her with an open and honest expression. "She has her reasons. I already proposed years ago, but she didn't think either of us were ready, and as much as I hate to admit it, she was right. Since then, circumstances just haven't been ideal, what with the emperor, Goler, and what I've got going on with camp. So, I keep waiting for the time to be right." He grinned. "It's got to come one of these days, so I'll just keep trying."

Kyrin shared in his smile. He and Anne would surely be perfect for each other when the right time came.

A half an hour after they left Marlton, they came upon a road where they drew the horses to a halt. Trask looked both ways, listening, but only birds and chattering squirrels disturbed the forest.

"Just another few miles from here," he said.

They crossed the road and entered the forest on the other side. After some time of winding along this way and that, the scent of wood smoke wafted through the trees. Kyrin's pulse picked up and her stomach fluttered, though not uncomfortably. They must be close. She rose up a little in the stirrups to see if she could spot camp, but the terrain was too hilly. Besides the smoke, she could find no true sign of human population. However, when they came up over a gradual slope, the campsite appeared, seemingly out of nowhere.

Kyrin's breath caught. This gathering of canvas tents and cabins nestled into a subtle bowl-shaped clearing in the forest would be her new home. She smiled. How peaceful it all looked compared to Valcré. Peaceful and safe. The security of this hidden place wrapped around her, warm and comfortable. Oh, if only Kaden were with her, then all would be perfect.

Their arrival sparked a wave of interest. The men who'd been busy at work set it aside and gathered to meet them as Kyrin and Trask dismounted in the center of camp. Drawing her to the front, Trask announced, "Everyone, this is Kyrin Altair."

He took the time to introduce her to each of the present members of camp. The men greeted her kindly with a few comments on her actions in Valcré. At their words of admiration, her cheeks warmed. Her actions usually weren't so well-received, but near martyr or not, she hoped their curiosity and fascination would wear off in time. She had no desire for them to treat her as something special. All she wanted was to live and be normal, and finally she would have a chance to do so.

As kind and welcoming as the men were, the only female face among them drew Kyrin's greatest interest. A lovely woman in her late forties, she had a quality of wisdom, yet also a spark of youthfulness in her dark blue eyes. She was about the same height as Kyrin and slim. A light brown braid fell over one shoulder. She smiled warmly when Trask introduced her as Lenae.

"Kyrin, I'm so very pleased to meet you. Come, let's get you settled in," she said. She looked at a young man who shared her hair and eye color. "Jeremy, will you bring her things into the cabin? And maybe someone else will take care of her horse."

Kyrin smiled to herself when at least three young men volunteered. Leaving them to sort things out, she walked along with Lenae to the nearest completed cabin. They stepped inside, and Kyrin paused to take it in. The one-room dwelling was small, but cozy and inviting. In just the few days Lenae had lived there, she had transformed it into a home. Shelves held an assortment of cooking and personal items, a good-sized dining room table and benches occupied the center of the cabin with a bed in one corner, and curtains even hung on the windows.

Lenae motioned to the loft above them. "We set up a bed for you up there. I hope you don't mind. I thought it would offer you some privacy."

Though no palace bedroom, it would be more than comfortable compared to life at Auréa. "It'll be perfect," she told Lenae with a smile.

She stepped away from the door to let Jeremy carry her

belongings inside and up to the loft. When he came back down, he turned to her with a striking smile.

"Is there anything else?"

"No, that's everything."

He just stood there a moment as if he wanted to say something but did not yet know the words. He fidgeted with his hands, and Kyrin smiled at him. He was cute and endearing— so different from the charming but overly confident Collin— and refreshingly innocent. He didn't have Collin's smooth tongue either. Apparently giving up on whatever he'd wanted to say, he glanced at his mother. "I guess I better get back to work."

On his way out, he flashed another wide smile at Kyrin. When he was gone, Lenae chuckled.

"I think you'll have many of the young men in camp enamored with you for a while, including my son."

Kyrin looked over her shoulder, out the door, to the men milling around. "That will be different. Only one boy at Tarvin Hall ever paid much attention to me, at least that sort of attention."

"Well, you're a lovely young woman."

Kyrin's eyes jumped back to Lenae. No one but her father had called her lovely before. All she'd ever heard and believed was that she was very plain, except, of course, when she was all painted up. But then she wasn't even herself. Warmth filled her chest with the knowledge that a beautiful woman like Lenae thought she was pretty, especially considering how she looked right now. Most would look at her and see only the shame of her shorn hair.

Lenae's bright expression softened, her voice gentle. "You know, I've always wanted a daughter. I prayed for one for many years. I only ended up with sons, and Jeremy is all I have left, but perhaps Elôm has answered my prayers with you."

Kyrin's lips lifted, but moisture prickled her eyes. "Growing up at Tarvin Hall, I really haven't had much in the way of a mother's care."

"Then I'd say Elôm is fulfilling the needs and desires of us both."

The afternoon hours passed with a comfort and peace Kyrin had not found since living at home as a child. Lenae helped her unpack her things and turn the loft into her own personal space before they shared lunch at the table with Jeremy. Though the young man struggled at first with just what to say, once he got going, he and his mother told her all about their life in Landale and transition to the forest. They'd lived such simple, yet fulfilling lives. Would it have been the same for her back in Mernin had she and Kaden not had to leave? Perhaps, but she would never know.

After lunch, Lenae showed her around camp. They stopped to talk along the way with the men who had many questions about the emperor, Valcré, and Kyrin's abilities. The afternoon flew by, and evening soon neared.

"I usually start supper about now," Lenae said on the way back to their cabin. "Trask insists I don't have to cook for everyone, but I enjoy it, and I know they do too. It's my way of contributing to Trask's vision for this camp."

"Is there anything I can do to help?" Kyrin asked, anxious to make her own contribution. "I'm afraid I don't know anything about cooking though. That wasn't the sort of thing we were taught at Tarvin Hall." She frowned. There were a good number of life skills Tarvin Hall didn't deem important.

Lenae gave her the heartwarming smile she was coming to love. "Of course, and I'll be happy to teach you."

They visited the supply shack and began making supper. Lenae showed Kyrin how to prepare venison and cook it over the fire. While it heated, the two of them peeled potatoes, sharing stories and laughter. The shadows lengthened around them, and by the time the forest grew dim, they had enough venison, savory gravy, and mashed potatoes for everyone. The men gathered from all around camp with eager eyes and filled their plates while expressing their gratitude for the meal. Everyone found seats around the fire on long benches made of half logs. They squeezed in, chatting and laughing companionably. With the entire camp together, many requested Kyrin recount what had taken place in Valcré, both of her promotion and standing up to the emperor. She ducked her head at their attention and fussing, but couldn't refuse them.

They paid close attention to her and quickly became engrossed in her words—so much so that she alone spotted another man entering camp. The growing darkness made him difficult to distinguish, but he was tall, and the shape of a slain deer draped his shoulders. A shadow moved to his right and drew Kyrin's eyes to a black wolf trotting at his side.

She fell silent in distraction, and everyone else looked up. With one glimpse of the newcomer, they just as quickly refocused on their food, except for one man, Rayad. He rose to meet the other man. They spoke quietly and passed close by the fire on the way to the supply shack. The firelight provided Kyrin a better look at the younger man's powerful build and raven black hair. Curiosity and intrigue tugged at her mind. There was something different about him.

"That's Jace," Lenae said. "He came here with Rayad."

"He's half ryrik," Jeremy added in a low tone.

Kyrin's eyes widened. "Half ryrik?"

Jeremy just nodded and stared at his plate.

Kyrin, however, turned to look over her shoulder, though she couldn't see much of Jace in the deepening darkness. Who had ever heard of such a thing? The people in Valcré would be astounded.

Her eyes drew back to her companions and scanned each of them. A definite hush had overtaken the previously eager and talkative group. The men either ate their food in silence or murmured and whispered amongst themselves. All except for Holden. He sat across the fire from Kyrin, and his eyes bored a flaming hole into Jace. She'd received some pretty scathing looks herself in the past, but this made her shiver.

The murmurs all died and everything fell silent but for the crackle and snap of the fire. Jace approached the nearby table and dished up a plate of supper. A pang of discomfort constricted Kyrin's middle, the weight of the silence pressing on her. How many times had she met with such silence in a group? Jace acted as though not a single one of them existed, but when he looked up, his eyes met hers.

She stilled under the clear, startling blue gaze. Ryrik eyes, yet lacking the fiery hatred she'd always attributed to them. Without that burning, devouring light, she could appreciate their unique brightness and beauty—just like the vivid aqua waters along the coast in Valcré. However, though hatred was absent, something just as great filled them. *Pain*. Despite their bright color, pain and hopelessness lurked in the shadows behind it.

The moment seemed to freeze around them, but Jace turned abruptly and snapped Kyrin from her thoughts. Still, she watched him. He didn't even look for a seat among the men, instead walking off to sit near a tree at the far edge of camp, with the wolf following. She then looked around the fire. Lenae sent her son a disapproving look, to which he hung his head, and Rayad returned to his seat, but never did finish his supper. He just sat with his brows furrowed and shoulders hunched, as if carrying a heavy weight. Conversation resumed around Kyrin, but her eyes drifted back to Jace's lone figure in the dark.

KYRIN STOOD OUTSIDE in the sun and scrubbed the breakfast dishes while Lenae swept and tidied the cabin. It was lovely to be outdoors without the bustling of a city full of people—only the happy sounds of conversation and the men working on the second cabin nearby. She gazed around camp and took mental note of each man present. So far, she'd seen no sign of Jace this morning. She placed another plate into the washtub and looked around again. He was probably gone hunting, considering the deer she'd seen last night. She would have liked to catch a glimpse of him though, now that it was daylight. His incredible but pained eyes had floated in and out of her thoughts ever since the moment at the fire.

When she finished the dishes, she dried her hands and stood for a long moment as her thoughts drifted. She looked up as one of the men named Mick approached. They hadn't spoken beyond greeting each other. He left the impression of being one of the quieter men, but kind and friendly. Kyrin offered him a smile.

"Jace always sleeps off in the forest and is gone hunting all day," he said. Kyrin stared at him in question, and he shrugged. "You seemed to be looking for someone. I figured it was Jace, since he isn't around."

"I guess I was." She frowned, processing his words. "Why doesn't he sleep in camp?"

"Nightmares. They wake him up at night. I think it embarrasses him to wake the rest of us, so he took to sleeping away from camp."

Kyrin glanced toward the trees, where Jace spent so much time alone. "Everyone acts like they're afraid of him."

"Most are. They think his ryrik blood makes him dangerous. It started with Holden. His parents were killed by ryriks, and he doesn't think Jace is any different. He's got a lot of the others believing the same."

"But not you?"

Mick shook his head. "Not me. I don't judge a man by what type of blood he has. Besides, humans can be just as cruel as any ryrik."

Kyrin's mind flashed back to the crowd gathered around her in Valcré—how they chanted for her death and reached for her in an attempt to kill her themselves. Ice prickled up her arms.

"That's true," she murmured as she rubbed the goose bumps.

"I've tried to make him feel welcome, but I don't think he trusts any of us. The Korvic brothers over there"—Mick gestured to three young men working on a cabin—"beat him up pretty bad a couple of weeks ago."

Heaviness settled in Kyrin's chest. More bullies. Just like the ones back at Tarvin Hall who always beat Kaden up. They seemed to show up everywhere. But somehow she didn't think Jace escaped from the mental afflictions of his tormentors as easily as Kaden made it seem he disposed of theirs, and her curiosity was piqued.

"Where did Jace come from? What's his story?"

"I only know a little from what Warin told me," Mick replied. "You should probably talk to Rayad. If you'll excuse me, I've got work to see to anyway."

"Sure," Kyrin said with a nod.

Mick walked off and left her once again to her contemplations. She sent the Korvic brothers a frowning glance. The youngest spotted her and grinned. She looked away. No man who treated others so cruelly would ever gain her interest.

Jace appeared again that night, but just briefly before he walked off with his supper. And once again, he was nowhere to be found the next morning, not that Kyrin could blame him after the reception he always received. It was uncomfortable to see him treated as she so often had been at Tarvin Hall. True, it was an odd thing to know someone whose bloodline was virtually unheard of, but surely Trask would have done something if he were a real threat.

She stayed busy helping Lenae in the cabin, but her mind kept wandering back to the things Mick had told her, leaving her with questions about this intriguing man she felt such a strange connection to. When an opportunity presented itself, she set out to satisfy her curiosity. She found Rayad working on a cabin door with Warin, but now that she approached him, she was suddenly tongue-tied. If only Kaden were here to start the conversation. She might have turned around if Rayad hadn't looked up with a smile.

"Did you need something, Kyrin?"

"I was wondering if I could talk to you . . . about Jace."

Rayad and Warin exchanged a look.

"I can finish this," Warin said.

Rayad set his tools aside and turned to face Kyrin. "What is it you want to know?"

"I guess I'm curious where he came from . . . how he got here."

Rayad seemed reluctant, protective, yet there was a look about him that spoke of much struggle. He looked around and motioned to a nearby log. "Why don't we sit down?"

Once they had, he looked at her, his brown eyes deep and serious. "Why are you curious about Jace?"

Kyrin considered his question and asked herself the same. It wasn't like her to pry into other people's lives and approach someone she hardly knew. "I guess I feel bad for him. I notice how most of the men treat him." She clasped her hands firmly in her lap and lowered her voice as her own memories and feelings welled to the surface. "It's not easy being the outcast."

At hearing the pain of experience behind her words, Rayad's eyes softened and, with a nod, he began to tell the story of Jace's life, from his early childhood and teen years as a slave to his time as a gladiator. He recounted finding Jace, and the three years he'd spent helping him and teaching him about Elôm. By the time he finished telling of Kalli and Aldor's recent deaths and the turmoil Jace experienced here, despair weighed his worn expression.

"He's slipping away, and if Elôm doesn't intervene . . ." He gave a helpless shrug. "I've done everything I know to do. I had hoped hunting would help bring purpose back to his life, but it has just separated us further. He'll hardly speak to me anymore. He's lost the will to live. He just exists now. If only I could snap him out of it, but the more I try, the more he pulls away."

His voice had grown rough, and he shook his head. Kyrin had been struck by the pain in Jace's eyes but never guessed just how much lay behind it. The turmoil inside him must be excruciating.

The two of them sat quietly for a moment before Rayad took a rejuvenating breath. His eyes cleared as he turned to study Kyrin.

"Altair," he said, more to himself than to her.

Kyrin tensed as her mind jumped immediately to the deeds of her grandfather. But she laughed inside. How much more shame had she brought to their name?

"You're not old enough to have known your grandfather, are you?" Rayad asked.

Kyrin shook her head. "No, he was killed quite a few years before I was born."

She stared at her lap and smoothed her dress over her knees. After all these years, she should be used to this, but the shame still crept in.

"Mm, yes, that was nearly thirty years ago now," Rayad said as if well-acquainted with the incident. "What have you heard about him?"

Kyrin raised her eyes but found no condemnation or disdain in Rayad's expression. If anything, it offered understanding.

"He abandoned his men in battle and then turned on them." She winced at the unflattering image. Though now bearing the label of traitor as well, at least she had not hurt anyone in the process, despite the emperor's claims. "Most of the soldiers were killed before someone took my grandfather down."

"I see," Rayad murmured. "Who were the enemies they were fighting?"

Kyrin stared at him, and her forehead wrinkled. How odd she had no answer for that. "I . . . guess no one ever told me."

Rayad gave a slow nod. "No, they wouldn't have. Few truly know the answer. They were villagers from a small settlement called Ilmar—both men and a few women, untrained to fight, but determined to defend their families."

"Villagers? But . . . why?"

"They were followers of Elôm, ordered to build a temple for Aertus and Vilai. When they refused, Daican sent men to either force them to comply or exterminate them. Your grand-father was the captain. But, when he arrived and witnessed the villagers' determination, something changed in him and several of his men as well. He ordered his company back to the barracks, but the men still loyal to Daican chose to fight.

"Your grandfather and a handful of his men stood with the villagers. Some escaped, but most were killed. Your grandfather was captured near the end. He was executed and branded a traitor throughout Arcacia."

Two warm tears slipped down Kyrin's cheeks. Her grand-father was really a hero?

"How do you know this?" she asked, her voice trembling.

"I was there," Rayad responded with a sad sigh. "Warin and I both. We'd come to sell horses, but ended up caught in the struggle. We helped some of the villagers get away, but stayed close enough to see how it ended."

Kyrin wiped her cheeks, but more tears flowed. For all her life, her grandfather had lived as a villain in her mind. How horribly wrong they'd all been.

"You saw my grandfather die?"

Rayad nodded solemnly. "I did, and let me tell you, it's one of my greatest regrets that I couldn't have stopped it."

Kyrin clenched her fists. How could the emperor do this to her family? To her father, who'd borne the brunt of the shame all these years? She tried to swallow the aching lump in her throat and the acidic burn of anger that came with the realization that he was doing the exact same thing to her. Would people speak her name in disgust thirty years from now, just like they did with her grandfather? Kaden and her father would know the truth, but would the rest of her family duck their heads in shame whenever anyone spoke of her?

The anger churned inside her, but her ire slowly gave way to a burdening need for encouragement. Wiping her eyes again, she looked at Rayad. "Do you think he believed in Elôm?"

"I can't say for sure, but in my heart I believe he did. He faced death like a man who is confident of where he's going."

Kyrin's lips lifted in a wobbly smile. "Thank you. I can't tell you what it means to me to hear that."

"I'm glad I could tell you. The way your grandfather has been reviled has bothered me for years. It gives me some peace to know at least one member of his family knows the truth and can see him for what he really was." He rested his hand on Kyrin's shoulder. "And it looks to me like his courage was passed on."

Jace trudged into camp just as the sun set with a red glow through the trees. Voices and laughter drifted from where everyone gathered around the fire for supper, as usual, but it wouldn't last long. He steeled himself as he approached. Would he ever get used to the hush he caused? He set his eyes on the large pot of what smelled like stew.

He had no game to tend to today. His mind just wasn't on hunting. He'd dreamt about Kalli and Aldor the night before. Though not his usual nightmares, they were just as painful, reopening the ragged holes in his heart he didn't believe anything could ever fill again. He never slept after that. With the nightmares still plaguing him, he only found a couple of hours of rest each night, if that, and it had begun to tell on his body. His reflexes and senses weren't as sharp as they should be. He never missed such an easy target as the deer he'd failed to bring down this afternoon. But the worst part was that he didn't even care.

Near the fire, he glanced at the group and his eyes paused on Rayad. He sat next to the new girl in camp. They spoke, and Rayad smiled. Jace hadn't seen him do that in a while. Something clenched like a cold vice around his heart. He could be sitting there, or at least sitting with Rayad somewhere. Rayad would be quick to join him if he just asked. But they'd grown so far apart now. It was his own fault. All of it.

He looked away from Rayad, cursing the way his eyes stung. But, as he dropped a ladleful of stew into a bowl, his eyes were drawn to the new girl again. She was watching him. His empty stomach twisted with a desire to hide from eyes that seemed to cut right into him, past his shield of protection, seeing everything—every weakness, every vulnerability. Yet, while he felt himself laid bare before her, she gave away nothing about herself.

He spun around and retreated to the solitude of the trees at the edge of camp.

When he sat, he cast a glance back to the fire as he considered the way she had watched him the last couple of nights. He'd heard something about her having the ability to read people. Just what did she see in him? Did she see the monster he was?

Days had passed since he let his thoughts turn to Elôm. He leaned his head back against the tree, his heart aching to cry, to release the pain. *Why?* Why did this happen to him? He waited for Elôm to speak, but the answer that filtered into his mind was nothing like what Rayad would have told him and not at all comforting.

Because you're an animal. Everything you touch is killed or destroyed.

Jace closed his eyes. He'd reached this devastating conclusion recently and believed it more and more every day. Nearly everything he'd ever cared about was gone, and it terrified him that this curse would manifest itself again by destroying Rayad, the only person he had left. For this reason alone, he still thought daily of leaving—of getting as far away as he could from anyone or anything he cared about so they could never be harmed because of him.

He wrestled with this until Tyra's whining penetrated the shadows of his thoughts. His eyes popped open. She stared at him with her head slightly cocked. He glanced at the bowl of stew that had gone cold and set it on the ground.

"You eat it. I'm not hungry."

Tyra looked down at the bowl, but then just stared at him again.

KYRIN HADN'T KNOWN such a peaceful existence in years. Forest life was every bit as wonderful as she'd imagined, and she loved Lenae and being amongst people who believed as she did. But then there came times she missed Kaden so much her heart broke. She prayed daily he would show up in camp with Tane, or she would at least receive word of his safety, but she lived in fear of learning something had happened to him.

Though falling into a routine, she still felt a little out of place and uncertain without her brother. She'd relied on his strength and presence so heavily over the years. Too heavily, perhaps. Needing time alone to gather her own strength, she wandered into the woods not too far from camp, where she sat on a fallen log surrounded by trilliums and violets. The delicate blooms swayed and quivered around her feet as silent witnesses to the gathering of tears in her eyes.

"I miss Kaden," she whispered into the quiet of the forest. "I worry about him, though I know You have his life guarded, just as You do mine. Help me trust that, and please bring him here safely. I want to enjoy it with him. He would love it so much." She bit her lip and closed her eyes. "I just want him to be safe."

Tears leaked past her lids and dribbled down her cheeks as her thoughts went to her last night in Valcré. The ache of riding away from the city without him still cut deeply. She hadn't even been able to say goodbye.

Something rustled in the grass, and Kyrin's eyes popped open. "Oh!"

Jace's black wolf stood staring up at her.

"Hello, girl," she said softly.

The wolf's tail wagged, and the animal took a step closer. Kyrin extended her hand, admiring the animal's beautiful eyes and shiny black coat. Tyra sniffed her and let her rub the soft fur under her chin.

As with Tyra, Kyrin didn't hear him come, but when she looked up, Jace stood a couple of feet away. He looked at her oddly as his eyes shifted between her and Tyra. Kyrin pulled her hand away from the wolf and smudged the tear tracks from her face. Clearing her clogged throat, she said, "She's very beautiful."

She offered a tentative smile, not sure how he would react to her touching his wolf. He just stared and barely murmured what sounded like "thanks" before walking off. Tyra trotted after him.

Kyrin twisted around to watch them. This was the closest she had seen Jace, and in full daylight. Despite all she had learned from Rayad, it had not prepared her for the sight of the dark shadows under his eyes and sunken cheeks. Though built like Kaden, he clearly wasn't eating the way her brother did. No wonder Rayad worried.

Wiping away the last remnants of tears, Kyrin returned to her prayers, but with a newfound focus as a burden settled on her heart. Jace needed help, and like Rayad, she prayed for divine intervention.

A couple of days later, Kyrin raced from the cabin the moment she learned Trask had ridden into camp with Tane. Wondering what news the talcrin would bring left her breathless, but the smile he met her with didn't speak of bad news.

"Kyrin, you're looking very well," he said.

"I am well," she told him as she worked to catch her breath. "How's Kaden?"

"He's all right for now," Tane assured her. "I'm afraid he's still watched closely, but we'll get him out as soon as we have the opportunity."

Kyrin nodded with a mix of relief and disappointment. At least he was safe, but he must be going out of his mind waiting to leave. He never was the most patient. "I know you will."

"How are things in Valcré?" Rayad asked as he came up behind Kyrin.

By now, most of the men had left their work to gather around.

"Not good," Tane answered, shaking his head. "As we feared, there have been many arrests due to citizens refusing to worship Aertus and Vilai. And it's not just in Valcré, but the surrounding area as well. Soon it will spread throughout the country. Friends and neighbors will be turning each other in all over the place."

"Have there been any executions?" Warin wanted to know.

"Not yet, but I'm sure there will be soon." Tane paused with a grave expression. "There's been talk concerning the arena in Valcré. Another year or two and it'll be complete. I don't think it's wrong to assume that's not a coincidence."

Rayad crossed his arms. "You think the emperor will make a sport out of killing us."

Tane shrugged, but said, "It's exactly what I'd expect of him."

Murmurs and silent looks passed through the group, and Kyrin shivered. It had been terrifying to face the crowd from the execution platform. How much more so would it be to stand in a giant arena and die providing entertainment to a crowd?

"We need to increase work on the cabins," Trask announced, drawing Kyrin's attention back to the group. "Tane and the others will try to warn the families who are in danger and direct them here. I don't know how many will make it or when, but we must be ready. This is why we're here."

With renewed purpose, the men returned to their work. Kyrin lingered to speak further with Tane, but Trask motioned her over to his horse.

"I brought something for you." He pulled a bundle from his saddle to reveal a small recurve bow. He placed it in her hands along with a quiver of gray and blue fletched arrows. "It should meet your specifications."

Kyrin smiled widely as she slipped the quiver over her shoulder and ran her hand along the smooth, dark wood of the bow. She'd asked him for one, but never anticipated it would be of such quality. "Thank you so much. It's perfect."

"You're very welcome." He grinned with a mischievous twinkle in his eyes. "Now, impress me."

Kyrin's brows went up, first in question and then uncertainty. She'd never shown off for anyone in her life, but she followed him to the edge of camp, where he stuck a square of cloth to a tree thirty yards away. She eyed the small target. Though she hadn't used a bow in some time, she'd had plenty of practice over the years.

She strung the bow and pulled out an arrow to fit to the bowstring. Sensing movement behind her, she glanced over her shoulder. A few of the men gathered to watch, including Jeremy and the youngest Korvic. Her stomach fluttered nervously, but she settled it by taking a deep breath. With her eyes fixed on the target, she raised the bow and drew it back smoothly. She paused a moment to aim and let the string slip. The arrow sliced the air and slammed into the tree about two inches above the target. Trask nodded approvingly. Not a bad shot, but Kyrin frowned.

She drew another arrow, aimed, and fired again. This one lodged itself about an inch from the target. Still, she knew she could do better. She reached for her third arrow and released more quickly this time. It streaked across the distance to the tree. A thrill raced through her when the arrow hit close to the center of the cloth. She fired off two more, and both hit within a centimeter of the third.

Applause trickled from the men, and Kyrin's cheeks flushed.

Trask grinned again. "Impressive indeed."

She shrugged and unstrung the bow. There were certainly better archers and a big difference between a tree and a moving target—a big difference between a living and non-living target. Even so, possessing skill with the weapon fit in perfectly with the plan developing in her mind.

Just after lunch, Kyrin sought out Rayad. Everyone was particularly busy since receiving the news from Tane. As much as Kyrin also desired to help the people who would be escaping the emperor as she had, Elôm seemed to be calling her to a different need, and she couldn't ignore it.

Rayad had a ready smile for her when she neared. They had shared some good talks since he'd told her about her grandfather. Kyrin enjoyed his stories and hearing of the places he and Warin had seen. She already held a deep respect for him. Now she needed his advice and honest opinion.

"That was good shooting earlier," he praised her.

Kyrin smiled and shrugged. "Thanks. It's one form of defense girls are allowed to learn at Tarvin Hall. I had a good teacher and practiced a lot."

"It's a good skill to know." After a pause, Rayad asked, "Can I help you with something?"

"I hope so." Kyrin's idea had grown to such a nagging ember in the back of her mind, she had to believe Elôm had put it there for a purpose. "I've been doing a lot of thinking, and I really want to help Jace."

"Not many people have ever felt that way."

"That's partly why I do. I was bullied at Tarvin Hall right up until I left, and I've always tried to help others like me." Except that those others had always been children like Meredith, not grown men. She hesitated at the uncertainty and unlikelihood of such a task, but every time she contemplated letting go of the idea, it was as if Elôm sent her a little nudge.

"That seems to be a rare gift these days."

"The problem is, I'm not quite sure how to get closer to Jace so I can help him."

Rayad loosed a sigh. "It's a hard thing. I'm not even sure how to do that myself anymore. I think it rests on Jace, whether or not he'll open up to anyone."

Kyrin sent him an uncertain look. If Jace's closest friend, his mentor, couldn't get through to him, what made her think she could? Jace didn't even know her. But she couldn't give up. Not without trying, at least.

"I have an idea, but I need to know what you think. Part of the problem is how Jace is always gone, so I thought, maybe he'd let me go out hunting with him."

Rayad gave her a gentle but regretful look. "I'm afraid that's quite unlikely."

"I know, and I'm prepared for that, but what I need to know is . . ." She hesitated as doubts pricked her resolve. This was not like anything she'd done before, and it would be so much easier to let it go. She struggled with it a moment, but pressed on. "You know him better than anyone. If I did go with him, would I be safe?"

Understanding lit Rayad's eyes. "What I can tell you is, no matter what anyone thinks, no matter what Jace himself thinks, I know he's not dangerous. I've seen him at his worst, and aside from when we first met, I've never once feared for my life or the lives of anyone innocent. It may not be the wisest move on your part for appearance's sake, but Jace would never harm you."

"Thank you. That's all I wanted to know."

Kyrin shivered. Dawn was chilly. She leaned against the cabin as best she could with her quiver and bow strapped to her back and wrapped her arms around herself. Her thoughts drifted to the warm bed she had left a short time ago. It had been hard to leave it, but she reminded herself this was more important than temporary comfort.

She'd gone over it so many times, this urging she had to befriend Jace, and spent much of the previous day praying about it. In the end, she always came to the same conclusion. Jace needed help, and for some reason, despite her doubts and uncertainties, she felt compelled to give it. She'd made her final decision after discussing it with Lenae before bed. Both believed Elôm was prompting her to act.

She waited in the dark and watched the trees for any sign of movement. Everything was so still, and peace settled inside her. But at the first glow of sun peeking through the trees, disappointment lurked. According to Rayad, Jace usually came by camp for supplies before setting out for the day. Would this be the one day he didn't? *Please let him come.* She'd worked herself up to this, and didn't want to have to do so again.

Just before she gave up hope, a shadowed figure approached the supply shack. She straightened. Actually seeing him brought all her doubts to the forefront. How did she expect to accomplish this? How would she even talk to him? She had to admit that the thought of going out alone with him suddenly intimidated her even more than it had yesterday, regardless of Rayad's assurance. *Elôm, don't let me back out now if You don't want me to.*

Jace gathered his supplies and then headed away from camp without ever noticing her outside the cabin. Before he went too far, Kyrin took a fortifying breath and set out after him. Her heart thundered. She glanced back to the security of the cabin, but kept on. Still Jace didn't seem aware of her presence. When she reached the edge of camp, she licked her lips and called his name.

He stopped and spun around. His wide eyes glinted pale blue even in the low light. Beside him, Tyra gave a wag of her tail. Kyrin hesitated under the guarded intensity with which Jace watched her. What in Ilyon was she doing? She cleared her throat to work her voice loose.

"I have a favor to ask of you." She paused to say a quick prayer. Jace's eyes bored into her. "Would you teach me how to hunt?"

His brows dipped low, shadowing his eyes. He stared at her and appeared to wonder if he'd heard her right. Deciding he had, he shook his head. "No."

He turned to go, but Kyrin hurried to stop him.

"Jace, wait."

He turned back and eyed her as if she'd grown an extra set of arms. His eyes narrowed warily. After all, how many people would ever come to him with such a request, especially a young woman like her? She spoke carefully to convince him of her sincerity and appeal to his sympathies.

"I sometimes feel a little out of place here. I love camp and the forest, but it's so different from what I'm used to. My brother is still trapped in Valcré, and I really miss him. He always helped me in new situations." She sure could use him right now. He would have been a better one to do this. "I love helping Lenae, but I'd like to help in other ways too. I've noticed the game you bring back and how much everyone eats. I'm a good archer so, I thought, maybe . . . I could help hunt."

Jace's expression barely changed, intense and indecisive.

She went on. "I've never hunted before, and I realize I have a lot to learn, but I promise I'll quit if I'm too much of a burden. I'd just like a chance."

She held her breath. *Please Elôm.*

Jace peered at her long and hard. When he spoke at last, his voice was tinged with suspicion. "You do know I'm half ryrik?"

Kyrin nodded while projecting as much openness and honesty as she could. "Yes."

"They'll think you're crazy."

Kyrin let out a breathy laugh that bubbled up with her nerves. "I'm used to that."

She held his probing gaze steadily despite the urge to shrink away. She had to convince him that she didn't share the same fear as the others. It was the first crucial step in earning his trust. He glanced past her, toward camp, before staring at her again. A storm of emotions flickered in his eyes. With a wince, he shook his head and muttered, "Fine."

Kyrin's heart gave a stuttering leap. *Thank You, Elôm!*

Without another word, Jace strode away as if to put more distance between them. Kyrin hurried to catch up. Whatever the rest of the day brought, at least she had made it this far.

Kyrin's foot snagged on a branch, and she gasped when she nearly fell . . . again. Panting, she glanced ahead to make sure she hadn't lost sight of Jace. How did someone his size move with such ease through the tangle of underbrush? He barely even made a sound and didn't say a word. She may as well have been out here alone.

She tugged on her sweat-soaked dress and pressed forward. The chill of dawn completely disappeared as the sun worked its way above the trees. But she wouldn't complain. She wouldn't even allow the temptation in her mind for more than a moment. Not after what it took to get here, though it didn't seem to be accomplishing much good at the moment. Did Jace even remember she'd tagged along?

Without warning, he stopped, and she nearly smacked into his back. She stumbled away with another gasp and looked up as he turned piercing blue eyes on her. Though they had to have come miles already, she asked, "Are we going to keep on?"

She hoped to sound willing, but her voice came out winded. So much for being in good shape. This was much more taxing than wandering the streets of Valcré. Jace stared at her for a good, long moment—something she would have to get used to. She tried to read his expression, but he made it difficult by so skillfully guarding his emotions. He stared at her the way Master Zocar did when trying to figure her out.

"We'll rest here."

Kyrin could have jumped for joy had her legs cooperated. They just about collapsed of their own volition, and she sank into the grass and old leaves. Grabbing her waterskin, she took a long drink. Though distracted by the relief, she felt Jace still watching her, but then he sat down a few feet away. A moment later, he dug around in his bag and surprised Kyrin by offering her a piece of jerky.

"Thank you," she said, "but why don't you eat it?" She smiled and pulled a pouch containing her lunch off her shoulder. "I came prepared."

Jace's eyes widened the tiniest bit, perhaps in surprise, but he didn't look at her long enough for her to be sure. He took a bite of the jerky and fed the rest to Tyra. No wonder he was so thin. The wolf probably ate more of his food than he did.

Kyrin ate her lunch in silence, while discreetly watching Jace, who stared off into the forest, never once relaxing. She didn't even taste her food as she racked her brain for the perfect thing to say to him. In fact, she begged Elôm for the right words, but nothing came. Why couldn't Kaden be there? He'd think of something.

The moment she finished her last bite, Jace pushed to his feet. Kyrin jumped up to follow him, and off they went again. As before, Jace quickly worked his way ahead and left her to trip and stumble after him. A branch slapped her in the face and tears seared her eyes, but more from frustration than pain. How did she ever think she could do this? Did Elôm even want her to, or had she just made herself think so? Because she was doing a terrible job of it. What would it benefit if she only managed to be a dead weight for Jace to drag around all day? She couldn't even find a single word to say to him during lunch, probably her one chance at speaking to him at all. Just like with Daniel, she'd failed at her opportunity.

Sometime later, Jace heaved a sigh and stopped again. She tried to catch her breath as she waited for him to either turn around or continue on, but finally he turned to her with in intimidating frown.

"I don't think we're going to see anything if you can't walk more quietly." Though he spoke evenly, frustration bled out through his voice.

Kyrin ducked her head, cheeks flaming. "Sorry."

Really, she had tried to be quiet, but there always seemed to be a stick or dry leaves to crunch under her feet and branches to snap and crash when she pushed through them. Tears threatened again, but she swallowed them back. She would not get teary in front of him. She'd ruined things enough without turning into an unskilled, noisy, *and* weepy girl.

Jace sighed again and stuck his fists on his hips. He frowned into the forest, which was void of even the hint of game, no doubt ruing the moment he'd allowed her to come along. Kyrin shifted and stared awkwardly at a nearby trillium. When Jace did look at her again, his expression had softened a little.

"When you walk, put your heel down first, carefully. Then shift your weight forward, but on the outside of your foot."

Kyrin looked at her feet. She took an experimental step. "Like this?"

She glanced up, and he nodded.

She took a few more steps. It seemed unnatural and put her

off balance, but with time and practice, she could get the hang of it.

"Always scan the terrain to see what's ahead," he told her. "Take advantage of large rocks and bare ground."

They moved along a short distance. Kyrin was quieter, but not nearly so much as Jace. He glanced over his shoulder.

"Softer boots would help. It's better when you can feel what you're walking on."

She glanced at his well-worn, soft leather boots. Maybe Trask could find her a similar pair.

For the rest of the afternoon, Kyrin practiced the new walking technique with nominal success. Focusing on every step, she fell far behind, forcing Jace to wait for her; but when she tried to keep up, quietness was impossible. By the time the sun set, her head throbbed and her legs burned. She didn't know what she'd expected, but this wasn't it.

Though she was never even aware they had made a direction change, they suddenly arrived in camp, where the men were just gathering for supper. The smell of it made Kyrin's mouth water and her stomach growl. She moved toward the fire, aching to sit down, but Jace hung back. She paused and turned to him. Careful to keep any frustration out of her voice, she said, "Thanks for teaching me about walking today. I'll keep practicing."

Jace said nothing, and Kyrin did not linger. He was probably eager to be rid of her. At the fire, she met Lenae.

"How did it go?" The woman studied her face. "You look worn-out."

Kyrin exhaled loudly. "It would've gone better if my crashing through the forest wouldn't have scared all the game away. Turns out I'm not a very stealthy hunter."

Lenae gave her a sympathetic smile. "These things take practice. I'm sure you'll be better next time."

If there was a next time.

DESPITE THE DISASTER of the previous day, Kyrin waited outside the cabin before dawn the next morning. She'd dragged herself out of bed, aching from the miles she had traveled, but she wouldn't give up. Not as long as Jace let her join him. *If* he let her join him.

She peered into the trees where he had appeared yesterday, but nothing moved in the last bit of nighttime darkness. Only a slight breeze rustled the trees, not that she would have heard him coming anyway. After another few minutes, a bird chirped nearby, and others soon joined in as the sky glowed pink in the east. Kyrin's expectation rose, but sank again when the other men woke and one by one left their tents to start the day. Jace would never show up now. With a heavy sigh, she turned and stepped quietly back into the cabin. She couldn't blame him. She had proven to be a liability, but defeat stung.

Kyrin returned her bow to her room in the loft and spent a little time there to pray before joining Lenae, who had begun work on breakfast.

"No hunting today?" she asked.

"He didn't come by this morning. He probably knew I'd be waiting for him. I don't know what I'll do now."

"Don't get discouraged just yet," Lenae comforted. "You may get another chance."

"I hope so." Kyrin walked over to the shelf to measure out coffee for the pot. Jeremy loved his morning coffee. "I still want to help him."

"Give him a little time. I think he'll eventually see that."

Kyrin looked over at her. If only she didn't feel like such a failure already. "Do you really think I can get through to him?"

"You?" Lenae shook her head. "No. But Elôm? Yes. And it just might be you're the one He uses. It may take days, weeks, or even months, but be patient and don't give up. It was a big step that he even let you go with him yesterday."

The encouraging words brought a smile to Kyrin's lips. It might not feel like much of a step, but Lenae was right, and she prayed for patience and perseverance.

Kyrin kept a close watch for Jace throughout the morning, just in case he showed up, though she didn't know what she would say to him if he did. But she trusted that Elôm would work something out. At least she could be one person to make him feel welcome and offer him friendship.

Just after lunch, she headed toward the edge of camp, but a voice called out to stop her. She turned to see Holden and frowned. She knew little about him since he kept to himself, but he was the one who had started the hostility toward Jace. Regardless of his reasons, it made it difficult for her to like him. Still, she tried not to pass judgment before she had a chance to get to know him.

"Yes?" she asked, her eyes following the determined lines in his face. His voice was just as unyielding.

"Where were you yesterday?"

Kyrin's frown deepened, wondering why it was any of his business, but she answered simply, "I was out hunting. With Jace."

"Alone?" His blue-gray eyes resembled Ardaluin Bay when a storm approached. Kyrin nodded, and he asked, "You're not going again, are you?"

"Maybe, if he'll take me."

Holden's sharp gaze flickered to the trees as if expecting a monster to emerge from them. "You can't do that. It's dangerous."

Kyrin shook her head. "I know how you feel about Jace, but I don't believe he's dangerous."

"He is," Holden insisted tightly. "His ryrik blood makes him dangerous. You can't trust him."

Kyrin read the real concern in his eyes. He truly believed every word he spoke, and deep down he had reason to. She kept this in mind and spoke evenly. "Perhaps, but I do trust Rayad. He said Jace would never harm me, and I believe him."

"He can't know for sure." Holden's voice rose. She might have been afraid of him if his own fear wasn't so evident. "That ryrik blood could take hold at any moment. You'd be no match for him."

Kyrin took in a deep breath to both restrain her need to defend Jace and to gather her sympathy for Holden's past. She would probably be afraid of Jace too if ryriks had killed her parents. Didn't she fear the emperor and his men the same way?

"I understand why you're telling me this, and I'm not naïve. I've seen ryriks before. I know what they do. I've seen the burning hatred and rage in their eyes, the desire to kill, but I haven't seen any of that in Jace. All I see is deep pain and loneliness." She sighed, picturing the image of his sunken face in her mind. "Who knows? Maybe in the end you'll be right, but I can't ignore the desire to help him. If Elôm can use me to do that then I'm willing, regardless of the risk."

Holden rubbed his hand across the back of his neck in agitation. "I don't think it's a good idea." But he must have understood that she would not change her mind. "Just be careful," he muttered and walked off toward a tent.

Kyrin watched him over her shoulder for a moment before going her own way. She would not be deterred. A short distance beyond the edge of camp, she came to a nice quiet spot and glanced back to make sure no one had followed her. Satisfied that she was alone, she looked down at her feet and took a couple of steps the way Jace had taught her. If she practiced enough and wasn't such a liability, maybe he would be more willing to take her hunting.

For the next couple of hours, she moved around the perimeter of camp as stealthily as she could. At one point, she pulled off her boots and went barefoot to get used to the feel of the terrain. If her classmates back at Tarvin Hall could see her now, they'd think she had lost her mind. How little they really knew of the world outside their bubble of unquestioning loyalty to the emperor.

When sunset approached, Kyrin leaned against a stump to pull her boots on and hurried back to camp to help Lenae with supper. Partridge was on the menu, but tonight, Mick joined in to show them how he'd learned to prepare it with wild onion. It gave Kyrin a chance to get to know him better. She never would have guessed that he came from a wealthy mining family. As much as she could tell he loved and missed them, they had turned him in for his faith in Elôm. After escaping the authorities, he'd wandered along, begging and struggling for food until he came to Landale and met Trask.

Despite the hardship he had endured, his story and perseverance inspired Kyrin. She took a seat beside him after they served supper and was so interested in what he had to say that she nearly missed Jace's arrival. She caught his eye as he dished his supper and smiled at him, but he didn't hold her gaze before ducking away into the darkness, as if propelled by guilt.

Kyrin blinked the sleepiness out of her eyes. Darkness cloaked the cabin, but it must be close to dawn. A rhythmic pattering pelted the roof. Even so, she pushed aside her covers and got out of bed. Rain or shine, if Jace came by today, she wasn't going to miss him. Maybe the wet ground would make her quieter. She pulled on her clothes and climbed down from the loft, tiptoeing to the cupboard where she buttered a roll for breakfast and packed her lunch. At the door, she slipped on her boots, cloak, and quiver. With a glance at Lenae who slept in the corner, she eased the door open and stepped outside.

A steady rain made its way through the forest canopy. She pulled the cloak close and stood against the door, where she had a little shelter. And she waited. The light of dawn came slowly because of the clouded sky. It took longer than usual before she could make out the distinct shape of tents in the murky gloom. By this time, her clothing clung damply to her skin, but she still waited another twenty minutes with eyes always on the forest. Same as yesterday, nothing moved in the trees. Not even the birds entertained her with their usual chorus this morning.

After over an hour, she gave up the wait and went inside, relishing the warmth of the fire Lenae had already been up to stoke.

"Nothing today?"

"No." Though she wasn't especially disappointed. It would have been a wet and miserable day to hunt. She slipped off her cloak and hung it and her quiver on a peg beside the door. "I hope it's because of the rain and he sought shelter in one of the tents at least. It's really coming down out there."

"If you see Rayad, maybe you can ask him," Lenae suggested. "And if you happen to see any of the other men close by, I want to let them know I'll serve breakfast for them in here. We can't have them all at once, but they can take turns. Then they can warm up and dry off while they eat."

Kyrin helped Lenae cook up a mound of eggs and bacon and gallons of coffee. Offering to get the extra supplies from the supply shack, she ran out into the rain and let Warin know of the meal arrangement so he could inform the others. A short time later, the first group of men showed up at the door.

Kyrin dished out food and filled coffee cups while Lenae continued cooking. Every time someone walked in, she looked up with hopeful expectation, but it was never Jace. However, when Rayad walked in, she met him at the door.

"Have you seen Jace?"

"He's in the tent. He came in just after the rain started."

"Good," she said, truly relieved. She'd hated the thought of him out alone without shelter in this nasty weather. "Is he coming in for breakfast?"

Rayad looked at her regretfully. "I don't think so. He's got food out there."

Simply happy he wasn't in the rain, Kyrin returned to serving. A cheery atmosphere filled the cabin, which was packed nearly full of people and glowing with the fire and candles in contrast to the dreariness outside. Kyrin enjoyed the conversations and laughter. It was so much more agreeable than all the gossiping at Tarvin Hall.

Though busy, she kept an eye on Rayad, and when he finished and was about to leave, she filled a large mug of coffee.

"Will you take this out to Jace?" she asked him.

He gave her a warm smile of gratitude. "I'd be glad to."

Jace stared out into the gloom as the rain drummed the tent canvas, but his thoughts were far away from this place. They took him back to the farm—back to better days. During rainy times like this, warmth, life, and the delicious smell of Kalli's baking had filled the cabin. She almost always made him his favorite shortbread cookies when the weather turned bad. Maybe because she knew how he hated being cooped up indoors. But it wasn't so bad at the farm. After the necessary chores, the men always found something to do, and Kalli had entertained him with stories of her childhood with nine rambunctious siblings.

Someone entered the tent, and the memories scattered. He cleared his throat and blinked several times, but a deep ache throbbed in his chest. He glanced up when Rayad offered him a steaming cup of coffee.

"Kyrin asked me to bring this out to you."

Jace wrapped his fingers around the warm mug, frowning at thoughts of Kyrin. He'd seen her waiting outside the cabin yesterday and this morning, even in the rain. Why would she be so persistent? Didn't she understand what he was? First Rebekah and now Kyrin. He shook his head. Young women were a mystery.

The rain beat down throughout the day and halted work around camp. The men congregated in their tents or Lenae's cabin, where there appeared to be a never-ending supply of hot coffee. No one seemed to mind the weather as their muted voices and laughter drifted through the rain. No one but Jace. He glowered into the soggy dimness. Being confined to the small tent stifled him. Tyra had been his only companion most of the day. When Rayad did come in, they didn't talk, though it wasn't for lack of Rayad trying. Jace just didn't have anything to say.

By evening, he was ready to forget the rain and take off. If it made him deathly ill, so be it. But, before he could act, Rayad came to the tent once again.

"Why don't you come and get supper with me?"

Jace eyed Lenae's cabin through the parted tent flap. It was sure to be crowded.

"You don't have to eat in the cabin," Rayad told him, tone firm, "but you can at least come and get a warm meal."

Jace still hesitated. Yes, the idea of facing the men repelled him, but that wasn't the main reason. Blast his nagging conscience. It wasn't his fault Kyrin stood waiting outside the cabin every morning. He'd never said she could go with him more than that one time, and even that had been a mistake. So why feel guilty about it?

In the end, his need to get out of the tent outweighed his discomfort, and he rose to follow Rayad. Though a chilly rain fell around them, the air refreshed his taut nerves. Comforting warmth enveloped them when they stepped into the cabin. At the mixed aroma of chicken and baked goods, Jace's stomach growled like it hadn't in a while. His eyes roamed over the men who sat at the table and stood around with plates. A few glanced at him, but the good food and company earned their full attention. Lenae stood at the hearth, and Kyrin moved around the cabin filling plates and mugs. Turning, she caught sight of him, and a smile lit up her face.

Jace ducked his head. So few people had ever offered him such a genuine smile. He stared at the floor and followed Rayad deeper into the cabin. He just had to get his plate and go. He didn't even care what was on it.

"Hungry?"

He cringed at the nearness of Kyrin's voice.

"Mm, yes," Rayad responded. "The food smells delicious."

Jace chanced a peek at Kyrin. Her face still glowed with a smile as she dished up generous portions of chicken and potatoes onto two plates. Before she finished, she asked, "Would you like a slice of pie? Lenae taught me how to make them this afternoon."

"I would love one," Rayad answered enthusiastically. He always had loved pie.

"Jace?"

He started at his name, and this time met her gaze. What was it about her that left him incapable of saying no? He nodded.

She put a large slice of berry pie on his plate and handed it to him, her eyes kind and encouraging. "There you go."

"Thanks," he murmured, just loud enough for her to hear, and immediately turned for the door. Back out in the tent, he watched the cabin with a frown, giving little thought to his food. Even so, for the first time in weeks, he ate everything on his plate.

KYRIN PROPPED HERSELF up on her elbow. Even though it hadn't rained the day before, Jace still had not come by. She had to admit, she missed sleeping in. Did it really pay to get up again when Jace hadn't shown for three mornings in a row? She should probably give up and face facts. He didn't want her hunting with him. She glanced down at her pillow, still warm and inviting. She wavered for a moment, but she was more stubborn than that. Just one more morning. Then she would have to wait to see if Elôm provided her with a different approach.

She changed into her hunting clothes and went to the door. With a little prayer, she reached for the knob and prepared herself for disappointment, but when the door opened halfway, her eyes rounded.

Jace and Tyra stood just outside.

It took two or three heartbeats for her to trust her own eyes. Not for a second had she truly expected him to be there. Getting a hold of herself, she stepped out and quietly closed the door. With a hand still on the knob, she stared up at Jace in the silence that hung between them.

Jace broke it with an uncertain glance toward the trees. "Do you want to go hunting?"

Kyrin tried to hide her smile. "I'd love to."

Jace cleared his throat and gave an awkward nod. Kyrin worked to school her features. She didn't want to scare him off with her enthusiasm, but giddiness bubbled through her as she followed him across camp and into the forest. *Thank You, Elôm, and forgive my doubting.*

Jace seemed to move more slowly today, perhaps to allow her to keep up. As the sun peeked through the foliage ahead of them, the forest came alive, delighting Kyrin with the freshness of a new morning, but she focused her concentration on walking silently. Though not nearly as quiet as she would like to be, there must have been a difference. About a mile in, Jace glanced over his shoulder at her and murmured, "You're improving."

"I hope so," Kyrin replied earnestly. "I've been practicing."

His brows hiked up, and she grinned to herself when he looked away.

The morning wore on Kyrin, but not as much as last time. The slower pace helped. Though Jace didn't speak again, the silence wasn't so uncomfortable until noon came and they paused for lunch. Kyrin couldn't waste this opportunity to get to know him. A third chance wasn't likely if she failed this one.

As she pulled food from her pouch, her mind raced all over for something to say. What would Kaden say in this situation, or anyone else for that matter? But then, neither she nor Jace had lived normal lives or had anything normal to talk about. She frowned down at the roll in her hand as if it might hold answers and tore off a piece to chew while she thought. She glanced over at Jace and found the same type of frown on his face. Suddenly, he looked up and met her eyes.

"So, you can remember everything?"

She blinked. He'd actually beat her to saying something. She gulped down her bite of roll to answer him. "Yes. If I see or hear something, I'll remember it." She paused, but seized on the opportunity to keep the conversation going and not let silence take over again. "A book, for instance. If I get a good look at a page, I can go back later and read it in my mind. It takes more concentration than simply reading it though."

Jace stared at her with widened eyes, but then looked away as a grimace flashed across his face. Clearly, he remembered enough of his past without having her abilities.

He cleared his throat and asked, "When did it start?"

"When I was four."

He looked at her again, his eyes vivid with interest and more openness than he had shown in their previous encounters. "You remember everything since you were four?"

Kyrin nodded, and Jace responded by shaking his head. "How do you process it all?"

She shrugged. "I just do, I guess, but it can be very overwhelming. I get bad headaches in new or stressful situations when I have a lot to take in. Especially in crowds. Sometimes I start to panic. I used to faint a lot, but I haven't in a while."

Quiet returned. She should ask something about him, but what would he be keen on sharing? She nibbled on her roll again. Her eyes fell on the wolf sitting at his side, and she perked up.

"How did you get Tyra?"

The wolf turned her head at the sound of her name, and Jace rubbed her back. "I came across her while hunting. She was just a pup, but someone had shot her. I brought her back to the farm and . . ." His voice caught, and he clenched his jaw. "Kalli helped me fix her up. She never left after that."

Kyrin offered him a compassionate smile, but a sharp ache jabbed her chest, and the smile faded when he looked away.

No way Kaden could pull this off . . . but it was mandatory. The order came straight from Emperor Daican. He swallowed, his dratted uniform pressing against his throat. He reached up to unfasten the top clasp, but it didn't seem to help when he swallowed hard again. If he didn't keep it together today, all would be lost and his change in behavior would be for naught.

He scanned the courtyard. Every student over fourteen trickled from the Hall and gathered around him. Thank Elôm the younger children weren't required to attend. His gaze snagged on Sam. The talcrin's face was set in a tight, grim expression.

When the final stragglers joined them, they and most of Tarvin Hall's staff filed out of the gate. En masse, they trooped to the city square. A crowd already filled the center, preventing them from getting much closer, but this was close enough. Kaden eyed the platform. Cold sludge filled his veins. He could still see Kyrin standing there—a sight from a nightmare.

He sucked air into lungs constricted by anxiety, and his eyes darted to his surroundings. If only he could bolt now while outside of Tarvin Hall. It had certainly crossed his mind since the emperor's order came. But his scan of the area destroyed such hopes. His two guards stood only a couple of paces behind him. Even if he could break past them, a hundred of his fellow students surrounded him, who would be quick to step in and stop him. He had no choice but to endure this.

His eyes settled once more on the platform as his hands turned slick and a cold sweat beaded on his back. The executioner stood waiting just as they were. Anticipation rippled through the murmurs around him. But something heavy and dark permeated the air and raised goose bumps across Kaden's skin—something far more sinister than he'd sensed at any ryrik executions. At least those executions had been just.

The commotion started at the far side of the square and rolled toward them. The hard hammering of Kaden's heart pummeled his ribcage, and he gnashed his teeth together. He couldn't be here without reliving the moment that Daican's men brought Kyrin to the platform. The last time he'd seen his sister. He looked away, fighting the hot burn in his chest that threatened to make him scream and fight his way out of this. His fists clenched, and he wished for a sword hilt between them. Maybe then he could stop this.

When he dragged his gaze back, a group of people ascended the platform, all but three of them guards. Two men and a woman lined up for the crowd to see. Kaden's eyes touched each of their drawn, dirt-smudged faces. The woman was especially pale. She wasn't much older than Kyrin and had the same shade of brown hair shorn just above her shoulders. Kaden struggled to breathe. They stared out at the crowd, their eyes wide, but a determined strength seemed to surround them as it had Kyrin. The restrictive bands around Kaden's chest drew tighter. These men and this woman weren't here for murder or any other heinous crime. They were here because of their belief in King Elôm—the very same belief he shared. And today, they would die for it.

Sir Richard stepped forward. The murmuring crowd quieted to let him speak.

"These three prisoners before you have publically renounced our sovereign gods, Aertus and Vilai, and have chosen instead to follow after myths. They have willfully turned on their gods, their emperor, and their country. For their treason, they have been sentenced to death, as is fitting for all such traitors to our empire."

Shouts of assent burst forth from all around Kaden. He tried to swallow, but his throat locked up. His hands trembled with the desire to grab the nearest person and shake some sense into them.

Sir Richard stepped back, and one of the guards reached for the woman. Tears streamed down her face, and she wilted in his grasp. Kaden choked down a cry for the madness to stop. Before the guard led her forward, one of the captive men stepped up and said something Kaden could not hear. The guard led him forward instead, toward the execution block.

Kaden dropped his eyes to the ground. Required or not, he couldn't bear to watch.

Not a single one of the prisoners begged for mercy. They met their deaths bravely and faithfully despite the hostile uproar of the crowd. By the end, tears tore viciously at Kaden's eyes. He stood frozen, his thoughts a hazy, roaring chaos. What little he had for breakfast threatened to come up. But if he reacted, he would soon be on that platform himself.

The crowd broke up, his classmates turning to return to Tarvin Hall, but Kaden couldn't move until someone took his arm. He looked up into Sam's watery gold eyes. He guided him around, and Kaden followed, a blank mask falling into place. But inside, he cried out to Elôm for intervention and justice for the murder of innocent lives.

Evening approached. They surely hadn't covered as much ground as they had on their first hunting trip due to how slowly Kyrin moved, but at least she was quieter. Hopefully that counted for something. She placed her foot down carefully alongside a dead branch and glanced up right as Jace halted and held up his hand. She froze. Just ahead, Tyra stood stone-still and stared intently into the trees. Very slowly, Jace reached back for an arrow from his quiver and nocked it to his bowstring. With stealthy steps, he moved a little farther ahead and to the right.

Kyrin scanned the forest. Nothing moved in the shadows, but then a flicker drew her attention to a deer twenty yards ahead. Her eyes darted between the animal and Jace and her pulse quickened. Jace drew back his bowstring. She held her breath.

At the deep twang of Jace's bow, the deer jumped and bolted. Tyra ran after it, but it fell before she reached it. Kyrin blew out a breath and looked at Jace. It hadn't even been her shot, but her blood surged with the exhilaration of the hunt.

"Good shot."

Jace glanced at her quizzically. "Thanks."

She followed him to the downed deer, where Tyra waited. Jace patted the wolf on the head and pulled out his hunting knife. He knelt near the deer, but paused and looked up at Kyrin.

"Will you be all right with this?"

She smiled at his concern and the fact that he would even think to ask. And people thought he was some sort of monster. "Don't worry. My family had a few farm animals when I was young, and my brothers cured me of squeamishness a long time ago."

Satisfied, Jace went to work gutting the deer. Kyrin stayed close and watched with interest. It probably would never be necessary to do it herself, but she could still learn.

"So, did Tyra see it first or did you?" she asked.

Jace shrugged. "About the same time."

Kyrin thought on this and glanced at Tyra, who waited patiently for Jace to toss her bits of scraps. It was fascinating to consider what type of abilities Jace might have that she did not. She wanted to know more, but how far could she question him without making him uncomfortable? With great care, she spoke. "I hope this question doesn't offend you, but are you able to sense things faster than, say, Rayad or I would?"

She watched his face and bit the inside of her lip.

He paused, but didn't appear upset. "It seems so."

What would it be like to have a heightened sense of awareness? But she didn't question him any further. They'd had a good day, and she wouldn't risk ending it on a bad note.

Once Jace finished, he lifted the deer up over his shoulders and led the way toward camp. It turned out they didn't have far to go. Again, Kyrin hadn't even been aware they'd headed back. Coming alongside Jace as they entered camp, she looked up at him.

"Perhaps you could teach me how to find my way in the forest. I had no idea where we were all day."

He glanced at her. "Maybe tomorrow I can show you."

A deep sense of pleasure welled inside Kyrin. She'd come so close to giving up, but today was even more than she could have hoped for. By all appearances, she'd made a breakthrough with Jace.

Near the fire, they parted, and Kyrin approached Lenae.

"That smile says a lot."

Kyrin didn't realize she had been smiling, but it grew into a wide grin. "It was a very good day."

"I'm happy to hear it. I could tell it in Jace's face."

"Really?" Kyrin glanced back at him. She was getting better at reading him, but it was good to hear that Lenae shared her observations.

In less than an hour, the men gathered for supper. Kyrin filled her plate, but didn't move to her usual spot next to Lenae or Rayad. On the other side of the cooking pot, Jace dished up and headed for his tree as always. Kyrin's gaze shifted back to the fire. If Holden knew of her hunting trip with Jace, no doubt the rest of camp did. It would explain the questioning looks she received.

She drew her shoulders back. She had come this far. Now it had to be all or nothing. Setting her eyes on Jace, she strode away from the fire and joined him at the edge of camp. His eyes, shining bright even in the twilight shadows, widened in open astonishment. She nestled down in the grass across from him and met his penetrating stare.

"You don't have to talk. I don't want you to feel pressure to do that. I know what it's like, and I'm not good at it myself. But I just wanted you to know that no matter what kind of blood you have, it makes no difference to me, and I don't care what any of those men down by the fire might say or think."

SUNSHINE FILTERED THROUGH the canopy, falling warm on Jace's face, and birdsong filled his ears. His eyes flashed open, and he bolted upright. Tyra lay stretched out beside him as she basked in the sun at their campsite by the stream. He rubbed his hands over his eyes, and it hit him. He'd slept through the night. For the first time in weeks, the nightmares had not tormented him. He breathed out a deep breath, refreshed by the rest. When was the last time he had slept so late?

Kyrin. She would think he left her behind. Strange how much that bothered him. They'd gone hunting every day for almost a week. At first, he did it only to ease the guilt that wouldn't let him rest, but, if he was truly honest, he now rather liked her company. Somehow, she understood him. Maybe even more than Rayad—a startling surprise. But she knew what it was like to be different.

Jace threw aside his blanket and pushed to his feet. Tyra jumped up to follow him, and he strapped on his sword. He wouldn't be unprepared if he and Kyrin ever came upon trouble. Her safety was far more important than his fear of hurting someone. Bow and quiver in hand, he strode toward camp.

He slowed at the edge and looked around. A long time had passed since he'd seen camp during the day. He wasn't used to so much activity, and his instincts shied away from it, but he pressed on with a purpose.

At Lenae's cabin, the door stood open to let in the warm fresh air. Jace stepped up to the doorway. Lenae and Kyrin stood at the table with their hands covered in flour. The older woman instructed Kyrin on something to do with baking. Jace knocked lightly on the doorframe, and they looked up.

"Jace." Kyrin's tone held a little surprise, but if she was upset, he couldn't tell.

"I overslept." He shrugged sheepishly. "I didn't want you to think I left you behind."

A bright smile bloomed on Kyrin's face, and she shook her head. "That's all right. And anyway, you don't have to take me every day . . . not if you don't want to."

But he did, even though he didn't say so. "I thought we could go now." He hesitated. "But I don't want to take you away from what you're doing."

Kyrin glanced at the dough she worked with. "It won't be much longer; otherwise, you can go. I don't want to keep you either."

"You go on, Kyrin," Lenae told her. "I'll finish."

"Are you sure?"

Lenae nodded, and Kyrin wiped her floury hands on her apron before setting it aside and giving Jace a quick smile. "I just need to get my bow."

She climbed the ladder to the loft, and Lenae turned to smile at him. It was kind of the woman to finish for Kyrin. Most people would have discouraged her from going.

"Have you had any breakfast?"

"No," he admitted. In his haste, eating hadn't even occurred to him.

"Well, take this at least." Lenae brought him a large sweet roll and a cup of coffee.

He accepted gladly, appetite fully returned. Taking his first bite of the roll, the sugary softness nearly melted in his mouth and reminded him of Kalli's delicious baked goods. Before he could voice a compliment, Lenae said, "Kyrin made them this morning."

Jace's eyes shifted to her as she came down from the loft. "They're very good."

A little pink dusted her cheeks, and she gave a modest shrug. "It's one of my first attempts. I knew nothing about baking and cooking when I arrived here, but Lenae is fixing that."

Jace took another bite, but this one went down hard. Kalli would have loved Kyrin. He could almost imagine her in Lenae's place, and how the two of them would have talked and laughed. A hot knife pierced his heart. He cleared his throat and pushed away the pain just before Kyrin looked back at him from over near the shelf.

"Do you have anything for lunch?"

He shook his head to give himself a second to moderate his voice, though it lacked the steadiness he intended. "No, I forgot it by the stream."

She stared at him for a moment with those perceptive, but kind, eyes. He glanced away, and she turned back to the shelf, tucking extra food into her pouch, including two more sweet rolls.

"I'll see you at supper," she told Lenae as she joined Jace.

"Have fun," she replied with a smile.

Jace let Kyrin precede him through the door and came alongside her as they walked through camp. The ache in his chest still throbbed faintly, but everything felt right until he caught Holden's watchful eyes. The intensity and mistrust in his expression turned Jace's stomach. He looked away, but the other man's accusation followed him. It was just like Rebekah and Laytan all over again, and it hurt Jace more than he wanted to admit. The last thing he would ever do was harm Kyrin, but Holden would never believe that.

"Don't worry about him." Kyrin's comforting words pulled his attention back to her. "His concern comes from what he experienced, not from you personally." She gave him a reassuring smile. "He doesn't know you."

Simple words didn't often encourage Jace, but something about hers had the power to lift his spirits, and he was able to leave all thought of Holden behind when they entered the forest.

Even with a late start, they covered a lot of ground. Kyrin's skill improved with every trip, and she learned much from Jace—how to find her way, how to spot and track animal signs, and which plants were edible. She'd questioned him one day as to how he'd acquired the knowledge. Most information had come from Rayad, but the rest he'd learned through experience, practice, and instinct. During this time together, Jace opened up a little more every day. Although they still avoided any serious topics, she sensed he was closer to sharing his deeper thoughts and feelings with her. After all, even someone as strong as Jace surely needed someone to lean on once in a while. He'd looked so sad for that moment in the cabin.

But such thoughts couldn't be dwelt on as she scanned the forest for any sign of game. It was one of the biggest things she learned from Jace—to always be aware of her senses and tune them in to her surroundings. She stepped along with care, deep in concentration.

When she reached to push aside the dense underbrush, an ear-piercing shriek rang out to her right as something exploded from the leaves. She jumped back, her foot snagging, and let out a little scream as she landed in a bed of ferns. Her rounded eyes followed a plump, chicken-sized bird that fluttered off deeper into the forest. Heart rattling against her ribs, she looked up at Jace. He gripped his sword, but he let his hand fall back to his side as he too watched the bird disappear from sight.

"What was that?" Kyrin gasped.

"Rock pheasant." He turned to her. "Are you all right?"

Kyrin nodded and took in long, deep breaths. "I've *never* seen or heard one of those in my life." She let her head hang back and willed her pulse to return to normal. Then, a nervous giggle bubbled out. She hadn't screamed like that since she was little and her brothers played pranks on her.

"Just about scared the life out of me," she laughed.

She raised her head to look at Jace again, and her heart skipped in surprise. A smile had broken out on his face—a comfortable, genuine smile that brought a sparkle to his eyes and transformed his expression from one that often made her ache with compassion to one that filled her with joy. Caught in the wonder of it, she could only stare. Slowly, his smile faded, replaced by self-consciousness.

"What?"

Kyrin shook her head and snapped to her senses. "Nothing, it's just . . . this is the first time I've seen you smile."

Jace's eyes dropped to the ground, and he shrugged. "I guess I haven't had much to smile about these days."

"Well," she said gently, "I hope that changes." That smile had been one of the most wonderful things she'd witnessed since arriving here. It thrilled her inside.

Jace said nothing, but reached down to offer her a hand. She gripped it, and he pulled her up out of the ferns. As she brushed herself off, he scanned the area. "I suppose we'll have lunch here."

"Since I scared all the game away?" She gave him a wry grin.

"The pheasant took care of that. It's too bad we didn't realize he was there sooner. They're good eating."

He led her to a fallen log nearby. They sat down, and Kyrin pulled food from her pouch.

"I take it you've encountered quite a few of these rock pheasants," she said as she split the lunch between them. "I didn't notice you react."

Now that he'd done it once, a smile came more easily to Jace as if the cage of despair trapping his joy finally unlocked. "Yes, they're pretty common, but they only shriek like that when they're startled."

Kyrin let out another amused laugh. "I think I was the one who was startled. I can't believe I didn't see him."

"They're well-camouflaged. I didn't see him either, or I would've warned you."

Kyrin just smiled with delight that he so easily talked with her now—not at all like their first hunting trip. His friendship meant so much to her after these few short days. She'd set out hoping to help yet another victim of cruelty and bullying, but he was so much more than that, filling a little of the hole left in the separation from Kaden. Through Jace, Elôm taught her how to let go of the familiar security of her brother and open up to others.

She chuckled quietly to herself. Jace would be astounded by such thoughts.

He gave her a questioning look, and she shook her head. "I was just thinking about my brother and how strange life is." She gazed around at the summer beauty surrounding them. Longing squeezed her chest. As much as Jace had enriched her days, she still ached for Kaden to be a part of it too. "I can't wait until Kaden can see all this. I'm not sure where he got the idea, but he's always talked about living off in the forest." She returned her attention to Jace. "I look forward to you meeting him."

A shadow crossed his face, flight instincts glinting in his eyes, but Kyrin was quick to reassure him. "He won't be like the others. He might be a little wary at first, but that's just because he's very protective of me. He'd be that way with anyone."

She offered a comforting smile. Once Kaden did arrive, and she held strongly to the belief he would, she was certain he would treat Jace as he deserved.

The hesitation slowly drained from Jace's expression. "He sounds like a good brother."

Kyrin gave a hearty nod, but her smile faded, and she dropped her voice to a more serious tone. "Do you know if you have any siblings?"

Jace met her eyes for only a brief moment, but it was long enough to reveal the empty hole in his heart. He gave a tiny shake of his head. "No."

He bit off a piece of his roll, and Kyrin read it as the end of their conversation. She focused on her own lunch, and for a long time they didn't say anything, but then Jace spoke again.

"My earliest memories are of working as a slave. I worked and slept with the other slave children until I was strong enough for harder labor. I don't even know who cared for me as a baby. No one told me where I came from, just that I was half ryrik . . . an animal."

Kyrin drew a quick breath, her eyes stinging because it was clear he still believed it. People were so horribly cruel. How could anyone look at Jace and see an animal? She couldn't help but hate the people who had done this to him, warping his perception of himself for all this time, and she prayed for calm and the ability to help him. The anger dissipated into more encouraging thoughts. "But then Elôm brought Rayad along to rescue you."

Jace hung his head.

"You don't believe that?"

He stared at his hands and murmured, "I don't know if it was for me."

"Oh, Jace, of course it was." She almost reached out to touch his arm, but held back.

He shook his head and fell silent again. She studied him and the doubt etched in every curve of his face. *Elôm, I want to help him so much, but how? Please show me.*

"I'm praying." He glanced at her, and she went on, her voice low with conviction. "I'm praying He will show you beyond any doubt that no matter what you believe right now, He loves you. I know He does."

Now Jace did hold her gaze for a moment. The longing glowed dimly in his eyes, but was strangled by fear. Too many betrayals, damaging words, and demons from his past destroyed any confidence he might have had, and the struggle played out on his face.

Elôm, Rayad said he believed once. Please show him his faith was real, that he does belong to You, that You do love him. He needs assurance so badly. She forced a lighter tone to her voice.

"Well, do you think we should get moving?"

Neither one had touched their remaining lunch for a while.

Jace nodded and looked eager to put the conversation behind him.

They packed up the uneaten food and set off again. This time, Kyrin paid particular attention to what might be hiding in the leaves and underbrush, but her thoughts lingered on Jace and his struggle. He had to have a soul. Rayad believed he did, and so did she. After all these days spent with him, no one could convince her otherwise. She wanted to help him believe it too, but only Elôm could truly do that.

When evening closed in on them, it appeared they would return to camp empty-handed this time. However, drawing near to camp, Jace stopped. Instead of pulling an arrow from his quiver as he usually did when he and Tyra spotted game, he looked over his shoulder and motioned Kyrin forward. With painstaking movements, she came to his side, where he pointed ahead. Kyrin peered into the trees. Her eyes picked out movement and landed on a small, yearling doe.

She looked up at Jace. He nodded to her and then to the deer. She pointed to herself and mouthed, "Me?" He nodded again, and her pulse pattered to a higher rate. What if she missed? She hated for such a good meal to get away. But something lit Jace's eyes she had not seen before. Confidence—in her. Her heart rate spiked again with a surge of determination.

She reached back for an arrow and slowly moved into a better position. The deer's head shot up, and Kyrin froze. It stared right at her, and she held her breath. For a long moment, all was still. At last, the deer put its head down again to nibble at the grass. Kyrin raised her bow and drew back the string. She forced herself to draw a long, slow breath. If she rushed the shot now, she would surely miss. Everything stilled and quieted inside her. The bowstring slipped off the tips of her fingers.

The arrow flew away, and the doe leaped forward, but crumpled. She'd done it. Her first deer. She looked back at Jace. A smile lifted his lips.

"Good shot."

She grinned, and her breath rushed out with a short laugh. "Thank you."

Together, they walked over to the deer.

"A very good shot," Jace said, and Kyrin delighted in the tone of admiration in his voice.

She walked around the doe and knelt down. Looking up at Jace, she held out her hand. "Can I borrow your knife?"

His expression lifted in surprise, but he reached down and pulled out his knife, handing it to her hilt first. Under his expert guidance, she gutted the doe. When she had finished, she wiped her hands in the leaves, and Jace picked up the deer to carry to camp. Just before they arrived, however, he paused and turned to Kyrin.

"Do you want to carry it into camp? It's your kill."

Now Kyrin lifted her brows as she considered it.

"Take off your quiver and turn around," Jace told her with a smile in his voice.

She did as he instructed.

Carefully, he draped the deer around her shoulders. "Got it?"

"I think so."

It was heavy, but manageable, being a yearling. Once he was sure she had a good grip, Jace picked up her quiver and they walked on.

She chuckled. "If only Kaden could see me now."

What a thought, considering his reaction to her all dressed up at the palace. No doubt he'd be just as shocked, but much more pleased. He wouldn't be the only one.

"If only my father could see me." She smiled wistfully with the distinct feeling he would be proud.

They walked into camp, and the sight of Kyrin caught everyone's attention. The men ahead of them talked and pointed, and soon gathered around. Now they'd really be enamored with her. She smiled as they questioned her about the deer and tried to minimize it, but they still made a fuss. She glanced at Jace, who stayed outside the ring of admirers. The little smile twinkling in his eyes made it worth it.

Once the men let her pass, she continued with Jace to the supply shack. Neither said anything, but the comfortable sense of camaraderie between them brought Kyrin much happiness and contentment.

"SEE THESE TRACKS?"

Kyrin knelt next to Jace and nodded. A narrow path was worn into the forest floor, the soft ground imprinted with many little paw prints.

"This trail is used often. It leads back to the spring." Jace pointed the way they had come. "It's an ideal location to set a snare."

Kyrin listened intently. They had plenty of meat at camp, so Jace turned his focus on teaching her other survival and hunting techniques. She welcomed not only the knowledge, but the reason to spend most of the day in the forest. Her worries and thoughts of the emperor seemed to fade in the quiet and peaceful green surroundings.

"This sapling will work well." Jace grasped the small tree and bent it down to show her how to rig the snare. "I usually prefer to hunt, but in the winter snares are helpful when game is harder to find." He tripped the snare and motioned to her. "You try it."

She traded places with him and reset it exactly as he'd shown her.

He gave her a nod of approval. "We'll check it tomorrow to see if you caught anything."

Kyrin rose with him, and they headed in the direction of a wild raspberry patch they'd discovered. If they brought enough back to camp, Lenae promised to make hand pies like the ones Kyrin had enjoyed so much back in Valcré. Maybe she could learn to make her own before Kaden showed up. She could just see him trying to sneak some of her baked goods. The thought brought a grin to her lips. Those days couldn't come soon enough.

"I never imagined I'd love living like this so much," she remarked, enjoying a walk without the worry of scaring off game. "I don't know what it would be like to live in the city again."

Jace glanced at her and wrinkled his nose in distaste. "I could never live in the city. Especially not Valcré."

"Have you seen Valcré?"

"Twice."

He still looked like he'd swallowed something nasty, but Kyrin's thoughts went beyond the city itself. "We came that close to meeting, but both ended up here."

Jace considered this in silence. She tried to read his expression. He seemed hesitant about such a notion; no doubt because of the life he'd lived at the time. Hating to spoil a beautiful day, she searched for a lighter topic to discuss.

She opened her mouth to speak again, but Jace stopped and held up his hand. Kyrin halted. A low growl rumbled from Tyra, who stared into the trees, the hair rising around her neck. Kyrin scanned the vegetation, but nothing stirred. She looked up at Jace. His eyes, bright with alertness, swept the area.

"What is it?" she whispered.

He shook his head. "I don't know."

Kyrin's eyes flicked down. His fingers wrapped around the hilt of his sword, and he withdrew it slowly.

"Stay close," he murmured.

Her heartbeat quickened. Jace spent so much time in the forest that nothing would concern him unless it presented real danger. She drew a breath to calm her nerves. After all, they had no idea what *it* was yet. Still, she reached for an arrow, feeling a lot more confident with the projectile fitted to her bowstring, ready for use.

Tyra growled again, and Jace followed her line of sight. Kyrin looked too, but sunlight and bright green leaves offered her a deceptively calm view. Too calm. The forest had become unnaturally quiet. A chill washed down her back, and Jace moved to stand in front of her. Something crackled the leaves several yards away. He straightened, and his forearms flexed as he squeezed the hilt of his sword.

"Someone's out there."

Kyrin gulped. Had the emperor's men found them? Her fingers sweat as she gripped her bow tightly. They wouldn't take her back to Valcré. She'd fight it first.

Jace's voice rang out, hard and demanding, to break the stillness. "Who's out there? Show yourself!"

Silence followed. Kyrin's eyes jumped from the trees to Jace and back again as she waited for the emergence of black and gold.

"Look what we have here."

She almost choked on her own breath as she and Jace spun around. Tyra snarled. Kyrin took a quick step closer to Jace as she witnessed every Arcacian citizen's worst nightmare. Less than four yards away stood three black-haired, wild-eyed, burly ryriks. With the snapping of brush, three more appeared behind Jace and Kyrin, cutting off any escape.

At Tyra's menacing growl, Jace murmured, "Easy," his eyes trained on the ryriks.

The head ryrik, the biggest and fiercest of the group, examined the three of them. A wickedly satisfied grin spread across his bearded face.

"We've stumbled upon quite a prize, now haven't we?" He glanced at the other ryriks, who grinned their agreement. His almost glowing eyes settled on Kyrin. Repulsion skittered under her skin, and she shivered hard. "Aren't you a pretty young thing?"

She tried to swallow back the rising tide of fear, but her throat convulsed. *Elôm, help us!* Her heart thrashed violently and ignited a panic she fought to contain. Every gruesome story she'd ever heard of ryrik attacks screamed through her mind.

Jace's firm hand closed around her arm, and he pulled her behind him to shield her from the leader's lecherous gaze. The ryrik gave a low chuckle, and Kyrin peeked around Jace's shoulder.

"You can't keep her from us, boy." The man eyed Jace, and his expression sank into a frown. "Wait . . . you're a ryrik."

"Half ryrik," Jace ground out.

The ryrik's eyes widened. "Half ryrik? Now there's a surprise." He considered Jace, looking him up and down. "Tell you what, since I'm in a generous mood, I'll make a deal with you. You leave your weapons and supplies, and I'll let you and your wolf walk away."

Jace nodded his head back at Kyrin. "She comes with me."

"I don't think so. The girl stays here."

Kyrin's stomach lurched up toward her throat, and she almost gagged. A tremor ran through her body straight down to her toes. She looked at the three ryriks behind her, and their vicious eyes froze her blood. She shrank back against Jace.

"I'm only giving you this one chance, boy," the lead ryrik said, his voice echoing his impatience. "You stay, you die."

Kyrin glanced up over her shoulder. If only she could see Jace's face! The frantic drumming of her heart dizzied her and brought a wave of unwanted thoughts of him leaving her to these monsters. Her eyes burned. *No.* He wouldn't do that.

"Tyra."

His voice helped her refocus.

The wolf looked up at him.

"Rayad," he murmured. Tyra cocked her head and he repeated the name. She watched him intently. Kyrin's heart pounded the seconds before he shouted, "Go!"

Tyra shot off like an arrow. One of the ryriks lunged for

her. His hand grazed her back leg, and she tumbled to the ground. Kyrin gasped, but the wolf jumped back to her feet and took off again, disappearing in the underbrush. Kyrin loosed a great sigh, but any relief died at the head ryrik's biting voice.

"Not a smart move."

Kyrin looked around Jace. A growing fire flamed behind the ryrik's eyes. She had seen that look before, but no chains or guards restrained this man. He dropped his pack and drew his sword. Each of the other ryriks followed his lead. Panic throbbed in Kyrin's muscles, and her breaths came in shallow gasps. Her hands trembled so badly she almost dropped her arrow. How would they ever get out of this? Blood thrummed in her ears, and her thoughts grew hazy. She gritted her teeth and shook the haze away. She must think clearly.

"Jace." Her voice cracked. She didn't take her eyes from the three ryriks she faced. "I will only be able to shoot one of them before they reach me." And they would reach her.

His shoulders moved against her in a slow breath. Voice quiet, but as sure she'd ever heard it, he said, "I won't let them have you."

She drew a steadying breath of her own. "I trust you."

"Last chance, boy," the ryrik growled. "Give up the girl."

"Never."

The strength and determination in his voice imparted just the courage Kyrin needed. She set her eyes on the nearest ryrik in anticipation of the attack. She had to make this one shot count. Ryriks were too resilient for her to fire just anywhere. She focused on his chest and pinned her eyes on where his heart was located. Her fingers still trembled, and she licked her lips. She'd never had to kill anyone before. *Stay calm.* But her pulse wouldn't cooperate and kicked up yet again. *Elôm!*

The ryriks lunged toward them. Kyrin raised her bow, drawing at the same time. The shot came purely out of instinct and buried deep in the ryrik's chest. Her gaze flew to the next man nearly upon her. She swung her bow. It caught him in the shoulder, but did little harm. He ripped the weapon from her hands. The third ryrik grabbed her by the arm. Hot adrenaline raced through Kyrin's blood, and she yanked and twisted, kicked and scratched. Anything to get away.

"Let go of me!" she screamed.

But her struggles were laughable compared to the strength of the ryrik. He grabbed her hair and dragged her a couple of yards away, where he forced her to her knees.

Gulping in air, she locked eyes on Jace. He stood surrounded by four ryriks. The one she shot lay unmoving. Sword ready, Jace turned in a slow circle, eyeing each of his opponents. For a brief moment, his eyes caught with Kyrin's, and she saw it—the fire, the intensity, building in them. Yet, it didn't contain hate and fury—only desperation and a strong will for survival. And right now, it was her only hope they would survive this.

The ryriks took advantage of his distraction and charged in. Kyrin sucked in her breath and held it, but with lightning reflexes and perfect accuracy, Jace met each sword hurtling toward him. The forest rang with the crash of metal. Moving constantly, Jace turned, and ducked, and blocked one attack after another. He fought masterfully and matched the strength, speed, and explosiveness of the other ryriks. But could he keep it up for long?

Kyrin struggled again, but her captor reached into his pack for a coil of rope and shoved her face-first into the leaves, pinning her there. He gripped her arm and yanked it back. Though her shoulder had mostly healed, pain shot through it, and she hissed in a breath. The ryrik hastily wrapped the rope around her wrists and tugged it tight, but Kyrin fought against him with all her strength. He used the other end of the rope to bind her ankles, and then snatched up his sword as he rose.

Kyrin rolled to her side and lifted her head. The ryrik rushed toward the fight and straight at Jace, who had his back turned.

Kyrin gasped, but Jace whirled around, his blade catching the ryrik in the arm and then driving into his side. The man stumbled away with blood pouring down his shirt. The four remaining ryriks redoubled their attack, but so did Jace. Kyrin could barely follow their movements. Many times, she braced herself to witness Jace's fall, but he somehow avoided it with moves he must have learned in the arenas.

Keeping her eyes locked on the fight, Kyrin twisted her wrists and pulled against her bindings. Her previous struggles and the ryrik's haste in tying her had created a little slack. If only she could loosen the ropes a bit more.

A second ryrik fell under Jace's sword, which left only three, including the leader. Their eyes burning in their desire to take him down, they came at him in a rage. Sweat darkened Jace's clothes, and his chest heaved. Kyrin begged Elôm to give him the strength to keep fighting, to win. But then he grunted in pain and grabbed for his side. Red seeped onto his jerkin.

"No!" Kyrin yanked at the ropes, not caring how the rough fibers dug into her skin.

The ryrik who'd injured Jace stepped in to finish him off. *Please, Elôm, no!* But Jace wasn't through. Rallying a reserve of strength, he caught the ryrik off guard. They traded crushing blows. Jace drove the man back and off balance until, at last, he threw down his opponent. Now only two remained.

Their glares bored into one another. Jace's heavy breathing filled the momentary silence. A wicked, sneering grin came to the ryrik leader's face and revealed no sign of fatigue.

"You're good, boy," he growled through bared teeth. "But not good enough."

The ryrik's blade sliced in a deadly arc toward Jace's throat. A small cry broke from Kyrin, but Jace jumped back just in time. The ryrik swung again. Jace managed to block, but the heavy ice sliding through Kyrin's veins told her this would be the end for both of them. Though eating and sleeping better, Jace still had not regained full strength. It was too clear in the way his arms shook as his sword collided with his enemy's.

Yet, somehow, some way, whether it was his ryrik blood, pure determination, or Elôm's aid, Jace again rallied his strength and launched his own attack. Hope rekindled in Kyrin. With one more strong pull, one of her hands slipped free. She scrambled up and reached for the rope around her ankles. Her eyes shifted between them and Jace as she tugged at the knots.

When Jace's sword locked with his opponent's, leaving him open from behind, Kyrin's heart stalled. Jace tried and failed to push the ryrik away and put space between them. Triumph lit in the lead ryrik's eyes as the second man raised his sword, but Kyrin jerked her feet free and lunged forward, locking her fingers around her bow. She reached for an arrow and drew back without even a pause for breath.

A gargled choke burst out. Jace looked over his shoulder as the second ryrik slumped to his knees with Kyrin's arrow piercing his throat. His eyes met hers a moment before flying back to the lead ryrik. Kyrin reached for a second arrow. The ryrik turned and bolted into the forest. She sent her arrow after him, but it deflected on a branch and missed him by inches. He disappeared before she could nock a third.

Jace turned to face her, and a breath rushed out of his lungs. Neither one moved for a long moment.

"Are you . . . all right?" he asked as he panted for air.

Kyrin's voice stuck in her throat. Fresh tremors passed down her arms and through her legs. Was she all right? Could she be? She forced out, "Yes, I'm all right." She gulped in a deep breath, and her eyes dropped to Jace's side. "But you're not."

She rushed over to him. Blood stained the side of his jerkin. He looked down as if just becoming aware of the wound and winced, but said nothing.

"Come, sit down," she told him, fighting the tremor in her voice.

She led him away from the dead ryriks. As the adrenaline and heat of battle wore off, Jace stumbled, but Kyrin kept a firm, supporting hand on his arm and walked steadily, though her bones were like willow twigs. The last ryrik she shot moaned as they passed, and his hand fumbled in the grass as if searching for his sword. He struggled once to rise, but collapsed again. She glanced at the gruesome sight with a grimace and gave him a wide berth.

Jace eased down into the grass, but his eyes trained on the forest. His right hand still gripped his sword. "We have to get out of here in case he comes back."

Kyrin glanced into the trees and swallowed. If she could, she'd run straight back to camp and not stop until she reached the safety of Lenae's cabin, but Jace needed tending. "You won't get far if you keep bleeding like this."

She attempted to inspect the wound through his ripped shirt and jerkin. The blood-soaked fabric stuck to his skin, but she caught a glimpse of torn flesh. Her stomach heaved and she choked it back, praying the wound wasn't as serious as all the blood made it appear. Of all the skills they'd taught at Tarvin Hall, why couldn't first aid have been one of them? Praying for guidance, she pulled out Jace's knife and slashed a panel from her split skirt. She cut it into a long strip and wrapped it tightly around Jace's middle to cover the wound.

"There. Hopefully that will help until we get back to camp."

Jace gave her an affirming nod, and she helped pull him up. Once on his feet, he kept her close and directed her away from the site of the battle. His eyes darted among the trees, and he did not return his sword to the scabbard. The ryrik could be anywhere, stalking them. No wonder Jace was so quiet in the woods. She realized now it must be an inherent ryrik skill.

Shaking off the uncomfortable chill that needled her body, Kyrin focused on Jace. He no longer panted so heavily, but his breaths still came out labored. Though his expression didn't show pain, he must feel some. She glanced at his bloodstained jerkin again. They were a good three miles from camp. Would he make it? *Please bring us help.*

The answer to her heart-whispered prayer came when Tyra bounded out of the underbrush toward them, followed closely by Rayad, Trask, Warin, and Mick. Kyrin blew out a sigh. "Thank You, Elôm."

When the men reached them, Rayad grabbed Jace's shoulder. "What happened?"

"Ryriks," Kyrin told them. A shudder passed through her.

The men traded looks, and Trask asked, "Where?"

"Back that way." Jace motioned. "There were six of them. Only one got away."

Rayad seemed far more concerned about Jace's condition than the ryriks. A little blood had seeped through the makeshift bandage. "Your wound, is it serious?"

Jace shook his head. "I don't think so."

Rayad looked pointedly at Kyrin.

"I didn't get a good look at it," she said. "I just wanted to get the bleeding stopped."

"You did well," he told her. "What about you? Are you hurt?"

Mentally, it would take time to recover, but physically she was unharmed—a miracle. "No, I'm all right."

"Good," Rayad breathed. "Let's get you back to camp."

It was a long walk, and Kyrin was thankful to have Rayad there to help support Jace as his strength wore away. When they arrived, the men drew around them to see what the fuss was about.

"Holden," Trask called out.

He stepped forward and cast a suspicious glance at Jace.

"Choose a couple of the men," Trask told him. "Arm yourselves, and get your horses. Ryriks attacked Jace and Kyrin. One got away. I want to make sure he isn't hanging around."

Holden's eyes rounded, and his face might have paled a little. But he nodded and turned to carry out Trask's orders. At least now he would get to expend his hatred on someone other than Jace.

As the men set off to track down the ryrik, Lenae beckoned Kyrin, Jace, and Rayad to the cabin and ushered them inside. Kyrin thanked Elôm that Lenae's husband had been Landale's physician and that she had assisted him. She would know just what to do for Jace. After guiding him to a bench at the table, Lenae addressed Kyrin.

"Will you fill a basin of water and bring it and clean cloths to the table?"

Kyrin rushed to gather the items while Lenae and Rayad removed the bandage and helped Jace pull off his jerkin and shirt. She set the basin and cloths on the table near them. The long gash below Jace's ribs drew her eyes. Lenae pressed a cloth to the still-bleeding wound and looked up again at Kyrin.

"There's a medical kit in the cabinet. Make sure your hands are clean and hold a needle to a flame for a few seconds. Then thread it for me and collect some bandages."

She spoke in a calm voice that eased the fitful churning of Kyrin's stomach. Kyrin followed her instructions and stood close by, ready to do anything else she could. She didn't mean to stare, but her eyes followed the pale, raised scars crisscrossing Jace's shoulders, back, and chest—deep scars from wounds he must have received in the arena, as well as whip scars. Tightness ached in her throat.

He looked up and caught her staring. She tried to pretend she hadn't noticed, and they both looked away uncomfortably.

When Lenae began stitching the wound, Jace grimaced, and his breath caught. Kyrin bit her lip.

"You should take it easy for a few days," Lenae said when she finished and covered the wound with fresh bandages. "I'll check it again tonight."

Jace stood slowly. He reached for his shirt and jerkin, but Lenae stopped him.

"You can leave them. I'll wash them and mend them for you."

"Thank you," he told her quietly.

He glanced at Kyrin and then walked outside. Rayad too thanked Lenae and followed him.

Silence settled inside the cabin. Lenae turned warm and gentle eyes to Kyrin. She'd acted so calmly, but now concern broke through. "Are you all right?"

Kyrin released a heavy breath. Moisture gushed into her eyes. "That's a good question." She sank down on the bench, and Lenae took a seat next to her. Tears spilled over. She swiped away the first ones, but more followed. "I was really scared . . . for both of us. They almost killed him."

Lenae put her arm around her and hugged her close.

"I've seen ryriks before," Kyrin said, sniffing, "but I never realized how terrifying they are . . . how utterly powerless you feel. If Jace hadn't been there . . ." She clenched her fists, shuddering, and couldn't get the ryrik leader's leering face out of her mind. She never would.

Lenae held her tightly. "But he was there," she replied softly. "Elôm didn't leave you defenseless."

Kyrin nodded and wiped her cheeks again. The tremors subsided and exhaustion set in.

"I'm going to go up and change," she murmured.

Lenae let her go, and she climbed up into the loft with heavy limbs. But when she had changed out of her torn dress, she stepped outside. Jace sat near the tent, resting. She walked over to him. Today was far too horrible to let any discomfort linger between them. He looked up, and she gave him a weary little smile.

"Thank you," she said, right from the deepest part of her heart, "for not leaving me to them. You saved my life."

Jace gave his head a slight shake. "I should be the one thanking you. You stopped the ryrik from killing me."

Her mind flashed back to the shot she'd made. "I just did what I had to." A fuller smile grew on her face. "I guess that makes us even."

The barest hint of a smile touched Jace's lips in return, but didn't fully materialize. Kyrin crinkled her forehead. Something troubled him, she was sure of it, but she didn't want to press him.

Trask and the others didn't return until late that evening. They came to the fire where the rest of camp ate supper, and Warin asked, "Did you find him?"

Trask shook his head. "We followed his trail a good eight miles south. I don't expect he'll come back, but I think it would be a good idea to post sentries from now on. At least at night, and no one should go out alone."

The men agreed, and as they discussed these new security measures, Kyrin worked her way around to one member of the tracking party in particular. She'd prepared for this all afternoon.

"Holden."

He turned to face her.

"I understand now," she said, her heartbeat a little elevated. She wasn't sure if it had completely settled at all yet. "Truly understand. But I do think you should know Jace was prepared to die before he'd let the ryriks have me. They realized he was part ryrik and offered to let him go, but he chose to protect me. He very nearly died doing so."

Holden stood silent as the orange firelight flickered on his hard expression. Doubt lurked, but Kyrin pressed on.

"I saw it in Jace's eyes, that fire and energy ryriks have, but it wasn't like the others. It had no hatred or cruelty behind it. What I do know for sure is, if Jace didn't have any ryrik blood, we would both be dead right now."

Whether this set Holden's mind to changing or not was impossible to know for sure, but she felt much better for having told him.

"No!"

The agonized cry broke free, but if it was just in his mind or real, Jace didn't know. He scrambled up. Pain ripped through his side, but it was eclipsed by the pain in his heart. He stumbled out of the tent as if to escape the horror, but it followed him, and the weight of it forced him to his knees. Gasping for air, he buried his face in his hands.

"Jace?" Rayad touched his shoulder.

He ripped away and staggered back to his feet. He didn't want anyone near him—*couldn't* let anyone near him.

"What's wrong?" Rayad asked.

Jace shook his head vehemently, afraid that speaking might make the dream real. Still panting, he backed away from Rayad.

"Jace, wait."

But he kept going as fear drove him out of camp. He hadn't gone far before the recurring images from his dream crippled him, and he dropped to his knees. It felt so horrifyingly real. Tears poured into his eyes, pooling on the rims, but not quite falling. With shallow, ragged breaths, he clenched his fists and swore he'd never let the dream come true. No matter what it took.

KYRIN CLIMBED DOWN the ladder to the sound of Lenae preparing breakfast. She glanced at the window where sunlight streamed in and was glad of the morning. Though she found a few hours of sleep, many times she woke up sweating and scared and would have to sit and pray before rest would come again. It made for a long night.

"I expected you to sleep in this morning."

Kyrin's attention returned to Lenae, and she shrugged. "I'm used to getting up early."

Lenae's eyes rested on her for a moment as if searching. She'd likely heard her wake up during the night.

"I'm all right," she assured her. "My mind just needs time to settle."

Lenae gave her an encouraging smile before focusing on the coffee.

Kyrin glanced at the door. "I think I'll go see how Jace is. I'll be back in a bit."

"Tell him to come in later so I can clean the wound and change the bandages."

"I will."

She opened the door and stepped outside. It was strange not to have Jace there waiting. It had become such a normal and familiar part of her day. Her eyes swept through camp. Several of the men were up, but Jace wasn't among them. Maybe he was still asleep. He could use the rest. She walked over to Rayad.

"Is Jace . . ." Seeing Rayad's tired and troubled eyes, the question died on her lips. "What's wrong?"

"He had a nightmare and went off during the night." Rayad shook his head, and lines deeply creased his forehead. "I don't know what he dreamed about, but I don't think I've ever seen him that upset before."

Worry splashed into the pit of Kyrin's stomach like a cold bucket of water. They'd come too far to have it all fall apart now. She turned to the forest. "I'll go look for him."

She started off, but Rayad warned, "Don't go far."

Kyrin swallowed as the coldness spread up through her chest and into her arms. The thought of being in the forest alone, even a short distance from camp, scared her more than she wanted to admit. But her concern for Jace outweighed even that. "I won't," she said and went on.

At the edge of camp, she paused to look around for any sign of where Jace had gone. If only she had his tracking expertise. The terrain didn't give up any answers to her barely trained eye. She pressed on a little farther and called his name, but received no response. She walked the perimeter of camp slowly, often looking over her shoulder. It would take time to shake the fear of someone stalking her, and she lamented the forest losing its peaceful touch. She whispered prayers, mostly for Jace, but also some for courage.

It didn't take long to circle camp. Of course, Jace was capable of taking care of himself, but Rayad's words left a gnawing ache inside her. Maybe it had to do with the way Jace acted after the attack. Something just felt wrong.

Arriving back where she started, she stopped and her shoulders drooped. Did she dare go farther? Moisture fled her throat. She didn't even have her bow with her. She turned to go back for it and caught a dark shape out of the corner of her eye.

Her heart almost crashed through her ribs, but she blew out a sigh when she realized it was Tyra and pressed her hand to her chest. The wolf appeared fully from behind a stand of close-growing maples. She stared at Kyrin, and then turned. Kyrin hurried toward the trees.

When she drew near, Jace stood. She halted. All the rest and health he'd regained seemed sucked right out of him. The healthy glow was gone, and his eyes were red, almost feverish. She glanced at his shirt. A small splotch of blood stained it.

"Jace, are you all right?" She took a step closer, and he shrank back as if afraid to have her near.

"You shouldn't be out here." His deep voice faltered. "You need to go back to camp . . . away from me."

Kyrin frowned, but spoke gently. "What's wrong?"

He just shook his head, unwilling to meet her eyes. "I can't take you hunting anymore."

The declaration hit her with an invisible force that stole her breath. "But . . . why?"

"You need to stay away from me."

She leaned in a bit to try to get him to look at her. "Is this because of your dream?" His face paled to an ashen hue. "Jace, what did you see in the dream?"

He dragged in a labored breath and shook his head again, but Kyrin persisted. "It will be better if you come out with it. Suffering alone won't help you."

Jace grimaced, but finally he spoke in a halting voice. "It . . . was you. You were . . . dead." His fists and jaw clenched, and he closed his eyes with a wince as if in terrible pain. "I did it."

Kyrin let this sink in and considered her reply. "Jace?" She waited until he finally looked at her. "It was only a dream. It wasn't real. I'm right here. You never have and never would hurt me."

He choked on a short pain-filled laugh. "How do you know?"

"Why would you?"

"Because, I'm a *monster*." He ground the words out, condemning himself, and as he held her gaze, the glint and shadows in his eyes writhed with the full extent of the pain he'd lived with for so long. "I'm an animal, Kyrin, just like they said. You can't trust me—"

"No!"

Her vehemence shocked them both. She cleared her throat, surprised by the force in her own voice, but she wouldn't let him do this. Not now, not after everything they'd been through. He might be willing to let himself sink back into despair, but she wasn't.

"No," she repeated, more softly this time. "You are not evil, you are not a monster, you are not *any* of the horrible things you've been led to think you are. You've been lied to from the time you could understand. You told me so yourself. But it's just not true, Jace. You must believe that."

Her words collided with his lifelong beliefs. He grimaced at the struggle. "Even if I wouldn't hurt you, people always get hurt around me. Look at Kalli and Aldor. Look at what nearly happened to you yesterday."

"You had nothing to do with the ryriks or with the men who killed Kalli and Aldor. You saved my life yesterday."

"But it's true. Bad things happen to the people I'm close to."

"No." She put her hands on her hips. She could be stubborn too, just like her brother. "If you're trying to tell me you're cursed, that won't work either. It's another lie. Things happen, Jace. Any of us could die at any time. That's in the hands of Elôm. You have nothing to do with it."

A fire had lit inside her now. She'd fought too hard to help him open up and always treaded so carefully so she wouldn't destroy their progress. It would not end with him closing himself off again out of fear something might happen to her.

She crossed the distance between them and reached out, gripping his arms to focus his attention. "You must listen to me.

I'm your friend. I care about you. You may try to push me away because you think it will make me safer, but I won't let you do it."

He stared down into her eyes.

"Stop believing the lies," she urged. "Please stop believing them."

Jace inhaled deeply and let it out in a rush. She felt the tension drain from his muscles. He might not be able to dispel all that had been drilled into him for so many years, but she saw in his eyes that he took the first steps.

Over the following days, Kyrin witnessed a subtle but sure change in Jace, as if the deeply rooted burdens he carried were finally falling away. She even coaxed him to join the group around the fire for meals. It wasn't comfortable for him, but at least the men seemed to have laid aside their fear and mistrust. Most of them anyway. Whether or not Jace's doubts were gone for good or would return in time was impossible to say, but she thanked Elôm for the progress. As she knew well by now, the future was too uncertain to dwell on for long.

Three days after her discussion with Jace, Trask rode into camp with an extra packhorse, but he brought more than just supplies. Kyrin approached just in time to hear him tell Warin, "I think I was followed on the way here."

"Did you see who it was?" Warin asked.

Trask shook his head, and his eyes lacked their usual sparkle. "I only caught a quick glimpse of movement, but I suspect one of Goler's men. I made sure to lose him well before I neared camp."

"What's Goler been up to lately?"

"That's the thing. I haven't seen him at all, and that concerns me. He's usually poking his nose around Landale more often."

Warin crossed his arms and shook his head. "I don't like the sound of it. You'll have to be wary."

"I will," Trask assured him.

He turned to unpack the horse and distributed supplies to the waiting men. Spotting Kyrin, he smiled and reached for something.

"Another gift specifically for you," he told her.

Despite the concerning news, Kyrin grinned and reached for the smooth oak quarterstaff she'd requested the day after the ryrik attack. Though she never could have matched them, she would have felt more secure with a weapon other than her bow— something she was even more familiar with.

"I also talked to the leatherworker in the village. He made this for you." Trask withdrew another item from the supplies— a quiver of sorts, but with a much longer and narrower leather tube. "Now you can take your staff with you without having to carry it."

Kyrin's eyes widened at the ingenious invention. She buckled the quiver over her shoulder and tipped her staff back to slide into the tube. It worked perfectly. She smiled again at Trask.

"Thank you for doing this for me."

He gave a short nod. "I didn't want you to find yourself unprepared in the future."

Kyrin pulled the staff out again and walked over to Jace. He eyed the new weapon with interest.

"It's not a blade," she said, "but trust me, it hurts, and can break bone."

Jace nodded in approval. "Most of the time that's all you need. Just a distraction so you can get away."

Kyrin agreed. She had no desire to stand and fight anyone.

"I'll try to find out what Goler is up to before I return tomorrow." Trask tugged his horse's cinch strap snug and glanced back at Warin and Rayad. The two older men had fallen into the leadership role in camp whenever he was not around, and he appreciated how smoothly they kept things running. There hadn't been any major problems since the incident with the Korvic brothers. The three seemed to have learned their lesson, especially now that Kyrin spent so much time with Jace. It amused him how the youngest Korvic moped over it.

"Don't dig too deep," Warin told him, bringing his thoughts back to Goler. "It might only stir up trouble."

"I won't." Trask grabbed the reins and mounted. With a last nod at them, he left camp and was meticulous in his care not to leave tracks. It would only take one mistake to jeopardize the entire camp and their mission. No doubt they'd all be executed for treason, even someone as innocent as Lenae.

When he arrived at the road, he made a thorough search. A set of tracks from earlier confirmed his suspicions. Determined to find answers, he urged his horse on toward Landale. The shadows of evening closed in as he trotted into the castle courtyard. Several horses were tied out front, including a tall, surly bay—Goler's horse. Well, at least he wouldn't have to go far for information.

Preparing himself for the confrontation, and with a word of prayer, he dismounted and strode inside. He was all set to deliver a sarcastic greeting to the captain when he entered the parlor, but caught the seriousness in his father's eyes and refrained. Goler turned to face him, appearing far too pleased. "Ah, Trask."

Trask stiffened his back and gave him a hard look. "I believe that's *Lord* Trask to you."

Typically, this would have infuriated Goler, but not this time. Strong warning signals fired off in Trask's brain. It took all of his control to keep his hand at his side and not reach for the hilt of his sword. He flexed his tingling fingers as Goler stepped closer, the man's probing eyes spearing into his own.

"Where have you been?"

Trask stared right back at him. "I think we've had this conversation once before."

"Perhaps you'd like to explain what you've been doing with all the supplies you disappear with." The captain's eyes narrowed. "Some of which might be considered for a young woman."

Trask shifted his jaw. Either someone had been spying on him or Goler had forced the local merchants into giving up information. Probably both. He drew a breath to remain calm and responded coolly, "Again, Captain, what I do with my time and money doesn't concern you."

"Oh, but it does if it involves aiding enemies of the emperor."

Trask ground his molars together and refused to respond. Now anger did flare in Goler's expression and transferred to his voice.

"You are hiding the girl, aren't you?"

No rested on the tip of his tongue, but the lie would not come out. Again, he said nothing, but stood in firm resolve. Triumph lit Goler's eyes and erased the anger.

"I know you are."

Very calmly, Trask replied, "You can't prove that."

"Doesn't matter. I can hold you on suspicion until one of the emperor's men arrives. You see, I sent word to Valcré just this morning."

Trask glanced from side to side. Goler's men had closed in around them during the conversation. Hot, followed by icy cold, slithered down his back and into his gut. He'd known this day would come. They couldn't prove his guilt, but, in this situation, it probably wouldn't matter.

"I'm taking you in," Goler sneered. "I suggest you come along quietly."

Trask looked to his father. The older man's face had paled, and his eyes clouded with uncertainty. Trask tried to convey to him not to take any action. Landale needed his leadership. The camp relied on his information and resources.

Trask returned his eyes to Goler, sorely tempted to bend his crooked nose further since they were arresting him anyway. With a sigh of resignation, he put his hands up, away from his weapons. He still had a chance to be cleared as long as he cooperated.

Goler grinned savagely. "Wise decision."

The soldiers promptly relieved Trask of all his weapons and clamped heavy chains around his wrists. The cold, rough metal sent chills up his arms and into his spine. Though it surely broke his heart, Baron Grey remained passive in the background. Trask traded a glance with him just before the soldiers yanked him around to lead him away.

Outside, he mounted his horse and one of the men took the reins. Goler mounted nearby, and Trask sent him a scathing look. With a clatter of hooves, they rode out of the courtyard. At the gate, Trask looked over his shoulder. His father stood alone in the castle entrance. Cold fingers squeezed Trask's throat. This could very well be the last time he saw his father. Turning back around, he hung his head and prayed.

Five miles outside of Landale, the group of riders came upon the barracks—a large area cleared of trees and surrounded by a wood palisade. In the growing shadows, it appeared far from friendly. A sense of doom weighed on Trask, but he held on to the hope that with no solid evidence, Goler would be forced to release him.

Inside the barracks compound, everything was dreary gray wood and dirt—not a patch of greenery and no color except for the stark contrasts of black and gold uniforms and banners. Trask longed for the forest. The group halted, and Goler jumped down.

Striding over to Trask, he took him by the arm and pulled him out of the saddle.

Faces mere inches apart, Trask said, "You've been waiting a long time for this, haven't you?"

"You have no idea."

Goler's fist smashed into Trask's ribs. He gasped and doubled over, wincing as pain spread through his chest. Straightening, he glared at the captain.

"Once I'm free, you'll regret that."

Goler laughed in his face. "I don't think so. I might not have enough evidence to hold you for aiding criminals, but I'm quite sure I'll soon have proof of something else, and you won't be going anywhere but in the ground."

Goler shoved him forward and, as he took in the sights of the compound, Trask's gaze landed on the building straight ahead. He drew in a sharp breath, and Goler gave a low chuckle.

Despite his reluctant steps, the captain forced Trask into the barracks temple. Only a couple of candles lit the dim, open space, but enough to draw Trask's eyes straight to the two carved idols standing on a ledge at the back. Goler pulled him to a halt in front of them.

"Kneel," he ordered. "Prove your devotion to the gods and the emperor they have chosen."

So this was it then. Trask breathed out, all his dreams falling about him—the camp, their mission . . . Anne. But acceptance and indignation settled in their place. He narrowed his eyes and looked at Goler.

"I will never bow and worship mute, blind, dead—"

Another solid fist to the ribs cut him off, and Goler drove him to his knees, but a declaration had never felt so good. Though Trask grimaced, a short laugh came out with it.

"You may force me to kneel, but it means nothing. In my heart I'm bowing before my King."

He braced himself, but it didn't lessen the impact of the

powerful kick to his stomach. Falling to the floor with a groan, he tried to catch his breath as the pain worked up through his lungs. After a moment, he pushed back to his knees. Goler caught him by the arm and hauled him to his feet. Digging his fingers in Trask's arm, he growled, "You and I have a few things to discuss."

He dragged Trask out of the temple, straight to the barracks headquarters and into a small interrogation room, where he threw him down into a chair. Trask sat up straighter and tried to convince himself not to hate the man. He should have hit him back at the castle. He'd probably missed his one and only chance.

Goler glared down at him. "Where's the girl?"

There was no point in pretending now. It wouldn't change anything. Either way, he was a dead man. Though his expression was blank at first, a slow smirk crept to his lips. The very same kind Goler had worn not too long ago. He leaned forward a little.

"Wouldn't you like to know?"

Goler's fist connected with his jaw, and his head snapped around.

"Tell me where she is."

"Why? So you can claim the reward for her capture?"

Goler hit him again. This time warmth oozed down his chin, and he almost tipped out of the chair. He blinked stars out of his vision. Goler grabbed his shoulder and jerked him up, bending close to look him in the eyes with a murderous flame flickering in his own.

"I can keep this up all night, all day, if I have to. You won't escape death, but you could spare yourself a lot of pain in the meantime."

Trask shook his head. "I would never give Kyrin up to a monster like you." He rested back in the chair. "And if I'm going to die anyway, I'd just as soon go with the knowledge I kept you from getting what you wanted."

RAYAD WALKED UP the small rise at the edge of camp and joined
Warin, who stared into the forest. The sun was a warm glow in
the west, and shadows stretched out behind him. His friend gave a
heavy sigh as he approached.

"It's late," Warin murmured. "He should've been here this
morning."

Rayad frowned, his own eyes searching the trees, but he
spoke in an encouraging tone. "He could've been detained by
anything."

Warin looked grimly at him. "Do you believe that?"

Now Rayad sighed. He couldn't ignore the unrest building
inside him any more than Warin could. "Not really."

Warin nodded as if that answer made up his mind. "I'm
going to ride into Landale after dark and see the baron. I only
pray Trask will be there. Will you come with me?"

"Of course."

"There you go, girl." Anne smiled as her white mare contentedly crunched away at a pail of oats. She ran her hand down
the horse's smooth neck. One of these nights, she would have
to ask her father to go for a ride. She loved summer evenings.

Her smile widened. Trask used to take her sometimes. It was during one of these rides he'd stolen his first kiss. She'd shoved him off his horse and galloped back to Marlton, though she had secretly fantasized about it for days.

The sound of horses approached outside. She leaned past the stall door, almost daring to hope it was Trask, but instead caught a glimpse of gold.

"Great," she muttered.

And it had been such a nice long while since Goler had stopped by. Raising up her defenses, she set off for the house. Two soldiers sat on their horses, but Goler was already inside.

"Let him leave quickly," she whispered in prayer. "And don't let him ask again about a ride."

On the porch, she glanced at the soldiers and glared at their lengthy perusal of her. But what more could be expected with Goler as their leader? Some example he set. She stepped inside with the purpose to send him off as quickly as possible. He turned at the clap of her shoes with a look of unnerving satisfaction in his eyes.

"Captain," she greeted just politely enough to hide her true feelings. Her attention shifted to her parents and landed first on her mother's pale face before locking eyes with her father. His gaze held both regret and sympathy. Trask and Kyrin flashed to Anne's mind.

"What is it?" She tried to keep her voice even.

Goler stepped closer, his nearness making it hard to breathe. She eyed him with the urge to step back, but stood her ground.

"Last evening, I took Trask into custody on suspicion of harboring criminals and traitors to the emperor. As a result, I confirmed something I've long suspected. He too is one of the traitors who have renounced our gods."

Anne's heart stopped before floundering to establish even a sluggish beat. She couldn't take in a breath and dizziness overtook her, but all the while, her brain screamed not to react in front of

Goler. If he saw her distress, she would be just as doomed as Trask. She swallowed, though she had no moisture to accomplish the task.

"Are you sure?" She somehow kept her expression neutral, and prayed Goler missed the slight tremor in her voice.

"I brought him into the temple myself. He refused to bow before Aertus and Vilai, and furthermore, had the audacity to profane them inside the sanctuary."

Pride swelled in Anne's chest, but fear sucked it away again and burned her eyes.

"What will happen to him?" she asked, carefully enunciating each word.

"He'll be executed." Pleasure dripped from his voice, and a knife stabbed into her chest as surely as if it were the one hanging on his belt. "Just as soon as one of the emperor's men has had a chance to question him on the whereabouts of the girl he's hiding. So far he's refused to give me her location, but one way or another, we'll get it out of him."

Anne didn't trust herself to speak. Her hands trembled with the desire to slap that hateful smugness off his ugly face. She stared blankly at the floor and willed herself to breathe, though her ribs shrank around her lungs.

"I know he was sweet on you."

Her eyes lifted slowly back to Goler, who watched her with a dangerous intensity. It was easy to minimize her relationship with Trask when he was safe, but this would be much harder. She forced a shrug.

"I suppose he was." By some miracle, she managed an indifferent tone.

"But he'll soon be gone," his voice slithered around her like snakes, "and you'll be free to entertain the attentions of a different admirer."

He grinned, and she resisted a shudder.

"Perhaps . . . but I would have to give it some thought."

The grin disappeared from the captain's face. "What's there to think about?"

At the bite in his voice, Anne's indignation flared to the surface. "I'll not be rushed, Captain."

"Very well, but don't think about it too long. My patience only goes so far."

"Captain," her father snapped, "you will not threaten my daughter. She has every right to decline your affections."

Goler stiffened, clearly carried away by his triumph over Trask's arrest.

"I apologize." His voice was smooth, contrite even. After all, as a knight, Anne's father still outranked him. "It was no threat. It's just that I most deeply desire the approval to court your daughter."

"Well, you don't have it," John told him shortly as he came to Anne and drew her close. "Now, you've brought your news. I'd appreciate it if you and your men would leave us to the rest of our evening, and I would ask that you not call on Anne again without my express approval."

Goler's eyes grew dark, but he just as quickly smiled, though it appeared sickeningly false. "As you wish." He nodded at Anne and her mother. "My ladies." His gaze landed once more on John, something dangerous in his expression. "Sir."

With a little bow, he turned on his heel and strode out.

No one moved inside the house for a long moment. Then John promptly shut and locked the door. Anne put a hand to her stomach, sure she would be sick, and reached for the back of a chair to steady herself. Her breaths came out shallow and ragged. John put his hands on her shoulders.

"Are you all right?"

She looked up, her head spinning. "Trask," she cried. "What are we going to do about Trask?"

Speaking his name opened the floodgates of her tears, and they poured down her cheeks.

"I don't know," John murmured.

Desperation and panic clamored for Anne to take action. She pulled away from her father and headed for the door. "I have to go to camp. They have to know."

But her father caught her by the arm. "You can't. If Goler suspects Trask is hiding Kyrin, then he probably has men watching the roads. You could be caught yourself or accidently lead someone to the camp."

Anne resisted him at first, but then the full import of the situation robbed her of strength. Her legs wobbled, and she choked out a sob.

"But we have to do something."

Her father pulled her into his arms and held her tight. "Anne, the only thing we can do right now is pray."

Footsteps echoed in Trask's throbbing skull. His body protested every movement, but he pushed himself up off the floor of his cell and gained his feet just before Goler appeared. The captain glared through the bars and looked to be in a foul mood.

"Here to tell me again of my coming fate?" Trask asked. His swollen jaw ached with every word, but he would fight this man to his last breath.

Goler scowled and unlocked the door. He strode in, grabbed Trask by the collar, and slammed him back against the wall. Trask gasped for the air forced from his lungs and winced at the pain streaking through his head. He jerked against Goler, but couldn't break his hold. The man growled in his face, "No, but you will tell me how to win over Lady Anne."

The fight left Trask for a moment. "Lady Anne?" His heart reacted to the thought of her and how difficult this must be. If only he had some way to send her words of comfort and let her know how deeply he loved her. Then Goler's words fully sank in and defiance flooded back. He scoffed. "You think I'd ever tell you how to win her affections?"

"No," Goler replied, his voice ready to snap. "But I'll still enjoy trying to beat it out of you."

A thick blanket of clouds hid the light of Aertus and Vilai and provided the needed cover. Warin motioned to Rayad, and they crept to a small service door in the wall at the rear of Landale Castle. He pulled one of two keys from his pocket.

"Trask gave me these so we could get inside if we needed to," he whispered.

Easing the door open, he peered into the courtyard. Nothing moved amongst the shadows. At least Goler didn't have guards stationed here. That was a good sign. They crossed the open space to the castle itself. Here, Warin unlocked one of the back doors. Inside, pitch-black surrounded them. Warin put his hand to the wall and led the way. They wound around in the darkness until they reached a torch-lit hall and followed it to Baron Grey's office.

Morris sat hunched over, staring unfocused at the paperwork strewn across his desk. At the creak of the door, his head shot up. His eyes widened, but weariness dragged down his expression.

"Warin, thank the King you're here," he breathed. "Please, come in and see the baron."

Warin's heart sank at the older man's reaction to them, which all but confirmed his fears. The secretary hurried to the office door and looked in. "My lord, it's Warin and Rayad."

The two of them walked in as the baron rose from his desk. The same weariness dogged his face, his eyes bloodshot and in need of rest. Desperation flashed in them as if devouring him from the inside.

"What's happened?" Warin asked, skipping any formalities.

Baron Grey leaned on his desk and appeared more like a frail old man than a strong lord. "Goler arrested Trask yesterday. He knows he's hiding Miss Altair and that he's a follower of Elôm."

Though expected, the news punched Warin right in the gut. He and Trask had discussed this scenario, Trask making sure he'd continue to run the camp if he were gone. But it surely didn't make it any easier to accept.

Grey sank back into his chair. "Goler sent word to Valcré of his suspicions about Miss Altair and expects the emperor to send men to investigate. Once they decide whether or not Trask can or will provide any information . . . he'll be executed."

The last phrase was barely audible.

Warin cleared the tightness in his throat. Trask would want him to make sure this didn't jeopardize the mission. "Do you think Goler suspects you of disloyalty?"

Grey shook his head. "I've done my best to appear apathetic." Something changed in his expression, and a fiery look came to his eyes as his fingers dug into the arms of his chair. "But I won't let him do this to my son."

Warin winced. He'd be right there with the baron in any attempt to break Trask free if he didn't have to consider the far-reaching consequences of any rash actions. "I can't imagine how difficult this is for you, but you must uphold your pretense of loyalty." He winced. The words tasted so wrong. "I implore you, my lord, do not take action in this."

The baron's lips set in a grim line, and he glared at him. Warin had never before seen him display any anger toward one of his friends.

"How do you expect me to stand back and watch my son be tortured and killed?"

Warin sighed with a heavy heart. "By remembering the people. I know it's a hard choice to make, but Landale needs your leadership."

Grey shook his head again and rose abruptly to pace. "I just don't think I can do it." His fists clenched. Without looking at Warin, he said in a thick voice, "He's my son."

Warin grimaced, sharing the man's pain, but sometimes leadership meant sacrifice. Too many people counted on them. "We still have time. Hold off any action, at least until there's no other way. I don't know yet what we can do, but you know we won't just stand by and watch him die. Please, my lord. Trask wouldn't want any of us to put him before the people of Landale. He would want them taken care of first. That's why he set up camp and is in custody now, because of his desire to help people."

Grey hung his head and morphed again into a mere shadow of a man. "It's only a matter of time before I'm discovered too."

"Perhaps," Warin acknowledged, "but Landale needs you for as long as you can keep up appearances." He glanced at Rayad, still unsure the baron would heed his words and make the necessary choice between leader and father—an unimaginable choice.

Rayad stepped up, his voice understanding, yet firm. "I apologize, my lord, but there's nothing you can do for Trask. Not on your own. You would only be arrested and executed right along with him. What would that accomplish?"

Grey just stared off at nothing with glazed eyes and didn't respond. Had he even heard Rayad?

At last, he looked up, his expression sagging. "Please, there must be a way to save him."

Warin rubbed his beard, knowing of no way to give the man hope. "We can't break him out. There are too many men stationed at the barracks." He glanced away from the man's stricken face, wanting a way as much as the baron did. "We'll set watches at the barracks. Our best chance at saving him would be if he's moved. He wouldn't be under such heavy guard then."

"Do you think he will be moved?"

"Not until they're ready to execute him, either here or in Valcré."

Grey's eyes misted. "But you think you have a chance of stopping it?"

"We'll certainly try," Warin promised and whispered a prayer inside.

THE TRAINING SWORDS met with a violent crack. Kaden pushed his advantage and forced his instructor back two steps. Sweat rolled down his face, and he panted, but did not slow. He pressed forward, attack after attack, moving almost recklessly, but right on the edge of precision. The frustration burning inside him needed an outlet.

Another ten minutes passed, maybe fifteen, before his instructor stepped back and called the match to a halt. Kaden frowned at him, far from ready to quit. He would fight until he practically dropped just to be rid of the restlessness that gnawed at him. His instructor nodded past him, and he looked over his shoulder. Two of his guards approached. A third stood at the edge of the training field.

When the men reached him, one ordered, "Go inside and change. The emperor has summoned you to the palace."

The news doused Kaden like ice water. His shoulders sagged and his arms fell heavily to his sides. He'd finally run out of time. He filled his lungs and let the air out slowly. Somehow, he'd known all along that he wouldn't escape.

His fist tightened around the practice sword, but he handed it over to his instructor and trudged up to the Hall in silence. Upstairs, the guards waited outside while he stepped into his room and closed the door. Stopping in the center of the room, he just stood—his only moment of privacy to prepare for meeting the emperor. He closed his eyes. *Elôm, whatever happens, help me stay strong and faithful to You . . . like Kyrin did.*

Instinct urged him to fight this with everything in his power, but common sense called for compliance, if only to see if a better opportunity presented itself. So he changed into a clean uniform and joined the guards. They passed through the Hall and out to the courtyard. Along the way, Kaden spotted Sam. Remorse etched his friend's face—helpless to intervene. Kaden just met his gaze with grim acceptance. He'd anticipated this for so long he was ready to get it over and done with. He couldn't live this way anymore. The next execution would have made him snap anyway.

They followed the same path Kyrin had taken when this all started. Kaden had wished to take her place that morning after the promotion, but at least she was safe now.

The guards escorted him inside the palace, but never once said a word to clue him in on what this meeting entailed. Not that any meeting with the emperor could really end well at this point. He glanced down the halls they passed. Cold, empty halls. Without Kyrin, they lost any hint of warmth or welcome. Not a single familiar face met them. But for Elôm, he was on his own.

A large door loomed ahead, and nausea turned his stomach. They entered the emperor's office, and he set eyes on Daican for the first time. He'd never met him face to face. The closest had been the day they brought Kyrin to the square. A lot of good those memories did to calm his unease, but they kept the fight burning inside him. His hands warmed as he took stock of the emperor. He could probably take him, given the chance. But the guards would never allow the opportunity. He'd get a sword to the throat first.

The men stepped away and left Kaden standing in the center of the room. Daican approached him.

"Kaden Altair," he said, his voice smooth, pleasant even, giving Kaden a firsthand look at the mask he so skillfully employed with Kyrin. But Kaden had already seen behind the mask—what it hid.

"Your Majesty," he replied cautiously as he fought the impulse to speak what was really on his mind. It left a horrible taste in his mouth, but if he didn't proceed with extreme caution, his fate truly would be sealed.

Daican's gaze bored straight into him and said far more than his relaxed expression. "I'm sure you're wondering about this meeting."

"It's not every day one of us is summoned from Tarvin Hall."

"No," Daican agreed. He clasped his hands behind his back. "I thought you should be one of the first to know the status on your sister."

Kaden's chest constricted. Had she been caught? If so, he would fight to the death to free her, guards or no guards. *Please, let her be safe.*

"I've received word on where she might be hiding," Daican continued, and Kaden let out his breath as slow as he could to hide his relief. "One of my captains has a man in custody who might be the one harboring her. It's only a matter of time before we discover her location."

The emperor measured his reaction without so much as a blink. Despite the intense scrutiny, Kaden kept a straight face. He'd gotten good at that.

"What do you think of this news?" Daican pressed.

The question was a snare—one of dozens Kaden could fall into. Maybe he was in one already, and it just hadn't closed on him yet. He shrugged. "It is what it is."

"Indeed," Daican murmured. He paced a couple of steps before facing Kaden again. "You two were close, were you not? You are twins, after all."

"Yes, but I can't change the way things are or what's happened."

Again, Kaden received the full intensity of Daican's stare that was determined to wrench the truth out of him one way or another. Well, he'd have to try a lot harder.

"I'm told you share some of your sister's skills—that you, too, are good at reading people."

Suspicion clawed the edges of Kaden's mind. "I'm pretty good."

With a sweeping look, Daican said, "It's a shame. Your sister was quite valuable before she turned on my kindness and generosity." He paused to wait for a reaction Kaden never provided. "So, tell me, Kaden, how do *you* read me?"

A dangerous question that was. But he wouldn't pander to the emperor. "I don't believe you're as kind and generous as you make yourself out to be. I think it's something you use, when it suits you."

A smile curved Daican's lips, but a cold, hard glimmer appeared in his eyes. "And you don't like me very much, do you?"

Kaden's jaw tightened, and the hot coals that had smoldered since Kyrin's near execution seared his insides. His restraint slipped a little. "What do you expect after I saw my sister humiliated, injured, and made out to be a criminal?"

Daican seemed almost amused by the heat in his voice. He stepped closer, eye to eye with Kaden. The fact that Kaden was taller was nothing compared to Daican's confidence in the power he held. "The question is, will you serve me? Will you take your sister's place here at Auréa?"

So that was his game—to replace Kyrin with the next best thing. But could Kaden do it? Could he keep up this perilous charade with so many deaths around him, some of which he may even cause by serving the emperor? The act was hard enough to maintain back at Tarvin Hall. Yet, what was the alternative? At least this still left him with the possibility of escape. He had to try.

"I'll do what I must," he answered even as it sickened him inside.

"A wise answer," Daican replied. The cruel smile resurfaced.

"But, of course, it will have to be tested." He inclined his head toward the doors. "Let's take a walk to the temple, shall we?"

Kaden's heart sputtered. Of course, it could never end any other way. It was foolish of him to think otherwise. He breathed harder, heat reclaiming his chest, and drew himself up taller. "Don't bother. I refuse to bow to any but King Elôm, the one true God of Ilyon."

Kaden winced as he struggled to draw in a breath past his throbbing ribs. He coughed, and pain ripped through his chest. Fog swirled in his brain, disjointing his thoughts, but he hadn't given Sam up. He knew that much for sure, and it offered a comforting satisfaction amidst the pain.

"Put him in this one," Aric's voice echoed ahead of him.

Kaden raised his head with effort as the guards pushed him into a dungeon cell. No longer supported by them, his knees buckled and hit the stone hard. The cell door clanked shut, the grating shriek tearing through his pounding skull. He glanced around the area, though one eye was almost swollen shut. In the wavering torchlight, his gaze caught on a man in the cell beside his. He blinked.

"Trev?"

The name barely made it past his lips, but the other man looked at him, his face a bruised and bloodied mess. Trev glanced out of the cell at Aric just before the guards all turned and marched away. The light faded with them. In the darkness, Kaden crawled to the back of the cell and leaned against the wall where he breathed out a cross between a sigh and a groan. The bullies at Tarvin Hall never beat him up quite this badly. He gingerly wiped his sleeve across the blood dripping from his chin and spit some out of his mouth. The thick tang coated his throat, and he longed for water to wash it down.

"Daican finally went after you too?" Trev's hoarse voice filled the empty space.

"Yeah."

The other man's long sigh rasped in Kaden's ears. Kaden looked in his direction, though pitch-blackness hid everything. "How did you end up down here?"

"I helped Kyrin escape."

This sent a shock through Kaden's sore muscles. Sam never told him who helped Kyrin out of the dungeon.

"The investigation was heating up," Trev explained. "I didn't want them digging any deeper, so I turned myself in."

Kaden breathed slowly in and out, his lungs hitching at every stab of pain through his ribs. "Thank you for helping her." It was little consolation for being down here, but it meant everything to him.

"I was glad to do it," Trev replied without regret. He moved farther back in his own cell with a grunt and sucked in his breath. Finally, he settled.

"How long have you been down here?" Kaden asked.

"A few days. A week, maybe. It's impossible to say." He shifted again. "They've been working on me to find out who helped Kyrin once she was outside the palace."

Kaden rested his head back. How many times had Trev faced the same sort of interrogation he just had, and yet remained unbroken? "They wanted to know if I knew anything . . . and who told me and Kyrin about Elôm." He paused. "So, you believe in Elôm too?"

"Yes."

"I suppose we'll both be executed in the square then."

"I expect so," Trev said with a tone of resignation. "Just as soon as they realize we won't talk."

Kaden put his arm around his ribs and tried to draw a deeper breath. The darkness was almost suffocating, and his pulse elevated. It must be a little of the same claustrophobia Kyrin suffered from so often. If so, he'd have to get used to it quickly. No telling how long he and Trev would sit here before meeting their fate.

Icy water crashed into Trask's face and jolted him cruelly into a painful consciousness. He sputtered and choked, and then groaned when he tried to move. Every single muscle screamed in agony. Blinking for clarity, he tipped his head up. Goler stood over him.

"What do you want now?" he rasped. He wanted to get up, not lie helplessly at the captain's feet, but he wasn't sure his limbs would cooperate.

"Just to see you awake and suffering."

Trask let out a dry laugh. "Of course." He clenched his jaw and slowly lifted himself into a sitting position. That was about as far as he could go. The walls tilted in on him, and he blinked hard before looking up at Goler again. The man drew far too much enjoyment from his struggle. "You don't even know what kindness is, do you?"

Goler smirked. "Why don't you teach me?"

Trask blew out a sigh. "If I thought you would actually listen, I might try."

Goler's lip curled. "So righteous."

"Is that why you hate me?"

The captain shrugged.

"No, really," Trask persisted. "Why do you hate me? It can't only be about Lady Anne. There must be something." He shook his head. "What did I ever do to you?"

"You," Goler laughed scornfully, but his expression was set in loathing. "You had everything handed to you from the moment you were born. You didn't have to work for any of it. Now me, I've worked for years, and this here," he spread his arms and gestured around him, "is as grand as it's going to get for me."

Trask scowled. Ignorant beast. "So you're jealous, is that it? Well, it may be true I was born a noble, but that doesn't mean it all came freely. It takes work to rule Landale, to lead the people, to make sure they're all fed and faring well. I serve and protect them. It's not all riches and ease. You may lead a company of men, but you have no idea what true leadership is."

Goler crossed his arms, entirely too pleased after such an insult. "I'll soon find out."

Trask frowned and dread wormed through his insides. Goler gave a harsh laugh at his confusion and bent closer.

"You see, once I've disposed of you and the girl is found, I'll have gained special favor with the emperor. As soon as I figure out how to get rid of your father, I expect the emperor will be quite generous and glad to name me as baron of Landale. I'm sure your father has something to hide. He can't be without blame having a son like you. All I have to do is dig."

Trask's breathing grew shallow. It would be his fault if his father was found out and executed. He was the one who had drawn Goler's suspicion, his ire.

"I'm right, aren't I?"

"Leave my father out of this," Trask forced through his teeth.

Goler snorted. "It's too late for that. And once I'm baron, there will be nothing to keep me from Lady Anne. Not you, not her father, not anyone. She'll be all mine."

Heat burst through Trask. He shoved to his feet. But Goler was ready, and drove his knee right up into Trask's gut. Trask collapsed with a groan, and his vision grayed around the edges. It took several moments for him to catch his breath and will the pain to subside. Gasping, he ground out, "You . . . are . . . despicable."

Goler gave a low chuckle.

Trask looked up at him. "Why don't you unchain me, let me out of this cell, and face me like a real man?"

"I'm quite content with you exactly where you are."

Kaden awoke to the same blackness. Not a sound broke the silence except for Trev's uneven breathing. He shivered, the coldness of the stone sinking right into his bones. The only benefit was that it dulled the ache in his muscles, but how had Trev endured it for so long? Or Kyrin?

He pushed up. His head pounded. He held it in his hands for a few minutes, and then lightly touched his swollen jaw. His stomach let out a low, pinching grumble and felt emptier than it had his entire life. To his left, Trev sighed.

"Any idea how long it's been?" Kaden asked.

"Hours, at least. But it gets harder and harder to tell, especially when you're out for a while."

Kaden rubbed his stomach, which cramped in protest of the meals it had missed. "Do you ever get any food and water?"

"Sometimes. Just enough to keep you alive and alert for questioning."

Kaden grimaced. Perhaps it would be better to just refuse food and die that way, though he sure never expected to die of hunger. But Daican would probably just execute him before that happened.

His thoughts drifted to the last execution. Would he be as brave as those men and that woman? Hunger turned to a nauseous churning of apprehension at the thought of taking those steps up to the execution platform. Would others be with him? Would Trev? That would be the worst—seeing others go before him. He swallowed, but his throat squeezed shut with the phantom feel of the block against his neck. His blood ran cold. *Elôm, I really don't want to die, but please help me when the time comes.* How had Kyrin appeared so strong and determined standing up on that platform alone?

Kaden shook himself and forced thoughts of execution to the outer edges of his mind. He reached for more distracting memories such as home and people he hadn't thought of in a long time—childhood friends who probably barely remembered him. Life had just gone on outside the strict and structured existence of Tarvin Hall. Where would he and Kyrin be now if they'd never had to leave home? He'd surely be a soldier, stationed somewhere with Marcus and Liam. His grandfather would have seen to that. Would he and Kyrin still be close?

The engulfing darkness hung like a timeless void, but a good while passed before Kaden caught the sound of footsteps. Torchlight forced away the blackness. A set of guards marched down the hall and halted at Kaden's cell to unlock the door. Kaden pushed stiffly to his feet as they walked in. His bruised muscles burned. They chained his wrists and pulled him out. He looked back at Trev.

"Stay strong," he encouraged Kaden. "Don't give them anything."

"Shut up," one of the guards growled, but Kaden nodded. He wouldn't. He'd die first.

The guards dragged Kaden with them, down the hall to the same interrogation room they'd used before. Shoving him into the center of the room, one of the guards left. Kaden stood, waiting. He didn't relish the prospect of further questioning, but he didn't fear it either. Whether here or at Tarvin Hall, he was used to beatings.

The knob turned, and he set his jaw defiantly. Let them try to make him talk. But his brows dipped in a deep frown when the door swung open and a feminine figure slipped inside. Davira. No mistaking her. Kyrin had described her well enough. She wore a form-fitted, revealing gown, and he set his gaze on her face. The cold light in her emerald eyes sent a prickling sensation down his back. No wonder Kyrin was afraid of her. She sidled up to him.

"Oh," she crooned, eyeing his injured face. "My father's men can be rather cruel."

Just like her father.

She reached up and brushed her fingers lightly across his cheek. He jerked his head away. Undeterred, her hand dropped to splay on his chest, and his heart pounded uncomfortably. She was much too close.

"You know, Kaden," she said in a silky whisper that raised the hair on his arms. "My father listens to me. I could get him to go easier on you. Maybe even your sister too. I only need you to answer a couple of my questions."

Kaden peered down at her, his stubbornness still intact, and swallowed down the dry catch in his throat. "I know what you're doing. I'm not stupid." He pulled his shoulders back. "You won't get anything from me."

"Oh, come now, you don't really want to do things this way, do you?" Her finger traced a little design on his shirt right above his heart, and she gave him a long-lashed, sultry smile. "I'm sure we can come to some sort of agreement."

He stared at her for a moment and then snorted. Her act slipped.

"This may work for you on most occasions," he said, "but not with me."

Davira's eyes narrowed to dark slits. She took her hand from his chest but leaned in to whisper icily near his ear, "You may think you're not stupid, but you are. You've chosen to follow ancient myths and set yourself against my father, the most powerful man in Ilyon. For that, you will pay dearly. Very dearly."

She turned with a whirl of her dress and strode to the door.

"You can take him now," she told the guards without looking back.

Kaden resisted the urge to touch his ear, still cold from her breath. There was something unnatural about her.

The guard still in the room shoved him forward. He stumbled into the hall, where he met Trev. There could be only one reason for them both to be brought from their cells. He gulped down a spike of fear as the guards led them through the halls and up out of the dungeon.

KYRIN SAT ACROSS from Jace at the tent and practiced what he had taught her about fletching arrows. But it couldn't completely distract her from the mood surrounding camp. A heavy gloom had fallen after news of Trask's arrest, and all they could do was wait. Kyrin hated it. It left a sickening ache in her stomach that wouldn't go away. He'd done so much for all of them, yet they could do nothing for him. She frowned at her arrow, though she didn't really see it, and prayed Elôm would provide the opportunity to rescue their leader and keep him safe in the meantime.

"Is that Tane?" Jace asked.

Kyrin's gaze jumped to him. He stared past her, and she looked over her shoulder. Across camp, Tane stood speaking with Rayad and Warin. At the same moment, all three set their eyes on her with grim expressions. A breath-snatching jolt streaked through Kyrin.

"Kaden," she gasped. She pushed to her feet, but stood paralyzed. What if he was gone already? Executed. *Elôm, no!* Her knees almost buckled, but the need to know pushed her forward. *Please, Elôm!* The moment she reached them, the question burst out of her, though she'd never been so terrified in her life. "Is he alive?"

"Yes," Tane answered.

Kyrin grew lightheaded and wobbled, but Jace grabbed her arm to steady her. She sucked in air and willed her racing heart not to fail her. Kaden was alive, but that brief moment of wondering left her weak. Once she could speak again, she questioned, "What's happened? Is he all right?"

Tane grimaced, and Kyrin thought she would be sick with these intense up-and-down emotions.

"The emperor brought him in and he declared his faith."

Thankfully, Jace still had a hold on her. She needed the link to someone close to her as she came to terms with her worst fear. Tears scalded her eyes and choked her throat. She swallowed down the sob that threatened to break free.

"When . . ." She swallowed again, voice rough and hoarse. "When will he be executed?"

"They're bringing him here to Landale."

A new wave of shock blasted right through her. Her eyes went wide. Was this a miracle or a cruel game? "What? Why would they do that?"

Tane sighed wearily. "They intend to use him as bait to capture you."

The ache inside Kyrin intensified and gnawed away at her core. "When will he get here?"

"He may have already arrived. They had a head start on me, and I kept to the forest. They're taking him to the barracks."

So close! After all this time, only a few miles separated her from her brother.

"I have to find out," she said, ready to saddle Maera this very minute.

Rayad stepped in and put his hand on her shoulder. "One of our scouts will bring word when anyone shows up at the barracks."

Kyrin clenched her fists, fighting down the overwhelming impulse to go anyway, just to be closer. This waiting was going to kill her.

"Kyrin, there's more," Tane broke into her struggle.

Her shoulders sagged. Could she take any more bad news?

"They aren't only bringing Kaden. They have Trev with them too."

"Trev?"

Tane gave a regretful nod. "Things were getting pretty heated at the palace. Trev gave himself up to keep suspicion from working its way to Aric. They're bringing him as extra incentive."

Kyrin's strength finally gave out, and she sank to the forest floor, Jace's grip letting her down gently. She covered her face with her hands and pressed her fingers to her eyes to hold back tears. She wanted to face this in a calm, clearheaded manner, but mounting despair forced a groan to her lips. If they couldn't take action to save Trask, they couldn't save her brother or Trev either. *Why, Elôm? Why this?*

The dark, thick-walled prison coach bumped and rocked down the rough path through the countryside. Kaden winced when one side came down hard over the edge of a large rock. Two and a half days of this had jarred his bones and deepened the aches in his already battered body.

He glanced at Trev. Light slanted through one of the barred windows and fell across his face. His jaw was clenched, eyes closed, but Kaden didn't believe he was actually asleep. That was impossible while moving. His gaze dropped to Trev's arms, which were wrapped around his broken ribs. Kaden's pain couldn't be anything compared to what Trev must be suffering at every jolt. They had better reach their destination soon. The pallor of Trev's skin concerned him.

His legs cramped, Kaden gripped the side of the coach and pulled himself up, though he had to duck under the low ceiling. He peered through the bars of the window. Dense forest passed on either side of them. Nothing to offer much distraction. He lowered himself back to the floor and closed his eyes to think of anything to shut out the constant lurching and banging.

Another uncomfortable hour passed before outside voices broke into his thoughts. His eyes popped open, and so did Trev's. Kaden scrambled up to peer out the window again as they passed through the gate of a tall palisade.

"Looks like we've made it."

The coach rolled into the barracks and up to the headquarters, at last coming to a stop. Kaden remained at the window to take in what little was visible from his vantage point. The men in their escort dismounted. A minute later, a blond man exited the building and met the leader of their group.

"Captain Goler," he introduced himself with a salute.

"Sir Richard Blaine, one of His Majesty's chief advisors." A little taller than Goler, Richard peered down his nose at the captain. Disgust laced his superior and far more cultured tone. "He sent me in regard to your message. Have you located the girl?"

Goler hesitated. "No, but I have the man responsible for aiding her in custody. Despite much persuasion, he has so far refused to talk."

"It doesn't matter now," Richard said. "I've brought with me two prisoners to lure her out." He gestured back at the coach. "I trust you have the necessary facilities to secure them."

Goler gave a sharp nod. "Yes, sir. No one could get in or out."

"Good." Richard turned to his men. "Bring out the prisoners."

The men came around the coach and unlocked the door. Trev struggled to his feet, his movements slow and careful. Kaden reached out to help him. Bent over, he sucked in a breath through his teeth. Kaden kept a hand under his arm to keep him steady. The door opened and light poured inside.

"Out, both of you," a guard ordered.

They stepped to the door, and the guards grabbed Kaden first to drag him out. Trev came behind. He stumbled as his feet hit the ground. Kaden tried to reach back to help him, but the guard yanked him away. Somehow, Trev stayed upright, and the guards shoved them forward to face Goler—a devious, predatory man by the looks of him. He wouldn't get anywhere near Kyrin if Kaden had anything to do with it.

"This is the girl's twin brother and the man who helped her escape," Richard explained. "She won't turn her back on them."

A cruel smirk lifted Goler's lips. "This way," he said, and led them all to the barracks' jailhouse.

They entered the building, and Kaden did a quick sweep of the interior. It was dim, with only a few windows for light. Thick iron bars blocked them from any means of escape. The place looked as solid as Auréa's dungeon.

Around a corner, they reached the cellblock. Kaden's eyes roamed each cell and landed on the man occupying one. He was conscious and watched them with alert eyes, but he'd obviously endured treatment similar to theirs.

As they passed his cell, he looked at Goler, his voice thick with sarcasm. "Thoughtful of you to bring me company."

"Enjoy it while you can," Goler growled. "Now that they're here, you've outlived your usefulness."

One of the guards pushed Kaden into the cell beside the other man's and Trev into the next one. With a glare from Sir Richard, he and the other captors strode away. The jail door banged shut with a solid confirmation of their predicament. Trev moved to the back of his cell and sank to the floor.

"Are you all right?" Kaden asked him.

Trev only nodded.

Kaden looked over and caught the eyes of their fellow prisoner. They studied each other a moment.

"You're Kaden, aren't you?"

"Yeah."

"You do look very much like your sister." Moving with slow

effort, the man pushed to his feet and steadied himself against the wall. He then walked to the bars separating them. "I'm Trask, son of Baron Grey and fellow follower of the King."

He extended his hand through the bars.

Kaden took his arm. "Pleased to meet you, though it's not exactly ideal circumstances."

Trask chuckled dryly. "No." He glanced past Kaden and greeted Trev.

"So, you know where my sister is?" Kaden asked.

"Yes."

"And she's safe?"

"She's safe," Trask assured him. "And doing well."

Finally, some assurance from someone who had seen her recently. But how long would it last?

"I just hope she stays that way. We were brought here to lure her out." Kaden hung his head and prayed she wouldn't take the bait. But why wouldn't she? He would give himself up in a heartbeat if she were the one in trouble.

Trask seemed to understand his concern. "Don't worry. There are others with her. They'll keep her safe."

"We need to make certain the Altair girl is in the area," Richard said as he reclined at Goler's table. He took a bite of the dry beef the captain offered and almost scowled. It was dreadful compared to the fare at Auréa. One more reason to get things done quickly.

"I'm sure she is," Goler replied with irritating confidence.

Richard peered at him and made the captain squirm. "I'll believe that when I see her."

He took a sip of wine and grimaced. Next time he had to leave the city, he'd bring his own. "You say you believe there are others working with this Trask who may be harboring the girl now?"

"No doubt. He's purchased and disappeared with supplies for more than one person."

"Do you have any idea who these people are?"

Goler shrugged. "A couple of troublemakers and outcasts have disappeared from the village. I think the villagers know more than they let on. They have strong loyalty to him." Bitterness leaked into his tone.

Richard pinned him with another hard look. "That could present a problem for His Majesty. We won't tolerate these rebellious factions. I trust you'll see to it that this rebelliousness is subdued and extinguished."

"Of course." Goler licked his lips, speaking with care. "Actually, I thought, perhaps, should the current baron prove uncooperative, the emperor might consider me a viable replacement. He wouldn't have to worry about any rebellion under my watch."

Richard eyed him. A bold move for this sorry country captain, but it could be of benefit. He considered him a moment. "You don't think the baron is loyal to the emperor?"

"With his son as the instigator behind all this, I think he too knows more than he will tell me. I have no proof, yet, but I have no doubt something would surface with a bit of pushing and digging."

Goler waited, breath held, and Richard left him in suspense for several seconds. Once he was satisfied, he said casually, "If this proves true, I suppose I could put in a word with the emperor on your behalf."

Goler's lips upturned a little, and a spark of glee lit in his eyes.

"But," Richard said, effectively squelching some of that delight, "you would have to make good on your promises to destroy any rebellion if it isn't finished when I'm through here. Even a couple of rebellious outcasts can embolden others."

"You can count on it."

Richard took another sip of sour wine and focused again on the matter at hand and his desire to return to civilization. "Now, about the girl. I want to see her. Tomorrow, send men into the village. Let it be known that I have her brother and I want to speak with her. If the villagers are in on this, as you say, word should reach her. I will set up and wait for her outside the barracks. She can either choose to give herself up, or I can make it clear to her what will happen should she refuse."

"DO YOU THINK it's a trap?"

Kyrin looked at Rayad, who scanned the area from their hiding place in the trees. An open field stretched out a couple of hundred yards before them and met the barracks' palisade. About a hundred yards from the barracks itself, a group of soldiers milled about a dark coach. One man reclined in a high-backed chair while the others waited on his every need.

"I don't think so," Rayad answered. "They're in the open and don't have any men hiding in the trees. They know we can easily make our escape back into the forest. No, they just want to talk and are overconfident in your choice."

Kyrin sent a glare across the distance to Sir Richard, but her eyes switched to the coach. *Kaden*. No doubt he was inside. "So, I go down and talk to them then?"

Rayad gave a slow nod. "Yes, but just to talk."

Kyrin glanced at him, and then at Jace. She'd had to convince them to let her come. Whatever happened during this meeting, Kaden would still be a captive. That wouldn't change, but, regardless of the outcome, she had to go out there. Though she didn't want to face the thought of it, this might be her one and only chance ever to see her brother again. It would be difficult not to give in to Richard's demands with Kaden's life on the line, but neither one of her friends would let her do it. Whether or not she was glad of this was too soon to tell, but she couldn't trust her own emotions under these circumstances.

"All right. Let's go down," she murmured.

They turned to where the other men waited with the horses.

"Do you want me to go with you?" Tane asked.

Kyrin looked up into his eyes. His presence would bring added comfort, but she shook her head. "No, you're still needed in Valcré. We can't let them see you. Besides, the less men they know we have, the better." She sighed. "I'll be all right."

She mounted up with Jace, Rayad, and Warin. The three men would be enough to offer her immediate protection and counsel, while the others could cover their escape if necessary. Just before leaving the forest, Kyrin whispered a plea to Elôm for strength and guidance.

She stiffened her spine and nudged Maera. The men followed her out into the open. Commotion rose among the soldiers the moment they appeared, but Kyrin's eyes stayed fixed on Richard. Though difficult to tell at this distance, she was sure of the wicked smile on his face. She could almost feel it. When they drew nearer, he rose from his chair, and his men, including Goler, took up defensive positions around him.

Several yards away, Kyrin and her companions dismounted. She reached back for her bow, needing the confidence boost of being armed. To her right, Jace gripped his. He met her eyes and gave her a reassuring nod. She forced a quick smile, though it barely touched her lips, and turned to face Richard again. They walked a couple of yards closer to talk, but maintained adequate room for escape.

Richard's satisfaction was plain now, and mingled with loathing. "Miss Altair. You're looking well, though I can't say that with any pleasure."

"The feeling is mutual," Kyrin replied.

"Well then, let's dispense with formalities and get down to business."

He motioned to the soldiers. Two of them opened the doors of the coach. Kyrin pressed her free hand to her stomach and held her breath. A moment later, they dragged out Kaden and Trev. Tears flooded her eyes at not only seeing Kaden's face, but the blood and bruises too. She ached to rush over to him, but held it together even though her voice broke when she gasped his name.

"Hey," he replied with a small smile.

She nearly burst into sobs. After so many weeks apart, she couldn't even give him a hug. Struggling to gain better control over her voice, she looked between him and Trev and asked, "Are you all right?"

"We're fine," Kaden answered.

Of course he would say that.

"Now that you've seen them, Miss Altair," Richard cut in, "let's discuss their fates."

She tore her eyes from Kaden. Her stomach rolled. She was not at all ready for this.

"Here's what I have to offer," Richard said as if it were nothing more than a simple business transaction. "Hand yourself over to me, and the emperor will consider showing them leniency."

Kyrin let out a short, mirthless laugh, strangled by threatening tears. "You're lying."

Richard shrugged. "If you return to Valcré, you'll be able to plead their cases. It's a better chance than they stand now."

It was all lies. As if Emperor Daican would listen to a word she said. He'd sooner use her brother and Trev as means to torture her.

Richard took a step forward, and his voice changed immediately to hard-edged cruelty. "Let's put it this way. If you don't give yourself up, I will take those two back to Valcré, and they won't just be killed. No, I'll make it my personal mission to see they are tortured—long, slow, painful torture—until they have only enough life left to be dragged into the square and executed in front of the whole city."

With each vicious word, Kyrin's chest heaved. Such horrific images left her cold and without strength. The malicious hint of a smile crossed Richard's lips, and he pressed his advantage.

"You know I'll do it. So spare them that, at least, and give yourself up."

For that brief, horror-induced moment, she almost did it—almost threw down her bow and offered herself up, but Kaden's voice cut into these fear-driven contemplations and pulled her eyes back to him.

"Don't do it." Their gazes fused, fueled by the determination lighting his eyes. He strained against his guard. "He'll just torture and kill us anyway. You know that. Don't believe a word—"

The soldier punched Kaden in the stomach, and he sagged to his knees with a groan. Kyrin let out a cry and instinctively reached for an arrow.

"I wouldn't," Richard warned with a voice like steel. "Neither you nor your friend."

Kyrin glanced over at Jace. He too had a hand to his quiver.

"You can't kill all of us. Not before your brother reaps the consequences."

At the hiss of a blade, Kyrin's focus darted back to Kaden. The soldier pressed the tip of a dagger under her brother's chin, and she lowered her shaking hand back to her side.

"Now, Miss Altair, what is your choice? Will you abandon them to torture, or will you do the noble thing and give them a chance for mercy, or at least a mercifully quick end? It's up to you."

Kyrin's eyes never left Kaden as the crushing pain inside begged her to do whatever she must to save him. But Kaden shook his head, his eyes intense, pleading even. She glanced at Trev and found the same urging in his expression. A hand grasped her shoulder. She flinched and looked back at Rayad.

"I think we should go," he said gently, but firmly.

Kyrin just stood and looked between him and Kaden with

her muscles locked in indecision. Wisdom tugged her one way while her heart pulled her in the other, and right now, her heart was stronger. Kaden needed her. After all the bullies he'd fought and beatings he'd taken on her behalf, how could she just walk away? They'd never abandoned each other. Her eyes locked with his again, and he mouthed, "Go."

Clenching her teeth and fighting every instinct she possessed, she backed slowly toward the horses.

"Miss Altair."

She paused at Richard's razor-edged tone.

"I won't wait indefinitely for you to think it over. Every day you refuse to show up here in surrender, they will neither eat nor drink, and when I come to the end of my patience, which you're already trying, I will begin torturing them here." A monstrous glint flickered in his eyes. "I can send bits and pieces of them to the villagers to give to you. Maybe then you'll change your mind."

Kyrin's stomach nearly emptied, and cold washed over her. The ground tipped underneath her but righted when Jace took her by the arm. She looked up at him, though her vision wavered with tears. Shared pain and sympathy filled his eyes, but also immovable determination.

"Come, Kyrin," he said in a low voice.

Nearly paralyzed, she followed along numbly as he led her to her horse and helped her mount. She settled in, and Jace sent a searing look back at Sir Richard. Gripping the reins, Kyrin sought Kaden's face again.

"I'm sorry," she could only whisper as tears welled until she could hardly see him.

He shook his head. He wanted this as surely as she would in his place.

Before Richard could say another word, Jace took hold of Maera's bridle and led her around with Niton. With Rayad and Warin covering their back, they rode for the forest and joined the others.

"Let's get back to camp," Rayad said. He cast a concerned glance at Kyrin.

Everyone turned, but Kyrin looked back to the field. The coach containing her brother and Trev was just disappearing into the barracks. She couldn't breathe, and a strangled sob worked its way free. *Elôm!* She covered her mouth and struggled to retain the last failing grip she had on the torrent rising inside her. She forced herself to turn away and found Jace waiting for her. His strength gave her just enough will to prompt Maera forward.

Caught up in a dark, sinking daze, Kyrin saw nothing of the ride back—only Kaden and Trev's faces and the threat of what Richard would do to them. When they arrived in camp, she slid down from her horse, her stomach a roiling pot she fought to keep down. Those who had stayed behind gathered for news, but Kyrin brushed past them and stumbled off to the far edge of camp. Here, she surrendered to the overpowering weight of despair. Her tears let loose and streamed down her cheeks. She felt as though someone had reached in to crush her heart between iron fingers. Her body convulsed with choking sobs, and she begged Elôm with all her soul to save them.

Kyrin's mournful cries carried to everyone across camp, but Jace made the first move to approach her. He moved slowly, uncertain. It was the first time in his life he was in the position to offer comfort to another. But he understood her pain and grief, and it hurt him deep inside to see her, his true friend, in such agony. The last three weeks he'd spent with her had reminded him that some things in life were worth living for. She shouldn't have to suffer so much after everything she'd done for him.

She must have sensed him coming and looked up. Her lips trembled as tear after tear rolled down her cheeks. She shook her head, nearly delirious with emotional pain.

"I want to give myself up." She choked out the words. "I do, I really do. I can't bear knowing what will happen if I don't."

Jace grimaced, but spoke as gently as he knew how. "Kyrin . . . you can't."

She squeezed her eyes shut as another heart-ripping sob broke free.

Jace took a step closer. What might happen if he couldn't get through to her? "Your brother was right. Richard will torture them regardless of whether or not you give yourself up." He shook his head, knowing too well the truth of his next words. "Men like him love inflicting pain. He won't keep his word. If you surrender yourself, it will only give him more pleasure in hurting them."

"I know," Kyrin cried in utter despair. Deep sobs gripped her again.

Jace ached to know how to help her. He glanced skyward in desperation. *I don't know what to do.* It was such unfamiliar territory. Hesitantly, he put his hand on her shoulder. The next thing he knew, she had her arms around him, crying desperately into his chest. He stood stunned for a moment, but then wrapped his arms around her. It felt right to offer her this comfort. How many times while growing up had he longed for someone to do the same for him?

He didn't say anything, just held her and closed his eyes. *Elôm, I still don't know for sure if You can hear me, but I hope so, at least for this one prayer. Please, rescue her brother and Trev, and protect them from further harm. And stop men like Richard from inflicting such pain.* He swallowed down his hatred for the emperor and his men.

Evening fell, matching the darkness in Kyrin's mind. She stared at the flames of the campfire, but found no comfort in them. Endless scenarios for rescue spun her mind in circles.

The men gathered for supper, but she didn't respond to any of them until someone offered her a bowl of soup. She looked up, and her eyes found Jace. Her stomach recoiled at the mere idea of food, but she took the bowl anyway as he sat down beside her.

"Thank you," she murmured.

It didn't escape her notice what he had done for her today and what a feat it was for him. His quiet concern meant more to her than all the other condolences she'd received. Despite her lack of appetite, she ate the soup just to satisfy him.

Long into the evening, she remained at the fire, and Jace never left her side, even as most of the camp turned in for the night. They didn't say much, but Kyrin welcomed his presence. After all they'd been through, she didn't mind him seeing her brokenness.

Sometime near midnight, after a long reign of silence, Jace said softly, "You should go in and try to rest."

Kyrin turned weary eyes to his. Her mind dragged more heavily than her body, but sleep would surely elude her tonight. Yet sitting here served no purpose. She knew too well that wishing wouldn't rescue Kaden. She nodded.

"I can try."

Jace rose and helped her up. He stared at her, clearly struggling for more to say.

"Thank you for what you've done," she told him. "You're just the friend I need right now."

His expression eased. "If there's anything you need, I'll be right here."

Letting her head hang, Kyrin huddled on her bed until the slow-growing light of morning sun drew her attention. Sleep had come in only short periods. The rest of the time she'd tossed and turned while straining her mind until her skull felt as if it were being pried apart. At that point, she'd dissolved into silent, wracking sobs that left her utterly spent. But it was in that darkest moment that the first tiny threads of hope began to take shape. She'd spent every minute since then in prayer.

Now, with the first bird trill outside, she threw aside her covers and dressed. Her body reacted sluggishly, though she tried to ignore it and the persistent throbbing in her head. She descended the ladder quietly, but Lenae was just getting out of bed.

"How are you this morning?" she asked. Her eyes were shadowed with concern and lack of sleep.

Kyrin let out a slow breath, congested from all her tears. "I'm not quite sure yet. I have to talk to Rayad and Warin."

She walked to the door and let herself out. The forest was still dim, but a glow came from the flicker of small flames at the fire. Jace still sat there with Tyra, just as he had promised. The warmth of this sight soothed her. Tyra met her as she approached and nudged her face into Kyrin's hands. Kyrin rubbed her head and sat down next to Jace.

"Have you seen Rayad and Warin yet?"

He shook his head. "Not yet. It probably won't be long though."

Kyrin gave a nod and forced herself to wait. Thankfully, it wasn't long. A few minutes later, the two older men joined them. Gathering her thoughts and determination, Kyrin stood.

"I'm going to give myself up."

The men looked at each other, and she caught Jace's horrified expression as he pushed to his feet.

"You can't," Rayad said only a second before Jace surely would have. "I know it's difficult, but giving yourself up won't save your brother."

"It might," Kyrin replied. "This isn't what you're thinking. Like Trask, the only way to rescue Kaden and Trev is if they're

441

taken out of the barracks. The problem is, if we wait around for that to happen, Richard will start torturing my brother and . . ." She swallowed to wet her aching throat. " I just can't bear that. And now that they don't need Trask to tell them where I am, Goler could just kill him. It doesn't leave us any time to wait for a perfect opportunity that might never come."

"So, what's your plan?" Warin asked.

"If I give myself up, Richard won't have a reason to hold any of us in the barracks. He'll want to get us back to Valcré for execution. So, when they transport us out, you can rescue us. I'll just go in to get things moving."

Rayad exhaled with a deep frown of uncertainty. "I don't know. It's risky. There's no telling what will happen to you before you're transported, and there's always a chance he could just kill you there."

"I know, but I don't believe he will. The emperor wants our deaths, particularly mine, to be public. He'll want Richard to bring us all to Valcré. I know the risk and that things could go wrong, but I *have* to do it. For Kaden."

Rayad looked over at Warin, who shrugged and said, "It's more of a plan than we've had so far."

Rayad considered it for a long moment, his expression mirroring his hesitation, and Kyrin prayed he would not only agree, but that her plan would indeed work. She glanced at Jace. He stared at Rayad too, with an almost pleading look in his eyes.

Finally, Rayad nodded. "I'm not at all comfortable with putting you in harm's way, but . . ." He sent Jace an apologetic glance and continued, "You're right that we don't have time to search for other alternatives."

Jace released a worn breath and hung his head, but when he raised it again, determination had replaced his fear. "We'll have to scout the road and select an ambush point." He looked at Kyrin and his face softened. "We need to have everything ready and planned out before you go in."

Rayad agreed. "As soon as we've had our breakfast, we'll ride out and do some scouting."

RICHARD PICKED AT his lunch and scowled. Such a tasteless diet was not fitting for a man of his breeding. And his sleeping accommodations! He snorted. The flat straw mattress had left him itching and no doubt crawling with bugs. His bedroll on the ground had been more pleasant. That girl would pay for forcing him to come all the way out here to the wilderness and endure this. Oh, yes, she would pay. And the longer she kept him waiting, the more he would enjoy inflicting pain on her in any possible way he could conceive.

His mood darkening by the hour, he shoved back his chair and stormed out of the headquarters, leaving his half-eaten food to the flies. It wasn't fit for much else. He strode across the yard and climbed up to the watchers on the palisade tower.

"Anything?"

"No, sir."

Richard's eyes scanned the tree line and narrowed. Nothing stirred. *That's it.* He would not be kept waiting by this little ragtag group of traitors. He spun around and climbed back down. On the ground, he met Goler.

"It's been over twenty-four hours," he snapped. "Time to send a message."

Everything inside Jace rebelled at what was about to happen. His eyes rested on the barracks for only a moment before coming back to Kyrin. Rayad offered her a waterskin, and she took a gulping drink before handing it back. Her face appeared pale as she too looked out across the field.

"Ready?" Rayad asked, and she nodded.

Jace watched her struggle to draw breath just before she looked at him. She attempted a smile, though it resembled a wince, and his heart nearly broke.

"Are you sure about this?" he asked. His insides churned over what could happen to her. Now he wished he'd protested it more. He'd do almost anything to get her to reconsider.

But she stood up a little taller, and determination solidified in her eyes. "He's my brother. He's always thrown himself into any situation to protect me. I have to do this for him."

Jace let a long sigh seep out and glanced over her head to the barracks again and the distance she would have to cross by herself—or maybe not.

His gaze dropped to meet hers again, and his pulse quickened. "I should go in with you."

Her eyes widened a little, but she shook her head. "No, you can't. Richard would find any way he could to use you against me, and there would be nothing you could do anyway."

Jace didn't care what Richard did to him, and maybe he couldn't protect Kyrin in there, but she shouldn't have to walk in by herself.

"I have to go. Alone," she said. Her voice held a slight tremble, but she was good at hiding her fear. She looked up at him with hopeful eyes. "Pray for me?"

"I will," he promised without hesitation.

She managed another brief smile and turned away to walk into the clearing toward the barracks. Jace stood and watched, never taking his eyes off her. Halfway across, she glanced back, and he took a step forward. Those men could so easily kill her, just like Kalli and Aldor. A fresh sense of loss from that day knocked the wind out of him. He couldn't lose someone like that again. But Rayad grabbed his arm.

"This is her choice," he said quietly. "We have to stick with the plan and pray it works."

As Kyrin drew nearer and nearer to the barracks, Rayad's grip on his arm remained. How the overwhelming desire to protect her had developed in the last weeks, Jace didn't quite know, but it burned through him like fire. No one had ever found their way past his barrier walls and mistrust so quickly before—not even Kalli. But Kyrin had. She'd offered friendship and understanding in the midst of hostility, but greater than that, she'd brought back a stirring of hope that he thought had died on the farm. If this didn't go according to plan and Richard didn't bring her out in the next day or two, he would get to her one way or another. He'd tear that barracks apart if he had to.

Loud footsteps echoed through the jailhouse. Kaden glanced at Trev. Gut instinct warned him what was coming. Richard stalked toward the cell, followed by Goler and a trail of soldiers.

"Your sister must not care about your well-being," he said in a low snarl. "Either that, or she considers me a fool."

With a jangle of keys, Goler unlocked the cell door. Kaden scrambled to meet them on his feet. They could break his body, but not his spirit. He would never stop fighting. Still, his heart pounded and refused to slow.

Two soldiers seized him by the arms, igniting his adrenaline. He wrestled against them, but one drove his fist into Kaden's side, setting fire to his already bruised ribs. He gasped, his struggle weakened, and they shoved him up against the wall. His breathing came harder as he glared back at Richard. The man yanked out a dagger, and Goler grabbed Kaden's wrist, splaying his hand against the stone. He tried to wrench it away, but his strength was depleted after being starved in the days since his arrest.

"Let's see how stubborn she is after this," Richard sneered.

The soldiers' tightened their grip on Kaden even as his will to fight them exploded with the knowledge he was about to lose some part of his body. Richard's dagger pressed down on one of his fingers, and the sharp blade sliced into his skin. He bit back a groan at the fiery sting, but it clawed its way up his throat as the blade went deeper—all the way to the bone. Hot blood ran down his hand. He ground his teeth together and shut his eyes tightly. He would do this for Kyrin. Anything, as long as she stayed safe.

"Sir!"

Kaden's eyes popped open, and Richard whipped his head around. A soldier rushed to the cell door.

"Sir, she's here."

The pain vanished, and coldness gripped Kaden instead. He couldn't mean Kyrin. She wouldn't come . . . she couldn't.

Richard wiped his dagger clean and snapped it back into the sheath as he strode from the cell. Goler and his men followed, locking the door shut behind them. Kaden slumped against the wall and looked down at his hand. Blood still trickled from the wounded finger, the steady drip adding to the spatter on the floor. He clamped his hand over it, but his eyes rose back to the hall. If Kyrin showed up there . . . He let out an aching groan and prayed like never before.

Nothing prepared Kyrin for the terror of walking up to the barracks alone and unarmed. She'd walked into the temple at Auréa, but she'd had no choice. This was voluntary and went against every screaming sense of self-preservation or logic. Waves of heat and frosty cold rolled through her muscles. She drew a shallow breath, but tremors followed. What was she doing?

She looked over her shoulder, toward the trees where she had left her friends, and her feet dragged. She could still turn and run. With Niton, Jace could surely reach her before the soldiers did. *No.* She set her eyes back on the barracks and clenched her trembling fingers. Kaden was in there. If she turned back now, he'd be doomed to agonizing torture and death.

"Elôm," she prayed to drown out the blood thrashing in her head. "I believe this will work, but only if it's Your will. I ask for Your protection and rescue, for me, Kaden, Trev, and Trask. Please, let it work."

Shouting clamored from inside the barracks. Her steps faltered and her insides gave a savage twist, but she pressed forward. The palisade loomed above her now, and the gate swung open.

"And, Elôm, I pray for strength in whatever happens. Give me courage and help me trust You."

Just outside the gate, a soldier rushed out and seized her. She winced as he pulled her roughly inside. Her gaze swept the compound, taking it all into her memory, and fell on Richard as he emerged from a nearby stone building. Triumph gleamed in his eyes. Fresh blood smeared his hands. Kaden's blood—she was sure of it. *Please don't let me be too late!* The soldier yanked her to a halt in front of Richard.

"Miss Altair." He grabbed her arm in a bruising, vice-like hold and hauled her into the building he'd just exited. "I knew you'd come."

A chill sweat dampened Kyrin's back. The building's dim interior and iron bars brought back images of the palace dungeon—the suffocating darkness and cold. They rounded a corner. Regular intervals of small windows let dusty streams of light into each cell. Her gaze shot straight to Kaden, and she sagged with relief. He stood at the cell door, his intense, taut expression both horrified and demanding. His ice-blue eyes snapped with questions, but an explanation would have to wait.

Richard shoved her into a cell directly across from Kaden. She turned to the man, but was met with a solid slap across the face. She stumbled, catching herself against the wall, and grimaced. Heat radiated in her cheek from the sting of the impact, and she put her hand to it. Slowly, the sting wore off, but her lip continued to throb and blood welled. She pressed her sleeve to it and turned again to face Richard, but more cautiously this time.

He glared down at her. "You will learn very soon that you should *never* have played games with me or the emperor."

She flinched at the slamming of the cell door. Richard turned away, casting a glance at Kaden, who gave him a flaming look, and stormed off. Kyrin stood quietly at the bars until his footsteps faded. Then, she rested her eyes on her brother. The intensity of his expression had not diminished.

"Why are you here?" His raised voice broke the silence, but she understood it came from concern. "Why did you give yourself up?"

Before she could answer, she noticed his bloodstained hands. "Are you all right?"

Kaden frowned, then seemed to realize what she meant and looked down. "I'm fine," he muttered. He met her eyes again with the frown still in place.

"Richard was going to take your finger to send me, wasn't he?"

Kaden refused to answer and practically glared at her.

"That's exactly why I gave myself up. I couldn't let him do this to you. You would've done the exact same thing."

Kaden shook his head fiercely. "But you're a girl! You shouldn't be here. You should've just let it be. We'll still be tortured and killed anyway."

Kyrin bowed her head. She hated to upset him so.

"I know."

He threw his hands out, flinging droplets of blood. "Then why did you do it?"

Kyrin glanced down the hall. If only she could explain, but if anyone overheard, the mission would be over and they really would die. She looked back to his face and tried to appeal to him with her eyes.

"Just trust me."

Pink dusted the sky outside the jailhouse windows when the thud of footsteps interrupted the quiet conversation inside. Sitting against the bars, Kyrin peered out of her cell. Richard appeared first, and then Goler and his soldiers. She breathed a prayer that their escape had arrived, but when Richard reached her cell, he only glared in at her without moving to open it.

"Who besides that man"—he gestured to Trask—"have aided you?"

Slowly, she rose to her feet and glanced at Trask, but said nothing.

"His father?" Richard pressed.

Kyrin's eyes met his. "No."

"Landale's villagers?"

"No."

"Who then?"

Again, Kyrin fell silent.

Richard's voice rose. "Where have you been hiding, and who were the men with you?"

Not a word. Kyrin just stared at him and the deep shadows brewing in his eyes.

Barely restrained, Richard said, "You really should know by now not to try my patience."

He spun around and motioned to Kaden's cell. Goler un-locked it with a wicked grin. Kyrin's heart launched into her throat. *Please, not this.* They'd warned her back at camp of the possibility of Richard using Kaden to draw information from her. She'd had to promise, no matter what happened, she would not give up anything, and they trusted her with their lives.

"No," she gasped as the men entered Kaden's cell.

They dragged him forward and forced him to his knees facing her. Kyrin locked her fists around the bars and looked him in the eyes. His jaw set defiantly.

"You know, Miss Altair, just because you're here doesn't mean I can't go through with my threats," Richard said in a deceptively conversational tone. He grabbed Kaden by the hair and yanked his head back, placing the tip of his dagger just under Kaden's eye.

"No!" Kyrin cried.

Richard's glare slammed into her with the promise of action if she did not comply. "Then tell me who aided you and where you were hiding."

Her eyes jumped between him and Kaden. Her throat constricted and strangled her words. "I . . . can't."

"You'd prefer to see your brother lose an eye?"

She stared at the menacing glint of the dagger's sharp edge. The thought of Kaden so gruesomely harmed was too horrifying to imagine. There had to be another way.

"Miss Altair," Richard snapped. "Give me the information."

Moisture flooded her eyes, and her mind whirled. *Please.* She squeezed the bars, the rusted metal slivers digging into her fingers, and gritted her teeth. But she was powerless. She could do nothing without endangering the others. She gulped, throat aching.

Why did it have to be this way? Could Kaden forgive her for allowing him to suffer so? Could she live with it burnt into her memory for the rest of her life? Yet, she'd chosen to risk this very situation with the hope it would lead to their escape—to save their lives no matter what was left of them. She'd already made the choice, but to have to live it . . . Her mouth opened, but no voice came out.

"Kyrin."

Her blurry eyes focused on Kaden. His voice was quiet and a little shaky, yet firm.

"There are too many other lives at risk."

Richard's dagger cut into his cheek, just below his eye. He flinched and strained against the soldiers. Kyrin bit back a whimper. The blood trailing down her brother's face matched her tears.

"Last chance," Richard warned.

Kyrin scrunched her eyes closed, and her wobbly knees almost failed her. She'd choose to face Daican again, to face a murderous mob—anything but this. With an agonized groan, she cried, "Kaden, I'm so sorry."

"It's all right," he murmured.

Richard scowled. "Very well, Miss Altair, this is on you."

He squeezed the dagger, and Kaden sucked in a breath.

"No!" Kyrin screamed, the nightmare fully setting in. "Please! Don't do this! Elôm! Stop him, please!"

The point of the dagger hovered above Kaden's closed eye. Kyrin jerked at the bars, desperate to reach her brother, and cried for Richard to stop. After a moment, he looked over at her with a smirk of twisted satisfaction on his face. He straightened and stepped out of the cell to walk across to hers. Tears still streamed down Kyrin's face as she gulped in air. Richard reached in and grabbed her by the throat, drawing her against the bars with bruising force. Bending close, he sneered in her face, "I could keep at this, a little bit at a time, until he's completely unrecognizable. And lest you think your *god* has anything to do with this, no amount of pleading, crying, or screaming would stop me. I stop now only so His Majesty can watch you beg. Once we're back in Valcré, we'll finish this."

Kyrin hugged her knees and huddled in the dark. Sleep was impossible. Every time she closed her eyes, she could only see Richard and that dagger, so close to mutilating her brother. She swiped at a tear that worked its way out, and not for the first time wished Jace were here even though she knew it was good he'd stayed behind.

Rubbing her chilled arms, she shifted and looked over at Kaden and the others. To her eyes they were only dark, still figures, but their light breathing mingled with the chorus of bugs outside. They seemed to be asleep, though Trev was harder to tell. His breaths came hard and ragged, and he had to change positions often to get comfortable. Her own chest hurt with worry for him. With any more rough treatment, who could say if he'd survive?

The glow of dawn offered some relief as darkness only fed her fears, yet it brought a new day of uncertainties. Despite Richard's claim of waiting until they reached Valcré, she didn't trust him not to torture Kaden again, just for the pleasure of it. She put her head in her hands and reached out to Elôm.

The grating shriek of the door drew her head back up and jolted the men awake. Footsteps, more than usual, echoed in the hall. Richard, Goler, and several guards from Valcré entered. Without a word, they unlocked the cells and led everyone out. A spark of hope grew inside Kyrin. This could be their escape. *Oh, Elôm, please.* But she was careful not to let any of this hope reach her face.

Outside, the coach waited, confirming Kyrin's expectations. They marched toward it, but the group split. She stumbled to a halt and looked back as Goler led Trask off toward a group of horses. Her lungs seized. Richard grabbed her arm and tugged her forward. She pulled against him, but couldn't break his grasp.

"What are they doing with Trask?"

Richard pulled her close, his voice low and menacing. "He'll be executed in Landale Village as an example to the villagers of what happens when anyone, including nobility, defies the emperor."

A tremor of panic raced through Kyrin. It wasn't supposed to be this way! Not after all this. She struggled to look back again. This time Trask met her gaze. With just a look, he seemed to understand this wasn't the plan. Acceptance settled, dulling the green of his eyes. He gave her a nod—a farewell.

Richard's hard fingers crushed Kyrin's arm. "Get in."

She almost tripped when he shoved her forward. Limbs leaden, she climbed into the coach after Kaden and Trev. The door shut, trapping them in the dark interior, but Kyrin went to the window to watch in utter helplessness as Goler's men forced Trask to mount a horse. She grabbed the bars to steady herself as the coach lurched into motion, still watching until Trask disappeared from sight. Her heart plummeted.

"No." She sank to her knees.

"What is it?" Kaden asked.

Her wide eyes settled on him, and her voice wavered as she whispered, "Trask is supposed to be with us. I gave myself up so Richard would take us out of here. It's the only way the others can save us, but they're nine miles from here. Landale Village is only five. Trask and Goler will reach the village well before we're rescued."

NITON RACED THROUGH the trees, skirting around the brush and effortlessly leaping over logs at Jace's command. He was sure-footed, and Jace's expert guiding kept them at a fast pace. When a group of other horses came into view, Jace pulled the stallion to a halt and jumped down. Tane waited for him.

"Did you see them?"

Jace gave a quick nod and tossed Niton's reins to the talcrin before rushing on another hundred yards on foot. The pounding of his heartbeat matched his feet. Near the road, he came upon Rayad and the others in the cover of the underbrush.

"They're coming," he announced for all to hear. "They're only about a mile behind me."

Warin signaled to the men across the road, and everyone moved into position. Jace strung his bow and nocked an arrow before crouching behind the bushes that hid him while still offering a good view. Everything fell quiet, except for the birds. All was going according to plan. Thank Elôm they had not had to wait for more than a day.

Jace sent another glance up the road and turned his mind to prayer. Humbly, he asked that Elôm would protect the group, that Richard's men would surrender peacefully, and most of all, that Kyrin was safe. He sighed, exhausted. He hadn't slept for a moment last night thinking of all the ways Richard could hurt her.

The clop of hooves and creak of wagon wheels grabbed his attention. He stiffened and motioned to Rayad, who alerted the others. His heart kicked up a notch, his adrenaline rising and blood warming. But this time, he welcomed the heat. It would help if he had to fight to save Kyrin.

Moments later, the coach and escort rolled into view with Richard in the lead on a tall black horse. Jace gripped his bow, every sense heightened and prepared. The gap between them narrowed. He stared at the coach with only one thought as it rocked and swayed—to get to it and get Kyrin out. Heaven help Richard if he'd laid a finger on her. At least the solid walls of the coach would protect Kyrin and the others if Richard didn't give them up without a fight.

Finally, the man rode past his position. A second later, Warin stepped onto the road with his arms outstretched.

"Halt!"

Richard's horse stopped with a toss of its head and pawed at the ground. The others danced to a halt behind him, and confusion rippled through the men.

"What is the meaning of this?" Richard demanded until recognition dawned on him. His hand dropped to his sword. "I know you. You were with the girl."

Warin didn't respond to this. "Dismount and disarm and there will be no trouble. We don't want any bloodshed."

Richard's spine straightened, and Jace pulled back his bowstring just a little.

"You threaten a chief advisor to the emperor, as well as his officers. Step aside, or I'll have you executed on the spot for treason."

Warin shook his head. "Not until I have what I came for."

Richard laughed sharply into the rising tension, but his voice held no good humor. "The prisoners go to Valcré. You would not dare to oppose His Majesty unless you wish to see his full might unleashed on your pathetic rebellion."

"I wish only for you to release the prisoners without resorting to unnecessary violence."

"Fool!" Richard yanked out his sword and drove his heels into his horse. The animal lunged forward, but Jace was quicker. He drew and fired. Warin jumped to the side as the snorting horse clattered past him, and Richard toppled from the saddle with the arrow shot through his shoulder.

Swords hissed from their scabbards as the guards rushed to their leader's defense. Jace dropped his bow and whipped out his sword to join the others who burst from the trees. He ducked as his first opponent tried to take his head. The guard's horse pranced sideways and threw him off balance. Jace reached up to grab him and pulled him down. The man landed flat on his back in the dirt. He scrambled to rise, but Jace struck him across the head with the flat of his blade, and he fell back dazed.

A horse snorted just to Jace's right. He spun around and leapt aside just before he would have been battered by the horse's broad chest. The animal pounded past him, but its rider pivoted so it came around again. This time Jace was ready. The gleaming tip of the guard's sword plunged toward him. He shifted and swung his own sword upward. The guard's blade streaked just past his face, but his own arced up under the man's arm. The guard hunched over, his sword falling. A moment later, he too fell to the ground.

Gripping his sword in both hands, Jace looked around. The fight had already ended. Any guards left uninjured stood with their hands upraised in surrender.

Warin walked over to Richard, who knelt with the arrow still protruding from his back.

"You will all die for this," he hissed through clenched teeth.

"If the King allows it."

At these words, Richard growled and reached for his dagger. Instinctively, Jace lunged forward, but Warin saw it coming. He kicked Richard's hand away and grabbed the dagger himself.

"Warin!" Kyrin's voice called urgently from the coach.

Jace spun around and caught a glimpse of her face through the bars. Leaving the others to guard him, Warin took the keys from Richard and hurried over to unlock the door. Jace was right behind him. The moment it opened, Kyrin jumped out. Fury burst like flames through Jace's chest at seeing the reddened and slightly swollen cut through her lip. He shot a glare at Richard and fought the impulse to put another arrow through him. Good thing he didn't have his bow. His attention snapped back to Kyrin.

"We must get to Landale as fast as we can," she said in a rush. "Goler took Trask there to be executed!"

"Now?" Warin asked, his eyes wide.

"Yes! They left the same time we did."

Warin spun around to face the other men. "Tie everyone up. They'll work themselves loose eventually. We have to get back to the horses."

With Trask's life on the line, the men raced to obey.

Kaden exited the coach after Kyrin, and Jace helped him get Trev out. Warin unchained the three and ushered them toward the trees. After retrieving his bow, Jace hurried after them and stuck close to Kyrin's side. As far as he could tell, her split lip was the extent of her injuries. He was still sorely tempted to leave Richard with more than a single arrow wound, if only to avenge Kaden and Trev.

Back at the horses with Tane, Warin spoke, his voice calm, yet tinged with urgency. "Tane, help them back to camp." He motioned toward Kyrin and Kaden, who were supporting Trev between them. "Goler has Trask in the village, and there's no time to waste."

Tane immediately stepped in to help Trev to one of the extra horses. Kaden followed, but Kyrin stood looking from her brother to Warin with a torn expression. Maybe Jace couldn't read her like she did him, but she wanted to come and help save

Trask, that he could see. While it was an admirable desire, he wasn't about to let her ride into more danger. Not when they had her safely away from Daican's men.

She caught his eyes, and he motioned toward Maera. "Go." She hesitated and he added, praying it was true, "We'll save him."

Her expression slowly changed to one of acceptance, and she turned to follow her brother, who had waited for her. But she glanced back with pleading eyes. "Be careful."

Jace nodded. He waited until she mounted Maera, and then turned for Niton. Commotion filled the clearing with the arrival of the rest of the men. They claimed their horses and gathered around Warin.

"Let's go get Trask," he said.

With him in the lead, they all rode out. They had to take it slowly through the trees, but when they hit the road, they urged the horses into a gallop. Four miles lay between them and the outskirts of Landale Village. A slow ache knotted Jace's gut with the unpleasant urgency of passing time. No matter how fast they rode, it wouldn't feel fast enough, and every minute brought them perilously close to the brink of failure, if they had not failed already.

He grimaced. Trask had accepted him, and even Tyra, without question. He'd proven that people with such kindness were not quite as rare as Jace once believed. He should have been more appreciative. Would it be too late now to show Trask?

The distance seemed tripled before they finally pulled their panting mounts to a halt in a grove of trees just outside of Landale.

"We'll go on foot," Warin said. "It's too dangerous to charge in, for both us and Trask."

They dismounted and sprinted toward the center of the village. No villagers were in sight—not in the fields or any of the local shops they passed—which was odd on a beautiful day like this. A chill worked along Jace's skin and sank into his middle.

Sunshine or not, something ominous hung in the air, and he could only hope they weren't too late.

They crept between buildings, working their way closer to the village square, and, at last, caught a glimpse of gathered people. Goler's voice drifted from deeper within the crowd. Another few yards, and the square opened up before them. In the middle, Goler stood above everyone on top of a flat wagon. Two soldiers waited off to his side with Trask secured between them. Jace let out a breath. They'd made it.

"We're outnumbered," Warin murmured.

Jace scanned the area. Gold and black surrounded the wagon and dotted the crowd—at least twenty soldiers, if not more. He glanced at their rescue group. Eight, including himself.

"We'll have to get closer without letting them recognize us," Rayad said. "If Goler discovers we're here, he'll kill Trask before we can reach him."

Warin turned to the men. "Spread out. Get as close to the wagon as you can without drawing attention. Hopefully Trask will see one of us and be able to jump down. If not, we'll have to climb up and get him once we're all close enough. As soon as we have him, we get out. We can't fight them all."

The men split up, moving inconspicuously through the crowd. Jace kept his head down so no one would see his eyes and mistake him for a ryrik, but most of the people had their attention locked on Goler and Trask. Jace glanced at the wagon where Goler named off a list of Trask's crimes, no doubt milking this for all it was worth, reveling in the power he held over Trask. But no one in the crowd reacted. How could they? One look at their faces said everything, especially the women. More than one had tears streaming down her cheeks.

He slipped through them slowly, but it was a tight crowd. He looked around and caught a glimpse of Rayad. None of them had made it very close to the wagon. They would have to gain a lot of ground to reach Trask before things went south. He ducked his head when a soldier caught his eyes just as Goler's discourse neared its end.

"And for these vile acts against the emperor, he is sentenced to death. Let this be a reminder that no matter what your station, disloyalty and treason will not be tolerated."

The soldiers led Trask forward. Jace's heart tripped. They would never get to the wagon in time, and if they tried to rush it, the soldiers would intercept and Trask would be dead before they ever reached him. Something had to happen quickly. His eyes darted around the area, and his fingers crept to his bow slung over his shoulder, but it was too cramped and the soldiers were too close. He could never fire from here. His gaze caught on a barn to his left. Heat surged through his muscles. If he was going to do this, it had to be now. They'd run out of time.

Trask stepped forward with the soldiers, his eyes traveling over the faces of the villagers, most of whom he knew by name. Old childhood friends he had run off to the woods with, and the older women who'd treated him so kindly after his mother died. Goler was a beast for making them watch this.

He looked over at the captain and glared at him, tempted to throw his shackled hands around his throat. He still hadn't decided if he wanted to go out with dignified acceptance or die fighting.

His gaze returned to the people. Some aching part of him wished to find Anne among them, just to see her face once more, but he didn't want her here. Not for this. He lifted his eyes to his father, who sat on his horse at the edge of the crowd with a handful of soldiers hovering suspiciously around him. Seeing his father's ashen face and ill-concealed emotions turned Trask's stomach inside out. He gave the barest shake of his head. If his father tried anything, then Goler would win, and the people would suffer. They would need his leadership now more than ever. And for this reason, in the end, Trask would not fight, because if he fought, his father would too.

Goler stepped up beside him and locked his shoulder in a painful grip. Leaning closely, he murmured in his ear, "Time to watch you die."

He kicked Trask's legs, sending him to his knees. A hushed whimper came from more than one person in the crowd. Trask looked out at them again. If only he could leave them a few words of encouragement, but that would just further mark them as potential rebels. Right now, the more removed he was from them, the better, though it hurt worse than Goler's torture.

The captain's hand gripped the back of his neck and forced him down against the block. He swallowed roughly against the wood. The sensation of it pressed to his throat shot icy jolts through his nerves. His heart took up an irregular beat while beside him, the executioner's sword slid out of the scabbard. When he tried to swallow again, his throat was too tight. He closed his eyes and whispered, "I'm ready to meet You, Lord."

Jace scrambled up the ladder into the barn loft and sprinted across the straw-littered floor. Grabbing his bow, he pushed open the loft door, and the sight below him stole his breath. The executioner stood over Trask with his sword raised. Jace's hand flew to his quiver. He nocked, drew, and released without even pausing to contemplate a miss. The arrow sliced the air and slammed into the executioner's chest. The man gave a loud grunt and toppled off the wagon.

Half a second of stillness, and then pandemonium. Shouts and screams rose from the crowd as the soldiers unsheathed their swords. Goler looked about, and his eyes landed on Jace. Teeth bared, he whipped out his sword and swung at Trask. But Jace had a second arrow on the way. It plunged high into Goler's left shoulder and halted his attack. He screamed, grabbing at the wound, but blinding anger overcame the pain. He raised his sword again. This time, Trask rolled off the wagon before the blade could find him.

In the mass of confusion and scurrying villagers, someone grabbed Trask from the ground and dragged him up. Warin. Jace scanned the panicking crowd. The rest of the men worked their way toward escape, but the soldiers were on to them.

He spun around and climbed down the ladder. On the ground again, he put his bow over his head and shoulder and yanked out his sword. Metal clashed close by and echoed amongst shouts and cries. Jace dashed out of the barn and nearly collided with a soldier. The man swung at his head. Jace ducked and sliced the soldier's legs, leaving him writhing and cursing while he rushed into the fray.

The villagers had scattered for cover, while most in the rescue group found themselves embroiled in battle with Goler's men. Jace threw down another soldier who blocked his path and ran to Rayad, who was with Warin and Trask. Warin called out to the men and motioned them toward their escape. They were close now, if they could just break away and get to the horses.

Then someone fell.

Holden crashed to the ground, his shoulder oozing blood and his sword out of reach. He tried to rise, but the soldier kicked him back down and raised his sword. Jace broke from the group and sprinted back to help. He threw his sword blade into the path of the soldier's. Metal shrieked on impact, driving Jace's sword into the ground, but both blades missed Holden.

The soldier was quick. His sword came up in an instant, straight for Jace's throat. As Jace jumped back, the tip of the blade narrowly missed his neck and nicked his shoulder. Fire pulsed through his limbs, but a swift and powerful counterstrike left the soldier unarmed and bleeding from a deep wound to his arm.

Jace grabbed Holden by the jerkin, hauled him to his feet, and guided him toward the others. They were the last two to join their group. The soldiers converged to cut off their escape, but they dashed through the narrow gap and raced away from the village. When Jace glanced back, a couple of soldiers were in pursuit, but most scrambled for their horses. They reached their own mounts without a second to spare. Hoof beats pounded behind them as Jace swung up onto Niton's back.

The group sent their horses into a gallop, riding hard across country, but the soldiers kept pace. Jace looked back again. This chase would be the doom of their rescue. Already tired from the ride to the village, their horses would never outlast the soldiers' fresher mounts. Niton's deep, snorting pants confirmed this. They couldn't keep the pace long, let alone widen the gap to make an escape. If Goler were to capture all of them, there would be no one left at camp to lead it as Trask intended. It could all fall apart. Then Kyrin would have no place to go. Not unless something slowed the soldiers.

A steady rise lay ahead of them. Eyes set on it, Jace lifted his bow from his shoulder. If he failed, he would become the first to fall back into Goler's hands, but a calm settled inside him. Regardless of what happened to him, the others needed this chance.

At the top of the rise, he pulled Niton to a skidding halt and spun the stallion around. Dropping the reins, he reached for an arrow. The first soldier up the hill took the projectile to the chest and toppled out of the saddle. Fitting a second arrow, Jace fired in a rush with another rider almost upon him. It grazed the man's side. He jerked on the reins, and his horse lost its footing, rolling over on top of him and almost taking out the third rider. Jace set his sights on him with a third arrow already drawn. The soldier stopped a few feet below him while the other eleven pranced at the bottom of the hill.

Their eyes locked. The soldier slowly raised his hand, his expression one of pleading. The bowstring slipped a little, but Jace held it. Backing down a couple of steps, the soldier turned his horse in a hasty retreat. The others followed his example. Jace held his bow until his arm started to shake and then lowered it. By now, the fleeing hoof beats were fading away into the distance.

Quiet settled around him. He sank back in his saddle with a sigh and hung his head, catching his breath. Taking up the reins again, he turned Niton around and rode on to catch up with the others.

KYRIN CAREFULLY CLEANED the deep cut to Kaden's finger and wrapped a thin strip of bandages around it. He barely seemed to notice, intent on devouring the plate of rolls and cheese wedges Lenae had set before him. Kyrin looked across the table where the other woman was bandaging Trev's badly bruised chest. She winced, but at least he could rest now and give his ribs a chance to mend. Her eyes shifted to Tane, who stood at the door peering out at camp. She drew a nervous breath. Her heavily thumping heart kept tricking her into thinking she heard horses.

"I'm sure they'll be all right."

Her attention returned to her brother and his encouraging half smile. If they weren't both sitting, she'd hug him again. She attempted a small smile of her own, but every minute of waiting was torture. Praying with all her might, she finished up with Kaden's injuries.

Ten minutes later, Tane's voice sent a jolt of energy through her. "They're here."

She froze, not quite prepared for what news might await. But the desperation to know propelled her to her feet, and she dashed out of the cabin after Tane. The riders gathered near the corral, and Kyrin did a rapid head count. The moment she saw Trask and realized that no one was missing, her breath rushed out of her lungs, and she ran the remaining distance.

Most of the men had dismounted by now. Trask climbed out of the saddle slowly, but very much alive, and Warin assisted Holden, whose sleeve and side were stained with blood. Kyrin caught a glimpse of red on Jace's shoulder, but everyone else appeared unharmed.

"You made it," she breathed.

Trask turned to her with a weary, yet bright smile. "We did." He nodded over his shoulder. "Thanks to Jace."

Her eyes shifted to him, as did a few others. He looked at them in surprise, but then ducked his head and focused on Niton. A slow smile feathered across Kyrin's lips.

Warin came up behind Trask and put his hand on his shoulder. "Let's get those chains off you and get you and Holden inside to Lenae."

The three of them walked toward the cabin while the rest of the men cared for the horses. Kyrin lingered behind and approached Jace, running her hand down Niton's face as she watched him loosen the saddle. "You'll have to tell me what you did."

He glanced at her and shook his head. "It was nothing."

She traded a look with Rayad as he passed by. Maybe Jace wouldn't tell her, but Rayad would. Her focus drifted over to Lenae's cabin. The woman had come out and had just released Trask from her embrace with a beautiful smile on her face. Kaden stood in the cabin doorway behind her. The sight brought an instant rush of moisture to Kyrin's eyes, and she struggled for a full breath.

"Are you all right?"

She turned her head around. Jace's brilliant blue eyes regarded her with almost grave concern. With a wobbly smile, her lungs freed up a bit.

"It just hit me . . . it's over. Kaden's here, and for now . . . we're all safe."

Lying in bed in the early morning quiet, Kyrin smiled up at the ceiling and basked in how right things felt in that moment. With Kaden just in the next cabin, everything was as it should be, and she cherished it. The last couple of months had brought much pain and hardship, but, in many ways, things were better for it. *Thank You.*

Below her, Lenae worked on breakfast—such a peaceful, now familiar sound that added to Kyrin's joy. Ready to face a day full of such thrilling newness, she slipped out of bed and dressed. Downstairs, Lenae smiled at her, mirroring her contentment.

"Anything I can help with?" Kyrin asked.

Lenae shook her head. "I think I've got everything nearly finished. Besides, you're going to rest and enjoy these days. I insist."

Kyrin smiled as gratitude filled her heart. The woman had become such a dear friend and mentor. On impulse, she walked up and gave her a hug. Lenae let out a little noise of surprise and squeezed her tightly in return.

"Thank you so much for everything you've done for me these past weeks," Kyrin told her.

As they parted, Lenae's lovely eyes were a little watery, and she cupped Kyrin's face in her hands. "You're welcome. I enjoyed every moment of it."

They shared another smile, and Kyrin stepped away to the window to admire the beauty of the bright forest right outside. Her gaze fell on Jace sitting with Tyra nearby. Rayad had told her all about what he'd done in Landale and during their escape, much to Jace's chagrin. He clearly didn't want the recognition of a hero, but that was how she would see him. And it wasn't only because of Landale. He had saved her life too, after all.

She opened the door and walked out to him. Tyra wagged her tail in greeting, and Jace rose to meet her. She smiled at them, glad of the opportunity to talk to Jace. He'd kept his distance after returning to camp the day before. The excitement would have certainly made him uncomfortable, but she suspected something more.

"Good morning," she said cheerfully.

Jace echoed her with enough of a smile on his face to make her happy.

"It's a beautiful day," Kyrin went on as she breathed in the fresh, earthy air.

"It is."

She stared at him for a long moment until his expression grew uncomfortable, but she couldn't help but marvel at the change in him since the first night she saw him at the fire. With such clear images of his tortured eyes in her mind, it was easy to compare the difference to their vivid sparkle now. And for some reason beyond her understanding, Elôm had used her to make it happen. What a thrilling transformation to be a part of.

Following the same impulse as before, she stepped forward and closed her arms around him. He tensed but returned the embrace, a bit awkwardly at first, and she bit back a chuckle. When they parted, he stared down at her with an amusing crinkle in his brow.

She smiled and gave a shrug. "I just wanted you to know how much you mean to me, really. Kaden may be here now, but you will always be one of my best friends, and I don't ever want to lose you. You can count on me for anything."

Relief cleared the confusion from his face. So it was as she suspected. He had worried that Kaden's presence would change things. He looked away from her and swallowed as if working to control his emotions. She waited for him to turn back to her. When he did, his expression was the most open she had ever seen, and his voice came out a little rough. "I don't want to lose you either."

"You won't," Kyrin promised. "Not by my choice."

A full smile emerged on his face—one of such true joy, Kyrin could have cried. Perhaps the doubts, the lies, the pain would still come around to haunt him, but for right now, he had found peace.

Off to the side, movement caught her attention. Holden approached them slowly, his arm in a sling. Just like with Jace, the look in his eyes had completely changed since the days he'd glowered in mistrust. Contrition filled them instead.

"Looks like he has a lot on his mind." She looked up at Jace to make sure he was comfortable. "I'll let you two talk."

Jace's eyes followed Kyrin for a short distance as his mind still lingered on how he had come to care for her in only a few short weeks. She was special. She hadn't given up on him when many others would have, even when he tried to push her away. That was the true definition of a friend.

Finally, his focus fell on Holden. Though unsure of his intentions, none of the old apprehension surfaced. Something else settled inside him—something nearly foreign. Confidence. Whatever the man might say, those who mattered most would stick by him, and that offered a calming assurance.

Holden came near and seemed unable to meet Jace's eyes until he stood directly in front of him.

"I needed to talk to you . . . because of yesterday." He paused and rubbed his shoulder as a clear struggle played out on his face. But determination set in, the expression of a man owning up to his mistakes. "I was wrong. Everything I said and thought about you was wrong." He shook his head. "I was a fool and went against everything Elôm has been trying to teach me. I'm sorry. I don't know if you can grant it, but I ask for your forgiveness."

Jace had to let this sink in. Not a single person in all his life had ever apologized or sought his forgiveness for their actions against him. He wasn't even sure how to accept it. But Holden waited, his eyes earnest—such a stark contrast to the scathing looks he'd previously cast Jace's way. Realization settled inside Jace that forgiveness was a difficult thing for him. It always had been. Yet, didn't he so desperately crave it for the things he'd done? Things far worse than what this man had done to him? Who was he to withhold it?

"I forgive you," Jace declared, and the gratification that washed through him was instantaneous.

Holden breathed a deep sigh. "Thank you for that, and thank you for saving my life. I didn't deserve it."

He extended his hand. Jace looked at it for a moment and then gripped his arm. For the first time, Holden smiled at him.

He turned to go then, but glanced back. "By the way, I don't believe your wolf is possessed."

Jace chuckled softly and reached down to rub Tyra's ears.

The moment Kaden left his cabin, Kyrin walked over to him with a huge grin springing to her lips. Though it would take time for the bruises and signs of beatings to fade, just one full night of sleep and good food had already lessened the effects of captivity. It brought her such joy to see him that she had to keep hugging him to be sure she wasn't dreaming.

"You're here. I can't believe it."

"Neither can I. It's unreal." His grin matched hers—a wonderfully familiar sight. "I told you we'd make it. It just took a little longer than I expected."

She laughed, thinking back to the bell tower. "A lot longer and with a lot more difficulty. If I'd known then half of what I do now, I would've escaped that very day."

Kaden shrugged. "It turned out all right in the end."

"It did." As much as she would have liked to be spared the heartache and pain they had both experienced, anything different may have ended disastrously or not happened at all, such as befriending Jace. That she would not want changed.

"So, this is it. This is home," Kaden said as he surveyed camp.

She took in the sight as well. It was the same as always, yet it felt more complete to her now, and a deep fondness for it welled inside her. "Yes, this is home."

"I always did want to live in the woods."

Kyrin chuckled a little. Their grandfather's face had turned so red when Kaden had mentioned this dream back in Auréa. "Elôm gave you exactly what you wanted."

"What about you?"

"My biggest concern was the two of us being split up, but we're both here and surrounded by good people and good friends. That's enough for me."

Kaden didn't say anything, but she felt his eyes on her. She looked up at him.

"What?"

"You've changed."

"Have I?"

He gave a definite nod. "I'm not sure how, exactly. You're more outgoing, I guess. The way you helped Lenae with the injured and how you interact with everyone. I don't think the Tarvin Hall Kyrin would've been so quick to do that."

She contemplated this. She hadn't even thought before she'd acted yesterday. "I guess I hadn't really noticed."

"It's good."

Kyrin smiled in appreciation of his praise and linked her arm with his to give it a little hug. Her eyes drifted to the center of camp where Jace and Holden had finished talking. From the look on Jace's face, it had gone well. She smiled up at Kaden and said, "You haven't officially met Jace yet."

Kaden also looked at him, curiosity in his voice. "Is he . . . ?"

"He's half ryrik."

Kaden's eyes grew a little wider, but after everything that had taken place in the last weeks, it couldn't be as shocking as it might once have been.

"He's taught me a lot since I got here. Besides Sam, I've never had a friend like him. I hope you and he will be friends."

"Your friends are my friends," Kaden said without hesitation.

She smiled, and just to cement his feelings, she added, "He saved my life when we came upon a band of ryriks a couple of weeks ago."

Kaden's brows lifted.

Having achieved the desired effect, she tugged on his arm. "Come on."

She led him over to Jace and Tyra. Jace looked a little nervous, but Kyrin offered him an encouraging smile. She trusted her brother completely to treat him with compassion and to befriend him just as she had.

"Jace, I would like you to officially meet my brother, Kaden."

Kaden was quick to extend his hand, and Jace took it with little hesitation.

"I'm pleased to meet you," Kaden told him.

"And you," Jace replied.

"Thank you for taking care of my sister. I'm glad to know someone's been looking out for her."

Jace shrugged, but a small smile came to his face. "I think she's looked out for me more."

Kaden grinned and glanced at her. "She's good at that."

It wasn't long before Anne showed up in camp. Kyrin smiled at her teary reunion with Trask. They hugged tightly for a very long moment before Trask stole a quick kiss when he thought no one was looking and claimed her hand to lead her into camp.

To celebrate the blessing of having everyone alive and well, and in honor of the camp's newest members, Lenae cooked a special lunch. At noon, the entire camp, including Anne, gathered for the meal. Their conversations were light and filled with laughter. For Kyrin, the experience was far more meaningful and enjoyable than any banquet she'd taken part in at Tarvin Hall. Claiming a seat between Jace and Kaden, an overwhelming flood of joy pushed tears to her eyes, but she could not stop smiling.

They shared their small feast and the stories that had brought them to this moment. Near the end, Trask rose from his place beside Anne and walked into the center of the gathering. Conversation quieted as they all looked at him.

"I'd like to say a few things," he announced. He turned in a circle to look at everyone. "First, I'd like to formally welcome the newest members of our camp, Kaden and Trev." He motioned to them and everyone smiled their way.

"I also want to thank all of you." His voice took on a more serious tone. "You saved my life, and I wanted to say, well done. This group is exactly what I hoped and prayed for when Elôm compelled me to do this. You worked well together, and I'm proud of each of you and what you've accomplished."

He paused, letting his words truly touch their hearts, before going on somberly, "All of us have now seen just what the emperor and his supporters are capable of. Many of us experienced it firsthand."

Kyrin exchanged a glance with her brother, considering what the two of them had suffered at the hands of Daican and Richard, and the miracle of sitting here in this group still in one piece.

"Evil is spreading through our country like a sickness, and the more it grows, the more people it will affect and endanger. We might not be able to put a stop to it, but we can stand up to it. The path we're on to offer aid is a dangerous one. Chances are we won't all survive to see the end, if there even is an end.

We might be fighting toward a goal that can't be reached, at least not in our lifetimes."

Kyrin looked around at all the faces focused on their leader's every word. Despite the uncertainty, despite the danger, only determination burned in their eyes, and she felt it deep within her own soul.

"But, my friends, we must resist this evil. We must never be idle while it destroys lives and hope around us. If we don't stand, who will? Everywhere, people will be choosing whether to stand up or bow to the emperor's wishes. Most will bow, but if we stand, we can give hope to those who may feel they're standing alone.

"We will stand for what is right, and good, and true. We will protect and aid each other and all those Elôm brings into our path. We will remain faithful to Him, even when it may cost us our lives, and we will stand firm against the evil that will soon surround us. We will not back down. Each of us, right here, right now—we are the resistance."

RACE PROFILES

Ryriks

HOMELAND: Wildmor

PHYSICAL APPEARANCE: Ryriks tend to be large-bodied, muscular, and very athletic. They average between six, to six and a half feet tall. They have thick black hair that is usually worn long. All have aqua-blue colored eyes that appear almost luminescent, especially during intense or emotional situations. Their ears are pointed, which makes them very distinct from the other races. They have strong, striking features, though they can pass as humans by letting their hair hide their ears and avoiding eye contact. Ryriks typically dress in rough, sturdy clothing—whatever they find by stealing.

PHYSICAL CHARACTERISTICS: Ryriks are a very hardy race and incredibly resistant to physical abuse and sickness; however, they have one great weakness. Their lungs are highly sensitive to harsh air conditions, pollutants, and respiratory illness. Under these conditions, their lungs bleed. Short exposure causes great discomfort, but is not life-threatening. More severe, prolonged exposure, however, could cause their lungs to fill with blood and suffocate them. It is said to be a curse from choosing to follow the path of evil. Ryriks' eyes are very sensitive, able to pick out the slightest movement, and they can see well in the dark. Both their sense of hearing and smell are very keen—much higher than that of humans. In times of great distress or anger, ryriks can react with devastating bursts of speed and strength.

RACE CHARACTERISTICS: Ryriks are the center of fireside tales all across Ilyon. They are seen as a savage people, very fierce and cunning. To other races, they seem to have almost animal-like instincts; therefore, it is commonly believed they don't have souls. They are a hot-blooded people and quick to action, especially when roused. They have quick tempers and are easily driven to blind rage. They prefer decisive action over conversation. Most have a barbaric thirst for bloodshed and inflicting pain. They view fear and pain as weaknesses and like to see them in others. They are typically forest dwellers and feel most comfortable in cover they can use to their advantage.

SKILLS: Ryriks are highly skilled in the woods and living off the land. They are excellent hunters and especially proficient in setting ambushes. They're experts in taming and raising almost any type of animal. They make the fiercest of any warriors. A ryrik's favorite weapons are a heavy broadsword and a large dagger. Ryriks aren't masters of any type of craft or art. Most of their possessions come from stealing. What they can't gain by thieving, they make for themselves, but not anything of quality. They think art, music, or any such thing to be frivolous. Most ryriks can't read or write and have no desire to.

SOCIAL: Ryriks are not a very social race. Settlements are scattered and usually small. They have no major cities. Families often live on small farms in the forest and consist of no more than four to six people. Children are typically on their own by the time they are sixteen or seventeen—even younger for some males. Ryriks have a poor view of women. They see them as a necessity and more of a possession than a partner. Once claimed, a ryrik woman almost never leaves her home. She is required to care for the farm while the men are away. Most ryrik men group together in raiding parties, pillaging and destroying unprotected villages and preying on unsuspecting travelers. Ryriks have an intense hatred of other races, particularly humans.

GOVERNMENT: Ryriks have no acting government. Raiding parties and settlements are dictated by the strongest or fiercest ryrik, so the position can be challenged by anyone and changes often.

PREFERRED OCCUPATIONS: The vast majority of ryriks are thieves. A few hold positions as blacksmiths and other necessary professions.

FAITH: Ryriks disdain religion of any kind. They were the first to rebel against King Elôm and led others to do so as well.

TALCRINS

HOMELAND: Arda

PHYSICAL APPEARANCE: Talcrins are a tall, powerful people. Talcrin men are seldom less than six feet tall. They have rich, dark skin and black hair of various lengths and styles. Their most unique feature besides their dark skin is their metallic-looking eyes. They have a very regal, graceful appearance. Men often dress in long, expertly crafted jerkins, while women wear simple but elegant flowing gowns of rich colors, particularly deep purple.

RACE CHARACTERISTICS: Talcrins are considered the wisest of all Ilyon's peoples. Some of their greatest pleasures are learning and teaching. Reading is one of their favorite pastimes. They have excellent memories and intellects. Talcrins are a calm people, adept at hiding and controlling strong emotion. They are peace-loving and prefer to solve problems with diplomacy, but if all else fails, they can fight fiercely. They have a deep sense of morality, justice, loyalty, and above all, honesty. They are an astute people and don't miss much, particularly when it comes to others. Besides learning, they are also fond of art and music. Most talcrins are city dwellers, preferring large cities where libraries and universities can be found. Of all the races, they live the longest and reach ages of one hundred fifty, though many live even longer. Because of this, they age slower than the other races. Talcrin names are known to be very long, though they use shortened versions outside of Arda.

SKILLS: Talcrins excel in everything pertaining to books, languages, legal matters, and history, and are excellent at passing on their wisdom. They are often sought as advisors for their ability to easily think through situations and assess different outcomes. They are master storytellers and delight in entertaining people in this way. Though they strive for peace, most talcrin men train as warriors when they are young. They make incredible fighters who are highly skilled with long swords, high-power longbows, and spears. When not reading, many talcrin women enjoy painting and weaving. Their tapestries are among the most sought after. Both men and women enjoy music and dancing. They are expert harpists. Beautiful two-person dances are very popular in talcrin culture and are considered an art form. Metal-working is another skill in which talcrins are considered experts. Their gold and silver jewelry and armor are some of the finest in Ilyon.

SOCIAL: Talcrins are a family-oriented people and fiercely loyal to both family and friends alike. Families are average in size, with between three to seven children. Men are very protective of their families and believe their well-being is of utmost importance. Their island country of Arda is almost exclusively populated with talcrins. Scholars from the Ilyon mainland often come to visit their famous libraries, but other races rarely settle there. Many talcrins inhabit the mainland as well, but are widely scattered. The highest population is found in Valcré, the capital of Arcacia. They get along well with all races, except for ryriks. Though generally kindhearted, they can hold themselves at a distance and consider others ignorant.

GOVERNMENT: The governing lord in Arda is voted into authority by the talcrin people and serves for a period of two years at a time, but may be elected an unlimited number of times. His word is seen as final, but he is surrounded by a large number of advisors, who are also chosen by the people, and is expected to include them in all decisions. Those living on the mainland are under the authority of the king or lord of whichever country they inhabit.

PREFERRED OCCUPATIONS: Scholars, lawyers, and positions in government are the talcrins' choice occupations, as well as positions in artistry.

FAITH: Talcrins are the most faithful of all races in following King Elôm. The majority of those living in Arda are firm believers, but this has become less so among those living on the mainland.

CRETES

HOMELAND: Arcacia and Dorland

PHYSICAL APPEARANCE: Cretes are a slim people, yet very agile and strong. They are the shortest of Ilyon's races, and stand between five foot and five foot ten inches tall. It is rare for one to reach six feet. They are brown-skinned and have straight, dark hair. Black is most common. It is never lighter than dark brown unless they are of mixed blood. Both men and women let it grow long. They like to decorate their hair with braids, beads, leather, and feathers. Crete men do not grow facial hair. A crete's eyes are a bit larger than a human's, and very bright and colorful. A full-blood crete will never have brown eyes. They dress in earthy colors and lots of leather. All cretes have intricate brown tattoos depicting family symbols and genealogy.

PHYSICAL CHARACTERISTICS: The crete's body is far more resilient to the elements and sickness than other races. They are very tolerant of the cold and other harsh conditions. Their larger eyes give them excellent vision and enable them to see well in the dark. They don't need as much sleep as other races and sleep only for a couple of hours before dawn. Their bodies heal and recuperate quickly.

RACE CHARACTERISTICS: Cretes are tree dwellers and never build on the ground except when absolutely necessary. They love heights and flying and have a superb sense of balance. They are very daring and enjoy a thrilling adventure. They mature a bit more quickly than other races. A crete is considered nearly an adult by fifteen or sixteen and a mature adult by eighteen. They are a high-energy race and prone to taking quick action. Cretes are straightforward and blunt, coming across as rather abrupt at times. They are not the most patient, nor understanding, and they have high expectations for themselves and others. They are a stubborn, proud, and independent people, and don't like to conform to the laws and standards of other races.

SKILLS: Cretes are excellent climbers, even from a very young age, able to race up trees effortlessly and scale the most impassible cliffs and obstacles. Because of this fearlessness and love for heights, they are renowned dragon trainers. They are masters at blending in with their surroundings and moving silently, which makes them excellent hunters. All crete males, as well as many females, are trained as skilled warriors. Their choice weapons are bows and throwing knives, though they can be equally skilled with lightweight swords. Cretes are also a musical race, their favorite instruments being small flutes and hand drums.

SOCIAL: Cretes live in close communities and often have very large families, maintaining close connections with extended family. They are very proud of their family line and make sure each generation is well-educated in their particular traditions and histories. They consider it a tragedy when a family line is broken. Still, all children are cherished, both sons and daughters. Every crete is part of one of twelve clans named after various animals. Men are always part of whichever clan they are born into. When a woman marries, she becomes part of her husband's clan. Though cretes are proud of their clans, they show no discrimination, and their cities always have a mixed-clan population. Cretes are hospitable to their own people and well-known acquaintances, but suspicious and aloof when it comes to strangers. It takes time to earn one's trust, and even longer to earn their respect.

GOVERNMENT: The highest governing official is the crete lord. He is essentially a king, but directly below him are twelve men who serve as representatives of each of the twelve clans. The lord is unable to make any drastic decisions without the cooperation of the majority of the twelve clan leaders. Each crete city has a governing official who answers to the twelve representatives. Directly below him is a council of men consisting of the elders of each major family in the city. In the past, the cretes ultimately fell under the authority of the king of Arcacia, but with the deterioration of the Arcacian government, they've pulled away from its rule.

PREFERRED OCCUPATIONS: Hunters, dragon trainers, and warriors are the favored occupations of the cretes. But leather-working is another desirable occupation. This is typically done by the women of a household.

FAITH: Most cretes have remained faithful to King Elôm, or at least are aware of Him.

GIANTS
(Also known as **Dorlanders**)

HOMELAND: Dorland

PHYSICAL APPEARANCE: Giants are the largest race in Ilyon. Standing between seven to nine feet tall, they tower above most other peoples. They are heavily built and powerful, but can be surprisingly quick and agile when the occasion calls for it. They are fair-skinned, and their hair and eye color varies greatly like humans. They dress simply and practically in sturdy, homespun clothing.

RACE CHARACTERISTICS: Despite their great size and power, giants are a very quiet and gentle people. They dislike confrontation and will avoid it at all cost. They are naturally good-natured and honest, and enjoy simple lives and hard work. To those who don't take the time to get to know them, they can seem slow and ignorant, but they are very methodical thinkers, thinking things over carefully and thoroughly. While not quick-witted, they are very knowledgeable in their fields of interest. They are generally a humble race and easy to get along with. They tend to see the best in everyone. Their biggest failing is that, in their methodical manner, it often takes too long for them to decide to take action when it is needed.

SKILLS: Giants are very skilled in anything to do with the land. Much of the gold, silver, and jewels in Ilyon come from the giants' mines in the mountains of northern Dorland. They are also excellent builders. While lacking in style or decoration, the architecture of their structures is strong and durable, built to last for centuries. They have often been hired to build fortifications and strongholds. Unlike other races, it is not common for giants to train as warriors. Only the king's men are required to be able to fight. While not a musical or artistic race, giants do love a good story, and they've been said to have, beautiful, powerful singing voices.

SOCIAL: Giants typically live in tight farming or mining communities. Family and friends are important. Families usually consist of two to three children who remain in the household for as long as they wish. Many children remain on their parents' farm after they are married, and the farm expands. Giants are known throughout Ilyon for their hospitality. They'll invite almost anyone into their homes. Some people even find them too hospitable and generous. They are very averse to cruelty, dishonesty, and seeing their own hurt. Despite moving slowly in most other areas, justice is swift and decisive.

GOVERNMENT: Giants are ruled over by a king who comes to power through succession. However, most communities more or less govern themselves. The only time the king's rule is evident is when large numbers of giants are required to gather for a certain purpose.

PREFERRED OCCUPATIONS: The majority of giants are farmers, miners, or builders.

FAITH: Almost all giants agree King Elôm is real, but in their simplistic and practical mindset, fewer giants have actually come to a true trusting faith.

THE KING'S SCROLLS

ILYON CHRONICLES – BOOK TWO

When a mysterious group of dragon-riding cretes arrive at camp, those in Landale must join their mission to rescue a teacher of Elôm and the last known copies of the King's Scrolls before the emperor's men can locate them.

COMING 2015

For more "behind the scenes" information on Ilyon Chronicles, visit: **www.ilyonchronicles.blogspot.com**

To see Jaye's inspiration boards and character "casting" visit: **www.pinterest.com/jayelknight**

ACKNOWLEDGEMENTS

Above all, I have to thank God for entrusting me with this incredible story. Never have I seen His hand so clearly in my writing. The way He has given me the different characters and plots has been an amazing experience that will always leave me awestruck.

My mom deserves a huge amount of credit for this book. She spent almost as many countless hours laboring over it as I did and always helped me work through things whenever I'd begin to freak out about how to fix something. Our final read-through left us both bleary-eyed and ready to fall into bed every night for a week. It wouldn't be what it is without her. Thank you so much, Mom! I couldn't do this without you.

Thank you to my beta readers, Jordyn, Morgan, Rebekah, Addyson, and especially Kara and Erika. Your feedback helped tremendously. I thank each of you for the time you took to read through such a long book and let me know what did and didn't work.

I thank my proofreader and publicist, Amber Stokes, for not only giving *Resistance* the final polish, but also making its release such a fun and exciting experience.

I want to give a special thanks to Donita K. Paul for writing *DragonQuest*, which was the book God used to sow the first small seed of inspiration that grew into *Ilyon Chronicles*.

ABOUT THE AUTHOR

JAYE L. KNIGHT is a homeschool graduated indie author with a passion for writing Christian fantasy and clean new adult fiction. Armed with an active imagination and love for adventure, Jaye weaves stories of truth, faith, and courage with the message that even in the deepest darkness, God's love shines as a light to offer hope. She has been penning stories since the age of eight and resides in the Northwoods of Wisconsin.

To learn more about Jaye and her work, visit:
www.jayelknight.com

16577591R00314

Made in the USA
Middletown, DE
18 December 2014